SHE THAT PLAYS THE QUEEN

in three Acts

Aline Waites

Published by Aline Waites
Publishing partner: Paragon Publishing, Rothersthorpe
First published 2016
© Aline Waites 2016

The rights of Aline Waites to be identified as the author of this work have been asserted by her in accordance with the Copyright, Designs and Patents Act of 1988.

All rights reserved; no part of this publication may be reproduced, stored in a retrieval system, or transmitted in any form or by any means, electronic, mechanical, photocopying, recording or otherwise without the prior written consent of the publisher or a licence permitting copying in the UK issued by the Copyright Licensing Agency Ltd. www.cla.co.uk

ISBN 978-1-78222-495-2

Book design, layout and production management by Into Print
www.intoprint.net
+44 (0)1604 832149

Printed and bound in UK and USA by Lightning Source

Contents

ACT ONE: 5
The White Fur Coat, 1941

ACT TWO: 111
Return of the Warriors

ACT THREE: 249
Curtain Up

Act One:

The White Fur Coat
1941

1.

'We are now *two bus* people,' cried little Maxine to her Aunt Irene as they left the chocolate coloured East Yorkshire bus to pick up a blue Hull Corporation one.

The bus was full and all the front seats were taken so they sat near the back facing the passengers on the other side and as soon as the journey began, the girl conductor came round to collect the fares. The young woman had just returned to her post by the door when there was a juddering, grinding halt, jarring the bones of the elderly passengers and bringing forth a stream of invective from the Clippie who grabbed hastily at her pole to avoid falling full length on the platform. The stream of curses faltered and dwindled into an apologetic laugh as she became aware of the eyes of the seven-year-old child fixed upon her.

'Pardon my French,' she said to her shaken passengers.

'It's them new drivers,' she confided, 'the real ones get called up. There is a war on, you know.'

They nodded sagely, 'Aye, there's a war on,' they told each other.

She turned her attention to Irene and Maxine.

'Next stop Paradise Street, Madam Reenie,' she said. 'No need to rush, Driver can't get bus moving till I ring bell,' she added – proud of her new found dominance over the male sex,

Maxine surveyed the clippie with awe. She looked dashing in her navy blue trousers and peaked cap. It wasn't just the costume, but the sights and sounds that were even more enthralling. Across one shoulder, a black money bag made a merry jingle every time she put coins into it. Over the other shoulder, the ticket punch which made a ti ting tong sound. But best of all were the actual tickets – Blue, red, green, yellow, orange all strapped together with black elastic into neat packs on their narrow oblong board.

Irene took Maxine by the hand, and Maxine held on tight, proud that her aunt was known by such a distinguished individual – the kind of person who used exotic words that she had never heard before.

'She knows your name. She called you Madam Reenie,' she whispered as they got to their feet and made their way down the aisle 'You must be very famous.'

Irene laughed, 'That is Lucy Benson. She's in one of my keep fit classes.'

'Tara Madam Reenie, See you on Wednesday. Tara Maxine', cried Lucy as the two of them leapt from the bus. Irene and Maxine stood and watched as the clippie performed her magic ritual. A ring on the bell, a cry of 'eh up' and the bus lurched into action.

'I want to be a clippie when I grow up,' said Maxine to her aunt.

'Good idea,' said Irene, who did not believe in inhibiting a child's ambitions.

Maxine's eyes were bright with excitement as the two of them looked around them. Despite the slight February chill, there was a trace of defiant sunshine making patterns across the flagged pavement. Maxine was full of high spirits and chattered as she skipped along.

'I really really want to go to Paradise Street,' she cried.

'Don't expect too much,' said Irene. 'It's only a street like any other.'

All the street signs had been removed to confuse possible German paratroopers, and Irene had never made the journey on foot before, but she'd consulted a map and worked out the route.

She took her niece by the hand, and they made the sharp turn into the narrow alley that had, at some time in the past, been mistakenly named Paradise Street.

As they did so, a rush of icy air assailed them, dampening their good spirits and both woman and child involuntarily put their hands to their noses.

Seven years ago, Irene had arrived in Hull's Paragon Station for the first time and been assaulted by the aggressive smell of fish that flooded the centre of the town when the wind blew in from the docks. She thought she had grown accustomed to it – until now. Her niece gave a shudder inside her white fur coat.

'Is this really the way to Daddy's office?' she asked with alarm.

Irene nodded. By car, the office was only five minutes away from town. The journey on foot was a new and not pleasant experience – but she had promised to look after the family business while her brother Tom was away fighting for King and country.

'I don't like it here,' said the little girl and her aunt suspected that tears were not far away. Irene felt like crying herself, but she bounced along in her Cuban-heeled lace ups, a martial figure in her square-shouldered suit and jaunty sailor hat, and hoped that her show of bravery would comfort the little girl.

Irene lived with Maxine and her parents at The Laurels, a substantial house on the respectable side of town near the University. Sherwood Park was a leafy crescent where trees and flowers grew in abundance, and the all-pervading smell was mint that covered the area like a weed.

By contrast, Paradise Street was in the filthiest slum area of town – a narrow river of gritty black slime with the blackened red brick houses on either side cutting out the sunlight.

The aroma of fish hung over the area like a noxious cloud. The children who screamed laughed and chased each other were whey-faced and skinny, their clothes ragged and filthy but they seemed happy enough. Their mothers, in floral aprons and turbans, stood around in groups, arms crossed, fags in their mouths, gossiping, breaking off to yell and swear at the children in their barely comprehensible dialect. 'What a nasty smell,' cried Maxine. 'It would make Mummy sick!'

Maxine's mother, Constance, possessed a delicate stomach and she would throw up at the slightest thing. Bad smell, bitter taste, even an ugly face could send her to the lavatory in an orgy of retching.

Irene felt a tug on her sleeve and Maxine pulled her aunt's head down to whisper in her ear.

'I'm frightened,' she said.

Irene didn't feel too confident herself, but she whispered back, gripping Maxine's hand hard. 'We're nearly there.'

'Shall we sing a song?' asked Maxine in a trembling voice.

It was a family custom to sing at awkward moments – like during the blitz when the bombs were dropping, and guns were banging away – but Irene was aware that this was one time and place where singing would be inappropriate.

'Wait till we get to Daddy's office,' she said, 'then we'll sing our hearts out.'

2.

The offices of Grantley and Fletcher Coles stood at the far end, down by the docks where the dock workers brought in the great slabs of marble to put on display for the buyers – builders, sculptors and monumental masons.

Irene's brother, Tom had resented being sent from the family home in Twickenham to take care of the northern branch of the family marble merchants. He had literary aspirations and little interest in the firm. However, as soon as he clapped his bonny blue eyes on Constance, the most beautiful woman in Yorkshire, he knew that he could survive anything – even the boredom of business life.

It wasn't too bad. Tom conducted most of his work from home, by telephone, only visiting the office once or twice a week, leaving everything to his office staff of two. At the weekends, he relaxed with his beautiful wife, his devoted sister, his small daughter and a magnificent set of golf clubs. Into this idyll came the war.

Nothing much happened at first, apart from the appearance of ration books, gas masks and air raid precautions. People made jokes about the phoney war and went about their everyday business, then, one summer night, the German bombers came thudding overhead, hell arrived, and jokes were not so easy to make.

The morning after that first raid, Tom set off for the office. He returned barely an hour later. He was deathly pale, shaking; his eyes looked raw in his face as if he hadn't closed his eyelids for a month. Constance rushed to him, surprised by his request for a drink at eleven o'clock in the morning.

'How was the office?' She asked, handing him a thick glass of whisky. He downed it quickly, and a little colour came back into his face.

'I couldn't find it,' he said.

'Couldn't find it? Don't be silly,' said Irene.

'The whole town is on fire. I didn't even get as far as Spring Bank. It was a ring of flames, piles of rubble. Impossible to find anything.'

He fell into an easy chair, the family grouped around him, not knowing what to do. Constance put her hand on his shoulder. Ada, the maid, took Maxine by the hand. 'Let's put kettle on,' she said and led her into the kitchen.

Irene looked at him, searching his face for some sign of a joke

'The whole town?'

'A wall of fire. The roads – Just rubble – Oh Connie' he grabbed his wife's hand and put it to his face. 'What's going to happen to us all?'

*

Tom went out after lunch and during the afternoon builders arrived to build a brick air raid shelter in the garden.

'I want to be sure you are safe while I am away' he said on his return.

'Away?'

'I've joined up. I have to go darling. I must do something positive about this terrible thing that's happening.'

They all sat around, silently, trying to understand what these changes in all their lives would mean to them. Ada came in and broke the silence.

'Tea's ready. You look like you need it!'

'But…Grantley's!' asked Irene 'What about our office? Did you find it?'

'Yes, it's there all right. Mind you nothing much will happen there for a while. The Italians won't be sending us much stuff while Musso's in power.'

He turned to his sister.

'Irene, would you mind dropping into the office now and again – just to make sure everything is all right.'

'Of course,' said Irene.

Constance looked from Tom to Irene and back again then she too rose from her chair.

'You've thought it all through,' she said and added with some reluctance, 'Would you like me to go to the office sometimes?'

Tom laughed.

'You know how you hate that place. Remember – dusty files, chipped cups, the smell of the fish dock? No, it's no place for a beautiful butterfly like you.'

She laughed and cried at the same time. Tom put his arms around her to comfort her, and they hugged each other.

'What about me?' shouted Maxine, pushing between them?

'And me' cried Irene.

They all hugged each other.

'Tea'll be getting stewed,' said Ada 'I'd best put kettle on again.'

3.

So Irene was walking down Paradise Street on a chilly February day and wondering why the hell she had allowed her little niece to come with her, but Maxine had ways and means of persuasion.

'I really really want to go to Daddy's office again,' she had said – her eyes shining with anticipation but watching her aunt carefully for the slightest sign of disagreement, and ready to shed the big fat tears with which she usually managed to clinch her deals. 'And see Scot and Cappy and Cuthbert. It's just my favourite place in all the world.'

Irene hadn't been able to say no.

Now both of them were having second thoughts.

As they passed down the street, the sullen looking women fell silent. Only a breathed 'Oh my god' and a click of the tongue indicated their scornful amazement at the vision.

'Obviously one shouldn't dress up to come down here. Who was I trying to impress?' muttered Irene.

She strode on through the mud, her red fox fur bobbing on the shoulder of her grey suit. Maxine looked up at her for reassurance. Maxine loved the way she looked, her stockings always of pure silk, her make up proudly visible, but impeccable in its application.

But if Irene's grace and dignity startled the apron clad women into silence, they were even more transfixed by the picture presented by little Maxine, who was unaware that she looked like an alien being in her white fur coat and ringlets. Not for the first time Irene wished her sister in law didn't insist on dressing up her pretty daughter like a doll. Her naturally straight hair had been curled up with rags and tied with champagne coloured satin ribbons to match her long champagne coloured socks, her Start rite sandals, and her tiny white kid gloves. One of her hands clutched a small kid purse, the other one held her aunt's hand.

Irene's grasp tightened reassuringly as the two alien beings walked past the dumbstruck women and continued on their way to the bottom of the street.

Irene had never been so pleased to see the untidy mess of barbed wire that now surrounded the offices of Grantley's. She was just about to breathe a sigh of relief when a little red headed girl – of about Maxine's age – ran out in front of them. The child stuck her piece of liquorice root into her mouth and with her grubby little hand grabbed hold of one of the blonde ringlets, pulling Maxine close to her. The other grubby little hand stroked the fur coat as if Maxine were a kind of huge teddy bear to play with. Maxine screamed loudly and clutched her aunt. 'Go away your hands are dirty.'

The little girl, startled by the sound, let go of the ringlet.

'Who the 'ell do you fink you are,' she said in her guttural accent, removing the liquorice from her mouth, 'bloody Shirley. Temple?'

Maxine stood rooted to the spot, and watched with horrified fascination as the little girl continued stroking her fur coat. Irene gently removed both dirty little hands, holding them for a while in hers.

'Your hands are freezing,' she said, 'And you haven't any shoes on. You'll get your death of cold.'

'Aint got no shoes' said the child with a sniff.

'You must ask your mother to get you some.'

The child gawped at her.

'Yer mean our mam?'

'Yes.'

'Our Mam's passed away.'

'I'm sorry,' said Irene.

The child looked at her quizzically, pulled away her hand and gave the coat another stroke.

'Are you Shirley Temple?' she asked.

Maxine was stung at last into replying, 'No, I'm not. I'm Maxine Fletcher.'

The child nodded.

'I'm Jessie Maffews,' she said with great authority.

One of the smoking women in the doorway called out harshly.

''Ere you Lil. Let 'er alone. You won't 'alf get a good 'idin' when I get 'old o' yer.'

The little girl screwed up her freckled face and looked beseechingly at Irene who, startled, saw that her eyes were pure beauty, soft and wet like purple pansies after the rain. She put her arms gently around the child, ignoring the filthy clothes, the smell of poverty and the possibility of bugs. The little girl looked up at her, startled by her kindness and began to weep silently. Irene turned to the woman who had spoken.

'She meant no harm. Please don't hurt her,' she said.

The woman lurched over.

'You, Lady Muck, you mind yer own bloody business,' she growled without taking the fag out of her mouth, and she grabbed the child by the arm.

Angry at being dragged away, the child let out a huge gob of liquorice coloured spit that landed right on target on the front of Maxine's white fur coat, wobbled a bit, then slid down to the hem. Maxine drew back and started wailing. The child, Lil, screamed as the woman belted her across the ear.

Irene and her niece continued on their way, the aunt disturbed and upset by what had occurred.

'Poor little kid,' she said, 'She wasn't doing any harm.'

Maxine looked at her aunt as though she had lost her mind.

'She was! She's spoiled my coat!' she cried. 'Look, there's spit and liquorice all over it.'

Irene glanced at the mess on the white fur.

'We'll give it to Ada to clean up,' She said, 'I'm sure it'll come clean,' she added with little conviction.

'She swore at me and pulled my hair. It hurt,' replied Maxine with an outraged sniff. '*And* she called me Shirley Temple! I *hate* Shirley Temple.'

Irene took Maxine's hand and they strode together down to the end of the road. The big iron fences that had surrounded Grantley's Yard had been taken away at the beginning of the war to make guns and it was now protected instead by an ugly mass of barbed wire. They approached the narrow entrance and opened the rickety gate that had replaced the grand old one. The sign was still there hanging drunkenly from one nail 'Grantley and Fletcher Coles Ltd' it said. Irene carefully bolted the gate behind them and they approached the office.

'Now we can sing,' said Irene.

But Maxine had lost the urge to sing or even to smile.

4.

It wasn't much of an office, just a one story brick building at one end of a large yard used for storing slabs of marble. It had been erected, as a temporary measure in the late twenties when Grantley and Fletcher-Coles set up a branch on the banks of the Humber and Tom was too lazy or too indifferent to make it more permanent.

There were sparse tufts of grass and weeds growing now where the marble had been. Although there were a few slabs of stone lying around, everyone knew there would be no more until the war was over.

By the entrance was a wooden hut, which was the habitat of Mr Capstick, the foreman, and any stonemasons or labourers who had formerly been employed but had now been called up for more important war work.

Mr Capstick came out of the hut when he saw Irene and Maxine approach. His rosy face broke into a broad beaming smile, and he tipped his cap respectfully as he greeted them and bowed them into his domain, showing them to the wooden chairs, newly dusted in their honour. Cappy was always delighted to see visitors and it was traditional for members of the family to drop in for a chat.

He looked alarmed when he saw Maxine's pale face. 'Eh what's up lass?' he said.

His kindly enquiry loosened her tongue; she needed no further encouragement to tell him breathlessly of her ghastly experience. He listened sympathetically.

'Them kids down street are all toe rags. Tek no notice love. They don't know nowt better.'

Irene saw that Maxine was beginning to enjoy the story of her humiliation and was afraid they would be there all day, so she hurried changed the subject.

'Keeping busy, Cappy?' asked Irene,

'Eh tha' knows. Nowt much to do since war started.'

Since the war, Cappy had reigned alone in his little kingdom. Every morning he arrived on his bike and opened up the hut. After taking off his bicycle clips, he lit his paraffin stove and put his kettle on to brew the tea. Then he would open up the office for Scot, the office manager, who was always there by eight thirty. After this, he would retire to his hut and mash his tea. From then on he spent his day pottering, playing cards with himself and reading the Daily Mirror only breaking off at lunchtime to eat the cheese and pickle sandwiches lovingly packed up by Mrs Capstick. Very occasionally he greeted prospective customers and showed them around the depleted stock of Carrera marble. Even more rarely, he made use of the big marble cutter to slice it up for them. Then when the office staff had left, he locked up, replaced his bicycle clips and rode off home.

Maxine grabbed delightedly at the Daily Mirror that lay on his little table and turning to the cartoon page, immediately became involved in the adventures of Belinda Blue eyes.

'Isn't it frightfully dull, having nothing to do?' asked Irene.

'Well, Miss Reen. As long as ah get me screw ah don't mind. It keeps me out of t'army.'

'You don't want to fight for your country?'

'Ah reckon as country's better off wi'out me. Ah've never bin no good at fightin'!'

After passing on information in answer to Cappy's eager enquiries regarding the health of the family, how they were coping with air raids, rationing, etc., Irene saw that Maxine had finished devouring Pip Squeak and Wilfred and, bored with grown up conversation was getting fretful and fidgety. She realised it was time to proceed with their journey.

'Look at the time,' she said nodding towards the big station clock that hung on the wall of his hut.

'Well I'd best get on then,' he said and respectfully escorted them down the crazy paving marble path to the office.

He opened the office door for them, doffed his cap again and retired to concentrate on the scantily clothed Jane and her dachshund Fritz.

The building had remained undamaged by the bombing, but over everything, there was a thick film of dust that was impossible to shift.

The general office was an oblong room with a high fixed bench table of solid oak, which ran across the whole length of it under the windows overlooking the yard. On the opposite side, facing the window, was the door to the managerial offices and on either side of the door were long banquettes covered in dark red leatherette, which in their heyday had been polished and shiny, but were now so covered in dust that it was evident few people ventured to sit there.

A door off to the left of the general office led to a tiny kitchenette with a gas ring, kettle and a rickety table on which reposed a big square biscuit tin which bore the insignia Huntley and Palmer; several cans of condensed milk; a hammer and chisel; some tin spoons; a brown teapot with a chipped spout and only half a lid; a screwdriver; a rusty hinge; a few sad looking cups and saucers of various designs and a tin tea caddy decorated with a picture of the little Princesses, Elizabeth and Margaret Rose. In the corner was a lavatory with WC and wash basin and a door hanging drunkenly on one single hinge – its partner obviously being the one residing on the kitchen table.

The general office was the domain of the office junior, Cuthbert and it was here he sat with pictures of tombstones and monuments, colouring in grass and flowers to bring alive the black and white photographs. He was also responsible for dealing with mundane things like petty cash and making the tea. Cuthbert was a slender youth with a pale, sensitive face, floppy blond hair and an Art School diploma. He lived with his mother and his collection of model aeroplanes in an old terraced cottage by the Land of Green Ginger where they spent their lives in a state of contented harmony working on tapestry cushions and fireguards.

Cuthbert greeted Irene with enormous respect as she came in and he showed her, and the eager-faced Maxine straight into her brother's office.

Tom's room, which looked out over the road was substantial with thick heavy furniture, rugs and an enormous desk on which resided a single foolscap pad, framed photographs of his family, a pencil box full of wonderfully sharpened pencils courtesy of Cuthbert who also watered each day the potted plant that had been thoughtfully provided by Tom's wife, Constance.

But it was clear that Scot McGregor, senior clerk, did all the real work in the office on the other side. Scot's desk, significantly smaller in area than Tom's, was completely concealed with piles of books and papers, which had even overflowed on the linoleum-covered floor. The filing cabinets always stood open, silent witness to the riffling through of files that went on all day

Each of the two largest offices had a two bar electric fire, and there was a free standing paraffin stove in the general office.

'It must be freezing here in winter,' said Irene as she looked around Tom's office, although it occurred to her that it would probably be a palace to some of the people out in Paradise Street.

'Well, hello there, Mrs – er Miss Fletcher!' said Scot McGregor, in his soft Edinburgh accent. He was, as always, rather in awe of the elegance and self-possession shown by his boss's sister; he was never quite sure what to call her, and he blushed when he met her steady gaze.

'Call me Irene,' she said with an encouraging smile.

He gave a quick, nervous laugh 'Irene' he said, trying it out.

Obviously, not satisfied with his attempt, he gave a self-disparaging shrug of his shoulders and quickly turned to the still solemn Maxine.

'So how's the wee missy, the day?' he asked.

Delighted by his attention, Maxine's sulky face lit up in a smile. Scot, with his strange accent, his long freckled face with its sizeable overbite and sandy moustache fascinated her. His light ginger hair grew straight up on his head like grass, and she always wanted to touch it to see if it felt prickly, like a doormat.

Scot was not his real name, he was christened Alistair, but Tom who loved to dish out nicknames, decided he resembled a Scottie dog and re-christened him accordingly.

'Cuthbert,' he called, 'Make the ladies a wee cup of tea and mebbe you could find a few digestives?'

Delighted to have company, the boy rushed off to do his master's bidding to make the tea and get out the digestive biscuits acquired especially for the occasion. Cuthbert wasn't his real name, he was called Leslie Daines, but Tom had named him Cuthbert and the boy never complained.

By now Scot had made up his mind what to call Irene.

'Your chair, Madame Renee,' he said with an elegant French accent, indicating the polished mahogany swivel armchair. Irene swung herself round in a circle. Maxine watched with shining eyes and longed to have a go herself.

'And this wee chair is especially for Maxine,' said Scot, bringing up a child-sized wooden kitchen seat.

Irene noted the way the child's lip trembled with disappointment. She got up from the swivelling chair and surrendered it to her niece. Maxine jumped into it and started whirling round and round. Scot watched with the faintly disapproving air of the childless. Irene witnessed his expression and laughed.

'What's happened to the tea, Scot?'

'It takes a while for the kettle to boil. We only have the gas ring you see'

'Marion sent you any mutton pies this week?'

Maxine gave a quick involuntary giggle, quickly suppressed by a sharp look from her aunt. Those pies were a family joke.

Scot had a wife up in Aberdeen who he worshipped and who made highly regarded mutton pies. Every week she would send a supply to Scot and he would always pass some over to Tom for a special treat for his family. Tom was much too soft hearted to let him know that they would all end in the rubbish bin. The very sight and texture of the long greyish pastry was enough to make Connie turn green.

The tea that Cuthbert brought in was strong, stewed and thick with sweet condensed milk. The cups, although politely accompanied by nearly matching saucers and superfluous teaspoons, were cracked and stained, and though Irene accepted hers with every expression of delight, she shook her head at Maxine and mouthed the words 'Leave it' then she cast her eyes to heaven and mouthed 'Men!'

Maxine, enjoying the feeling of intimacy and female solidarity, cast her own eyes heavenward in agreement.

'I hope it's mashed enough for you,' said Cuthbert in his gentle, hesitant voice.

'We'll water the plants with it, it's completely undrinkable, but it was kind of them to make it for us. We don't want to hurt their feelings'.

The child nodded, delighted to be in on a conspiracy and the tea was disposed of discreetly.

'There need to be a few changes made around here,' said Irene looking around the dusty room, 'A spot of charring for a start.'

As it turned out, the charring was unnecessary. That very night the Luftwaffe paid a visit.

5.

'Where's Ada?' asked Maxine as Irene came into the breakfast room with the teapot.

Irene put the pot down on the table.

'She's in her room. Don't bother her, darling; she's upset.'

Maxine pouted.

'But I wanted her to clean my coat. Before Mummy sees it.'

'Never mind', said Irene 'We shall get it cleaned up. Just don't worry her at the moment.'

Maxine poured milk on her cereal and took a big spoonful before asking, 'Why's she upset?'

Irene sighed and sat down at the table to face her niece.

'You'll find out sooner or later, so I might as well tell you.'

Maxine looked up expectantly. 'Her mother was killed in the bombing last night.'

'I didn't know she had a mother. I thought she was in our family.'

'Yes she is, but everybody has a mother.'

'Then why don't we ever see her?'

Irene considered this for a while.

'She – doesn't like going out,' she said at last and became too busy to explain further.

Irene considered that Maxine was simply too young to know the truth. She remembered only too well the day nearly eight years ago that Ada had arrived at The Laurels – fourteen years old, woefully thin and pregnant.

*

Capstick, Tom's foreman, had been early getting in that morning. He had a new labourer coming on, and he needed to have a look at him before he started work. Not only did they have to be good workmen, but also it was important that they had a sense of humour. Tom was a great practical joker, and it would be no good to have someone who took themselves too seriously or who might get angry or hurt.

After he had lit his paraffin stove and put on his kettle to boil He took his bunch of keys from the hook on the wall of his shed, picked out the ones that opened the office door and crossing the yard to the office, proceeded to unlock the door. Usually, the door swung open with a light push, but today it seemed to be stuck. After uttering a few local curses, he reminded himself to bring out a can of oil next time to grease the hinges. He pushed again, a bit harder, but it still didn't open. This was strange; he had never had a problem with this before. There was an obstruction on the inside. He took off his cap and rubbed his head, trying to remember the position of the door the night before. He had locked it as usual, and there was nothing in the way then.

He gave the door one last push and the door opened just a chink. To his surprise, he realised the chain was on the door. Somebody must have come in even earlier and for some reason put on the chain. He'd never known that happen before. Surely this couldn't be one of Tom's jokes?

All of a sudden he heard a flush of the toilet and the sound of light footsteps walking across the floor.

'Who is it?' he cried, and much to his surprise a scared little face appeared through the crack of the door.

''Ere you, open this door!' he ordered. 'Or I'll get the cops.'

Quickly the door shut again, and he could hear the chain being slipped off.

Standing there was a thin young girl of about fourteen years old, wearing an old but clean and slightly crumpled summer dress in check cotton. Her long brown hair had been newly washed and was neatly tied back with ribbon. Her face was also clean. In her hand, she had a toothbrush. Capstick saw that on the banquette was a blanket and a neat pile of clothing. The girl looked at Capstick appealingly. She was shaking a little but trying not to let her nervousness show. All these things Capstick took in with a glance but what was the most noticeable thing about the girl was the bump in her belly that could be clearly seen straining under the cotton of her dress. The child was about four months pregnant. He stood for a long moment on the threshold, not knowing how to start the conversation. She stood before him with her head lowered.

'Eh lass,' he said at last. 'Where'd you come from?'

'Paradise Street, please sir,' she said, and she lifted her big brown eyes on his face. Cappy took off his cap and started turning it around between his fingers. He didn't know what to think; he was too surprised to be angry and too aware of her plight, and yet he knew he should be calling the police. This little girl was, after all, an intruder.

'Will you come in, sir?' she said like a polite little girl who had temporarily forgotten her manners. She picked up the cushion that had been obstructing the door.

'That's Mr Tom's cushion! It belongs in his office,' he said.

'I ain't done it no harm, sir,' she protested. 'I covered it up with my blanket afore I put my head on it.'

She stepped back to allow him to advance further into the room. She put the cushion on the banquette

'I'll put it back in other room, sir.'

'I'm not a sir, so stop calling me one.'

'Sorry – sir – er – Mr.'

'You was sleepin' 'ere then. How did you get it?'

'Through that window Mr,' she said pointing at Tom's office, 'It was easy at first, but it in't so easy now.' and she put her small hands on her swelling belly.

'Have you pinched owt?'

'No sir, course not,' she said, blushing at the very idea. 'I've never stolen nothing in my life. Me mam would kill me if I did,' she picked up her pile of clothes and held it out to him.

'Look, this is all my stuff. I've not done no harm; I always tidy up. You'd never know I'd been here if you hadn't come in early this morning.'

'You've slept here before?' he asked.

She hung her head. 'Aye, for a couple of weeks.'

'Two weeks?'

'Well, mebbe three. Since I got big.'

'But why?'

'I've nowhere else to go.' She fixed her eyes on him, and her lip started to tremble.

'Don't tell on me, sir, please,' she said beseechingly. She gave a sniff and began to wrap her clothes in the blanket.

She turned to Capstick who still stood there, twiddling his cap.

'I'll just go and get my things from the lav. Then nobody will ever know.'

Capstick took her by the shoulder; it was painfully thin under his grasp.

'Here lass,' he said, 'How did you get in here.'

'I told you, through the window.'

'No –no how did you get into the yard?'

'Oh,' she gave a little laugh through her tears. 'Easy. One of them railings is loose. I just slipped through.'

By this time, she'd got all her things together and tied the blanket in a knot.

'Well, tata then,' she said.

'Ere!' Capstick grabbed her arm again. 'Where do you think you're going?'

'I've got to go to work.'

'No, you don't, lass,' he said, 'You've got to wait here for Mr Tom.'

'But I'll lose my job if I'm late.'

'You should of thought of that,' he said.

'Aye,' she said nodding. She studied her feet for a moment then.

'Shall I put kettle on then?' she asked. 'Sit down there, and I'll make tea. Look, it's my tea. I haven't touched any of theirs.' and she picked up her basket and showed him the contents.

'No, I can't do that, I've got a bloke to see in a minute,' said Capstick slowly, 'Any road, it wouldn't right for me to drink tea here. I drink tea in my place.'

'Is that your little shed? It looks real nice. I couldn't get in there.'

'No doubt you had a try.'

'Aye.'

'Mm. Well I'll tek you there now,' said Cappy. 'You won't skedaddle will yer?'

'I promise.'

'I'll mek you a cup of Bovril. Kettle will be boiling be now.'

Capstick put on his cap and picked up the little girl's bundle before she had a chance to do so. The girl took her basket and the two of them retired to Capstick's hut to drink Bovril and share the cheese sandwich Capstick had brought for his lunch.

When Tom arrived, it didn't take him long to get the truth out of her.

His kind face and soft voice made her cry but gave her confidence, and through her tears, she told him the story. She had run away from home with just a bundle of clothes. She was afraid to go home, convinced she would be in for a beating from her mother as soon as she knew about her daughter's condition.

'Your parents must be so worried about you,' he told her. 'You really must let them know that you are still alive. I'm sure they'll understand, eventually.'

She screamed and clung to him at the very notion.

'No, no,' she cried and then she whispered, 'They're very Religious!'

'Then, of course, they'll forgive you. Remember the Virgin Mary?'

The girl gave a gasp and looked at him with open mouth; he immediately wished he'd never said that.

'Tell you what,' he said, 'Why don't I come with you? Then I can explain it all to them.'

6.

Mr and Mrs Watson lived just down the road on the second floor of a terraced house in Paradise Street. Tom and Ada climbed the stairs, and he knocked on the door, as the shaking Ada hid behind his back.

A pale hatchet-faced woman in a white pinafore opened the door. With narrowed eyes the woman looked Tom up and down, then she espied the frightened girl hiding behind him. She showed no emotion at all.

'Ah see,' she said.

'This is me mam,' said Ada in a tiny voice.

'May we come in Mrs Watson?' asked Tom.

She looked him up and down once more.

'Aye,' she said after a pause and stood aside allowing them to pass into the room.

An overpowering smell of disinfectant greeted him. The room was so terrifyingly clean that Tom had a sudden violent urge to spit on the floor. The bare brick walls looked as if somebody had whitewashed them that very morning, and on the centre of the concrete floor was a single concession to comfort; a square of brown linoleum. The furnishings were just three wooden chairs, a table, and a dresser all scrubbed within an inch of their lives. In the middle of the room stood an unlit paraffin stove.

The windows offered no cheer; a plain white net curtain was stretched tightly across them – no suggestion of a frill to soften the harsh contours. There was a single unshaded light bulb in the centre of the ceiling. A Bible lay open on the dresser, and there was a large wooden cross hanging on the wall next to a newspaper picture of the Royal Family. Apart from a few utilitarian cups and plates on the dresser, there was nothing to suggest that anyone actually lived there. In pride of place, sinister and threatening, there was an evil looking cane hanging on its special hook.

Tom, dressed for summer, shivered in the freezing room, but the occupants didn't seem to notice. Mrs Watson wore a long black cotton dress under a white pinafore. Mr Watson – a small, wizened man wearing white shirtsleeves, a black waistcoat, a drooping moustache and a sad expression –

was sitting at the table. He didn't say a word, nor did he evince any interest in the return of his lost daughter.

'Hello Dad,' said Ada. He nodded.

The woman, ignoring the presence of Tom, took down the cane from its hook on the wall.

Ada whimpered 'Mam, no'.

Tom advanced on the woman, taking the cane from her and holding her firmly by the shoulders sat her down on the chair opposite her husband.

'Please, not so fast. Listen to me,' said Tom.

'Who are you that we should listen?'

'I'm Tom Fletcher – from Grantley's at the end of the road.'

The woman took a deep intake of breath, crossed herself and then clasped her hands on the table looked at him with narrowed eyes and pursed lips. Tom felt his confidence draining away, unaccountably intimidated by this dragon-like creature who seemed to think he was the devil incarnate. He took a deep breath.

'Your daughter was sleeping in my office.'

'Ah see,' said the woman looking at him with deepest venom.

'No you don't see,' said Tom, 'Please try to understand. You should be taking care of her.'

'She looks all right to me.'

'You don't understand. Ada is pregnant.'

The woman looked at him as if the word was not part of her vocabulary. He tried again.

'She is expecting a child.'

The woman rose to her feet with a scream and raised her clasped hands to heaven.

'God forgive us all,' she cried, 'Oh dad what are we going to do?'

Dad just shook his head without changing his expression, and Mrs Watson gave a loud sob and fell back into the chair plunging her face into her hands. Tom felt he was in a dream -the kind where you're on stage in a melodrama, and you don't know the lines. Despite the underlying seriousness of the girl's plight, he was only kept going by the thought of how amusing this scene would be in retrospect and was already looking forward to regaling Irene and Connie with the story. He tried to soothe the heaving creature and patted her awkwardly on the back.

'No no, don't cry, it's not the end of the world. I'm sure everything will turn out all right.'

She looked up.

'I don't want any bastards in this house,' she snapped.

'It may not come to that. . .' Tom began, but was not able to continue as Mrs Watson turned to her daughter and with a voice dipped in cyanide 'Get out of this house,' she said quietly and deliberately. 'Now.'

'But where'll I go?'

'Just get out. And don't come back here no more. Look at your father. He's too upset to speak.'

'Dad?' said Ada turning to him. He shook his head.

Tom looked around at the scene and realised he had only one option.

'Come back with me – just for now,' he said and, taking the girl's hand, made his way to the door.

The parents sat there wooden faced on their wooden chairs at the wooden table, immobilised with shock, staring into space. He went back to the table and taking out a card from his wallet said 'You can get me at Grantley's or you can ring me here if you want to talk about things.'

As there was no reply he went back to join Ada at the door.

'Toodle-oo then' said Ada idiotically to them before Tom shut the door behind them. They made their way down the stairs, and as soon as they hit the pavement, Tom's self-control broke down, and he dissolved into hysterical laughter.

'Sorry love,' he said, 'I know it's not funny.'

His laughter was infectious. Ada looked at him for a while and then joined in.

'Oh dear...Toodle-oo!' he muttered, wiping his eyes. And bundling Ada into the back of the car brought her back to the Laurels.

His sister greeted her kindly, fed her and put her to bed without asking any questions.

Later Tom told her the story.

'The whole thing is so tragic that it's funny,' he said to Irene.

'You always had a misplaced sense of humour,' she said, 'I'll bet you wouldn't even keep a straight face at my funeral.'

'Oh yes I would,' he said and started to laugh again at the very thought.

Ada took to life at the Laurels as to the manner born. She recovered from her fear and revealed a chirpy and cheerful nature. She was a loving creature and her obvious admiration of Connie captivated that lady who took the young girl into the family with enthusiasm, especially as she was a helpful and willing skivvy to have around the house. When Maxine began to fight her way into the world Ada was there to lend a helping hand, and Ada's baby came, without assistance, a few days later.

Tom tried several times to call on the Watsons – if only to collect report progress on the pregnancy, but they always refused to answer the door to him. After the birth, Tom yelled the news through the door, and Mrs Watson allowed him to come back into the room where the two of them were sitting exactly as he left them – at the wooden table. Mr Watson remained silent while Mrs Watson showed no interest in her grandchild and still refused to see her daughter. He left the house in disgust – but even in his anger, he managed to turn at the door to say, 'Toodle-oo then' – it still made him giggle.

After Ada had given up the child for adoption nothing more was heard of it. Instead, she was happy being Maxine's big sister, looking after her and lavishing on her the tenderness she might have given to a child of her own. Although not of the brightest intellect, Ada had a kind and loving nature – probably the cause of her downfall – and she loved every member of the family although her adoration of Tom practically amounted to worship. At the news of her father's death two years later she had shed a tear or two and insisted on attending the funeral only to be snubbed by her mother. After this, she disowned her old life just as her parents had disowned her, and she seemed none the worse for it. But the news of the death of her mother affected her deeply.

7.

'Doesn't like going out!' Irene had said.

Maxine was not satisfied with Irene's explanation. As soon as her aunt was out of the way Maxine went upstairs and knocked on Ada's door. Ada gave a muffled reply. Maxine opened the door and stood there looking at her friend who was sitting on her bed, crying into a soaking wet handkerchief.

'Ada what's the matter?' She said, 'I've never seen you cry before.'

Ada looked up and put out her arms and the little girl ran into them.

'Our mam's passed away,' said Ada and the two held each other for a while until Ada's tears began to soak Maxine's hair.

'You're spoiling my ringlets.' said Maxine as she drew back to look her friend in the eyes.

'Blow your nose,' she said, taking her handkerchief from her sleeve and handing it to Ada.

'It makes it better.'

Ada obediently blew.

Maxine's curiosity was aroused.

'Where did your mam live?'

'Paradise Street.'

Maxine nodded, *'No wonder she didn't like going out'* she thought.

'I've been to Paradise Street. My Daddy's office is there.'

'Mr Fletcher's office was bombed an' all, like rest of Paradise Street.'

'That's where the bombs were last night?'

'Aye, whole street blown to smithereens. The ARP man came and told us. Some of the bodies was so broken up and burnt they couldn't tell who was who. Some are buried, they're still diggin' for em.'

Maxine listened carefully, her mind spinning with strange thoughts.

'They're all dead then, the dirty people?'

'Dirty people?'

'Isn't your Mam one of the dirty people in Paradise Street? Is that why you don't go to see her?' she asked.

Ada was outraged.

'Not our mam. You could eat your dinner off her floors.'

'Then why don't you ever go and see her?'

'It's not her – it's me that's dirty. That's why she dun't like me, she thinks I'm a natural sinner and I brought shame on the family,' said Ada.

Maxine was outraged.

'That's just silly. You are the best and cleanest person in the world – well – except my Aunt Irene and my daddy and my mummy.'

Ada started to cry again.

Maxine put her arms about the crying girl and thought her own thoughts.

She was remembering someone else who had lived in Paradise Street; the little dirty girl with the liquorice root.

It gave her a creepy, almost enjoyable feeling to think that someone she had met might be in that strange state known as death. Lil had become, in Maxine's mind an enemy, someone to fear.

'Will she be in heaven?' she thought, *'Will she still be spitting at people?'*

She wasn't sure that God would allow that kind of behaviour and wondered how he would stop her.

Then another cold thought struck her. Maybe that stain of the liquorice spit on Maxine's fur coat was all that was left of Lil.

*

She woke up suddenly that night with Lil still on her mind. What must it be like to be dead? It was something she thought she would never find out. Well, not for years and years anyway. Every night she prayed to Jesus and she was positive he was listening.

'Please me live forever – or at least until I am a hundred and ten.'

But now a little girl had died in the blitz – a little girl about her own age. Could this possibly happen to her – to Maxine Fletcher? Could she become just a body – unrecognisable perhaps like the poor people in Paradise Street? Maybe little Lil hadn't bothered to pray to Jesus every night, maybe that's why he had let it happen. So Maxine got out of bed and knelt to pray even harder – just in case Jesus hadn't heard her the first time.

She stayed kneeling by the bed for a long time.

'Please let me live forever, please let me live forever.' until she gave a sneeze and realised she was freezing cold.

She decided that Jesus must certainly have heard her by this time and she crept back into bed and lay shivering. She reached for her hot water bottle, but found it had cooled off and only made matters worse. She thought of the fur coat in her wardrobe and considered getting it out to put on the bed.

Then another thought struck her. She knew about coughs and sneezes spreading diseases. Could spit spread death? She sneezed again.

'Mummy,' she cried out in panic, 'Mummy!', but there was no answering call from Connie. She tiptoed into her mother's room and saw Connie was lying there fast asleep, snoring gently.

She knew better than to try and wake her. The only thing that Connie would wake for now was the air raid siren; she was impervious to all other sounds. Maxine went back to her room and put on the light. She took the white fur coat from the back of the cupboard where she had hidden it and she held it at arm's length, looking away from it with disgust. The dirty spit marks were still there. Something of that dirty little girl was lurking in her wardrobe, making her feel dirty too. She couldn't mention it to her mother, knowing that any reference to the externalisation of bodily fluids would have her throwing up until Christmas.

She took the coat and went downstairs to the kitchen.

On a high shelf, well out of sight there was, she knew, a box of matches. Pulling over a chair, she climbed on to it and took down the box. She listened carefully to make sure nobody was about, and then clambering down, she took a match and struck it on the side of the box. The flame shot up high. Taking the coat, she applied the lighted match to where she supposed the death germs lurked, the place where the little girl's spittle had landed and rolled down the front of the coat. The fur blackened and shrivelled making a curious acrid smell. She put out the fire with water and went back to bed with the smell of burning fur in her nostrils – a smell that ever after would bring back the sight and sound of the little red haired girl.

*

Connie was furious when she found out, but Irene, who seemed somehow to understand, intervened and told her some story to placate her. What the story was Maxine never knew but she was never asked to explain. The coat was ruined, but the ever resourceful Connie, muttering 'Waste not, want not' cut it up into pieces to make trimmings and the whole family had to put up with white fur collars on their coats for years to come.

8.

Irene was at the Laurels, sitting alone at her desk in a mood of deep melancholy. Ian had been dead for eight years – it was the anniversary of his death. Despite the passing of the years, her unhappiness on this day never abated. She had loved him since she was a child – he had been everything in the world to her. It was for him she gave up her ambitions to be a ballerina. She had been five years old when she decided to marry him and it was during her years at the Royal Ballet school that she had found out he loved her too, had waited for her.

She was pleased when Scot arrived to bid them goodbye. The office of Grantley's had received a direct hit in the blitz and had been completely wiped out. Bereft of employment, Scot was free to return to Scotland and his beloved Marion.

'I brought this as a going away present,' he said, handing her a bottle of whisky.

She fetched a couple of glasses and poured out two strong tots and they retired to the drawing room and sat in the big easy chairs.

'Lucky I lighted a fire,' she said, 'Extravagant hussy that I am.'

Scot's former nervousness in her company had completely left him now that she was no longer his employer. They sat together, sipping contentedly like old friends.

'Leslie sends regrets,' he said. 'He would have come with me but, but er – he had pressing engagements.'

'Leslie?'

Scott laughed.

'Cuthbert! That was Tom's name for him. But Leslie reckons it's not a right name for a fighter pilot. He's proud of his real name. Leslie Howard was a special hero of his.'

'A fighter pilot! But he's such a child. Is he old enough?'

'Just about.'

'He never seemed like the heroic type.'

'People are unpredictable.'

They sat, quiet, for a while; thinking about the young man who had put himself in danger.

'What makes them want to do it?' said Irene at last, 'To risk their lives?'

'Who knows. He said he was sorry to miss the big scrap.'

'The Battle of Britain? I'm afraid there'll be more opportunities for him. I worry about his poor mother. She'll miss him dreadfully.'

Scot drained his glass.

'It'll be my turn soon. Wish me luck Irene.'

He had used her name for the very first time as if he no longer had to think of her as the boss's sister.

Irene was sad to see him go. She hadn't realised how much she had liked him. As he said, they could have been good friends if only things had turned out differently.

'Bloody Hitler,' she thought, 'he's got a lot to answer for.'

*

It had only been three months since Maxine's father had gone to war, but she was beginning to feel that he was a figment of her imagination. When she tried to bring him to mind, it was mostly single pictures that came in flashes like stills from a movie.

Sometimes it was the stern father – the one who unaccountably refused to give her a ha'penny for a bar of Five Boys chocolate despite the fact that all the other children had one.

'She must learn she can't have everything she wants!' he had remarked.

But then there was the jolly Daddy who took her for rides on his back, whinnying like a horse, and then mooing like a cow to make her laugh. That played the piano at her birthday party, singing *the laughing policeman* making all the other children envious.

Or the studious man who taught her to read, how to say some words of French and Italian. He helped her with her piano lessons and taught her how to use his typewriter correctly.

Very occasionally, she remembered the angry Daddy who got so furious when woken suddenly or interrupted when he was writing, erupting into a violence that made her run and hide.

And then there were whole scenes that stayed brightly in her memory.

The night last June when the bombs started falling on the town, he had carried her downstairs in her pyjamas and dressing gown, and joined Connie, Irene and Ada under the billiard table. She remembered with great clarity the way he made everyone laugh every time there was a bang. It had all seemed such fun, the four of them in their own little world, tucked under that great slate edifice, laughing at the bombs.

It was the next day that he arrived home to say the town was on fire – the day he joined up.

She remembered the flurry of busyness as his stuff was sorted out and his things were packed to go to the training camp near Huddersfield. Then off he went to catch his train.

'Be good, look after Mummy.' He hugged and kissed her. She could always bring to her mind the picture of how he was on that day – fresh faced, loving and kind with the floppy fair hair that he had combed back with brilliantine to stop it falling over his eyes, the smell of cigarettes and fresh air and saddle soap and bay rum. And most of all his clear forget-me-not blue eyes.

These images she carried with her and they meant even more than the letters he wrote, letters she could barely read and often didn't understand, but the latest of which she always carried like a talisman in her little purse.

*

Connie became angry and peevish when Tom had left her and she missed the loving flattery with which he always surrounded her. All she'd had to do was be beautiful and amusing, to entertain his guests. The sordid business of housekeeping, was all taken care of. Mrs Mears, the daily, kept the place clean and together Irene and Ada kept the house running smoothly. All she had to do was let them get on with it. One talent she allowed herself to display was for sewing and her main delight was making clothes for the rest of the family, her current speciality being the curious all-in-one known as The Siren Suit – familiarised by none other than Mr Churchill himself. She fabricated these hooded garments for every member of the family, but apart from that she still managed to spend a lot of time lying on the sofa, reading romantic novels by Denise Robbins and Ethel M Dell.

She'd had a qualm of jealousy when Tom did not even think of asking her to take charge while he was away. Why should he think that Irene would be more competent than she was? But then, she had never shown any interest in gravestones – found them a morbid topic of conversation, so she couldn't seriously complain.

There were other causes for complaint though when the war started getting nasty –all her daily luxuries, her make up; her silk dresses; and her expensive shoes all came from France or Italy and had become unobtainable. The laundry and dry cleaning people had joined up. Even her favourite hairdresser had got a job in munitions – but worst of all was the shortage of chocolate. That was something she felt impossible to accept. Her temper began to fray and the rest of the household avoided her.

'*Why is it,*' she thought to herself resentfully, '*Even my daughter doesn't care about me. She'd rather spend time with Ada than with her own mother?*'

9.

It was Sunday morning after breakfast. Irene was studying her accounts for the week and amusing herself by tuning in from time to time to Maxine who was having one of her frequent fruitless battles with her mother. As usual it was over a dress. Connie had made, with her own fair hands, a pretty little smock dress, hanging straight from neck to mid-thigh, in spinach green with floating yellow ribbons from a bow at the neck.

It was the dress that everyone exclaimed over, saying, 'What a pretty dress. Did your mother make it?'

Maxine longed to wear a dress that didn't look as if her mother had made it. She had seen girls in party dresses with waists and net skirts, just like grown up ballerinas and she envied them. Most of the time she kept her envy to herself, because even at that early age Maxine had found out that no matter what she said to her mother, Connie only ever heard what she wanted to hear.

'Maxine's favourite colour is green,' she always asserted with authority 'Most people with her colouring would wear blue but Maxine is sophisticated for her age, she much prefers green.'

Even her private school had a green uniform. Irene was of the secret opinion that it was the colour rather than the educational standards of the school that had influenced Connie's choice.

Maxine had a secret dream of wearing blue – the blue of forget-me-nots and the colour of her father's eyes, but if she mentioned it to Connie, her mother would just take on that far away, absent-minded look and say 'Yes darling' and no more would be said on the subject.

*

Today Maxine had decided to try something else.

'Can't I have a dress with a waist please?'

'A waist darling, whatever for?'

'So people stop thinking I look like Shirley Temple.'

Despite the fact that Connie always affected to despise anything to do with Hollywood, she gave a smirk at the comparison.

'Why should they think that? You are much prettier than Shirley Temple,' she said.

'Cos of my clothes. The little dirty girl called me Shirley Temple.'

'Don't be silly, when have you ever met any dirty little girls.'

Irene, sensing trouble, quickly intervened.

'I think Maxine is talking about the day we went to the office. There was a little girl in Paradise Street who thought she was Shirley Temple.'

Connie gave a shudder.

'I told you it was stupid taking the child to that horrible place. Heaven knows what those children are infested with. It's a wonder she didn't come back crawling.' A ghastly thought stuck her. 'She didn't actually touch you, did she?'

Irene suddenly had visions of weeks of fumigation and fine toothcombs and clenched her fists in anticipation of what the child might say. But Maxine was more interested in making her point.

'She called me Shirley Temple,' insisted Maxine.

Connie looked at her little daughter, head on one side.

'Well, I suppose you do look a little bit like Shirley Temple, the blonde curls and the dimples. But at least you don't have false teeth.'

'*Here comes the diversionary tactic*,' thought Irene to herself. She was not wrong; the idea of false teeth drove everything else out of her Maxine's head.

'Like Grandma Paget?' and she turned to Irene, 'Do you think she makes funny faces with them?'

Maxine and Irene together visualised Connie's late mother, who took out her teeth at night and kept them in a glass by her bed. Maxine was almost breathless with excitement when applying this picture to the famous child star.

Irene was also impressed by this image.

'What makes you think Shirley Temple has false teeth?'

'Of course she does. Have you ever seen her with a missing tooth? All children lose their teeth at some stage. She never did. It's disgraceful exploiting children in this way. Thank goodness Maxine has no desire to be a film star.'

This statement puzzled Maxine, who had always assumed that one day very soon that is exactly what she would be.

'Then why do I have dancing lessons every day?' she asked.

'Well, because of Aunt Irene's dancing school.'

'Don't blame me,' muttered Irene indignantly.

'Besides,' Connie went on 'Dancing lessons are essential for making a little girl into a graceful grown up lady. See how they cured Millicent Turner's knock-knees. Anyway it would be foolish not to when we have a dancing school right on the premises.'

'But I am going to be an actress, you know, Mummy – and I should start soon. Shirley Temple was a film star when she was my age! And I can dance just as well as she can. Can't I, Aunt Irene?'

Irene was about to reassure her but Connie jumped in.

'Better darling,' she said with pride and then added with great conviction.

'No darling, you are going to be a princess when you grow up. You don't want to end up kicking up your legs in the chorus. You can marry a Prince.'

'I don't know any princes.'

'You will darling. Just wait and see.'

'All right then,' the child said reluctantly, 'I'll be an actress first. Then I'll marry a prince later on when I'm old.'

'Princes don't marry chorus girls,' said Connie firmly 'And anyway' she added with great scorn. 'Shirley Temple is American.'

There was no more to be said. Connie began singing – a sure sign that she considered the conversation at an end.

Connie's favourite song was *'Someday my prince will come'* from *Snow White,* which she sang about the house in her sweet but somewhat uneven voice. She often sang the song to Maxine with an encouraging smile as if assuring her that one day she would be mingling her blood with royalty. Maxine at the age of seven had no hopes of this kind. Her heart was in Hollywood. But she silently decided that all further discussions of her future stage career would have to be with her aunt Irene.

'When I'm a famous actress. I'll wear dresses like forget-me-nots all the time – not horrid stinking spinach green and stupid Shirley Temple pink.'

Connie stood back to admire her offspring in her favourite green dress, and her champagne sandals and socks, her ringlets caught up with yellow ribbons. Everyone admired her mother's good taste and commented that Maxine was a lucky girl to have such a clever Mummy.

'That green dress really brings out that touch of green in your eyes,' Connie told her daughter proudly, 'Thank goodness you don't hanker after those horrible net dresses all the children are wearing these days. I suppose it helps the war effort – not using up all the valuable silks and things, but they are such frightfully bad taste.'

Maxine put on her hated pale green coat with the white fur collar and prepared herself for her Sunday morning walk. Unlike her parents, Maxine went to church – not locally but to a village outside town. The vicar was her mother's cousin and Connie believed fervently in nepotism.

'Ada, are you ready?' Maxine shouted.

Ada arrived in her best Sunday clothes, a brown hat perched on top of her little round face, a mustard coloured costume with the jacket open giving glimpses of the tight brown jumper stretched across her prominent breasts and on the collar of her jacket the white fur scarf that Connie had given her for her last birthday. Many people thought of Ada as mentally retarded and she politely allowed them to go on thinking so. She sensed that it would be unnerving for them to discern any signs of intelligence in a young woman from the wrong side of the tracks.

But in one respect Ada was foolish. She adored most men but was deeply, irrevocably in love with Tom who enjoyed many jokes at her expense.

'Ada,' he said one morning, 'The roses are looking a bit sad. I think we need manure for them.'

Anything Tom wanted he had to have so 'Aye Mr Fletcher,' she said and turned to rush off and procure some. A few minutes later, she returned.

'Where do I get it from?' she asked.

Tom laughed.

'Where do you think?'

'I dunno.'

'There are plenty of horses going up and down this road.'

'Oh I see,' she said and disappeared.

An hour later she arrived in Tom's study triumphantly bearing a bucket of steaming excrement. She put the bucket down at his feet.

'For roses,' she said proudly.

'Where did you get it?'

'Where you said. I follered milkman's horse, then coalman's horse. I stood be'ind 'em till they did it.'

Tom laughed immoderately. She watched him, puzzled.

'Sorry Ada, but I didn't really mean it. It was just a kind of…joke.'

'Oh' she said in a tiny voice. Shamefaced she picked up the bucket.

'I'll go and put it all back then!'

*

Ada was looking particularly blooming today. Maxine looked at her tummy closely.

'You're not getting another of those bumps are you?'

Ada shrugged and giggled at the same time.

The year before Ada had suddenly put on an enormous amount of weight. There had been a kind of roundness about her and a largeness of belly, which seemed to get bigger and bigger. Then she suddenly disappeared for a month and when she came back, the bump had gone.

Maxine made enquiries of her mother why this should be.

'Did she just burst or something?'

'It was a growth darling. It comes and goes,' said Connie with a nervous laugh.

Maxine had not found this explanation satisfactory, but could get no further sense out of her mother. Even Irene seemed to be reticent about this subject.

Ada and Maxine went off to church, both chattering excitedly. They enjoyed their Sunday morning walks through the lane – and Ada especially liked her visits to the church. There were several young men there who seemed to know her quite well. Even the curate grew a little pink when he spied her there in the churchyard.

'Why does Uncle John look at you all the time?' asked Maxine.

Ada laughed, 'He thinks I'm smashin' she said.

Maxine surveyed Ada, her mousy brown hair; her undistinguished grey eyes her round button face.

'Why are you so smashing, Ada?' asked Maxine as they picked their way through the muddy lane, jumping from clump to clump of grass to avoid getting their shoes messed up.

'Dunno,' Replied Ada, and after a moment's thought, 'maybe 'cos I let them think what they like about me. Folks don't like being in the wrong.'

Maxine looked at her unbelievingly, not quite understanding what she meant. But then she too thought Ada was a bit simple.

Having had such a religious upbringing, Ada was uneasy in church, so once she had got Maxine settled in the pew, with various friends and relations, she would leave her there, going away until the end of the service only to appear again pink and dishevelled at the church door ready to take her home.

Maxine never told her mother about this. It was just one of the many secrets that she and Ada shared.

10.

'Ey up Ladies!' shouted Edith Applegate as she bounded into Irene's studio, resplendent in her navy keep-fit shorts, white blouse and tennis shoes. Although the shirt had been newly bought for the classes, it was already straining across her rapidly growing bosom 'I must be the only lass who can put on weight in wartime' she would say with a burst of her loud, infectious laughter.

She kept the whole class laughing at her antics, especially with her vain efforts to keep her generous body under control.

'As the Keep Fit class's social secretary,' she announced to the assembled ladies.

'Since when?' asked Lucy Benson, the chippie 'one two three four one two three four' as she did her usual warm up, running on the spot.

'Since now! Stop jigging about love, I have news of great import!'

Lucy stopped jogging and contented herself with shaking her alternate feet in front of her 'One two three and, one two three and, one two three.'

'Now do them both at once,' cried Edith with another burst of laughter.

'Hurry up and spill the beans, Edie. We're agog.' put in Letty Parkes.

'OK!' said Edith. 'Guess what has arrived at the Cross Keys!'

'No!' cried Lucy 'at last!'

'What are you two idiots talking about?' said Letty.

With one voice Lucy and Edith cried, 'Gin!'

They now had the attention of the entire room.

'So I suggest we take a trip down there after class and sample it. To make sure it's fit for human consumption.'

'How do you know about the gin?'

Edith tapped her nose.

'Ways and means, love, ways and means.'

Edith worked in a sweet shop in the centre of town near and was in a prime position to discover information of this kind.

The Cross keys was a hostelry in the vicinity of the Town Hall – a pretty dangerous area during the blitz, but gin was in short supply and it was well worth it once you had made up your mind to take the journey. People were getting very bored with staying at home at night waiting for the sirens to sound.

'If it's got your name on it' was the feeling *'There's nowt you can do about it.'*

So, after class, the intrepid band of women, already chattering and laughing excitedly in anticipation of their treat, bussed into town for an hour's happy drinking. The Cross Keys, although on the outside was gloomy looking with massed sandbags and windows blanked out with heavy black curtain, it was cosy enough inside with its several small rooms served by one central mahogany bar. Renee's keep fit ladies went as usual to the Snug and their drinks were handed to them with a warning to 'keep it dark'.

As they were about to seat themselves around the table, the sound of chorus singing coming from the lounge made them change their minds and they wandered through the connecting door into the larger bar which boasted an ancient upright piano, played by an elderly, portly lady in a red felt hat and a floral gown.

'What a lot of people' remarked Lucy as they entered the lounge

'It must be the music that draws them,' replied Edith.

It was so full there was no table to accommodate the group, so they split up and sat at adjacent tables. Edith and Lucy managed to get chairs together and they sat themselves down, prepared to join in the singing. Sentimental songs like *'I'll be seeing you'* and *'We'll meet again'* were the fashion. Lucy had lost her husband who went off with the BEF to Dunkirk and had never returned. Edith had a string of boyfriends scattered over the globe and she spent every spare minute writing letters to them *'Safety in numbers'* was her motto.

The singing helped them to express their pent up emotions and they joined in with a will, hardly noticing the two little girls who crept in the room. Children were definitely not allowed in public houses, but as one, the assembled company kept their eyes averted and no comment was made on their presence. Just the same, Edith sensed that the singing was becoming more automatic and there was a feeling of anticipation, the distinct impression that something momentous was about to occur.

The two children crept quietly to the side of the room where the piano was standing.

The younger of the two was six or seven years old with an unruly mop of light auburn curls.

As she reached the piano, the elderly lady pianist gave a little smile and launched into the introduction to *'Somewhere Over the Rainbow'*.

The small child began to sing. She sang quietly at first and with perfect control. Then, as the song continued, the voice poured out of that tiny frame like liquid gold. It was a deep full throated with an underlying throb of passion and if filled the room soaring to the heights and sinking to the depths.

'My god, that child must have four octaves at least!' muttered Edith to Lucy, who was sitting there with her mouth open.

Lucy laughed – 'Impossible' she said.

But the voice was extraordinary. The voice of a grown up woman with silvery childlike overtones, the effect was devastating. Every person in that room had their own rainbow to long for, had their own wishes and hopes and the child's rainbow became theirs. She seemed to speak directly to each one of them, reaching their hearts.

No one noticed that, although fairly clean, her little pink dress was faded and split under the arm. They were enraptured by her voice and personality. She wore a scruffy pair of plimsolls that must have been worn and thrown out by dozens of children before, but as the song came to a close, she rose up on her toes and started to dance, as light and graceful as thistledown – she could have been wearing the most elegant of pumps as she allowed herself to be carried along by the music issuing from the piano.

As the song came to an end, the child stopped dancing and sang the coda *'If happy little blue birds fly – beyond the rainbow, why oh why can't I?'*

The voice rose higher and higher until it reached the final note which she left hanging, it seemed for ever, in the air until it faded away into nothing. As the music ended, there was a reverent silence before the tearful audience burst into a round of applause. The child curtsied in acknowledgement, but declined to repeat the performance and, running to Mrs Dewing, the landlady, took the piece of bread and jam that was offered and started devouring it hungrily.

The other child, a plain little girl of maybe ten or eleven with the same coloured hair to state the family resemblance, but with no other similarity, came around with a hat and took a collection. All the time, she looked apprehensively over her shoulder at Mrs Dewing as though she might suddenly give them the sign to get lost. Mrs Dewing was keeping her eyes on the door in case the police came in. She knew she was playing a dodgy game, but running a pub in the middle of a danger area and with a meagre ration of liquor was not the way to make a fortune or even a living. Any method of bringing in customers was a bonus and the entertainment she provided brought the people back time and time again to watch the little star.

When the collecting girl arrived at their table, Edith Applegate stopped her and asked her name.

The little girl curtsied politely.

'Janie Marsden Miss,' she said.

'And who's the one who did the singing?'

'Me sister, Miss,' the child replied. Edith turned to her friend Lucy who was searching in her purse for some suitable change.

'She really ought to go to Madam Renee'.

Lucy looked up from her search, startled.

'You are joking of course,' she whispered.

'What's Madam Renay?' asked Janie.

'She gives dancing lessons,' said Edith.

'I don't want dancing lessons. I can dance,' said a gruff voice behind her and the little girl stood, arms akimbo, jam on her face, looking at her belligerently.

'This is my sister, Miss,' said Janie, 'You mucky kid' and she pulled down the sleeve of her cardigan and spat on it, applying the dampened cardigan to her sister's jammy face.

'Aye,' said the scrap, as her sister carried out the impromptu ablutions, 'I'm Jessie Maffews, the film star.'

Edith laughed.

'I've never met a film star before'.

Sensing that she was being mocked, *Jessie Maffews* stuck out her chin pugnaciously and raised her fist, which Janie quickly grabbed.

'Her real name's Lil,' said the older girl, 'But she wants to be Jessie Maffews.'

'She's more like a young Deanna Durbin,' said Lucy, and the child scowled ferociously at the comparison.

'More Judy Garland I should say.' disagreed Edith and the child scowled even more.

Edith turned back to Janie.

'She can't waste that talent. She must go to stage school.'

'Doesn't that take money? We ain't got no money.'

'She could get work. She could do pantomime. That would help pay the tuition.'

'What's pantomime?' Janie wanted to know, her little face turned up to the lady and her eyes shining with interest.

'Oh you poor kid, have you never seen a pantomime?' asked Lucy.

Lil growled at being called a poor kid. Edith, seeing this and witnessing the puzzled look on Janie's face, tried to explain.

'All the theatres have them at Christmas. There are children in them.'

'Ah've never been. What's it like?'

'Want to go to toilet,' said Lil and pulled at her sister's hand.

Janie remained where she was, looking curiously at Edith.

'What's feeter?' she said.

'People go there to watch shows – acting, singing and dancing.'

'Like at Regal?'

'A bit, yes.'

'We go to pictures nearly every day,' boasted Janie, 'to learn dancing steps.'

'How do you pay for that if you don't have any money?'

Janie shook her head. She was considering an earlier remark by Edith.

'Do they get money for it, then? The pantomime?' she asked with new interest.

'Yes of course. But you have to take lessons from Madame Renee first.'

Edith jotted down the address on an old envelope she found in her purse.

'I done it,' said Lil as a little pool spread on the floor underneath her tennis shoes. Lil dipped her shoes into the puddle and skated it across the cheap brown linoleum.

'Yer daft bugger,' said Janie, grabbing her arm to stop her 'Couldn't you wait till we got outside?'

'No, I couldn't.'

'Come on, we better go,' said Janie, grabbing Lil's hand. As they left she turned and took the piece of paper from Edith.

She whispered in Edith's ear.

'Don't tell Mrs Dewing – what Lil done.'

'I won't, I promise,' said Edith.

As the little girls dodged out the side door, Edith took up her handkerchief and started mopping up the mess of the floor. Lucy looked at her in amazement.

'What are you going to do with that handkerchief?'

Edith shrugged. She took the sodden handkerchief into the ladies' room and rinsed it out in water. She looked for the soap, then realised that even if the landlady provided such a precious commodity it would have been taken long ago.

She looked around for something to wrap the handkerchief in, shrugged her shoulders and left it in the sink.

11.

The bombing never really let up. There were gaps, to be sure, when everyone began to think maybe things were back to normal and started cleaning out their air raid shelters, washing their blankets and moving back into their bedrooms. The lulls were merely temporary, however, and before they had a chance to get their blankets dry, the raids would start again.

In May 1941, to show he meant business, Hitler set about the total annihilation of the city. The Fletcher family abandoned their upstairs bedrooms altogether and moved outwards and downwards. Extra beds were made up in the cellar and bunks erected in the brick shelter in the garden.

However, the bombing brought another addition to the family, which turned out to be a key one.

The all clear had gone early that night. It was only just after midnight, and Connie, Irene and Ada were settling down in the kitchen with a cup of cocoa when there was an insistent ringing at the doorbell.

'Who on earth can that be?' asked Irene, glancing at her wristwatch.

Ada rushed to the door, to prevent further ringing from waking Maxine who had just got to sleep. On the doorstep was a wild-haired woman, shoeless; her bare feet filthy and bleeding, as were the tattered remnants of the long grey dinner dress that covered her spare form. Sparkling oddly in the midst of the dirt and rags was a diamond necklace, which hung around her throat. Despite her bedraggled state, the apparition laughed at Ada's startled face. She spoke in a powerful Yorkshire voice in accents of one used to command.

'It's all right, young woman. It's not a ghost. It's Constance's long lost Aunt Paget come to visit.'

And pushing Ada aside, she marched into the kitchen.

'Constance, where are you?'

Connie looked up from her cocoa, and after a while recognised her aunt.

'Aunt Paget! What on earth's happened to you?'

'We were dancing, and we got bombed,' she said with a rueful laugh.

'But why were you dancing during an air raid, all dressed up like a Christmas tree with your diamond necklace?'

'Have I still got that?' she asked, put her be-ringed hand up to her throat. 'Well, that's something.'

She sipped the cup of cocoa Ada had brought her.

'I don't suppose you've anything stronger? A gin and it would not go amiss.'

'You are joking of course,' said Connie sharply. 'But we do have a drop of Scotch which we've been saving for emergencies.'

'I presume you mean whisky, dear,' remarked Aunt Paget. 'Where do you get these common expressions? Certainly not from our side of the family.' And she looked accusingly at Irene – who raised her hands as if to say '*Not guilty.*'

'I'm not blaming you Irene. Southern folk can't help it. But I never understood why Constance couldn't marry a proper Yorkshire boy.'

Connie just smiled as she handed the glass to her aunt. Aunt Paget took a hearty slug of the drink and poured the remainder into the beaker of cocoa, which she balanced on her knee.

'This doesn't happen to people like us,' she said, 'It only happens to people who live down by the docks. I mean there we were at the ball, a load of pensioners raising money to fight the wretched Hun and they drop bombs on us. Damned impertinent, I'd say.'

'Then you weren't at home. Aunt?'

'Do I look as if I was having a quiet evening washing my hair? No, as I said. I was out dancing for the troops. There was this almighty explosion and the roof just came down right in the middle of the Dashing White Sergeant. It was quite a surprise. Well, I must have flaked out for a bit cos when I came to, there I was lying under a pile of rubble. So after deciding I was still alive, I started shoving off the plaster and stuff from the wall and ceiling on top of me; and feeling myself all over to see if it was all still there. As everything seemed to be in working order, I got myself out from under the wreckage and found my way out.'

'Were there many casualties?'

'I didn't wait to find out. There wasn't a lot I could do on my own. There were some unpleasant sights. Constance dear, you would have hated it. No. My first thought was to get help. I just looked for the nearest warden and told him what had happened. He was very kind and wanted to take me to hospital, but I said, 'Better look for the others' and he went off.'

Irene was looking at Aunt Paget in awe. Here was a woman she hardly knew; The Paget family – her in-laws were not exactly a close family and communicated rarely. Nevertheless, she was family, the first one to be involved in air raids and she was taking it incredibly calmly.

'Well, you did right to come straight here,' said Connie.

'No – why would I do that?'

'Well, you are here.'

'No. I went straight home. I started walking, and then a nice young soldier gave me a lift on his crossbar. So I went to West Ella, to my cottage.'

Aunt Paget's powerful tones, which had not faltered until now, let her down as she remembered the sight of her treasured house, destroyed and set on fire by a stray incendiary bomb.

'The rotten Boshe had got that too…'

'Oh no…not your cottage!'

'Four hundred years it had survived. We took such good care of it'. Aunt Paget brushed away the tears that had started to course down her face. She looked piteously at her niece.

'Would it be possible to have a bath?'

'Of course Aunt. There should be hot water, we've had the fire on all day. Oh dear Aunt, I'm so sorry about the cottage.'

'I realise how lucky I am to have somewhere to go. While the firemen were bringing me here, I couldn't help thinking of all the poor wretches who have been pushed out into the street, what happens to them eh?'

Connie took her Aunt's hand and then, moved beyond words by the tragedy, gave her a long hug. Her aunt allowed herself to be held for a while, then pushed her aside.

'Don't worry about me. I've only lost some stuff,' she said, 'But I have no clothes – only what you see. Maybe you could lend me some things until I get sorted out.'

'We are probably the same size,' said Irene 'My clothes would fit you,'

'Thank you, If you can find me something I'd be so grateful,' she said.

So it was that Aunt Paget settled herself down as a permanent resident at the Laurels. Connie immediately got her Singer working and fabricated yet another siren suit from the remnants she had procured. Nobody was allowed to ask how or where the bits of cloth came from. She had kitted out the entire family in those curious all in one zip up garments popularised by no less a person than Mr Churchill himself.

Maxine's was, of course, moss green, and lined with red flannelette. Realising she was doomed to wear it until the duration, she imagined the green into khaki and pretended to be a soldier in battle dress. After that, she quite enjoyed wearing it.

Aunt Paget certainly made her presence felt – a definite godsend. Ever resourceful, she took over the catering, in fact, the entire running of the household. She was digging for victory. Growing vegetables and fruit, making jam from rhubarb; beer from dandelions and nettles and sweets by mixing dried and condensed milk together. She followed all the recipes on the BBC and in the Hull Daily Mail and came up with dishes that were made of hardly anything and were frequently quite edible. All this activity left the rest of the household to concentrate on their war work. Irene, who was on the conscription list and expecting call up papers any minute, was running more keep fit classes every evening as the women of the town realised they needed to keep healthy to stay alive and working for the war effort.

During the day, the studio filled up with babies and little children. Many of the mothers were doing important war work, and they helped each other by babysitting in shifts.

Irene kept an eye on the crèche with input from Ada helped in the nursery in addition to her part-time work at the munitions factory The place was a hive of activity.

12.

But the biggest surprise of all was Connie – who joined the ARP.

Asked what drove her to it, she would reply tersely 'Boredom' but there had been a certain look in her eyes when Aunt Paget told her story which showed the family that at last she had become caught up in the country's plight. She became incensed every time she heard a radio news bulletin about the raids on Coventry. She would shout back at Frank Philips or Alvar Lidell,

'What about Hull then? Why don't you tell them about what we have to put up with?'

But of course they never did. Only the people who were actually there in Hull knew what was happening.

Aunt Paget's mishap had made her angry and brought out a streak of toughness in Connie that no one could ever have suspected. As a warden, she was reckless in her courage during the bombardment; Dashing here and there in her steel helmet, shepherding people to the shelters, rescuing them, their children and their animals from falling debris.

Even more astonishing was her work with the bombed out people. She became involved in a scheme to take over as many empty houses as could be found in the area, including the newly built North Hull Corporation estate, scrub them up and furnish them with whatever could be begged, borrowed or stolen in order to rehouse the refugees from the harder hit parts of town.

In theory it sounded wonderful but it was not entirely successful.

'Those families from the slums don't even know what plumbing is,' She remarked with a shudder, 'They've never known an inside lavatory – and don't know what to do with it.'

Many of the poor families felt embarrassed in their new, clean surroundings. They missed the cosiness and companionship of their former existence and often absconded, taking with them furniture, bedding, whatever they could carry. They left stains of urine, defecation and menstrual waste all over the floors and even up the walls and blocked up the lavatories with garbage. When they had gone Connie and the rest of the team had to go back in, delouse the properties and clean them up all over again for the next wave of refugees. But there were others who were happy and grateful just to have a roof over their heads and it was from these that the hardworking women got the incentive to carry on.

For a young woman who had an aversion to getting her hands dirty and who would throw up at any bad smell, it was a curious choice of career, but Connie didn't seem to find it strange. Jolly Edith Applegate was also part of the team and she became Connie's closest colleague and best friend. They worked well together and braced each other against all the horrors they encountered. As Connie would say, 'It's just a case of doing what had to be done.'

It provided her with a new lease of life. She no longer had time to lie on the sofa and long for chocolate, champagne and compliments. She became healthier, had a rosy glow about her and a renewed vitality as she lost that discontented expression that had never been far away. What is more, she happily put up with Aunt Paget's bullying, knowing that this was the older woman's only way of showing affection. As Aunt Paget often remarked

'I don't believe in all that kissy kissy stuff.'

Connie and Edith delighted in regaling the rest of the Laurels household about their ghastly experiences bringing forth such remarks from Aunt Paget as, 'They should be put those ungrateful wretches against a wall and shot. You didn't see me peeing in the bath after I'd been bombed out'.

*

Connie and Edith were hard at work one day tidying up a house that had been particularly badly treated and whose tenants had taken away every stick of furniture, every item of bedding, cutlery, pots and pans – even the light bulbs had been removed. All that was left were old, torn copies of the Daily Mail and a few strips of old sheet lying around.

'What would they be using these for?' asked Edith.

'I can't even begin to imagine' replied Connie with a shudder.

They went from room to room exclaiming about all the things that were missing.

'How could they carry all this stuff? Do you suppose they had a wheelbarrow?'

'Probably nicked one. 'said Edith.

'Where would they go? They must have somewhere to keep all the things.'

'Oh come on Connie, don't be so naïve. They've got a fence I bet. All that stuff will be on sale in the market next week. We'll probably be buying it back ourselves!' And Edith went to have a look at the state of the bathroom.

'Connie – what in hell is this?' cried Edith.

Connie came in to see what it was lying in the bath.

'It's just a bundle of old wallpaper.'

'What do you mean old? It's just been pulled off the wall. I only put it up last week.'

'New or old, it has to go,' she said and reached into the bath to remove the offending mass of paper.

As she did so, she gave a scream or horror and turned her face away.

'What is it?'

'I can't believe it.' gasped Connie, her hands over her face. Edith peered over her shoulder and saw there, in a mass of congealing blood, an aborted foetus.

'No wonder they left in such a hurry,' said Edith. 'Get me the bucket will you.'

She calmly extracted the bloody mess from the bathtub and put it into the bucket they had brought with them.

'I'd no idea there was so much... stuff involved. Have we really got all that inside us?' she said.

Connie turned her head away. 'Just shut up,' she said.

Edith nodded and swished the mess around in the bucket.

'What shall we do with it now?'

Connie was swilling the blood from the bath and vomiting into the lavatory pan at the same time.

'There's only one thing we can do. Bury it,' she said, between heaves.

She wiped her face and looked round for something she could use to dig a hole in the garden. She came back with a small coal shovel that had been left in the fireplace.

'This is about the only other thing they've left behind,' she said, 'Let's see if there's something else outside'

They took the bundle into the garden with them where they found a child's bucket and spade. It was old and battered, not worth selling and had been discarded by the absconding tenants.

So the two women, dressed in siren suits. Red and blue respectively, ventured into the yard with their implements, the blue suit holding its breath and the red one still retching, and with their improvised implements they dug a hole as deep as they could and, wrapping the unborn creature in the bits of sheets that had been lying around, they buried it at the bottom of the garden.

'Should we say a prayer or something?' asked Edith.

Connie shrugged.

'I'm not sure. I never know whether a thing that size is a person or not, do you?'

'I try not to think about it.'

'Mm,' said Connie, 'better not take any chances.'

So they stood and said a few silent words for the soul of the child that never was. Neighbours, catching sight of them, looked at each other and shrugged. People did a lot of digging during the war. 'Dig for Victory' was the catchphrase, and maybe they thought the odd prayer would help the crops along.

As they stood there, solemnly praying, Edith suddenly bubbled over with irrepressible laughter.

'Whatever's the matter?' enquired Connie.

Edith, gasping for breath leaned heavily against the garden fence.

'I don't know what I look like', she said, 'But you look exactly like a garden gnome in your Siren suit, with the red pixie hood and that shovel in your hand.'

Indignant at first that her handiwork was being made fun of, Connie was about to remonstrate when she too dissolved into giggles.

'You look pretty stupid as well,' she said, 'I wish I could see the two of us together.'

Still giggling, the two ladies put a cross and a heavy piece of stone above the grave.

'We wouldn't want anyone planting potatoes here,' remarked Connie, which produced another paroxysm of giggles from Edith.

Solemnities over, the two women went back into the house and started making it thoroughly ready for the next lot of refugees.

13.

'What was that?'

Irene looked up from her books as she heard a tiny sound at her front door. It was such a small knock, more like the scratching of a small animal. She went out into the hall. In the top of the front door there was a window, which was useful for seeing who was standing on the step, She peered out, but could see no one. She gave a sigh, thinking that the whole thing had been imagined and went back into the front drawing room. No sooner had she sat down than the scratching sound came again. This time it was at her window. The tapping became more and more insistent until at last she went to the window and drew aside the heavy lace curtain.

She caught the glimpse of a terrified child's face as the little one turned and ran down the front garden showing only a small pair of worn out soles as she disappeared into the street beyond. Irene rushed to the door.

'Stop! stop! I won't hurt you,' she cried.

She ran down the front garden path to the gate and looked up and down the road, but there was no sign of the child. She turned to go back into the house, but a slight movement caught her attention. She saw, hiding being the great privet bush on one corner of her fence a small red head peeping round the corner – the late sun glinting on steel rimmed spectacles, a glimpse of a tattered frock which blew out in the wind. She ran to the bush and peered behind it, but again there was nothing to be seen.

Again she cried out 'Come out, I won't hurt you' but there was no reply.

Eventually, she shrugged and went back into the house, conscious all the time of a pair of eyes watching her, but she couldn't tell where or how. She closed the door, angry now, and returned to her drawing room. It was time for the three o'clock class and the house was soon over run with children.

Children dressed in their practice clothes, their faces plump and rosy, and their clothes clean and well cared for. It was obvious that the small apparition had not been one of her pupils. She looked at them carefully and none showed signs of playing some kind of game with her. Even when she questioned them, no one owned up. She decided to let the incident go for the moment and she concentrated on her teaching.

She loved her work, it uplifted her. There was no doubt that Maxine, her niece, was the star of the class. She was such a pretty child, good-natured, never resenting criticism and only interested in working hard. Her talent and her capacity for hard work would stand her in good stead, but Renee had reservations about her. She felt that maybe Maxine had not the ruthless desire to succeed, the obsessive ambition that would make the difference between competence and brilliance. Maybe it was just that everything had come too easily to her.

She thought no more of her strange visitor until the following afternoon.

She was sitting, writing out her accounts when there was a knock at her study door. It was Aunt Paget, dragging behind her a little girl of about ten years old.

'I found this lurking in the back garden. I suppose I should have boxed its ears and sent it home. But it insisted it had to see you. I decided to give it the benefit of the doubt.'

The little creature was shaking all over with terror. With a trembling hand, she adjusted her steel rimmed spectacles, which had fallen over to one side in the panic.

'What do you want with me?' asked Irene kindly.

The child hung her head as two big tears came into her eyes and ran down her plain and very pale face. Irene found her strangely appealing.

'Won't you sit down?' she said 'How about some lemonade?'

The girl's face brightened and she nodded.

'Is there any lemonade Aunt Paget? And – a biscuit or something?'

'When did we last have biscuits?' asked Aunt Paget. 'Don't you know there's a war on?'

'There must be something in the larder. What about some of your lovely ground rice cheese cakes?'

The cheesecakes were a family joke. Cheesecakes or Chizzaks as they were called in Yorkshire came in two varieties, the ones made with curd cheese, butter and currants, and the ones with ground almonds. Both lots of ingredients were difficult to track down in wartime, but Aunt Paget had come up with a substitute using ground rice and almond essence, which was easier to find. It was not a successful experiment, they were universally loathed, but for some reason, Aunt Paget went on making them relentlessly, announcing,

'You'll be glad of these one day. Remember, there's a war on,' was her favourite cry.

For the first time Irene was glad of them, the request placated her aunt in law and she hustled out of the room.

'Sit down, won't you,' said Irene again.

The little girl went over to a pale yellow silk chair.

'No, not there' amended Irene suddenly as she noticed the child's muddy feet and legs.

'This chair is better for your back,' she explained kindly, indicating an upright kitchen chair.

The child gave the yellow chair a yearning look, then climbed obediently on to the upright chair and sat there awkwardly, her knees together, her feet hanging high above the ground. Irene tucked a stool under her feet.

'There, that's better,' she said. 'What can I do for you?'

The little girl, alarmed by such kind attention, was too frightened to speak, so Irene concentrated on trying to put her at her ease.

'Do you live around here?' she asked, 'I haven't seen you before!'

The child shook her head.

'I've lived in this town for a long time. I'm surprised we haven't bumped into each other before now,' Irene went on.

The child still sat there, mute, looking around here, taking in the furnishings of the room; the shelves of books, the piano in the corner with piles of music laid carelessly on the piano stool.

She looked at the table next to her and opened her eyes wide at the sight of the little china shepherdess that sat there. It seemed to hypnotise her and she stared and stared.

So there they were sitting when Aunt Paget arrived with a tray full of the despised cheesecakes, a pot of tea and a jug of her own homemade lemonade. She dumped the tray on a side table and bustled out.

'Would you like some lemonade?' asked Irene – pouring a glass and handing it to the child.

The child smiled excitedly and accepted the glass, taking it in both hands with great care. She took a sip and made a face.

'Tain't lemonade,' she said, 'no bubbles.'

Irene laughed.

'It's a different kind of lemonade,' she said, 'I'm awfully sorry, we don't have the fizzy kind. Maybe you'd prefer a cup of tea.'

The little girl shook her head and drank a little more. Irene was amused to see how the sourness of the lemonade made her face crumple up in a comical fashion.

'Sall right. Ah like it,' she said and her eyes rested on the plate of cakes.

'Would you like one of these?'

The child panicked, being faced with a problem of where to put the lemonade.

Irene took it from her and placed it on the table next to the shepherdess. The child nodded and took a cake, biting into it with obvious enjoyment and eating with great rapidity. Irene, without speaking, handed another.

The child was obviously hungry.

'Didn't you have any lunch?'

'I 'ad a chip butty for me dinner. But Dave stole it,' she explained.

'Then dig in,' said Irene 'I'm so glad you are enjoying them.'

The child took another cake.

'Oh ta,' she said, remembering her manners.
'Now maybe you can explain what you want.'
'Are you Madam Renay?' she asked.
'Yes I am. How do you know?'
'T'woman told me about you.'
'Woman?'
'Fat woman. In pub. Cross keys. You teach dancing – for pantomimes'.
'Yes I do – do help yourself to the buns.'
The child took another one – she was eating a little more slowly now.
'Now then,' thought Irene, 'now the appetite problem is solved, might get some sense out of her.'
'First you'd better tell me your name.'
'Janie Marsden,' she said.
'And are you interested in having dancing lessons?'
This was met by a burst of giggles.
Janie Marsden laughed and laughed, choking on her bun.
'Have I said something funny?' said Irene, patting heron the back.
'Tin't me,' explained Janie, 'I can't dance, me. But I can sew.'
'Very useful. Just as useful as dancing,' said Irene. 'But why do you want to know about the lessons?'
'Me sister, Lil can dance. She was dancing in pub when we met them ladies and one of 'em said I should bring her 'ere. She's good is our Lil,' she said all in one breath.
'How old is your sister?'
'Seven and a quarter.'
'Then if she's serious, she really should be having lessons.'
Janie nodded her head vehemently.
'Yeh, yes she is. She's good, Allus 'as been. She could be a film star – like Ginger Wogers.'
'What's her name?'
'Lil Marsden, but she says she's Jessie Maffews. Jessie Maffews was a poor girl an' all and now she's a big star and talks posh like you I've seen her at pictures. Lil can dance just like her. She's real clever is our Lil.'
'Where is she now?'
'Outside, waiting for me.'
'You mean outside in the street? You must bring her in at once. It's not safe out there.'
The child looked at her, puzzled.

'Why? There's no raid on?'

The blitz was the only danger she knew about.

'Go and get her at once.'

Janie clambered down from the chair. Irene stood, about to accompany the child but Janie put out her dirty little hand to stop her.

'Better you don't come. She's funny is our Lil.'

'How do you mean?'

'She's funny with strangers.'

14.

Janie came back a few minutes later, dragging behind her a tiny scrap of a child – looking younger than her seven years of age. She presented her to Irene.

'Here's our Lil.'

The little girl scowled.

'Ah'm Jessie Maffews,' she insisted, but her eye had caught the sight of the buns left on the table. She put out her hand to get one, and then looked at Janie for permission.

'Can she have a bun?' asked Janie.

'Of course she can.'

Lil took the plate of buns and emptied it into her skirt.

Janie slapped her on the wrist and the buns fell to the ground.

'She shouldn't of done that,' said Janie, 'but we'll pick them up again. Lil, pick 'em up again. And don't tread them into carpet.'

Lil picked up a bun from the floor and crammed it into her mouth.

Irene watched her in silence, aware that the child seemed vaguely familiar to her.

The child was eating very quickly now and suddenly she caught a crumb in her throat and started to cough. Janie, quickly and efficiently, patted her on the back to relieve the tension and the offending bit of cake flew out into Janie's waiting hand.

Janie turned to Irene.

'She does that 'she said chattily 'when she's 'ungry, she eats too fast, she gobbles it up and this 'appens.'

Janie looked at the piece of cake in her hand, not quite knowing what she should do with it. Lil made as if to snatch it from her. Irene silently handed over a waste paper basket and Janie dropped the soggy big of cake into it.

'Or'right now – our Lil?' she asked.

The child nodded and put out her hand for another cake.

Janie instead handed her the glass of lemonade and the child drank thirstily.

'When did you two last have something to eat?' asked Irene.

'Mrs Dewing gave us bread and marge last night,' replied Janie. 'She allus gives us summat when we've done singing.'

Irene thought this was no time for explanations. She could find out soon enough about the singing and who Mrs Dewing was. At this moment in time she was worried about the children, where they lived, what she was going to do with them. They obviously had a definite purpose in coming to see her which was nothing to do with Ground Rice Cheesecakes and lemonade.

Janie helped her out.

'Will you watch her dance?' she asked.

Irene nodded.

'Have you got a piano player?'

Irene laughed.

'Not here at the moment. I can play, but then I wouldn't see her. I have a better idea. Why can't she dance to the gramophone?'

'Where's that?' asked Janie looking around.

Irene indicated the large mahogany radiogram she kept in the corner.

'Can you play that?'

'Yes, do you want to hear it?'

Janie nodded and Lil kept on eating.

Irene selected some records, aware of Janie's eyes watching her, and Lil's total lack of interest.

'Do you like Vera Lynn?' she asked, 'Or something classical?'

'Dunno,' said Janie, 'Dunno what you mean.'

Irene put on just four records – the fairies dance from *Midsummer Night's Dream*, *We'll meet again*, the first movement of *the moonlight sonata* and *The Laughing Policeman* – A selection geared to assess the taste of the two children. It was exciting, finding out what these totally unlettered infants would be interested in hearing.

Lil was still concentrating on her cakes and lemonade when the music started.

As the strains of Mendelssohn's music filled the air, a strange transformation came over her, and forgetting her food, she got to her feet and let the music take over. She danced perfectly in rhythm and with a grace not even seen in all trained ballerinas. Her youthful joints were so supple and by some extraordinary osmosis they seemed to know exactly how to behave. Her control and her strength were phenomenal. She paid no attention to the two watching but carried on, in her own private world whirling and leaping and pirouetting.

When the music finished, she turned to Irene, pleading for the sound to continue. It took a little time for the next record to fall and she turned again to the plate of cakes. Just as she was about to take one, the music began again and she forgot all about them. A look of complete rapture came over the tiny face, and this time she began to sing along with Vera Lynn. Irene had never known anything like it. This was not the piping voice of a tiny seven-year-old child, but the voice of a mature woman highlighted with silvery childlike tones that added rather than took away from the magic. She sang the words, not quite understanding, but she phrased it to echo exactly the phrasing of Vera Lynn.

Janie and Irene still watched in silence. Janie knew and Irene was finding out that this was a precocious, phenomenal talent that must be nurtured at all costs.

As the moonlight sonata began there were yet more revelations. Lil slowed down the tempo of her dancing and moved in a dreamy sustained slowness which showed off her strength and her immediate response to the music.

Janie whispered to Irene 'Nice music', and Irene felt as if she was listening to it for the very first time.

As the child sank into a deep curtsey at the end of the record, there was an air of almost religious hush which was broken by Irene's delighted cry. The child looked at her for the first time, her tiny sulky face transformed, and as she looked into her eyes, Irene remembered her as the little girl she had met in Paradise Street months before. She was cleaner now, her hair was combed and she had shoes, but she knew from those pansy purple eyes that this was the same child.

Irene also knew that she had stumbled upon something. The child had quality, something Irene had occasionally recognised when she was a member of Sadler's Wells in London. It was because she had not recognised this in herself that she had willingly given up her career for teaching – and to marry Ian – and up and coming lawyer who later succumbed to the flu epidemic.

Nearly mad with grief, she left London altogether to live with her brother and start her school here in Hull. She had always dreamed of finding a star and she could hardly believe what was happening.

The laughing policeman broke the hush quite decisively and the three of them laughed along with the record, the ice now firmly broken. As soon as the record finished, the two children waited, expectantly for the next treat and were sad and disappointed when it didn't come.

Ada, attracted by the sounds coming from Irene's room, had come in to find out what it was all about; she sat down quietly and watched the show, unnoticed by the others who were completely engrossed in what they were doing. As the music came to an end, she got to her feet and prepared to take the dirty plates and glasses away.

Lil snatched them to her diminutive bosom. Ada laughed.

'Don't worry. I'm not thieving from you.'

The little girls smiled at the sound of a familiar accent and Ada felt her heart almost stop at the beauty of that smile.

Irene smiled too, surprised to find that she had spent her entire afternoon enjoying the company of the two children, but Janie suddenly announced.

'It's dark; we have to go to pub.'

Irene held them both, one under each arm.

'Which pub is this? You shouldn't be going to pubs.'

Janie gave a huge exasperated sigh and explained to Irene as if she was a mentally deficient child.

'Pub is where Lil does the singing.'

Lil interrupted her renewed consumption of cakes.

'Jessie Maffews!'

'Jessie Maffews sings and dances, I collect pennies. Mrs Dewing lets us sleep in her snug sometimes.'

Irene was brought up suddenly.

'Sleep in the snug? Haven't you anywhere else. No house or anything?'

'Course we have – lots of houses.'

'How do you mean?'

'We was bombed out. We keep moving.'

'Where are you now?'

Janie pointed in a southerly direction.

'Over there.'

'You don't know the address?'

'Forgotten!'

'What about your mother and father?'

'Mam's passed on,' explained Janie matter of factly. 'And step Dad just gets drunk and wallops us. We're better stopping at snug when he's like that.'

'Won't he worry?'

Janie shrugged.

'Don't fink so. Don't care if he does. He's got free other kids – and he's got Agnes his fancy woman. He won't miss us two.'

'They can stay with me in my room,' put in Ada who was standing, looking at the children with infinite compassion. Irene took up the offer.

'Yes, stay here tonight with Ada and I'll go over and have a word with your father.'

The two children burst into raucous laughter.

'What's the matter?'

'You can't speak to Dad after dinner,' said Janie.

'He's too shickered by then,' explained Lil.

'Then you've got to stay,' urged Ada.

'We'll be all right,' promised Janie.

'It's no bother, there's a spare bed. Big enough for both of you, or you can have the settee. It's comfy.'

'Don't wanna,' said Lil, 'Wanna go to pub.'

'We don't want to do that,' interpreted Janie, 'Mrs Dewing wants us at pub.'

She took Lil b the hand and pulled her to the door.

'Then you'll bring Lil back again on Saturday?'

'To the dance class?' said Janie. 'To get her into Pantomime?'

'I can dance,' said Lil. 'She just saw me.'

'You've got to have dance class to get into pantomime,' explained Janie and turned to Irene.

'She's only a bairn,' she said. 'She dunt understand.'

'So you will come back on Saturday. At about ten o'clock?'

'We ain't got a clock, but I'll get her here in morning.'

Irene asked Ada to pack up whatever food could be spared into a brown paper bag and she gave this to the two children before they started on their pilgrimage to the Cross Keys. Then she went to see if her sister-in-law had any information on the Marsden family.

15.

Connie Burst into Irene's study.

'I remember the Marsdens,' she exclaimed, 'Edith has just reminded me. They were one of our bombed out families.'

'Well done,' said Irene warmly, getting to her feet.

'Where do they live?'

'At the moment I don't know,' she said, 'I'll tell you as much as I can.'

Connie sat on the sofa, prepared for a good old gossip. She felt in the breast pocket of her uniform for her silver cigarette case, and carefully extracted the one remaining half cigarette in it. Since becoming a warden, Connie had taken up smoking in a big way and cut them in half in order to make them go further.

Irene threw her a box of matches and went back to her office chair, ready to take notes.

When she had approached Connie last night asking for information, Connie had replied rather pettishly that she couldn't be expected to remember all her waifs and strays. Now it seemed, she had changed her tune.

'They were rehoused about a year ago – after they got bombed out in Paradise Street. Since then they've moved about a bit. The last we knew, they were in Mersey Road, no 23.'

'Mersey Road?' she wrote down the address. 'Is that on the corporation estate?'

'Yes in quite a decent area! Anyway as it happens, Edith went round there to check up on them only a couple of weeks ago.'

'And?'

'The birds had flown, there was no sign of them. Just a woman who said they'd left with no forwarding address. She'd been a neighbour from Paradise Street and had been lodging with them. She was obviously respectable; the rent was up to date. and the house was in good nick, nothing missing, so there was no point in going any further.'

'How could that happen? How can people disappear – and how can somebody take over a house just like that? Can't you stop that kind of thing happening?'

'Honestly Irene, with the population moving about as it is, neither the civil defence nor the corporation can keep tabs on everybody. We've got other things to do with our time,' replied Connie somewhat crossly.

'Of course.'

'The woman seemed perfectly decent. It's not up to us to interfere in the lives of people who are reasonably content. There are too many sad cases who really need our help.'

Connie stubbed out her cigarette fiercely. 'Yes, yes I'm sorry. I didn't mean to criticise. I know how hard you work and how much you care for these people. Please don't be upset.'

Irene offered her sister in law a placatory cigarette from the alabaster box on her desk.

'How come you always have cigarettes?' said Connie sulkily.

'I have a friend who works in a tobacconist,' she laughed. 'You have the same friend but you smoke more than I do. That's the difference.'

'I have to smoke for my nerves. I have a lot to worry about. It's not all that easy taking care of people who don't understand they're being taken care of.'

'Of course,' said Irene soothingly, and tried to bring the conversation back on course. 'The Marsdens. Had you ever met any of them?'

'Yes, but only when they were first bombed out. Edith had more to do with them. She gave me the information.'

'What were they like?'

Connie wrinkled her brow, trying to remember.

'Difficult to tell. In a bad state of course, covered in smoke and grime, cuts and bruises, you couldn't tell what they looked like. How they got out of the building I don't know. We just bunged them all in the first property that was available – except for the second boy who had a broken leg and had to go to hospital.'

She drew heavily on her cigarette.

'Thanks for this,' she said, 'I'd forgotten how much better they taste when they aren't cut up.'

Irene opened the box and gave her another couple. Connie smiled her beautiful smile and put the cigarettes into her empty cigarette case.

Irene knew there was further information to come, a little more blood to be coaxed from the stone.

'They all had the usual horrible accent, impossible to understand them. I remember the father best, not in the services, don't know why. He worked on the fish dock – raffish sort of person, but I suppose you might call him good looking in a gypsyish kind of way.'

She paused, smiling, as if the memory was rather pleasing.

'And the children?' prompted Irene.

'A load of them, four – no five. The eldest boy would be about nearly fourteen, ready to leave school. Edith said he was going to start work at Reckitts and there was the other – the one with the broken leg, he was a bit younger. I think a couple of the young ones were step children.'

'Could you guess at the ages – of the younger ones?'

'Difficult to tell, they were a bit undernourished I should think. Father drinks of course, they usually do.'

Irene smiled a little to herself. Connie had a very well developed sense of 'us and them' which had been exacerbated by her recent personal experiences of 'them' and she talked about them with a kind of faraway look as if lecturing on the habits of some remote African tribe.

'Well, let me see, the little boy about five, little girl a year or so older, and the ugly one with the glasses – well… nine – it's just a guess.'

'You are wonderful, remembering all this!'

Connie looked pleased and Irene's approbation encouraged her to search her mind even further for memories of this unfamiliar tribe of creatures.

'What about the mother?' prompted Irene.

'There wasn't an actual mother. Died in childbirth maybe – quite a few of them do you know – but that's just a guess. Now – the two older children are dark and powerfully built – again a bit like gypsies. The others are red haired and scrawny, obviously from a different mother, may even have been stepchildren. It was a very disorganised sort of family. They had been living in appalling poverty even before the bombing. I think Mercer Road was a huge step up for them. Pity they had to go – at least they didn't take the bed linen with them – makes a change.'

'Was there no woman with them?'

'I believe there have been several. I'm not surprised, as I said he's very attractive. It was the older girl who seemed to be in charge of the housekeeping.'

'They sound like the ones I was asking about. Thank you very much for your trouble.'

'Glad to be of use.'

'You have a wonderful memory.'

'Thank you. I do my best. They were particularly memorable – you know with the handsome father and the three little kids all with red hair I'm only sorry I can't tell you where they are now.'

'I'm hoping to find that out on Saturday. They are coming here.'

Connie's eyes opened wide and she exploded with an inflection that Edith Evans would have been proud of.

'Coming? Here?'

'Yes I'm going to give the little girl dancing lessons,'

'The ugly little brat? The one with the glasses?'

'No, the other, younger, little brat.'

'Oh Irene is that wise?'

Irene laughed.

'Probably not. But it's an experiment – an adventure!' she said and kept her fingers crossed, uttering a prayer that they would actually turn up.

'Irene darling, these creatures are not like us you know. I've been finding that out recently. It may be a great mistake to bring them into our lives. They won't be happy and I promise you they won't thank you for it. I should know about that.'

'I wouldn't expect them to.'

Connie shrugged

'Please yourself. You always do,' she said pettishly as she flounced out of the study.

16.

Maxine remembered the day her life changed. Unusually for her Ada had been a little late for breakfast, but didn't vouchsafe any reason why. Maxine had Dalton's Wheat flakes, her favourite. They were very light and thin with a beautiful crispness that melted as soon as they were put into the mouth. Ada thought they were rubbish and preferred toast with margarine. Maxine didn't like margarine. It was a nasty colour and it left a coating on the roof of your mouth. If you didn't clean your teeth after breakfast, it stuck with you for the rest of the day. Aunt Paget had started mixing it with the butter ration to make it taste a bit better, but Maxine could still feel it on the roof of her mouth.

Ada was complaining about the war. She was pining for masculine company.

'I'm fed up with bloomin' war,' she said, 'I haven't seen a fella for months, except on films. All real ones'ave joined up.'

Maxine nodded.

'Like my Daddy,' she said, digging into the wheat flakes bringing up a large spoonful to her mouth. Ada looked at her with eyes starting to brim over. She was a soft touch was Ada.

'Do you miss him?' she asked.

'I think I do a bit,' replied Maxine gravely, 'But he writes me lots and lots of lovely letters. Mummy says I'll understand them when I grow up if I get really good at reading. People buy me books all the time, so I can practise.'

'Aye, well, you wouldn't do to be working in factory,' grumbled Ada, 'There's nowt much to read there. Just posters about not talking about what we're doing and recipes they hand out for cabbage rissoles and stuff.'

'What do you do at the factory?'

'We make things.'

'What kind of things?'

'Ey up young Maxine. You shouldn't ask questions like that. Careless talk costs lives. Anyway I don't know. We just make bits of things. We never get to see what they finish up as.'

'But you listen to the wireless all the time – I listen to *Workers playtime*. Don't you?'

'Avin' fellas on wireless in't even as good as seein' 'em at pictures,' said Ada spreading her toast with Aunt Paget's plum jam.

'But they have shows at the factory don't they? Real people singing and dancing?'

'Aye screeching women and nancy boys.'

'Oh.' there was nothing Maxine could think of to say that would console her, so she concentrated on finishing her breakfast.

'Are you coming to class with me?' she asked Ada.

'Might as well, then we can go and see Jack Buchanan after dinner.'

Ada was the ultimate film fan. She bought all the film magazines and knew all the personal details of the film stars – who was married to whom, how many children they had, what size was their swimming pool, what face cream they used.

Movie stars were portrayed in *Picturegoer* and *Photoplay* as the popular ideal with any whiff of scandal quickly suppressed by the studio. The lives of the stars were the stuff of dreams for young girls like Ada who fervently believed all the rubbish that the columnists printed.

Ada and Maxine were very close, despite the disparity in their ages. If it hadn't been for Ada's height and well-developed figure, it would have been a problem to tell which one was the younger of the two.

They ran, laughing, into the studio changing room to get ready for class.

Ada helped Maxine put on the uniform. A special costume designed by Connie and made up by the local W.I. sewing bee. Navy blue satin knickers and white satin blouses with a red M R (for Madame Renee) on the breast pocket The costumes were sold to the parents at a reasonable price and profits went to provide comforts for the troops.

The shoes came separately from the theatrical shoemaker in London. Each student had to have at least three pairs. Pink satin point shoes, red leather character shoes with taps and red leather ballet flats. These had to be specially ordered and the children's feet measured regularly to make provision for rapid growth.

The shoes were expensive and outgrown ones were never thrown away, but kept in a cupboard, as there was always a chance that supplies might dry up in wartime.

The ground floor of the house was Irene's domain. One half contained her office and her bedroom. Her studio took up one whole side of the double fronted house and was equipped with its own changing rooms and washing facilities. The studio had a specially sprung wooden floor with a practice barre and fully mirrored walls so the students could see their every move and attitude.

Maxine looked at herself in the mirror. She liked her face – but wished as always she could have had her mother's luxuriant chestnut curls rather than her own home made yellow ringlets. People would look at her and say 'What a pretty little girl' she liked that – although it never happened much when her mother was around, people were always too much involved in looking at Connie. Everyone looked at Connie – especially her father who still went weak at the knees when he caught sight of her unexpectedly.

But then Maxine had talents that her mother didn't. Maxine could sing and dance and she felt wonderful when she was on stage and knew that she was prettier and more talented than anybody else. Everyone looked at her then. She was just as beautiful as she wanted to be. She was the queen of the May, the fairy princess and she confidently believed that nobody could ever outshine her.

17.

Vera Delaney, one of Irene's full time students, always presided over the Saturday morning class. Vera took herself rather seriously these days since she had become a full-blown professional, engaged to appear as principal girl in the Christmas pantomime at the New Theatre. She had an undistinguished but pleasing face and a lithe dancer's body, which she showed off to its fullest advantage in her tights and leotard.

Her class was supposed to be for ten and eleven year olds, but as Maxine was so much more advanced, she was allowed to attend.

Lil had impressed Irene so much that she had decided to let the new girl take her chances with this same group. When she told her sister in law, Connie was struck dumb, unable to form a single syllable.

'I think it's a good idea. After all Lil and Maxine are both exceptionally advanced for their age, it might create a bonding between them.'

Connie looked at her, forming the word 'bonding' with her mouth but with no sound coming out.

'It will be good for Maxine to have someone of her own age to work with.'

At last Connie found her voice.

'You put her in the class with my Maxine!' protested Connie, 'That is appalling, – why should we want to create a bonding as you call it. Why she might start coming to tea, things like that. Even – God forbid – even staying overnight!'

Irene laughed.

'I don't expect them to become quite that close,' she said, 'but they will be company for each other.'

'It's a mistake, I'm telling you.'

Lil arrived, being tugged along by Janie, at eight o'clock in the morning. Connie, almost fainting at the sight of them, bundled them down to the basement where Ada was sent after them to check them for vermin and perform necessary ablutions after which Aunt Paget was to feed them breakfast – which she did with bad grace,

'We've not enough to feed ourselves, let alone waifs and strays,' she muttered and she spread margarine and rhubarb jam on toast for them, jealously withholding her best plum jam for the family.

'Renee's a typical southerner – all those communist ways.'

Irene managed to kit the newcomer out with a practise costume that

Maxine had grown out of, and shoes from the second hand cupboard. The child was such a skinny little creature, even Maxine's outgrown blouse and shorts hung on the tiny frame.

'The children will never notice.' Irene said to herself optimistically, as she made a mental note to get Ada to do some adjustments.

At ten o'clock Madame Renee took Lil to the studio and introduced her to the rest of the class.

'This is a new pupil. Her name is Lillian. Maxine I put her in your especial care – explain to her how things work. Vera will be along in a minute; she is just changing her shoes.'

She saw Ada peeping out from the dressing room.

'Ada,' she said, 'come with me.'

'Will you look after Janie for me?' she asked Ada as they made their way down to the basement where Janie and Mrs Paget sat, silently looking at each other, 'You could take her for a walk or something and bring her back in about an hour.'

But Janie was loath to go.

'I can't leave our Lil,' cried Janie. 'She'll be frightened. She don't like strangers.'

'They're not strangers anymore,' said Irene. 'They're nice girls. Lil will soon make friends with them.'

The girls all turned and looked at the little newcomer and were not impressed with what they saw. Her clothes were too big for her and obviously second hand. She was scrawny, had red hair and freckles. Her eyes looked enormous in her thin face and her hands were rough and scrubby.

Nevertheless, having been put in charge of the stranger, Maxine realised it was up to her to behave like the hostess and she graciously held out her hand.

'Hello Lillian,' she said.

Lil didn't take the proffered hand she just gawped.

'It's bloody Shirley Temple,' she said in her guttural voice.

Maxine's memories and all her horror came flooding back. For a moment she couldn't speak. She just stood there, looking at the dreadful sight in front of her. When she found her tongue, she didn't seem to be in control of what she said.

'Paradise Street,' she stammered, 'You're supposed to be dead.'

'What d'yer mean?' growled the little girl, and the girls standing around looked at Maxine in horror.

'What an awful thing to say,' said one of the other girls.

'She spat at me and put liquorice all over my white fur coat.' explained Maxine in her own defence, 'Then the Nazis came and bombed her. I thought she was killed.'

The girls were frightened; they too backed away from the scowling redhead as if her touch would contaminate them. Lil didn't respond to their reaction in any way. She just stood there glaring at Maxine, her nose wrinkled, mouthing the words *'Bloody Shirley Temple'*

So they stood, Lil at one end of the room, Maxine and the other girls at the other. The girls turned away and exchanged meaning looks with each other. Lil and Maxine just glared at each other.

Vera, who had now changed her shoes, came back into the studio, surprised to find everyone so quiet. She approached the new girl and shook her hand.

'Hello Lillian,' she said with a friendly smile.

Vera's kind manner made Maxine ashamed and she made another effort to be nice.

'I'm sorry Lillian. I made a mistake,' she said.

'Aye you did,' said Lil, 'Me name's Jessie.'

'Madame Renee said your name was Lillian,' said one of the older girls.

'She knows nowt,' said Lil, 'I'm Jessie.'

Vera spoke up,

'Have you ever had lessons before…Jessie?'

'Ah don't need lessons,' she snarled back. 'I can dance!'

'All right then, swank pot' said one of the girls, 'Let's see you then.'

'I think we should wait until Madame gets back,' Maxine protested.

This spurred Lil on to be contrary.

'I dun't mind dancing for yer,' she said.

'We should wait for Madame,' protested Maxine, but Vera, who objected to suggestions, disagreed. Vera took her job as teacher very seriously. After all, she was to play Jill in Jack and the Beanstalk. She didn't need any little seven-year-old, no matter how talented, to tell her what to do.

'I'll put on the music,' she said – and went over to the gramophone. She turned to Lil.

'Anything in particular?'

'Owt'll do,' said the little girl with a shrug.

Vera put on her favourite Ballet Egyptian.

Lil waited for a moment or two until she had the measure of the music and then she launched into a vigorous and spontaneous dance, her strong young limbs working in precise rhythm, her bodyline perfect. The rest of the class watched, open-mouthed. Even at their stage of development they recognised a phenomenon. As for Maxine she felt her heart sinking. She smelled danger, danger of losing her status as star pupil. When Lil had finished, the girls called for more and Lil, flushed with triumph, went into a Jessie Matthews' routine, her little feet tapping away and her legs whirling in circles above her head.

Maxine, realising she had to make some kind of gesture to keep the attention, started a round of over enthusiastic applause as soon as the music stopped.

This gave Vera time to adjust her enthusiasm.

'Yes, dear you can dance a little,' she said with a patronising smile. 'But you could still do with some lessons!'

'And some new clothes,' remarked Maxine with a sniff.

Lil stuck out her tongue.

'Not if I 'ave to look like bloody Shirley Temple I don't!'

Maxine had nothing to say to this and her heart sank to her ballet pumps.

*

Janie and Ada were down in the basement, knee-deep in film magazines when the class was over. Janie thanked Irene very much for having them. Lil was less gracious.

'Ah 'ate it,' she said as they walked home, 'They talk so bloody pale blue, I didn't know what they were on about – and they were real clean – in new clothes an' all. Just in't natural.'

'But them clothes Madame gave you – I can make 'em fit.' Janie showed Lil the pile of magazines she was carrying.

'Anyway Look at the Photoplays Ada gev me to look at. She din't say I could keep 'em. I'll 'ave to tek em back!'

'Yeah, well I in't goin' there no more. I don't care about bloody pantomime. I'd sooner stop at Cross Keys.'

'Ay well, we're done there. Cops have been in, saying we bin breaking law. Folks have complained.'

'Then I'll stop at 'ome. Dun't matter now Dad and his fancy woman have run off.'

Janie grabbed her by the arm and put her hand over the little girl's mouth.

'Don't you go telling folks he's gone, will you?'

'Course not,' promised Lil stoutly.

'We could be 'vacuated. Them social workers could take house away from us.'

'They'd not be bothered to do that.'

'Aye, they would. One of 'em came round t' other day. Spoke to Aggie. She thought they was from red caps!'

'What she say to em'

'She said Marsdens had flitted, din't know where, and it was her place now.'

'What they do?'

'Said *sorry to trouble you*' and went away.'

The two girls laughed at Janie's impersonation.

'Old Aggie wan't that bad', said Janie, 'Pity she had to go with him'.

Lil suddenly had a nasty thought.

'Ey, if they do find us, they wun't split us up?'

'I wun't let 'em,' said Janie with resolve, 'So long as you keep your big gob shut'.

She took out her key and opened the front door of the little house on Mersey Street.

Then she laughed,

'One good thing, Dad went so fast he din't take his ration book.'

'You mean we get 'is rations?'

The two of them laughed delightedly at the idea of extra food coming into the house.

''E won't come back, will he?' said Lil.

'He dursent, Not while war's on he can't, can he? Them soldiers in red hats'd come back and take him off.'

'And shoot him!' shouted Lil excitedly, clapping her hands.

For a moment their faces lit up at the idea. Then Janie said sorrowfully.

'They don't shoot deserters any more.'

'It's a real shame that.'

And the two children sat there, dreaming hopefully of the possible demise of their stepfather.

*

'So your little lambs have lost their way again, have they?' remarked Edith, putting twenty Players on Irene's desk.

'You shouldn't do this, you know. It practically amounts to Black market trading.'

'I call it a skimpy return for all you've done for me.'

Edith executed a deep plie with such a look of determination that Irene giggled.

'Excellent' she said, 'Maybe I deserve the fags after all. Thank you.'

And she slipped the contraband into her top drawer. Edith sat, waiting to hear what had occurred.

'Yes, the little birds have flown again. It is a shame I was looking forward to working on that little girl. She had something special, you know.'

'You don't have to tell me. I discovered her!' cried Edith, 'At the Cross Keys.'

'Of course you did.'

'Have you tried asking about them at the pub?'

'To be quite honest I haven't looked for them anywhere. It's been a particularly busy time, you see. It's always difficult to concentrate on anything extra when the panto rehearsals are going on. But last week Ada took a trip to the Cross Keys to see Mrs Dewing. It seems that the police had scared off the poor woman, so she denied all knowledge of them. One thing is certain, they're not working there any more.'

'So what next?'

'I don't know. You wouldn't believe that people could just vanish without a trace, could you – even in wartime?'

Edith shook her head.

'You'd be surprised, she said, 'It's impossible to keep track of anyone. Do you think some of the girls might have frightened her off?'

'How on earth could we do that? We're not frightening people!'

Edith laughed.

'I remember being a new girl at Newland High School – with all the posh kids. I was on a scholarship and didn't they let me know it! They used to get into groups to talk about me and there would be sudden silences when I entered the room. I was an alien creature. Even though there was a uniform to make everyone equal, mine was always different from theirs. My tunic was always too short and my blouse always covered in ink stains. If I put sweets in my tunic pocket, they would melt and make a horrible smell. These things just happened to me. I 'spose that's why I ate such a lot – for comfort – and got so fat. I was better off as a fat kid. They'd all joke about it and I would laugh with them and they started to like me. Funny, I didn't mind them laughing about me for being fat, but not for being common.'

'That's ludicrous. Surely the fact that you passed a scholarship meant that you were cleverer than they were?'

'Clever didn't count. It was nice clothes and clean blouses that really counted.'

'Good heavens.'

'Anyway, there's at least one person will be glad the child has disappeared.'

'Really, who?'

'Oh come on, don't be so naïve. Your niece Maxine of course. Lil fair put her nose out of joint.'

'Oh no,' said Irene, 'Maxine's a real little pro. I think she's old enough to understand about unusually gifted people. How it makes them somehow special – not to be judged like the rest of us.'

'You don't think Maxine thinks she is somehow special, too?'

'Maybe she does. She certainly is exceptionally pretty and she has brains and talent. But Lil has a kind of magic. I can't explain it exactly, but I think you saw it too. Oh I wish we hadn't lost her.'

*

Despite her vow to herself that she would track down the family Marsden, too many things were happening at the moment and quite took her mind off her little lost lambs.

Things began to change rapidly in Sherwood Park.

It started one day when Irene was taking a class and the doorbell rang. Thinking Aunt Paget was around, she didn't answer it at first, but after a couple of minutes the bell rang again.

'Take over for a minute, would you, Vera?' she said and she went down to answer the door.

On the doorstep was a young woman in the uniform of a WAAF officer.

'Mrs Fletcher?' said the young woman.

'I'm Miss Fletcher, her sister in-law. Mrs Fletcher is at the warden's post all day if you need her. But maybe I will do?'

'Well, yes. I need to speak to both of you really. I'm Pat Fraser, the billeting officer from the RAF station at the Chestnuts across the road.'

'Yes, how can I help?'

'As you probably know. We now occupy many of the properties in Sherwood Park. There are some new chaps arriving within a week or so and we need billets for them. I was wondering if you have any spare rooms here?'

Irene thought for a moment.

'Come in for a minute, will you? You look weary. Have you time for a cup of tea?'

The young woman thanked her and sank into the living room sofa.'

'You're exhausted.'

'Yes, it's not an easy job. So many of the wives are reluctant to make this sort of decision. Nervous about what their husbands will feel about it whilst they are away fighting the war.'

'Have they any option?'

'Not if it comes to the push. But let us hope it won't.... come to the push. We'd rather do it with their permission than without it. It doesn't make for happy households'.

'Yes, I see. It's a sort of gentle blackmail is it? Well we have a pretty full household here already.'

As Irene was talking they heard the sound of the front door opening again.

'Ah here comes Aunt Paget, saves me the job of making the tea, she always puts the kettle on immediately she comes in.'

'You're sure it's no trouble?'

'Not in the least.'

Aunt Paget looked at the stranger with suspicion, but nevertheless, dutiful to the laws of northern hospitality, she remarked.

'I'll just go and mash the tea.'

and went off to rustle up refreshment.

Irene offered the girl a cigarette and they both lit up, Irene thinking hard.

'As I said, we are a busy household and a pretty full one. My sister in law's Aunt who you saw just now lives in the basement. She was bombed out last year.'

'Oh bad luck.'

'Yes it was. It was lucky we had room for her. She acts as our housekeeper now; don't know how we managed without her. She hasn't a lot of spare room there as she shares the accommodation with Ada our maid and we all tend to flee down there during the air raids. I suppose it's possible that Ada may go into the forces soon, but she is in a reserved occupation just now.'

The girl made a note.

'You'll keep us up to date with that situation?'

'Naturally. Now half of this ground floor is a studio, which is constantly in use for dance classes and keep fit – and a crèche for young children, though, at a pinch it could provide temporary accommodation for quite a few. There are washing facilities there, which might be useful. Obviously we'd rather keep the school and the classes going, but if the worst should come to the worst…'

'I understand perfectly. Let us hope it won't come to that.'

'Then we do have one spare bedroom on the top floor if that would solve any of your problems…!'

'Sounds good,' said the girl, writing it down.

'But we none of us have the time to cook and clean, look after someone.'

'Most of our officers prefer to take their meals in the canteen, so you wouldn't have any extra cooking to do, in fact you'd get a few extra rations – and a small remuneration. It would be enormously helpful if you could help out.'

'Obviously I would have to discuss this with Mrs Fletcher.'

The girl smiled and accepted gratefully the cup of tea handed to her by Aunt Paget, but refused the ground rice cheesecake on the grounds that she had to watch her figure. Aunt Paget snorted and removed the plate.

'Of course, you mustn't make any snap decisions. Here is my number. I do hope you will at least consider it'.

*

To Irene's surprise Connie gave an unequivocal 'Yes' to the proposition.'

'To be quite frank, I'm sick to death of seeing nothing but women around the place. It would be nice just to hear a man's voice.'

'Shouldn't we consult with Tom first?'

'I shall write to him in Egypt and tell him not to worry. But by the time he gets the letter, the war may be over. It would be ridiculous to wait for his reply. How can he possibly object when we are only doing our bit for the war effort?'

Irene was not quite so sure, but decided it would not be politic to air her doubts.

Connie rang Pat Fraser and set the wheels in motion.

18.

Ada sank thankfully into her seat at the Regal. She'd been waiting outside for an hour and a half to see Rita Hayworth dance with Fred Astaire. Hollywood musicals were very popular and this was a great combination – worth queuing for.

The movie '*You'll never get Rich*' was about halfway through as she reached her seat. That didn't matter. She didn't mind about seeing the last bit first. Every Fred Astaire film had a happy ending anyway. The fun was seeing how they arrived at it and of course watching the wonderful dancing. The programme was continuous, so she could stay and see the whole film all over again if she felt like it. It was her day off and her time was her own.

She enjoyed every minute of her excursions to the movies and she had been known to sit through a film three or four times in one day.

In addition to the main film, there was a cowboy second feature; a short starring the Three Stooges and a Mickey Mouse cartoon. Then there was the news. She loved the way the news started with screen split into four each giving a clue as to what would come next, and the cockerel crowing in the middle.

Most of the news was about the war of course. She sat up when she realised the news was about North Africa where Tom Fletcher was and she watched carefully to see if there would be a glimpse of him – but he didn't appear and no place names could be mentioned. She was disappointed, she still loved Tom Fletcher more than anyone else in the world. He was her hero, her knight in shining armour. She relaxed again to watch the fashion tips – how to make do and mend, how to create a glamorous appearance by turning old clothes into fresh ones; cutting up two dresses to make one; turning scraps of material into patchwork quilts and cushions; making a sailor hat by pulling a felt hat over a plate and steaming it until it stayed in shape. Connie was brilliant at that and distributed 'sailor beware' hats to anyone who wanted one.

She settled into her seat ready to spend the rest of her day and half the evening here in the cinema. There was nothing else to do.

Idly she wondered whether her period would come soon. She hoped so. It just wouldn't be fair if she got pregnant yet again. In the last three months she'd only had one proper boyfriend – and then only for a weekend leave.

'Sometimes I wish I didn't like fellas so much,' she thought to herself, wistfully, and gave a shiver.

Although she had her cardigan with her, on that cool spring day, the cinema was chilly, but she knew it would be all right once the heat of the bodies started to warm the place up.

The lights came on briefly and she looked around her. People were just beginning to take off their outer garments. That was a good sign.

It was time for the adverts now – and the cherubic face of Maxine burst out from the screen as she acted out a scene in the Regal teashop. The camera loved her fresh perfect little face and her blonde curls and she returned the affection. She was the most completely natural child Ada had ever seen on the screen – it was as if Maxine was really there, in the flesh.

She watched the film through again along with the rest of the programme and decided she would stay and see Maxine's ad one more time. She smiled as the face came on the screen. She felt as if the child was actually talking to her and almost replied. But it was not her voice that came out. It was another that she seemed to recognise. Rough, but childish, the voice said:

'It's bloody Shirley Temple again.'

Ada's heart missed a beat and she laughed gleefully to herself. She knew who that must be and she knew that she must catch her before she disappeared again. She stood up and began to run the gauntlet of knees as she made her way to the end of the row, then she heard another voice. A man this time.

'It's you again is it, you little monkey. How many times have I told you? I don't pay good money for films for little brats like you to sneak in and see 'em for nowt. I've had enough.'

Ada turned to see the tearful face of Lil as the manager was roughly pushing her into the manager's office at the back of the stalls.

As he did so, Janie emerged from the ladies room, and running up to the manager tried to drag her sister away from his grip.

'Let her go, you bully.'

'You here as well are you? I'll tell yer dad on you,' he said 'so he can give you a leathering.'

'No, no!' cried Lil.

'Where do you live?'

'Don't tell him!' screamed Janie.

'Right that does it. It's the cop shop for you.'

And taking the two little girls by their collars he opened the door of the office.

Ada at last extricated herself from the row and marched purposefully down the aisle to the manager and addressed him in her best Connie manner.

'Excuse me,' she said, 'These children are with me.'

In his astonishment, the manager let go his grasp and the two little girls ran away towards the double doors that led to the foyer.

'Stop Janie, Lil.' shouted Ada. They stopped, shocked by the authority in the young woman's voice.

'Now what are you running away for, you daft buggers?' she said.

The manager tried to explain.

'They came in without paying. They do it all the time. I was just going to call the cops.'

Ada smiled her most bewitching smile and allowed her eyes to brim over slightly.

'They're just a pair of bains.'

And she lifted her gaze beseechingly, a move that pulled back her head and allowed her breasts to lift slightly beneath her sweater.

'But...' said the manager weakly and his gaze went from Ada's bewitching smile to her pert little breasts and then down to her shapely calves and ankles.

Ada, fully aware of his interest, gave a little wriggle and a pout.

'But they are two of Madame Renee's troupe. That little one is going to be a big film star one day... like Rita Hayworth.'

'Jessie Maffews,' put in Lil.

'Shut up stupid.' hissed Janie.

But the manager no longer cared about the two little girls. He was spellbound by Ada.

'Why don't we go and have a cup of tea? We can talk about it,' he suggested, 'The café is still open.'

The two little girls shouted with glee.

'Yes, yes. Can we have an ice cream?'

The manager looked crestfallen, not intending to include the children in the invitation.

Ada let him off the hook

'Another time,' she said, and she gave him a wink that sent him into a spin. 'I'll be here again next week.'

'Just ask for me,' said the manager, 'I'm Mr Johnson, Peter to you. I may be able to pass you in...you know.' and he gave her a wink in return.

'Well, thank you Mr Johnson,' said Ada, 'And my two little girls?'

He turned and saw the two eager faces. They each treated him to a smile as bewitching as Ada's. They didn't seem such bad kids after all. He nodded curtly and his gaze returned to Ada.

'As long as they are with you, they will be my guests,' he said.

As soon as she got the children out of the cinema, she gave them both a good shake and took them into the station milk bar, and bought them each a sarsaparilla.

'Now ... what are you playin' at?' she asked, dropping her Connie voice and reverting to her old manner.

'Lil has to see the picture. To get the steps for her turns.'

'Still at the Cross keys?'

'No. Red Lion. Cops got on to Mrs Dewing and we had to stop.'

'You shouldn't be going to pubs at all at your age.'

The little girls sucked at their straws.

'Now, tell me. Why don't you come to dance class?'

'Can dance. Don't need class,' said Lil.

'She says she don't need dance class,' translated Janie.

'Rita Hayworth still has dance classes and she was dancing on the stage when she was six!'

'Gerroff!' said the girls simultaneously.

Ada took out her Picturegoer she had bought at the cinema earlier and showed them a picture of Rita Hayworth at the barre.

'See!' said Ada triumphantly.

This threw the two little girls into deep thought as they finished their drinks with loud gurgling noises. She took them to the bus station.

'We can walk,' said Janie, 'We don't have money for bus.'

'But I'm coming with you.'

At this moment the bus came and the girls turned to fly away, but Ada, who was a strong girl and had anticipated their flight managed to grab them and manhandle them on to the platform, holding them tightly until the bus left the station.

Ada knew that the children were hiding something, but she had no idea what it might be. What was more she had no wish to pry into secrets they didn't want her to know. They were kindred spirits after all, street kids like she had been only a few years ago and she still remembered the days when she was dossing down in Tom's office. Like them she was devoted to motion pictures and like them, knew an illegal way in to every cinema in town. She knew just how they'd got into the Regal. Although nowadays she used more conventional methods, there were times, when broke, she could still find her way in. Just like the two children she had managed to see every movie, every week, in every cinema in town.

The three of them got off the bus at the end of Newland Avenue, and she practically frog marched them to Sherwood Park.

Still holding them by their collars, she knocked on Irene's door.

'Look what I found,' she said.

Irene looked up from her papers, and though her heart gave a leap she did not allow her emotions to show.

'Ah, there you are,' she said, 'I've been wondering what happened to you. What a pity, you missed the panto. Never mind.' She looked at her watch. 'Vera will be starting her class in twenty minutes. Just time for tea before you join her.' She turned to Ada, 'Ada, you have some film magazines to show Janie?'

19.

To her great relief, Ada's period started the very next day. She laughed a little. So many times she cursed the monthly flow, and yet, there were times in life when the sight of the blood gave her feelings of delight. She didn't want anything to interrupt her life at the moment.

She had made the decision to accept Peter Johnson as her new beau. Hardly her type admittedly, but she was a practical lass and it was awfully handy to have someone in a position of authority at the cinema, and candidly, any beau at this stage was a bonus. From now on if she went into the Regal, all she had to do was mention his name and free seats were produced. What was more, she never had to queue again, and if he did see the two children hiding in the back of the stalls or in the high circle, he turned a blind eye, so afraid he was of upsetting the light of his life.

He was exempt from the services because of his bad eyesight, his flat feet and his general bad health, but he was better than nothing. Anyway it felt good that she could contribute to the nurturing of Lil's precious talent.

Irene was delighted to have her prodigy back with her and the girls in the group seemed less actively hostile than before.

Connie was, of course, furious by the turn of events and felt Irene was giving an unnecessary amount of attention to a *'snotty nosed little ragamuffin'* to the detriment of her daughter and Irene's own niece.

Maxine kept her own council and didn't dare utter a word against Lil, realising that it would only put her in a bad light. She also knew that, like everyone else, Ada was besotted with the child and she feared to lose the woman's friendship if she forced her to take sides.

Irene was exhausted with emotion. Much as she had longed to find the child again, she realised the enormous responsibility she had taken on. She never managed to find out where the children were actually living, she was forced to trust Lil to turn up to class and was relieved to find that she had become totally reliable – she suspected that it was Janie who made sure of that.

Then just as she felt that life was once more getting under her control, the Air force moved in. Just the one. Slightly over medium height, the young man had a gentle Scottish accent, sandy hair, lustrous hazel eyes, and a long humorous face covered in freckles. He arrived unexpectedly one Saturday afternoon when everyone except Aunt Paget was out shopping.

Aunt Paget let him in after scrutinising him from head to foot and deciding that she liked what she saw. She sat him down, made him a pot of tea, produced the inevitable ground rice cheesecakes and settled down for a gossip about life in the services.

He was a polite young man and accepted the cheesecake, taking a slightly too large bite out of one before realising how dry it was. Having started, he was forced to finish it, taking copious mouthfuls of tea to get it down his throat. As he finished she immediately handed the plate to him again.

'Och no,' he said, reverting this native Scottishness, 'I'm doing fine, thanks.'

However, Aunt Paget put on the pressure and he was forced to a accept another. It was while he was trying to swallow a morsel whilst explaining that he was not actually in the Battle of Britain being a member of the *'Chair born division'* that the door opened and Irene walked in.

'This is Mr McGregor – our RAF man,' said Aunt Paget proudly.

Irene came toward him with a welcoming smile, then stopped short.

'Great Scot,' she cried.

'Correct,' he said with a laugh.

'Scottie!'

He laughed again, and before they even realised it, they had embraced. Both shaken and alarmed by this sudden flood of warmth, they separated and looked at each other.

'Madame Renee,' he said, 'I hoped you'd still be here.'

'Well I'm not dead if that's what you mean.'

Scottie flushed to the roots of his ginger hair.

'No, I mean I thought you might have joined the forces.'

'Not yet,' she said, 'Though I think it's only a matter of time.'

'Well you seem to know each other,' said Aunt Paget who had been watching them with confused but good-tempered amusement.

'Yes, he worked with my brother for years. What a strange coincidence.'

'I expect you'd like some tea,' said Aunt Paget and left them alone together.

They stood for a while, looking at each other. Scot was looking better than she remembered, younger, healthier. She put it down to the forces life style and the blue uniform, which suited him so well.

'You look fine,' he said.

'You look well too.'

'Your hair is different,' she said, remembering the ginger shaving brush of the past.

'The power of the Air force is incalculable. They even managed to control my hair' he laughed, 'Yours is just the same – as handsome as ever.'

She thanked him for the unexpected compliment and they ran out of conversation once more.

'Jolly good,' he said at last.

'Won't you sit down,' she said, 'I'll freshen your cup.'

As he sat, she saw his ebullience begin to desert him, and his face fall into folds of sadness.

She wondered what had happened in the two years since the office was bombed.

'Did you go back to Edinburgh?'

'Aye,' he said, 'Before I joined up.'

'How is Marion, still making her mutton pies?'

Scottish dropped his head.

'I don't know,' he said, 'We are getting a divorce.'

'Oh I 'm sorry,' was all she could say. She could see that Scot was upset and didn't know him well enough to pry any further.

Luckily Aunt Paget came to her rescue, bustling in with another cup for Irene and a pot of hot water. Declining the invitation to join them, she bustled out again saying she had things to do.

He insisted on pouring her tea.

'You know what this means?' she said 'Two people pouring the tea from the same pot? It means we'll have ginger twins,' Immediately she wished she hadn't said it.

'I can think of worse fates,' he said and his face reddened again. Irene felt herself growing hot under the collar. She had met all kinds of men in her life, but few who blushed quite so readily. She found it endearing, but thought it would be as well for both their sakes to change the subject.

'Heard anything of Cuthbert?' she said and realised that this was another mistake, alarmed to see his eyes become wet as he shook his head sadly.

'He was unlucky, he bought it.'

'Oh no, that's awful. That lovely boy.'

'He wanted to be a hero – and he got a posthumous DFC.'

'His poor mother must miss him dreadfully.'

'She never knew. She was killed in the blitz – before the message arrived.'

'I'm sorry.'

'That's the way it is.'

They sat in silence, sipping their tea. Irene looked at her watch.

'Connie will be back soon,' she said praying that she would be early; she felt the need of a little help. The return of Scot had filled her with a kind of unease that she couldn't altogether explain.

Scot also felt the awkwardness and after fifteen minutes of desultory conversation, he stood up.

'Maybe you could tell me where to put my stuff?'

Irene leapt to her feet.

'Oh of course. I'll show you. How very remiss of me.'

And, keeping a careful distance from him, she escorted him up the stairs.

20.

'On the right foot please. Ready. Five-six-seven-eight. Tap spring tap spring shuffle ball change tap spring shuffle hop step pick upstep shuffle hop step brush heel brush toe pick up step shuffle ball change tap spring.'

Panto time was coming round again. The little class was working hard on the routines.

At last Lil was to be in a panto and she was looking forward to it.

This year it was to be Cinderella and she and Maxine were to be a double dance act Fairy Rosebud and Fairy Snowdrop.

Though Lil still felt she had nothing in common with the other girls who followed Maxine's example in treating her politely but with little warmth, she had found a friend in Vera, Irene's assistant who was playing Cinderella. Vera found it strangely pleasurable that Maxine's nose had been put out of joint and took the new girl under her wing even calling her Jessie which was the name she preferred.

Vera had had a busy and successful year. Besides qualifying as a dance teacher, she had, with Irene's help developed for herself a song and dance routine intended for a tour with ENSA next year. As it happened she had already had a chance to try it out at the Tivoli, and the management of the theatre called on her whenever there was a gap in the variety bill.

Vera got Lil and Janie tickets to see her perform and both were amazed to find they didn't at first recognise her. The rather homely looking girl who was their friend was suddenly transformed into a gorgeous, glamorous creature with true film star looks. Vera had insisted that they come round to the dressing room afterwards, and the two girls were thrilled to see that Vera had a little room all to herself. There was a wardrobe with a mirrored door, a dressing table and chair and above the dressing table another big mirror with lights all the way round it. There was also just room for an easy chair so that Vera could relax when she was off stage.

'Not that I get much chance of that,' she laughed. 'I spend most of my off time changing my clothes. It's a busy show.'

'You looked like a film star,' said Janie with shining eyes.

'The magic of the footlights,' she said and added, 'Actually it's all artifice. Young Lil ought to learn about it. Why don't you both come along and watch me make up tomorrow. It takes me about half an hour every night!'

They accepted the invitation and presented themselves promptly at six o'clock. The show didn't go up until 7.30 but visitors were not allowed backstage after the half at 6.55.

Vera sat at the dressing table, her hair curled up and secured with Kirby grips and covered with a net.

'I put the pin curls in so that when I take my wig off I have lovely curly hair and don't look like a drowned rat. The wig makes my head sweat and sets my hair you see. So – tip number one, never forget to put your hair in pin curls when you wear a wig!' she said as she put on an elastic headband to protect her hair from the grease.

She sat at a table in front of the mirror with lights all around it.

On the dressing table were rows and rows of sticks, bottles, pots and tubes of make up. There was also a jar of cotton wool balls, some torn up old handkerchiefs and an old towel.

'Do you use all this?' asked Lil breathlessly.

'You bet,' laughed Vera, 'I need all the help I can get. Watch closely and learn, my puppet.'

First she used Crowe's Cremine to clean her face thoroughly and then squeezed out a cotton wool pad with glycerine and rosewater and rubbed it all over her face and neck.

'Freshens you up and gets rid of some of the grease,' she said.

She looked in a magnifying mirror at her eyebrows, and after dabbling surgical spirit on them, took her tweezers and pulled out a few stragglers.

The foundation came from a tube marked Spotlite Klear and this she spread evenly over her face.

'This is just a short cut. Spotlite Klear is five and nine ready mixed to make just the right colour. Peach to make me look healthy, otherwise I'll look washed out when the lights hit me.'

She sucked in her cheeks and put a spot of number nine greasepaint into the hollow of her cheeks, another at the temples in line with her eyes and down the sides of her nose.

'This is to give my face some shadows. Number nine gives me lovely cheekbones.'

'You look like a red Indian,' remarked Janie who was making careful notes in case Lil should forget something.

'Then, number five highlights the shadows and make the bones stand out.'

She put streaks of five on her cheekbones, her temples, under her eyebrows, on her jaw bones and outlined her top lip, blending them all in carefully with her fingertips, finishing with a straight line down the middle of her nose.

'My nose isn't straight in real life, but this makes it look straight on stage. The highlights and shadows stop me from looking like a blob. It will seem like wonderful bone structure, which as you probably realise I haven't got.' She laughed and selected a carmine two to colour the apple of her cheeks, her chin, the top of her nose and a spot under the eyebrow.

'Brightens up my face,' she said, 'very important, especially after a night out.'

Blue on the eyelids, deep just over the eye and then blended upwards so that it had faded to nothing by the time it met the highlight under her brow.

A narrow tube of twenty eight liner squeezed into a wedge shape was used next to draw a brown line across the top of her eyes from the inner corner to the outer one, finishing with a tiny flick up towards the eyebrow, and below the eye from the middle to the outside edge and extended a little to match upper one.

'Never join these lines together,' she said, 'It makes the eyes look deep set. The aim of the ingénue is to look doe-eyed and sweet like a baby animal so that people go *'Aah'* and fall in love.'

She filled the gap between the two lines at the side of her eyes with white to make her eyes look enormous. She laughed at herself in the mirror.

'Grandma what big eyes you've got!'

Then she put red dots in the corners.

'Don't ask me why, I've never found out,' she said, 'It's just something we do. Now for powder.'

This was applied generously with cotton wool and the surplus brushed of with a rabbit's foot.

'For luck,' she said with a laugh.

'Now some mascara,' and she spat on her cake of mascara and applied the black paint with something that looked like a tiny toothbrush.

'The wonders of modern science!' she exclaimed, picking up what looked like a pair of scissors with clamps on the end.

'Eyelash curlers,' she said as she held the instrument against her lashes until they set in an upward sweep.

'More mascara,' she said – and opening her mouth, put on another coat of black.

'You can do it without opening your mouth, but it's more comfortable if you do,' she explained.

'And the final piece of eye drama.'

She lit a candle over which she held a spoon, melting her hot black. She then applied it with a matchstick, drop-by-drop leaving a little blob on each individual lash. She laughed at the expressions on the faces of the two little girls as they watched her with their mouths open.

'And furthermore – extra glamour!'.

This time it was gutta-percha, which she used for filling in tiny gaps between her teeth before applying her tooth enamel to give her a white smile.

'Still more!' she said and with a brush of dark red lipstick she painted herself the outline of a totally new mouth with an upward tilt to her top lip.

'Carmine three,' she said, and as if she was filling in a child's colouring book, painted the lighter carmine two into the outline.

Finally, she added a smear of even lighter carmine one on the bottom lip to make her look fashionably sulky and voluptuous.

'Nearly done now,' and with a minute comb, she combed her eyebrows, fixing them in place with Vaseline. She blotted her lips with tissue paper and added another touch of Vaseline to make them shine.

'How do I look?'

'Wonderful!' breathed the two girls.

'Like Jessie Matthews?'

'No,' they chorused.

'More like Hedy Lamarr!' added Janie.

'Now I really am flattered. All I need to do now is transform the bod.'

'How do you do that?' cried Janie.

'You'll see. These are the dancer's lifelines. I don't need as much help as most dancers, but this is panto after all.'

She tucked her falsies into her brassiere and stuck her chest out to make the little girls giggle. She climbed into a wide elastic belt called a 'Roll on'.

'I can only wear this for a couple of hours, or I get stomach-ache,' she said. 'But it makes me pull my tummy in. Some girls wear bum pads as well, but mine is quite big enough already, thank you.'

'Thank God, my costumes all have shoulder pads stitched in to make the dresses hang better, but sometimes you have to put those in as well. Now these – are wonderful.'

'These' were elastic fish net tights, which made her legs even more Hollywood shaped than they were already.

The final touch was the lustrous curly blonde wig made of real hair.

'Now, do I look smashing or what?'

'Smashing!' they remarked fervently.

Lil who had been remarkably quiet during the whole operation, taking in every action as if photographing it, looked at the final vision, starry-eyed.

This was real magic, footlights magic. The only kind she would ever believe in.

21.

Irene brushed aside Connie's ragings with regret, she thought that without Connie's interference Maxine might have come to accept the presence of Lil. Anyway she had no time to remonstrate with her sister in law. Irene saw the friendship develop between Vera and the two little Marsden girls and had mixed feelings about it. Lil certainly blossomed as a result, and her defensive aggression gradually melted. But Irene had set her heart on turning Maxine and Lil into bosom buddies and she was disappointed to see that Maxine was always sulky in Lil's presence and the more cheerful Lil was, the sulkier and more aggressive Maxine became. Irene put it down to snobbishness on her part – a snobbishness encouraged by her mother Connie. Connie would allow Maxine to be seen with only the most respectable people and Lil would certainly not be entertained as any kind of companion for her precious daughter. She told Irene so in no uncertain terms and added that Maxine felt the same.

Irene had no time to argue with her sister in law, she was concentrating hard on the Pantomime, which she feared might be her last. It seemed there was another job for her on the horizon which would be even more fulfilling. Her talents were being held in readiness for something important to do with the war effort.

*

For the moment it was time for the first rehearsal on stage with the rest of the cast, so the children had to be perfect in their routines by then.

Lil was now resplendent in her new practice dress and new shoes. Janie had got herself an illegal evening job making buttonholes for army uniforms. It was hard close work and she had to wear even stronger spectacles, but she was happy. She was earning enough money to buy things for her sister, so she wouldn't feel embarrassed about her clothes.

Jack, the eldest Marsden, who was now sixteen, was at work in the factory bringing in nearly three pounds a week, which was enough to pay the rent and help feed the family. David had a paper round and his fourteenth birthday not far away. He knew he would easily get a good job. In wartime, there was always something to do for young men who were not yet old enough to join the forces. So the little band of children prospered, better fed and better cared for than it had ever been when it was in charge of the grownups.

Nobody at Sherwood Park ever found out that Bill Marsden had bunked off, pursued by the military police and Janie and Lil kept their secret, positive that if the authorities knew, they would be separated.

Nobody was interested enough, or had time enough to make enquiries of the family. From time to time Irene would enquire from Lil about the health of her father and Agnes. Each time Lil would say 'he's fine' and nobody ever questioned them any further. The children seemed fine, clean and well cared for and were doing well at school She usually managed to persuade the two girls to have some supper after classes – stew or soup, whatever could be spared and Irene was happy to see her little charges well fed and rosy looking.

*

When everyone had arrived at the rehearsal, Irene ran through the children's names quickly, knowing that it was pointless the actors trying to remember all the names straight away.

'The little ones play all the animals and the smallest fairies and the big girls are the grown up fairies, the dancers at the ball and the villagers. The two little girls, Maxine and Lillian are Fairy Snowdrop and Fairy Rosebud'

Nobody noticed Maxine's shudder as she heard her name partnered with her enemy. Lil's reappearance had been a sorry blow to her, but she was careful to avoid showing it, as her two favourite people Irene and Ada were both thoroughly impressed by Lil's expertise in learning steps. Lil had learned to take on board the information quickly before she was evicted from the movies she had attended illicitly.

Each of the dancers curtsied as their names were mentioned and the cast acknowledged their presence with a smile, a wink or a 'Hiya kids.'

Then Irene introduced the senior members of the cast.

'Girls you know Vera of course, who is playing Cinderella.'

'Yes Madame Renee,' chorused the children.

'Hello girls,' said Vera and they chorused 'Hello Vera' back, even though Vera had arrive along with the others from the school.

The children were all standing on the stage of the new Theatre and the rest of the actors were scattered about in the stalls. She addressed the actors and proceeded to present the children to them.

'Stand as I mention your names would you? Just so we can all get to know what you look like.'

The actors looked up and gave a murmur of consent.

'These two gentlemen in row three are Mr Jenkins and Mr Wallis. They are playing Ermintrude and Gertrude, the ugly sisters,' said Irene.

Lil turned to Ada who was on call as dresser and chaperone for the troupe, and said in a loud whisper.

'They're fellas!'

Ada laughed. She was an old hand. She knew all about pantomime.

'The dames – they are always played by men in pantomime.'

'Stupid. 'snorted Lil.

'No, it's a laugh, you'll see.'

Lil look curiously at the two men, one was a big burly creature that reminded her uncomfortably of her stepfather, and the other one was thin and weedy with a huge Adams apple. She wondered how they could possibly be made to look like women – ugly or not. Then she remembered Vera's transformation into a glamour girl and decided maybe it wasn't quite so farfetched after all.

'And the principal boy is played by a girl.'

'That's what I'm going to be one day,' broke in Maxine, 'A principal boy. I'm going to be Robin Hood.'

Lil was indignant. Robin Hood was one of her heroes. She had learned all about him at school and decided he was her kind of bloke. She couldn't imagine him being played by a girl, especially one she still thought of as Shirley Temple.

'You'd better off as Little Bo bloody Peep,' she hissed at Maxine.

'A little less chat please girls,' said Irene, thus depriving Maxine of a come back.

'Evelyn Shields who is to be Prince Charming and Dulcie Prescott as Dandini. The Baron – George Sharpe, The broker's men Lennon and McLain. Fairy Queen – Madeleine Townsend.'

Finally, Irene turned to a burly sandy haired man who was sitting all alone at a table on the side of the stage. He bared his flashing white teeth in a smile that didn't quite make it to his gooseberry green eyes.

'This is our star, Sonnie Pitts. He is playing Buttons.'

He got to his feet and walked slowly across the stage, surveying the row of children and he stopped when he came to Lil and Maxine who as Rosebud and Snowdrop were standing together at the head of the line.

'I want a young lass for my act' he said, lowering his pale green gaze upon Rosebud and Snowdrop who were suddenly agog with expectation 'One o' them two will do.'

Irene was suddenly nervous.

'I'm sure they can do it, but are you sure you only want one of them? Can't you use them both? They come as a pair.'

'No. Wouldn't be right. I sing this song, you see, – *All I want is a chucky chuck chuck*' – then I get lads and lasses in t'audience to sing it wi' me, you see? Then I get one of t'kids to do it on their own!'

'I see,' said Irene.

'Folks go mad at that. Then I say 'I bet you thought this kid were a plant, din't yer?' and they go 'Yes' you see, and I go 'Well, she's not and I'll prove it' so I say to t'kid, 'You've never seen me before in your life have you?' and she says, 'No Daddy!' Brings the house down.'

'But what if the little girl doesn't say No Daddy?' asked Maxine.

Sonnie replied shortly

'But she will.'

'But how can you be sure?'

'Cos she'll be a plant.'

'But you just said she wasn't.'

Sonnie Pitts raised his weary eyes to heaven and turned to Irene.

'I'll tek the red head,' he said 'that blonde's a bit mouthy for me.'

Irene took Sonnie aside.

'Are you sure Sonnie? This might be very awkward for me. Maxine is usually the one who does the solos.'

Sonnie turned his big red face on her and his gaze was as cold as green glass marbles.

'Listen here, Missus,' he said, 'whose act is this?'

Irene laughed nervously.

'Yours Sonnie, of course.'

'And who's going to bring in t'customers?'

'You are, of course.'

'Then what I sez goes – get it?'

'But...'

Sonnie saw her consternation and his face softened a little.

'Listen luv, we want somebody they'll believe in. Somebody common like me. That blonde is too a la posh!'

He did a couple of funny mincing steps and put on a high pseudo posh voice.

'Too Kingston upon Hull! She'd only get their backs up.'

'Oh dear,' said Irene, 'I do see.'

He turned away and called Lil to him, speaking to her in his soft country accent,

'Where's tha come from, lass?'

'Essle Rawd.'

He turned back to Irene.

'Ya see? A real 'Ull on 'Umber accent. That's what we want' he went back to the child.

'Can tha sing, love?'

'Course I can' she said 'Like Jessie Maffews.'

He laughed.

'Not with that accent you can't.'

'I can. I can be as pale blue as her.'

And to Sonnies astonishment she launched into *'Over my shoulder goes one care'* in a perfect imitation of her idol, finishing with a high circular kick over her head.

Sonnie turned to Irene,

'Well by go! I've never seen owt like that before. Don't tell me! Don't tell me! That bairn's a forty-year-old dwarf, in't she?'

And he laughed and patted Lil on the head.

22.

Dear Irene

I have received a letter from Connie, which has disturbed me quite a lot. It seems that there has been some friction between you. This is the last thing I want, or expect from you. As you know Connie is a fragile creature – hardly of this world – and I left her in your custody. It is cruel of you to torment her in this way.

It seems my little girl Maxine has been upset by your treatment of her. You know just as well as I do how talented she is and I feel it sad that you should be passing her over for someone who's obviously inferior.

Connie tells me that this other child is the daughter of a dockhand, a drunkard and a deserter from Paradise Street.

I know these people. I used to drive past them on my way to the office, and I can tell you how often I have had to run the gauntlet during that slow drive over the cobblestones. They would throw anything at all they could get their

hands on. Things that would cause Connie to take to her bed for a fortnight if she got a smell of them.

It seems odd that you could have taken such a creature and should be favouring her above your own brother's child. Please do what you can to make things right with Maxine and Connie. If only I were there to sort things out, but I'm sure you will understand what I'm talking about and do your best to see that our little family remains stable. Yours Tom

Irene put the letter from her and smiled wryly. She was surprised that a brother of hers should be so shallow minded, but then he had only had Connie's report on the matter and she knew what that would have been.

After Lil had been chosen to do the bit with Sonnie, poor helpless little Connie hadn't spoken to her sister in law for days.

'Maybe I have been a little insensitive,' she thought to herself. She was so used to the rough and tumble of the profession where it is a case of 'the best man wins' and hurt feelings maybe painful but are not to be nurtured. It had never occurred to her that Connie would feel insulted that her precious darling had been passed over. Mothers should be encouraged to keep their distance – difficult in this instance, but Maxine had always behaved so impeccably been so advanced for her age, it had been no problem to treat her with the respect she had deserved. Now Irene realised that Lil had usurped Maxine's position.

Irene tried to think of some way to placate Connie. It wasn't her fault that Sonnie Pitts had insisted on Lil, but Connie would never believe that the comedian could not have been persuaded.

Irene understood his point of view perfectly. Maxine was a clever little girl and with coaching, could easily have done it, but Lil was much more easily blended into the audience. Maxine with her exceptional appearance and presence always stood out a mile. She decided this was the line to take with Connie.

But first, as soon as she had a chance, she tackled her niece.

'Maxine darling, are you happy with what you are doing in the pantomime?'

Maxine's face flushed slightly, her green eyes flickered for a second and then looked at her aunt fearlessly.

'Yes of course. I always am.'

'You don't mind that Lil is doing the song in the audience?'

Maxine gave a little laugh.

'No. I would have hated it. I don't like mixing with the audience. Lil is... different. She can do the right accent and they understand her. I couldn't do it as well as she does.'

'I'm glad you understand that.'

At this point Connie entered hot foot from the warden's post. Her face burned with fury.

'What are you doing, talking to my little girl like that? Behind her mother's back?' and she clutched the child to her, pressing golden head against navy serge breast.

Irene kept calm as well as she could.

'She was telling me how much she would have hated being the girl in the audience!'

'That is absolute rubbish. She's heartbroken. Aren't you darling? She had set her heart on doing that bit.' and Connie blinked away the tears that had welled up in her eyes. Maxine tried to comfort her.

'Mummy, no. I didn't even know about it. I promise.'

'You see what she's like? The little Angel – trying to hide her terrible disappointment.'

Irene tried to explain.

'Lil has the right accent. It is easier for her to blend in with the crowd. Maxine is much too well bred and she has too much personality. She would stick out like a sore thumb amongst all those ordinary people.'

Connie was faintly placated.

'But she could have acted it, couldn't she?'

Irene counted to ten.

'Of course she could, but acting wasn't called for in this instance. Not real stage acting. Sonnie wanted someone common... like him he said ... otherwise the joke wouldn't work. Nobody could ever think of Maxine as a common person could they? Even you, her mother, can see how striking she is to look at.'

Connie was smiling by now and Irene heaved a sigh of relief. She could imagine the letter that would be winging its way to Tom, chiding him for being oversensitive and telling him how highly his sister valued his little girl.

It was Scot to whom Irene finally confided her worries.

'You have something on your mind,' he remarked when they were having a quiet breakfast together one morning.

She showed him the letter Tom had sent her. He agreed that Connie must have misrepresented the situation a little, but he had been aware that Maxine was missing out on attention since Lil had arrived – and especially since Sonnie had chosen the other girl to do a special bit in the pantomime.

'It would be unnatural if she really didn't mind,' he said. 'Nobody likes to be passed over, no matter how sensible the reason.'

'Maybe you're right,' she said slowly.

'I know I am,' he said gravely. 'I think maybe Maxine is a much better actress than any of us ever suspected.'

*

Lil had never been so happy in her young life. She loved everything about the panto. The make-up, the smell, the hard work, the rehearsals, the constant changing of clothes and the hustle and bustle of the dressing room. She loved the effect of Doctor Footlights, the way her usual winter sniffle would disappear the instant she started getting ready for the show.

She also loved the children in the audience. Most of them poor children like her – not like the girls she was working with.

Sonnie was pleased with everything she did. As he thought, she had a true common touch and her shock value, when it was revealed that she was part of the show, was immense. He was aware that the other girls in the troupe seemed to shun her and wondered if it was his fault. It worried him.

It was one day, just before Christmas when they were doing a few warm up shows ready for the big one on Boxing Day, Sonnie went up to the wardrobe for some running repairs on his costume and heard voices coming from the chorus room which was on the same floor. He knocked on the door. It was not on the latch and it swung open. There he found little Lil sitting with her sister, the other girls having gone off to get themselves fish and chips for their tea.

'Hullo young 'uns!' he said in as jovial a manner as he could manage. Although during his performance Sonnie gave the impression of all-encompassing warmth and love, offstage he was entirely different, cold and shy and all the girls were terrified of him.

Lil and Janie both jumped to their feet at the unaccustomed greeting.

'What's thee doin' lass all on thy own?' he peered at Janie 'Who's this? Got a visitor have you?'

'It's Janie me sister; she brings me samwidges.'

'Good for thee, lass,' he said heartily. 'She shouldn't stop here tha knows.'

'I never do, Mr Pitts. I ony bring the samwidges.'

He looked at the two children sitting there in their thin clothes, and a strange idea came into his head. Sonnie and his wife Avril never bothered much with Christmas. Sonnie was always working over the holidays, as were their three children who were also in the business. Christmas was the busiest time for their family. No time for fripperies.

'What's Father Christmas bringing you two?' he asked.

The little girls laughed nervously

'Dunno' said Lil.

'I 'spect your Dad's in Forces.'

'He's away.'

The little girls laughed again.

'Your mam'll be havin a bad time then.'

Janie shook her head.

'Ain't got no mam.'

'Mam's passed on,' added Lil.

'Ee well then' he heard himself saying 'Mebbe you could come to country wi' me, an we'll have Christmas together. I'll drive you after matinee on Christmas Eve, and we'll be back for Boxin Day.'

The girls looked excited for a moment, then after a glance at each other shook their heads.

'No.' they chorused.

'Why not?'

'We can't leave our brothers on their own.'

'Bring 'em all,' he said rashly.

The girls looked at him open-mouthed. He went to the door, then turned back.

'How many brothers is this?'

'Jack's sixteen and a half, David's just fourteen and Jamie's eight and a bit.'

'Blurry 'ell what have I done?' he muttered to himself.

'Fine,' he said, hoping that Avril would agree with him.

'They can come to show on Christmas Eve; then I'll drive you all to Little Weighton after.'

*

Avril had not been best pleased at first. It wasn't the little girls so much. 'Boys of sixteen. Remember what ours were like? They're horrible!' she said.

But as she got used to the idea, she began to look forward to it. Living on the farm in the country they had few food shortages, and it had been years since she had made a proper Christmas dinner. She went into Hull and spent lavishly on presents for the five young visitors.

'After all, it's only one day in the year,' she said to herself.

*

Little Jamie sat through the panto open mouthed, turning to stare at Janie and the other children in the audience as they cheered for Cinderella and booed the ugly sisters, until, tentatively, he started to join in.

The older boys started off with supercilious expressions on their faces, aware that they were much too grown up and sophisticated to believe in it or be part of it. Janie was dreading the moment when their sister stood up and volunteered to sing the song, even though she had warned them in advance so they wouldn't spoil the moment for everyone else. As it happened, they nudged each other and pointed as she stood up in the box, but laughed as heartily as the rest of the audience at the denouement. After that, they relaxed and enjoyed themselves until at the end they were laughing and shouting as much as everybody else.

They piled into Sonnie's car as soon as the actors had taken off their costumes.

'Leave t'slap on,' Sonnie had instructed Lil, 'You can all have a good bath when we get back.'

He had been fully prepared for the children to treat him with awe when they had just witnessed his performance. Instead, they greeted him as if he were any other stranger and as they drove out of town, they discussed the pantomime and, in particular, the character of Buttons, freely without any reference to Sonnie at all. Not only that but they also talked boldly about Button's little girl who sang.

'She di'n't arf show 'im up, di'n't she? Bet she di'n't arf gerra belt after'.

To the boys, the little girl had not been their sister, but the real life daughter of Buttons. Despite the fact that both of them were with them in the car, they saw no resemblance between them and the characters they had played. Sonnie decided to let it stay that way.

The country was also a first for the children – and Sonnie lived bang in the middle of it – a few miles away from Little Weighton.

As they drove down through the outskirts of town, past the big houses to the north, Sonnie told them about what it was like, before the war, when everybody had Christmas trees out there in their front gardens, all lit up with different coloured fairy lights.

'War's got a lot to answer for, 'he said, 'Now we got another kind of lightings up.'

It was pitch dark as they approached the Lane to Sonnie's farmhouse, but he was used to travelling there every night, and he swung into the drive hardly lowering his speed.

Avril was at the door to greet them; she gave each of them a big hug as they entered.

'Come on in loves. You must be frozen. I've got hot water on for a couple of baths; I'm sure you don't mind sharing do you. You'll soon get warmed up. It's none too warm in here, despite the log fires but I'll get you some big jumpers and things.'

In no time at all they were warm and cosy, sitting by the roaring log fire, in borrowed dressing gowns, eating cheese on toast and drinking mugs of hot cocoa.

Next morning, they got up very early and tucked into a huge Christmas Breakfast – Porridge with syrup, ham and eggs and fried potatoes, toast and strawberry jam. They couldn't wait to explore the farm. They were unprepared for the cold country weather, but Avril, who knew about townsfolk, provided coats jumpers, scarves and gloves to keep them warm and had put stone hot water bottles in their beds and told them to help themselves to Wellies from the huge pile that was always kept in a cupboard near the back door.

Lil and Janie were amazed to find that Sonnie was a farmer with cows, sheep, a retired racehorse called Bess and most exciting of all – his greyhounds in the outhouses at the back.

He told them that when the panto closed, he would take them all to watch the dogs race.

Avril's fears had been completely unjustified. The children were just too busy to be any trouble. The girls helped with the dinner, peeling potatoes and preparing sprouts without a single grumble. Then they joined the boys feeding the animals and had a go at milking. Sonnie was glad of the help as the farm manager always had Christmas day off.

All the Christmas preparations were so well ahead of schedule that Avril sent them off to church for the Christmas service. They walked across frosty fields and through muddy lanes to the village church and Sonnie arranged them in a pew near the back door. He had found out that the children's visits to church had been infrequent, to say the least, so he wanted to make sure they had an escape route if they got too bored.

'It's just like the pantomime,' muttered Janie as she settled in and picked up her hymnbook. Sonnie settled them in, gave them each a few pennies to put in the collection plate, and waited, interested in their reaction.

They picked up the tune of the opening carol quickly and enjoyed it, singing with gusto and total lack of understanding for the actual lyrics.

Then hysteria set in. The vicar's costumes, the choir boys with frills round their necks and the audience responses struck them as highly comical and got them giggling all the way through. Sonnie looked at them with amusement.

'They laughed more at Vicar than they ever did at panto,' said Sonnie to Avril when they got back 'Mebbe I'm in wrong business.'

The dinner was of lavishness unseen by the poor townies. The Pitts had their farm produce, and it was the biggest turkey ever seen, accompanied by crispy roast potatoes, two kinds of stuffing, little sausages, bacon, chestnuts, sprout and lovely rich gravy. Then a wartime Christmas pudding made mostly with grated carrots that was set alight with liquor and served with rum flavoured custard. And Finally Avril produced a huge plate of steaming hot mince pies, a bowl of apples and a big wedge of Cheshire cheese.

After lunch, everybody helped with the washing up and then they listened to the King's speech on the wireless. In the afternoon they all took turns in learning how to ride Black Bess, and Avril took them on jaunts in her pony trap. Despite the fact that they had consumed more in one day than they would usually have in a week, by teatime they were famished again and Avril produced Pork Pie and salad and Christmas cake.

*

The little family had never known such perfect happiness before. On Boxing Day, Sonnie dropped them back at Mersey Road before he and Lil went back to the theatre. When they returned to their home on Boxing Day, they began to realise what kind of life they had been missing.

On the following Thursday, New Year's Eve 1942, Lil and Janie sat up late after getting back from the theatre.

On the stroke of midnight, they made resolutions, not just for the New Year, but also for life.

'One day you're going to be a big film star, just like Jessie Matthews,' said Jane.

'We'll have a big house in the country just like Sonnie's,' said Lil.

And they both repeated the words of Scarlet O'Hara in 'Gone with the Wind.'

'As God is my witness. If I have to lie or cheat or kill, I'll never be hungry again, nor any of my folks.'

They swore the words solemnly and, licking their forefingers, crossed their throats

'That's wet; that's dry. God cut my throat if I tell a lie.'

And they went to bed, looking forward to a New Year and a new life.

23.

On the Sunday after the Panto finished, Sonnie gave a party at the theatre, starting mid-afternoon and lasting well on into the night. The whole company turned up, including the whole cast and the crew, and all the people who had contributed in some way to the success of the show.

The orchestra was already in the pit, playing popular songs 'This is the Army Mr Jones' was the latest number one favourite, due in some measure to the GIs that now over ran the country, bringing countless joys to the war torn Brits. Joys like cigarettes and liquor, scented soap and chocolate bars.

But best of all, they brought themselves and added greatly to the social life of those war torn spinsters. Ada had swiftly abandoned her cinema manager in favour of Chuck a big blonde redneck who displayed every charm known to womankind. Edith had added yet more pen friends to her already overburdened address book.

The two main dressing rooms were kept locked until most of the guests had arrived, and then, at three thirty, it was teatime, the dressing rooms were opened, a trestle table was set up on the stage and out came trays and trays of delicious food, borne by Avril, Edith and Ada – hostesses for the day.

Avril had brought along as much rare farm produce as she could manage and everyone had contributed something they could spare from their carefully hoarded rations and food parcels. But it was the GIs who had adopted the company and been regular stage door johnnies to the girls in the company who provided the most exotic fare in addition to crates of beer and cider. And lashings of this strange exotic substance called coca cola. Cigarettes were brought out to the grownups and sweets for the kids – Hershey bars, lifesavers and chewing gum. The long trestle table groaned with unusual delicacies and the frequent cry was *'You'd never know there was a war on!'*

Sonnie really liked to let his hair down on these occasions. He had brought along his accompanist who played for his variety show and the two of them set ball rolling with a twenty-minute act that had them all in stitches. Afterwards he insisted on getting members of the company to perform to this already warmed up audience, leading the applause and laughter himself. Lil sang some of the popular songs of the day and Maxine impressed everyone by her rendering of the Puck speech from *'A Midsummer Night's Dream'.*

'Couple of diamonds you've got there love. Her and young Lil,' he said to Irene 'Look after 'em. They'll both on 'em be stars one day.'

Irene relayed these words to Maxine as soon as she had the chance. Maxine was delighted to have his seal of approval, but was sad that even in her triumph, her name was still linked with that of *'the dirty girl'.*

*

Edith was detailed to ferry the Marsden children back to their homes despite their remonstrances. She was hoping that at last she would find out where and how they lived. However, Janie, who was still scared of anyone knowing their address, insisted on being dropped in a street quite a way from the Mersey Road. Edith gave in with a sigh and the two girls watched her drive away and hid for a while in some bushes until they were sure her car would have disappeared into the distance. Then they set off the walk the quarter of a mile back to their house.

As they approached, they saw a chink of light coming from number 23 which had obviously escaped the scrutiny of their Raid Wardens who were still enforcing the black out.

'They've waited up for us,' said Janie happily, determined never the less to give them a piece of her mind about the insufficient black out. But her smile turned to horror when she heard loud voices coming from inside.

They crept round to the back of the house and opening the door, slipped in and hid behind the window curtain.

Their gravest suspicions were confirmed when she saw Bill and his Agnes in there yelling at each other. Bill had young Jamie under his left arm and was beating him systematically with a stick in his right hand. The two girls started to shake and Janie was about to rush in to help the little boy when she saw the sturdy figure of Jack appear in the hall doorway. Jack gave a shout and, putting his head down, rammed Bill in the stomach so that he had to let go the child. Bill grabbed Jack by the throat and the woman Agnes stood by, wringing her hands and shouting. Lil kept tight hold of Janie's hand, to keep her from running into the scene.

'Stop out here Janie, you can't do nothing.'

At that point, Jack threw Bill off and got him to the g round. The man was blind drunk, not aware of what he was doing. His woman, Agnes, kicked his body several times, but he didn't stir.

'You stinkin' bastard,' she said and she left the house. As she came out she noticed the shadowy figures of the two little girls.

'Don't go in there, he's raving, 'she said, 'He said he wanted to see his kids, but 'e's mad to come here with them redcaps after him.'

After one glance at each other, the two girls turned on their heels and with the same thoughts in mind ran to the police box at the end of the road.

'We want to report a deserter,' said Janie.

The policeman got on to it at once and gave them a cup of tea while they were waiting for the redcaps to arrive. They watched in silence from the corner of the street, as the two burly MPs dragged him out of the house.

'Mebbe they will shoot him after all,' said Lil hopefully.

Even in his state of stupor, Bill noticed the girls standing there with their police escort and summed up the situation perfectly.

'You wait, you little bitches. When I get back you'll wish you'd never been born.'

But the two sisters didn't care.

'This is the Army Mr Jones.' They sang and laughed happily as he was carted off.

24.

Towards the end of March of that year an official looking envelope arrived on Irene's desk.

Irene sat down at the breakfast table and with her knife, slipped open the envelope, knowing quite well what was within. She took a slurp of tea before sliding out the contents.

'Oh this is it,' she said to Connie, 'my call to arms' and she handed over the call up papers.

'I wonder why it took so long,' remarked Connie.

'They've obviously been saving me for something special.'

'Something special, what do you think it is?' cried Maxine in excitement.

Irene laughed.

'A mission so important and so secret that I'm not allowed to talk about it!'

'Is it dangerous?' asked Maxine with badly controlled glee.

'I'm told it is not so dangerous as it was staying here in Hull, dodging the Luftwaffe.'

'I expect they want you to organise the Second Front,' remarked Connie.

'Really?' asked Maxine.

'Yes,' replied Connie, 'They say the Allies are planning an enormous invasion of the continent to drive out Hitler and all his forces.'

'And you believe I can do that single handed?'

'Without a doubt!'

Irene picked up the papers and stuffed them into her handbag.

'I think they just need a PT instructor to take keep fit classes – to energise the chaps. Anyway I have to report this afternoon!'

'They don't give you much time to pack!'

It was true, having had the initial interview she only had another day to say her farewells and then would have to leave for a destination unknown.

After the morning class, she called Lil into her study.

'Lil,' she said and she spoke with some difficulty 'There is something I must tell you.'

Lil sat down, ready to be lectured about some misdemeanour. Instead Irene led off with a compliment.

'I can't tell you how much you have improved during the past year. I'm so pleased with you. It is quite stunning how well your hard work has paid off.'

Lil smiled, delighted. Madame Renee was usually rather sparing of her praise.

'Thank you Madame Renee,' she said.

'Unfortunately, it will all have to come to a standstill for a while.'

Lil got to her feet to protest. 'Why? why?'

'Sit down child, let me finish.'

Irene took a cigarette from the Alabaster box on her desk and lit it.

'The fact is,' Irene herself rose and began pacing the room, 'The fact is, I am leaving here tomorrow'

'Why? You can't leave us. We need you.'

'It must be difficult for you to understand, but I have been called up to help in the fight against Hitler and I must go.'

The little girl leapt to her feet again, and running to Irene, grabbed at her skirt.

'We need you more than he does.'

Irene put Lil from her firmly, but still holding the small had sat down in order to put herself at the child's level.

'I must. You couldn't possibly understand, but there is something I can do to help us get rid of Hitler and his Nazis once and for all. I have felt a little ashamed up to now, running a dancing school when people were out there getting killed. Now at last I can be of more practical help.'

Irene was talking to herself. Lil stood there, not really understand anything of what was being said. All she had taken in was that Irene was going away.

'What about classes?'

Irene let go of the girl's hand and turned away slightly.

'I'm afraid they have to cease until the war is over.'

The child gave a cry, but Irene went on.

'There is nobody to take them.'

Lil was searching her mind for some solution to the problem

'Vera! She can do it.'

'She too is doing essential war work. It is very important to have people to entertain the troops.'

'I can do that. I can entertain!'

Irene had to smile a little at her eagerness, but it touched her more than tears could. Dancing was Lil's whole life. Irene was the one who had made it possible and now she was responsible for spoiling it for her

'Sadly no. You are too young'

'Well,' said the child, thinking hard, 'We can come here and do classes on our own.'

Irene put her hand on the little girl's shoulder. This was the most difficult part of all.

'I'm sorry, but the house will not be available anymore to you or to any of the girls. It is being taken over by the RAF.'

'All of it?'

'It is more use to them than to us.'

Lil tried to work out what was happening to her.

'So Madame Renee's will just stop?'

'Until after the war, yes. Let us pray it won't be too long now.'

Lil's eyes filled with tears and Irene surveyed the face that she had grown to love. She took the child in her arms.

'Please don't cry. Everything will be all right, you'll see. There is an old friend of mine who runs a ballet school in Cottingham. I will arrange that you and Maxine both go to him for classes!'

'Where the' ell is Cottingham?' she asked grumpily.

'Just a short distance away. A fifteen-minute walk. Or you could get an East Yorkshire bus.'

'But I don't want to go to nobody else.'

Irene laughed and took the little girl's chin in her hand.

'Now listen here, young woman. It is important that you keep working. M Revaux may be a little stricter than I am. He's quite an old man now and he comes from an old fashioned school of ballet – he's not just a dancing teacher like I am. But please try and put up with him, just until I return. I promise it won't be long. The war will soon be over. I'm sure of that.'

*

Scot was still stationed at the house and Irene had got used to seeing him about the place. He seemed like part of the family and it was taken for granted that he would be present at the farewell dinner the family had arranged for her. He was delighted to be there and provided champagne and even a bottle of Whisky.

Long after Maxine and her mother had gone to bed, Scot and Irene sat up, smoking and finishing the bottle of whisky.

'I'll be sorry to see you go, Madame Renee'

'Why do you never call me Irene?'

'Seems wrong somehow. I prefer called you Madame Renee. Does it worry you?'

'Not in the least. But you could cut out the Madame.'

'Okay Renee,' he said, trying it out, exaggerating the rhyme.

She smiled at him.

'I shall miss you, too, Scot.'

'Try Alistair.'

'All right I shall miss you too. Alistair.'

Scot emptied his glass of whisky and poured them another before his blushes subsided and he was able to speak again.

'Why should it affect you, when I call you Alistair?'

'Something to do with Marion I expect. Since Tom christened me Scot, nobody's called me anything else. Only Marion called me Alistair.'

'I never asked what happened about Marion. I suppose I thought you wouldn't want to talk about it.'

'It's Ok now.'

'So, what happened?'

'I suppose it's an old story. After the bomb that demolished the office there was nothing for me to do here in Hull anymore, so I went back to Edinburgh. I was going to tell her that I would be joining the forces as soon as I could, but she was in no mood to listen. When I got home, she was in bed with my best friend, Robbie. I suppose I should have called to warn her I was coming.'

'You wanted to surprise her.'

'Well I certainly did that,' he replied lightly. 'It seems the affair had been going on for some time. It's my own fault for leaving her alone for so long.'

He smiled ruefully, and then he gave a laugh and looked at her with a twinkle in his eyes.

'Anyway I found out the reason for all the mutton pies. Guilty conscience.' He laughed again and added mischievously, 'It was unfair of me to put you through that agony.'

'Unfair of you. You mean you knew we didn't like them?'

'I don't blame you, they were horrible. It just made me laugh when you were so polite about them.'

'You were playing tricks on us.'

'Listen Renee, since I met Tom, my life had been plagued with his practical jokes. It was an opportunity to get my own back.'

'I can't wait to tell Connie. She will die!' As they laughed, their glances locked for a moment. He was the first to break the silence.

'More whisky?'

'I shouldn't but – oh what the hell.'

As he poured the last drop into her glass, she felt there was something that had been left unsaid.

'And you couldn't find it in your heart to forgive her – patch things up?' Scot laughed.

'She didna want that. She wanted Robbie. Always had –or so she told me.'

'I'm sorry. It must have been an awful blow.'

'It was at the time. I thought I was finished. I rushed straight into the welcoming arms of the R.A.F. It's only since I...well...since I came here that my life seems to have got back on track again.'

Irene took a deep breath. Knowing what she wanted him to say and yet afraid of how she would feel if he did.

'What is the reason for that?'

He did not disappoint her. Nor did he need to answer the question with words. His kiss said everything.

25.

'Poor old Ada,' remarked Connie to Scot as they watched the RAF arrive. 'She's been complaining about the lack of men, now as soon as she gets herself into the ATS we get requisitioned by the Air Force.

It was good to have Scot there. A friendly face amidst all the strangers.

'Ada will be just fine in Scotland. There's always a load of men folk up there wanting to be kept warm.'

Connie was kept very busy, but had thankfully given up the scrubbing out of houses. The whole war was much more organised now on the home front, and as the bombing had slowed down, everyone was taking things more or less in their stride.

In fact, the arrival of the RAF bumped up Connie's social life no end. Tom's billiard table had never seen more activity. The studio was a perfect place for parties and Connie's talent was in much demand for running up dresses and making alterations for the two WAAF officers who moved into Aunt Paget's basement and became part of the family. After the initial grumbling, Aunt Paget really enjoyed having them around. They were nice girls, full of fun and one of them even became a helpless devotee of the ground rice cheesecakes, which pleased the manufacturer no end.

Although the keep fit classes had stopped, the girls didn't stop their visits. The sight of so many handsome men in blue was like a feast for their starving eyes. Edith popped in at least once every day on some pretext of another to try and catch a glimpse of some approachable male person.

Maxine surveyed the general hysteria and wondered what it was all about. She still hadn't caught up with some of her school friends who already talked in giggling whispers about boys. The officers loved the beautiful Connie and they treated her like a princess. Maxine watched the way her mother talked to the officers, the way her eyes began to sparkle and her cheeks to flush. They were none of them as handsome or funny as her father and she couldn't understand why Connie would ever find them attractive.

*

Maxine and Lil presented themselves at M. Revaux's academy. M Revaux was short and whippet thin and he carried a cane, which he found useful for inflicting stinging blows on recalcitrant limbs. Working with him was a much more serious affair than at Madame Renee's, where there was always time for a joke and a chat. Maxine was in her element. She loved the strict discipline of it and was never in any danger of receiving blows from that thin evil cane. It helped her concentrate and acted like a spur to her work.

Lil on the other hand, was terrified. She had lived all her young life under the threat of violence; it had been Madame Renee's kindness and patience that had allowed her to blossom. M Revaux frightened her. He didn't believe in making allowances for nervousness. Her confidence diminished and she performed less well whenever she was in his presence. She hated the school and she loathed M Revaux.

After her first lesson she came back and told Janie

'Well, I ain't goin' back there no more.'

'You said that about Madame Renee's.'

'Yes, but she was kind. Mongsewer is real nasty. It was the girls that put me off at Madame Renee's.'

'Are these girls any better?'

'Worse, even more snobby – but different. All they go on about is *'the ballet'* as if it was summat real special. It's still only dancing i'nt it same as the rest. Anyway I ain't goin' back tomorrow.'

Janie shrugged, 'It's up to you. But remember the vow *'As god is my witness!'* You won't be a big star or get that house in the country if you don't keep on at it.'

Mention of the vow made Lil stop and think. She knew Janie was right.

'OK,' she said. 'But I won't think about it now. I'll think about it tomorrow – after all...

And they chorused, *'Tomorrow is another day!'*

'Anyway, just stay until you've finished this lot of exams. Promise.'

So Lil returned to Mongsewer as she called him and continued working. But this time she was doing it, not for Irene, or for herself. This time it was for Janie and the family. She'd get that house in the country no matter what it cost. She loved her family even though she and the boys had little in common and nothing to talk about. Janie was a constant joy always encouraging and on her side although the boys often thought that the ballet school was just 'swank'. Janie protected her against any antagonism both at home and at school.

The girls from Madame Renee's had all dispersed, gone their separate ways. Even though she had never become intimate with any of them, she missed the classes and the company. She and Janie were thrown more and more into each other's company, and they began to spend more and more of their time at the movies again.

*

In June 1944, the allies landed in Normandy. It was the end of the beginning as Mr Churchill said. All sides had joined forces. The Russians in the East, the Americans and English and free Europeans from the west. And underground there were the resistance and the Maquis who were infiltrating enemy lines, causing disruption to the German forces.

Everything seemed to be going well with the little family in Mersey Road. Jack at seventeen was registered for call up and might be enlisted any minute, but in the meantime he was still earning good money at the factory and so was David – now 16. Janie was still sewing uniforms and Lil was at last understanding what school was about and her ballet classes were providing her with discipline she'd never had before.

She still pined for Irene, for Ada and Vera who were all now away living different lives. Janie was her only companion and the two girls became closer than ever. Whenever Janie had time off from her job the two of them would go to the movies.

*

Soon after the Normandy landings, Hitler responded with a new menace known irreverently as Doodlebugs. They were guided missiles or *'pilotless planes'* each containing a bomb that would explode when they arrived at Britain. London bore the brunt of the doodlebugs but quite a few managed to get as far as the North East coast. They were no respecters of people or buildings; they were aimless, just landing at random on whatever happened to be in their path. People just put up with them the way they had put up with the Blitz. No point in worrying. Just put them out of your mind, occupy yourself with other things. There was nothing that could be done except cope with them when they arrived.

'Hope exam goes all right,' said Janie, 'Shall I come with you and wait till you've done?'

'No, don't know what time I'll finish. You go to pictures. Ingrid Bergman's on at Dorchester. Don't you want to see it?'

'I'm not bothered. You go enjoy yourself.'

Janie seldom went to the movies on her own, but Lil's exam meant she would she would have to be locked in the town hall all day.

*

Like everyone else, Lil heard that unmistakable drone of the buzz bombs as they flew overhead. They all ran in the same terrifying routine. First the unearthly buzz, like the sound of an enormous bee, a sudden stop and there would be silence for a seemingly endless thirty seconds as the missile's engine switched off and finally the explosion as it found its random target.

Lil was happy with herself when the exam finished. She rushed out of the Town Hall, hoping that Janie would be home so she could tell her all about it.

Jack met her at the door. His usually ruddy complexion was ashen.

'In't Janie back yet?' asked Lil.

'Dorchester was hit by a doodle bug.'

'Is she all right?'

'Don't know. Was a direct hit.'

Janie's little body was found in the wreckage.

*

Lil busied herself with the funeral arrangements. Irene had gone somewhere far away and she saw no reason to contact Connie or Maxine. They'd never shown much interest in her or her family. Some of their neighbours turned up at the church service where Lil remained dry eyed throughout.

*

After the funeral, Lil had nowhere to go, nothing to do. She walked around like a zombie. She felt guilty because she had not been with her sister when she died. Irrationally she blamed her dancing for the tragedy and gave up her classes altoether – she must have been dancing when the little girl died. When the results of the exam came through, she threw them on the fire without even opening the envelope. For months later she expected Janie to come running in at any moment. But in her heart she knew it would never happen. Now it was up to her to keep the little family together, to try and take Janie's place.

Her dancing career – and with it her life – was finished.

She no longer had anything to live for. Thoughts of a country house disappeared into a distant memory.

Act Two:

The Warriors Return

1.

1945

Everyone expected Johnny to come marching home immediately. It just didn't work out that way.

Irene was the first to arrive back at the Laurels; She was lean, healthy and totally unaffected by her military experiences.

'It was like being back at Sadler's Wells,' she laughed. 'Except the Army food was better.'

She arrived one morning when Maxine was having a ballet class so one of her first actions was to go along to Jacques Revaux's ballet school to see how her pupils were getting on. M Revaux was delighted with Maxine's progress, but greeted Irene with mixed feelings.

'I am happy to see you Renee, but I expect that now you are back, you will be taking all my best pupils away from me.'

'I'm not back, Jacques. They haven't exactly chucked me out yet. This is my demobilisation leave. It means I can come home for a while and then I have to go back again while they write out all the papers to get me discharged.'

'Nevertheless, it is the .... thin end of the wedge?'

'Besides, I still haven't decided what I'm going to do in Civvy street,' she added.

Her romance with Scot had blossomed during the past couple of years. They had corresponded frequently and the question of marriage was hanging in the air. Scot had not yet sorted out his civilian lifestyle. He could hardly depend on Grantley and Fletcher-Coles for a living. Marble was a luxury item and the building trade had more to do with its money than to spend it on fripperies.

Jacques took Irene on a tour of the classes. Maxine's face lit up when she saw her aunt and she worked especially hard for her, showing off.

But after Irene had seen all the classes at work, she had a question to ask Jacques.

'The other little girl... Lil... How is she getting on?'

Jacques shrugged 'Who knows?'

'What do you mean? Why is she not here today?'

'Not today or any day. We haven't seen her for a year. Not since her last exams. She did surprisingly well, but she never came back.'

Irene treated Maxine to tea in *Jenny's* a little teashop near the theatre where all the actors used to hang out. Maxine was thrilled to see a couple of famous faces and practically fainted with delight when they recognised her aunt.

'You know everybody,' she said with a happy sigh as she cut up her toasted teacake, 'I'm going to be an actress you know, when I grow up. A real actress in rep. Not just a dancer'

Connie had warned Irene in advance of this ambition and had instructed her not to encourage Maxine in this direction. Irene thought Maxine had as good a chance as any of making a living. But it was not her business to say so. Instead she asked the question that was in the forefront of her mind.

'What about Lil, how is she doing?'

Maxine frowned slightly as if trying to remember who Lil was.

'Oh. Lil' she said at last 'She doesn't come to class any more.'

'So I gathered. How did it happen?'

'She just stopped coming. I think she was fed up with it. She didn't like Jacques. Didn't like the discipline'

As far as Maxine was concerned, that was the end of the matter

'When are you going to start the school again? I'm sick to death of being a ballet dancer. I want to be an actress'

'Does she still live in Mersey Road?'

Maxine shrugged.

'How should I know? She never was my friend you know.'

'I just thought that maybe…'

'What?'

Irene shook her head. 'Oh never mind.'

She had foolishly thought that Maxine might have kept up with Lil, even though she had absconded from the classes, but then why should she? Apart from the dancing they had nothing at all in common. Maxine had no reason at all to love Lil – or even like her. Toleration was about the extent of her involvement.

The following day, she had an hour to spare, so she took the journey to Mersey Road. The town was still devastated. They were beginning to clear up the ruins and a few prefabricated buildings had sprung up, but mostly there were just gaps where the buildings had been. The wind, never kind in the North East, now whistled through the bomb sites and seemed to freeze the bones, even in August. It would be a long time before there would be the money, the time, and the manpower to rebuild the whole city centre.

Mersey Road was a quiet little cul-de-sac full of neat tiny houses and Irene was agreeably surprised at the air of respectability. She tapped on the door of number 23. A young woman answered.

She took in Irene's smart appearance, her officer's uniform and smiled in a friendly manner.

'How can I help you?' she spoke with a transatlantic accent.

'I'm looking for a family who used to live here. The Marsdens.'

'Come on in,' said the woman 'You want coffee?'

Irene thanked her, introduced herself to the girl whose name was Cindy.

They went into the kitchen and Cindy put on the kettle. The house was decently but impersonally furnished as if it were meant for short time residents. Cindy explained that many of the houses, were the same. They had been taken over for people in transit or just waiting for permanent accommodation.

'I came over from Canada to be with my husband,' she said as she measured the coffee into an earthenware jug. 'As soon as I arrived, he was sent to Europe.'

'Typical,' said Irene.

'Yes. Anyhow he's back and we are waiting for our ship home to Toronto.'

Cindy put the coffee things on a tray and led the way into the sitting room

They sat down on the big comfortable armchairs and Cindy handed Irene a cup of coffee.

'Don't worry, it's the real thing,' she said.

'Forgive me,' said Cindy, 'I have asked you in under false pretences. I know nothing of the Marsdens so I'm no possible use to you. I invited you in because I do love listening to your English accent. We're all North Americans on this estate – we might as well be back home!'

'You still may be able to help. This is the last address we had for the family. They may have moved out some time ago. I was very remiss. I didn't keep up with them.'

'People come and go a lot around here,' Cindy put her cup down, 'But I have an idea. Excuse me there is someone I can call.' and she went back into the kitchen.

Irene sat back, to enjoy her coffee, and took out her packet of Senior Service.

'Do you mind if I smoke?' she shouted.

'Go ahead,' came the reply, 'How nice of you to ask.'

Cindy came back, looking pleased with her.

'My friend Jenny is coming over. She's lived here longer than most.'

She went to the sideboard and produced an ashtray.

'Neither of us smoke but all of our friends do. Do you care for Lucky's?'

'Well. Yes.'

'Then you can have all of ours. We have a generous ration from the PBX; we thought we'd take them to give out to the deserving British. So far you're the only one we've met. Socially, that is.'

There was a sharp ring at the doorbell and another young woman burst through the door.

This time Irene was luckier.

'The Marsdens? Yeah I know who you mean. They left before I arrived, but I have heard of them. A very young family. Three boys and a girl. Stepfather somewhere and his wife or girlfriend. They were never seen.'

'There were two little girls.' corrected Irene automatically.

'No. Just the one. Oh wait a minute. Oh dear yes, there was a tragedy. One of the girls was killed in a movie house I believe. One of those flying bombs.'

Irene felt sick. The room began to spin. Jenny was contrite.

'Oh Jeeze, I'm sorry, you didn't know? It must a shock for you.'

'Can I get you something – cognac?' asked Cindy. Without waiting for a reply she splashed a slug of brandy into a large balloon glass and handed it to Irene.

'Which one was it? The one who was killed?'

'I don't know. I'm sorry. The two boys were working at the factory. The little girl and the small boy were both at school still.'

'And that's all you know?'

'They didn't talk to people much. All I know is gossip.'

'Do you know where they went?'

'Not exactly. They were rehoused. I think they got a prefab someone over Sutton way.'

Irene thanked Jenny for the information sketchy though it was. She thanked Cindy for her hospitality, took her carton of Lucky Strikes and a month's supply of chocolate and made her way back to the Laurels.

When she told Maxine and Connie what had happened, they listened politely and changed the subject as soon as possible to things that held more relevance for them.

It was not until she was in bed that night, sated with American chocolate that Maxine went over what Irene had said. So it was possible that Lil, her rival, the dirty girl was dead. To her guilty horror she found she relived the elation she had felt when the bomb dropped on Paradise Street five years before and in her nostrils she could feel again the acrid smell of burning fur.

2.

Ada was the next to arrive at the Laurels. She burst in one day when Connie and Maxine were having tea. She was wearing civilian clothes, looking fit, healthy and pregnant.

'Oh no, not again,' cried Connie when she saw that familiar bump.

Ada gurgled with delight.

'This one's for me,' she cried as the removed her white cotton gloves and presented her left hand, showing off the golden wedding band on her finger. 'I've got wed!'

'Tell, tell', cried Maxine, 'What's he like?'

'He's smashing. Tom, he's called, like your dad – and he's got blue eyes like him and all.'

'Did you meet him in Scotland?'

'Aye he was in army up there, like me. But he'll be demobbed soon and then we'll live in Ponders End.'

'Where in the world is Ponders End?' asked Connie.

'Down South – in London,' she replied proudly. 'My Tom's a plumber in Civvy Street. He says there'll be lots of work for him down there once they start building again.'

'But where will you live? It may be not be easy to find somewhere after all the bombing!'

'That's the beauty of it. He's got a house already. He was engaged you see to a lass down there, but she ran off and got wed to a Yank a couple of years back.'

'I shall be able to come and stay with you when I go to London to be an actress.' cried Maxine.

'You'll be welcome lass, you always will. You and your folks have been real kind to me in the past.'

She looked around.

'Is Mr Fletcher back yet? I thought I might see him.'

'He'll be another week or so yet. It all seems to take so long,' sighed Connie.

'What has happened to Lil?' was her next question.

'She was killed by a doodle bug' and Maxine related the whole story as told by Irene. Ada was very upset and cried for a while, but her heart now belonged to her Tom in Ponders End and he and their child was now her priority.

*

Maxine, full of excitement, went with Connie to meet her father at the railway station. He was frailer than she remembered and still very brown from the African sun. His eyes seemed bluer than ever in his sunburned face.

As he stepped off the train, Connie rushed into his arms and they hugged each other close.

'What about me?' cried Maxine, and she tried to get between them as she had done when she was a child. But she had grown too tall. Tom loosened himself from Connie's grip and looked at his daughter as if she were a stranger.

'Maxie?' he said, 'You've grown up.'

He kissed her politely and gave her a cursory hug.

They got a taxi home from the station. The three of them sat together in the back seat with Tom in the middle. Maxine was conscious all the time that though he was next to her, he was turning away from her, addressing all his attention to Connie. The conversation in the cab was halting and was interrupted over and over by exclamations from Tom about landmarks that had disappeared since the bombing.

'I don't even know my own town any more,' he said.

The ten-minute drive seemed to last a lifetime.

Irene and Aunt Paget were peering through the drawing room curtains when they arrived.

Tom got out of the cab and looked at the Laurels from the outside.

'Looking a big drab,' he said.

Connie laughed nervously.

'There's been a war on,' she said jokingly.

She led the way up the path and through the front door. He looked around the hall.

'They haven't done as much damage as I expected,' he said.

'We didn't get any bombs.'

'Not the bombs,' he replied, 'The Brylcream boys.'

Irene and Aunt Paget exchanged significant looks. Irene knew Tom and had known that having the air force in his home would disturb him. Both stepped forward both to greet him and to try and reassure him, but before even greeting them, he set off on a tour of the house, Connie following behind, twittering like a broody hen. Maxine tried to stay with them on their peregrinations but Tom didn't seem to see her at all. On his face was a strange expression as if he didn't know exactly where he was.

'Where is my desk?' he said as they arrived at his study.

Connie indicated it to him.

'Over in the corner.'

'No, not that, my desk. Where is it?'

Connie went over to the desk and put her hand on it.

'That's not right,' he said.

'Yes, yes, it is, see' and she opened the flap to show him the neat arrangement of files and notebooks.

'It's not the same,' he said.

'Yes of course it is. Just as it always was.'

He turned on her.

'You've moved it!'

Connie gasped. It was possible. In five years so many things got moved around from place to place.

'Where do you want it?' she asked.

'Where it was before,' he snapped.

And so it went with everything around the house. Tom wanted everything to be exactly as he remembered it and Connie, taken off guard, fluttered about, all her newfound toughness and strength deserting her in her efforts to please this strange person who was her husband.

Eventually she managed to persuade him to sit down and have tea with Irene and Aunt Paget who were still waiting for him, not knowing what to make of things.

'I'll make some fresh tea,' said Aunt Paget.

'No no this will do,' he said.

'It will be icy cold. It won't take a minute to mash another pot.'

'I said it will do,' he snapped.

Aunt Paget shrugged and poured a cup of the cold tea for him.

'Then here you are, Tom. I shall make fresh for the rest of us' and she bustled away indignantly.

'That was most unkind,' said Irene, 'Poor Aunt Paget, she was being thoughtful. She was so excited about you coming home.'

'I don't need to be patronised,' he replied shortly.

*

As the days went by Maxine wondered what she had done to upset him. Maybe he was disappointed in her because she wasn't his little girl any more. It wasn't her fault. It was what she longed to be. She wanted the past five years to disappear so that she could be Daddy's little girl again. She longed to sit on his knee, hug him, and smell his wonderful tobacco smell. But when she got close, he always found that there was something more important for him to do and gently pushed her away.

Sometimes she caught him looking at her strangely, with criticism, with sadness and with a kind of fear.

'You're too thin,' he would say, 'Did you go hungry while I was away?'

Connie intervened quickly.

'We didn't have a lot of food, but we had enough,' she said.

'We didn't have any bananas. 'put in Maxine, hoping for a laugh. Bananas had completely disappeared and they had become a byword for unnecessary luxuries. Tom didn't laugh, that tragic look came back this face.

'We must fatten you up,' he said.

3.

Lil was glad they had moved into the prefab and away from Mersey Road where there were so many memories of happy times she had shared with Janie.

Although the prefab looked small, it was amazingly roomy inside, convenient and warm. The two big boys – the working men of the family – shared the master bedroom, which gave the two younger children a tiny room each for themselves. Davy was looking forward to the day when Jack would be called up his national service so that he too could have a room to himself. Davy would be a fully-fledged heating engineer when his apprenticeship was up. He was a steady, practical young man, only getting into scrapes when dragged into them by his big hot-tempered brother.

Lil worked a couple of evenings a week at the uniform factory which was now given over to making cheap off the peg demob suits. It was hard close work and the material felt rough and uncomfortable to her fingers, but suits were urgently needed for men returning from the forces, discarding the uniforms that they had been wearing for up to six years. She missed her dancing but tried not to think of it, although she practised each day to the wireless.

One Saturday in late September, the eldest boys had gone off to watch Hull Kingston Rovers. James, who had a bad cold was reading to her from 'A Tale Two Cities' as she darned socks.

When the doorbell rang, she jumped to her feet.

'I wonder who this can be,' she said. She always had a faint cold fear when strangers came to the door.

There was no hall in the little house, the front door opened directly onto the living room and she could see the shadow of a man through the net curtains on the window. For a moment she contemplated ignoring the bell, but knew that this was not the answer. She had to face what was waiting for her on the doorstep.

4.

The first thing she saw as she opened the door were those familiar light eyes. Eyes as translucent and as cold as the ice on a wintry green pond. They looked her up and down.

'You are Lil,' he said and he held out his arms to her. When she did not respond, he dropped his arms, but his eyes remained on her face.

'So little Janie bought it. I'm sorry.'

Lil stood, transfixed, like a rabbit in the headlamps of his pale penetrating eyes.

'Aren't you going to ask Daddy to come in?'

She took a step back and he pushed past her into the room where Jamie sat, still with the book in his hands.

'Baby Jamie?' he said.

Jamie got to his feet and backed against the wall. Lil felt sick when she saw the terror on his face.

'Give your old man a kiss,' he said. 'Baby James in't too old for a cuddle, is he?'

The two children stayed still, waiting to see what would happen next. Bill did not move either, just gave a harsh laugh, mocking them for their fear.

'Bit of a bloody job finding you,' said Bill. 'Mersey Road had never heard of you. But a father always knows where to find his young 'uns.'

At last Lil found her voice.

'Where's Agnes?'

'Bitch left me when they put me in the glasshouse' he said 'Can't rely on nobody, can you?' and he fixed his cold stare on Lil.

'At least my own kids wun't rat on me, would they?'

Lil found she couldn't look away.

'Would they?' he said, louder this time. Lil, not knowing what else to do, shook her head, limply. He laughed at her again.

'Got any grub? I'm starved' and he sat on the sofa and taking his basilisk gaze off Lil, concentrated for a while on Jamie, who quailed, but met his gaze bravely.

Lil, glad to get away from those penetrating eyes slipped out into the kitchen. There was a pan of mince on the cooker that she had ready for the boys when they came in from the football match. She put the potatoes on to boil and went back into the sitting room where Bill and Jamie were still looking at each other.

*

'I've put potatoes on,' she said.

'When I said I was starved. I meant now' he said 'Give me summat now.'

'Bread?'

'Aye, owt'll do' She went back into the kitchen, and slicing a thick piece of bread, she covered it with margarine and poured hot mince over it. She put the whole thing on a tray and added a knife and fork. After a moment's thought, she slipped the sharp bread knife down the back of the knife drawer. Bill seemed fairly calm at the moment, but she wouldn't trust him with a handy knife.

He sat down at the table and demolished the meal in seconds. He held out the plate.

'More' he said.

'It's our whole meat ration for the week,' she replied. 'It's for the boys' tea.'

'They been well fed. They can do wi'out for once,' he said.

She took the rest of the mince and poured it over another slice of bread, adding an extra slice of bread and Marge on a separate plate.

She brewed the tea in the brown teapot and brought it in with some cups, milk and sugar. She put milk into the cups conscious of his eyes upon her as he gulped down the food. He demolished everything in sight, slurping the tea with great satisfaction.

'Glad you learned to cook' he said, 'Couldn't live with a woman who couldn't cook!'

'Live with?'

'Where else would I go? Bosom of my family, where else?'

He finished his meal and, picking up his shabby kitbag said, 'Where do I sleep?'

'We haven't got room There's only enough for us'

'Then Somebody can sleep on sofa' he said and went into the room shared by Jack and David.

'I'll sleep here,' he said, putting his kitbag on the only bed. He threw himself down next to it and bounced a little to feel the springs, 'Aye, this'll do me,' he said.

Lil did not offer any protest; she just went back to Jamie who was sitting with the book still in his hands, staring at the wall. She took his hand and held it tightly. They dared not speak. Every word uttered in the prefab could be heard throughout the house. They just held each other by the hand and waited for what would happen next.

After a while, they heard Bill go into the kitchen and start rattling the kitchen jars in which they kept things like tea and sugar. She knew what he was doing. The family had always kept their housekeeping money hidden in one of the jars and Lil had carried on with the habit. She knew that he would be bound to find it sooner or later.

Sure enough Bill came out of the kitchen, jingling money in his pocket.

'I'll be out for a bit. My mucky clothes are in me kitbag. See they get done' he said and he left the little house, whistling.

'He's taken the housekeeping money,' said Lil in a low voice, 'He'll go out and get drunk. What do we do?'

'Kill him,' said the child without emphasis 'He should be killed'

Lil put her arms around the child.

'He's not worth sufferin for,' she said.

'We'll all suffer now he's back,' said Jamie.

She went into the boy's room and picked up the kitbag. It was very heavy. She emptied it out.

She took out a handful of filthy ragged underclothes, and then a battered tin mug and plate with fork, spoon and a blunt knife. She saw there was a whole bundle of other, ragged garments, so, loath to touch them, she up-turned the bag and the things fell out with a thump. There was an old grey woollen vest wrapped around something very hard and heavy. She picked it up. She knew instinctively what was and her heart started beating so heavily that she could feel the blood pounding and banging painfully in her ears.

She unwrapped the woollen vest and there it was. She had never seen a revolver before. It was black, it looked vicious. She placed it carefully on the bed and drew back from it.

Jamie called her.

'Lil, where have you gone?'

She wrapped up the gun again in the woollen vest, placed it back on the bed and, shutting the door behind her went to see what it was Jamie wanted. He was hungry and his tea had vanished down Bill's throat. As the potatoes had now boiled, she mashed them up with some cabbage from the garden and formed them into rissoles. She fried a couple of them in dripping and gave them to Jamie with some rice pudding she had put into the oven earlier. Then she sent him to his room to do his homework. The other rissoles she put aside for Jack and Dave who were usually hungry when they came back late after the match.

When the doorbell went again, she thought it was the boys who had forgotten their key. She rushed to the door, ready to tell them the news about Bill, but to her horror it was Bill himself who stood there, swaying gently, his face reddened and his eyes bloodshot.

'I'm not drunk' he said, 'There weren't enough money to get drunk on'

He staggered past her into the house.

'Something I forgot,' he said and he made his way into the bedroom.

*

When he saw the clothes laid on the bed, he turned and belted Lil across the face with the back of his hand.

'What you doing, spying on me. Opening my private things,' he said.

'You told me to do your washing,' she muttered, rubbing her reddened jaw.

He picked up the gun, which lay just as she had left it.

'You saw this, did you?'

She nodded.

'I got it specially' he said 'it had two bullets in it, but I only need one now.'

He came very close to her, and grabbing her collar, he held the gun to her chin. She could smell the alcohol on his breath.

'Do you know what that bullet is for?'

She whispered 'No.'

'Oh I think you do. It's for them as told on me to the Redcaps. Janie's gone poor little bitch, so I can't teach her the lesson. So who does that leave, eh?'

He let her go suddenly with a mighty shove and she crashed against the wall. She slid down the wall and stayed there, sitting on the floor as he looked at her with his face contorted with hate.

'It's no joke in glasshouse, you know. You're like a slave. They can do whatever they want to you.'

He licked his lips

'You don't know what that's like, do you?'

She shook her head.

'Well, you soon will' and clicked the gun 'And if I've any trouble from you –nobody would ever miss a little girl like you, would they? Even if they did, they'd never find you. Not dead they wouldn't. Not in the river, they wouldn't'

She was afraid to move or speak. She guessed that he was just trying to frighten her, but wasn't taking any chances.

'Now then' he said, 'Where's your bag? You must have some more cash somewhere'

'You can take all I have' she said, 'My purse is in my coat pocket. The grey one, hanging up there on the door'

He laughed, 'Good girl, that's the way. Now remember this. I'm head of this house now and I say what gets done with the money what comes in. You got that?'

'Yes'

He went to her pocket and took out her purse. There was five bob there, her wages for the week.

'Now then,' he said, 'You can start washing.'

He tucked the five shillings in the pocket of his reefer jacket, tossing the gun carelessly to the floor.

'Put that gun somewhere safe.'

'Can't you tek it with you?'

'Don't be daft. Asking for trouble that would' he said 'Stick it under mattress and don't go blabbing about it, understand? Not to anyone.'

As he went, slamming the door behind him, little Jamie came out of his room, white and shaking. He went to her and sat beside her on the floor, holding her close. They sat there, looking at the gun lying beside them until the key in the lock told them that Jack and Davy had returned at last.

5.

'What's for tea?' was the usual cry as the two boys came through the door.

'Cabbage rissoles,' said Jamie.

'But we always has mince on Satdays,' said Davy, and for the first time he caught a glimpse of the two white faces.

'What's been going on?' he said.

Jamie burst into tears and jack turned his attention to the children.

'Something happened while we were out?'

'You was such a long time. Where've you been?' and Lil threw herself into jack's arms and started to sob.

Jack put his arm around her and tried to calm her. Davy turned to Jamie.

'What's up?' he said again. Together Lil and Jamie tried to tell them what had happened.

Lil took Jack into the bedroom and showed him the gun, still lying on the floor where Bill had thrown it. Jack picked up the gun, flicked the chamber and took out the bullets.

'Least it's not loaded any more' he said.

'Please be careful,' cried Lil.

'It won't do no harm if it's not loaded' put in Davy.

'Don't you fret our Lil' said jack. 'There's four of us and only one of him. Davy and me, we're grown up now, he dun't realise that. He thinks we're still under his thumb – and we're not.'

'Can't you get rid of that thing?' Lil was still regarding the gun with terror.

'I'll see what I can do' he said 'But first, burn all that muck.'

'You mean his clothes?'

'Clothes – and all his papers. Poke up that fire and burn 'em, everything.'

'But why?'

'Don't ask questions. Just do as I say.'

Soon the fire was blazing nicely in the grate and the smell of burning cloth and papers filled the air. Anything that would not burn was put back into the kitbag along with the gun.

When the firs began to die down, Jack picked up the bag and slung it over his shoulder.

'Anyone see him?' he said, slipping the bullets into his pocket.

'Don't think so.'

'Come on our kid,' he said to Davy 'We've got summat to do,'

'Where you going?'

'Mind your own business,' replied Jack, 'Give that stuff a good raking and bury it. We don't want anybody to know he's been here!'

'What are you going to do?'

'Never you mind, lass,' said jack 'Best you don't know nowt'

'Can I come?' asked Jamie.

Jack rubbed the head of his little brother.

'No you can't. Remember you know nowt. Bill never came,' he said and he turned to Lil.

'Who's Bill?' said Jamie.

Jack laughed. 'Good lad', he said and turned to Lil.

'If anyone asks, tell 'em you haven't seen him,' he ordered.

And the two boys left the house.

When the clothes had turned to black dust, Lil cleaned out the grate and she and Jamie buried the ashes in the patch of dirt nearest the back door.

It was nearly midnight when the boys returned. They seemed in high spirits. They had rissoles, some bread and marge, rice pudding and a pot of tea. Then they went to bed – in their usual bed as if nothing had happened.

Bill never came back that night, or for the rest of the week.

Lil quizzed her brothers about the whereabouts of their father; they pretended they didn't know what she was talking about. It was as if the whole thing had been a terrible dream.

6.

It was a couple of weeks later that she answered the doorbell to two uniformed policemen who asked if they might come in.

'Do you recognise this man?' they asked, and they showed her picture of Bill.

'Yes,' she said in a low voice.

'He is your step father?'
She nodded.
'Have you seen him recently?'
'No not since – during the war. He was taken away by the military police.'
'We have reason to believe he has recently been in the neighbourhood. Are you quite sure you haven't seen him?'
She swallowed hard 'No, I haven't.'
'Where were you a week last Saturday?'
'I was here at home.'
'Alone?'
'Yes' she lied 'The boys were all at Craven Park.'
'A neighbour says that she thought she heard a man's voice coming from here.'
'No. Not possible,' then she added quickly, 'Oh, just a minute. It could have been the wireless. I always have it on for company when I'm here on my own.'
One of the policemen tapped her kindly on the shoulder.
'If you see him, please don't be afraid to tell us. He is a known criminal. You don't owe him any loyalty.'
'I know that,' she said.
'I promise you – no harm will come to you if you tell the truth.'
'I'll let you know if I see him.'
The policeman left.
'They know summat,' said Lil when Jack returned, 'The coppers know summat.'
Jack laughed, 'Listen kid, they're after him cos he's a criminal. In't that what they said? You mustn't worry. Everything's OK.'
Lil took a deep breath.
'If they come back I'll have to tell them he's been here. I can't go on lying.'
'What you saying?'
'I'm saying I can't go on pretending.
'Don't you be so fuckin' stupid,' said Jack – and he gripped her shoulder so hard that she cried out 'If you say a word to the rozzers, you'll be sorry – and you know why? I'll make bloody sure of it... *Understand?*'
She shivered at the unusually harsh note in Jack's voice.
'Look at me!' he said.
She looked up at him and there was something in his face she had never noticed before. It was a look she had seen in the eyes of his father – that

cold fanatical gleam, that look of vicious hatred. Jack was his father's son, he had the father's evil streak. People forgave Bill over and over again, always blaming the drink for his destructive urges. But Jack, even sober had that same streak of viciousness.

Lil found that suddenly she was afraid of someone she had known all her life.

'You've gotta swear. You won't say a word.'

And he shook her hard.

'Do you understand?'

She nodded, tears pouring down her face.

'I understand.'

*

The following Saturday evening, the police came back. Lil was in the bathroom and Jamie answered the door. She heard them ask about his father and he told them that as far as he knew Bill didn't even know their address. Her words rang true even to Lil lurking in the bathroom and she knew he was lying.

'We want to speak to your sister again.'

In the split second before Jamie said 'She's not here. She's gone to the shops. Perhaps you should come back later' she had snatched up her cardigan which was hanging on the bath rail, climbed up on the lavatory and was squeezing herself out of the bathroom window, which looked out on the piece of spare ground at the back of the bungalow.

'Thank you, we'll wait here for her.'

She tore her blouse on the bramble as she slipped out of the window and down the wall, but she clutched the cardigan to her as she pressed herself up against the wall, listening for any sound that might tell her what was happening inside.

She heard Jamie speak to the policemen.

'No, I told you, I think she went shopping Shall I make you some tea while you're waiting? She shouldn't be long.' Jamie was buying her time to get away.

Still not knowing quite what she intended to do, but knowing she had to do something, she started to run and run.

7.

Her only thought was to get away as far as possible, to find sanctuary. As she ran, avoiding the main thoroughfares, choosing back streets and alley ways, avoiding curious eyes, concealing herself when necessary behind high walls and hedges, slowing her pace is someone approached, but nobody seemed interested in her – a scrawny little red haired child in a torn cardigan.

She wasn't sure where she was going, but the image of Irene's face arose in her mind, followed swiftly by one of Ada. The images of her two friends reassured her, gave her hope and without any real intention, her feet seemed to carry her to Sherwood Park.

She hammered on the door of the Laurels, confident that here she would find a kind and familiar face. She had a vivid image of Ada, smiling, taking her into her arms, and she waited on the doorstep, eager to see her friend again.

A stranger opened the door – a young girl, who looked at this torn and bleeding person in alarm

Sorry,' said Lil 'Is Ada there?'

The girl giggled but did not ask her in.

'Ada is married and gone to London,' she said.

Lil looked around her. High trees surrounded the Laurels, and she felt that behind each one there could be a policeman hiding, watching her. She must somehow get into the house, into that safe haven.

'Is Madame Renee there?'

'I'm sorry, but there's no Madame Renee here.'

'Miss Fletcher.'

'Do you mean Maxine?'

'No I mean her aunt, Irene – the dancing teacher.'

'Oh Mrs McGregor, she is away in Scotland with Mr McGregor.'

'Is nobody in?'

'Mr and Mrs Fletcher are in Scotland as well until Monday, but do you want to see Mrs Paget?'

Lil knew that she was not Aunt Paget's favourite person.

'Is there no one else in?'

'Maxine is here.'

'Oh good,' said Lil in relief, 'Tell Maxine I'm here.'

'Very well,' said the girl, 'Who shall I say?'

'Lil.'

Relaxed now, she prepared herself to be admitted into the house. She could feel rather than see the eyes looking out at her from the first floor room.

The girl came back.

'Miss Maxine told me to say she is too busy to talk to you, and she can't let you come in without her parents' permission. Perhaps you would come back on Monday when Mrs Fletcher is here.'

'But we are old friends.'

'I still daresn't.'

'Please, please let me in.'

'Sorry,' and the girl shut the door in her face.

*

Maxine was trembling all over. She sighed with relief as she saw what she had taken to be Lil's ghost turn and walk away. The dirty little girl with the evil black spit had risen from the dead yet again. She tried to pull herself together. Of course she didn't believe in ghosts, maybe the report had been wrong. For the first time Max remembered that there had been a sister – maybe she was the one who had been killed by the doodlebug and the dreadful Lil was really still alive. Maybe she shouldn't have sent her away, but she had been so afraid. Lil had looked terrible – she looked just like the seven-year-old ragamuffin she had first met in Paradise Street. Maybe she should have consulted with Aunt Paget who spent most of her time writing letters these days about the rebuilding of her cottage. The damage had not been as extreme as she had first thought and in a year or so she would be able to move back in. Maxine told herself it would have been unfair to disturb her, after all she didn't owe Lil anything. She had been given many opportunities and in the end she had thrown them all away. She wondered what her mother would have done, and she knew that Connie's reaction would have been the same.

'We just don't need people like that hanging round our necks, especially since your father has not been well.'

Tom's strangeness had not improved.

He talked continually about places that had been bombed out and refused to believe that they no longer existed. Sometimes he appeared to have wiped from his mind all recollection of the past six years and for him the war had never existed.

At other times, he would seem perfectly lucid and normal – except for his relationship with Maxine. Meeting her unexpectedly he would have to be reminded of who she was. He couldn't accept her as an almost grown up person and asked repeatedly for 'little Maxine.'

Connie had consulted local doctors and specialists who all gave him drugs for his headaches and said he was suffering from post war anxiety. One of them suggested she try to discuss the war with him, to release some of the tension and she tried. He had always been prone to violent rages when woken up or when disturbed at his work. Now the rages became worse and mention of the war would always trigger them off. She was afraid to continue.

This particular weekend, Connie and Tom had gone to Scotland to see a doctor who it was said, knew all about this kind of illness and may be able to treat him. Maxine remained at home with Aunt Paget, happy to be on her own, away from Tom's depressing presence.

'Who was that at the door?' asked Aunt Paget as she emerged from her letter writing, her hair ruffled and ink on her fingers.

'Just a gypsy.' Maxine lied, without knowing why she did so.

'Did you send her away?' asked Aunt Paget 'We have enough clothes pegs to last us for ten years.'

*

Lil was still running. It was now getting dark, but she couldn't think of anything to do, she turned back towards the town thinking maybe she could find somewhere to get herself cleaned up. She couldn't for the moment think where.

It was as she was passing through the town centre, she saw the haven she was looking for The New Theatre.

Of course, The Theatre – she remembered it well from the pantomime. She knew the place like the back of her hand. There were plenty of places backstage where she could wash and clean up. Might even find some clean clothes. If only she could find a way in. After all she had managed with her sister to gain access to most of the cinemas in town. This shouldn't be all that difficult.

It was easier than she thought; her luck seemed to have changed. As she wandered around the theatre looking for a way in, she glanced up at the posters. 'The Lucky Revue' was having its final performance tonight – and there – fairly high up in the bill was the name Vera Delaney. At first she could hardly believe it and looked away, supposing that it was some kind of mirage and the name would not be there when she looked back. But it was, and her heart leapt with the first bit of hope she had since Maxine had turned her away.

She had no idea of what time it was, but it was pretty dark, so it seemed to her it might just be the second interval of the last house. There was no way the stage door man would let her in during the show, but on a Saturday night, they would be doing the get out. The dock doors were usually open to take the scenery out as each item finished. This would save time after the show and the van driver and stagehands would have a chance to relax, so that the van could make an early start in the morning before the Sunday traffic started blocking the roads.

Lil waited until a load of scenery came out of the dock doors to be loaded on to the lorry and, hiding behind the moving flats, she crept through the gap. Once in the building she found her way to the corridor in the area below stage where the dressing rooms were.

She found Vera's room easily by working out how far she was up the running order. The star always had number one dressing room and the rest came in order of their billing.

Dressing room number five was not locked and, sure enough it bore the name Vera Delaney on the door. Lil quietly opened the door and slipped through.

Vera was sitting in her easy chair having a cigarette. Lil held her finger to her lips.

'Please, just get me away from here.' Vera took in her look of distress and her good heart responded immediately.'

'OK,' she said, 'help me with the hooks.'

As Lil was struggling with the hooks, there was a knock on the door.

'It's Ok Elsie,' cried Vera 'I've managed, thank you,'

She turned to Lil 'That was Elsie, who usually does me up.'

'You don't half look a mess. I'll see what I can find for you. As soon as she was dressed for her last act number, Vera took up the box of soiled laundry that was waiting for collection by the wardrobe mistress and she picked out a reasonably clean pink blouse and a grey skirt and an unladdered pair of art silk stockings.

'They may smell a bit,' she said 'But from the way you look now I don't suppose you'll care all that much. I can't give you any shoes, so we'll have to clean up the ones you have on. Mine would be like boats on you.'

She stealthily smuggled Lil into the ladies toilet so she could clean herself up. Lil had a good wash and put on Vera's clothes. They were far too big for her, so she rolled up the sleeves and bunched up the skirt under her belt. She shuddered a little at the colour scheme, at the way the somewhat bright pink clashed with her red hair and she polished up her dusty shoes as best she could. By the time she had finished, the curtain had come down and members of the public were legitimately allowed back stage, so she went back to Vera's dressing room, her natural optimism beginning to dominate her feelings of rejection and fear.

8.

'You don't look too bad,' said Vera and she made one or two minor adjustments to Lil's costume. 'You are such a tiny thing,' she laughed as she tucked the over large blouse under the belt which was already bulging from the bunched up skirt.

As soon as Vera had taken off her makeup and put on her street clothes. 'You can come and stay with me tonight,' she said, 'Mum won't mind.'

Vera was staying with her parents during the Hull week of the tour.

Lil had a moment of panic.

'Your mother might recognise me!'

'How could she? I can say you are someone from the show – a chorus girl! She never notices anyone in the show except me. She'll be none the wiser. Better give you a new name,' she gave a chuckle 'How about Jessie Matthews?'

The two girls laughed together at old memories

'Aye Jessie's good,' said Lil, 'I've always thought I was Jessie. My birth name is O'Malley.'

'Jessie O'Malley, that'll do.'

Molly Delaney, a bright eyed ex dancer herself, did a double take as she recognised some of the clothes that Lil had on, but was too polite to comment.

'This is Jessie, Mum,' said Vera. 'She's in the chorus, you must remember her.'

'Oh yes,' said Molly, 'Who could forget such lovely red hair.'

'We are both getting a lift to Cardiff from the Stage Manager. I thought it would save time if she stayed with me tonight.'

'Glad to have you,' said Molly warmly and gave them a substantial supper of pork pie and salad, with apple pie and cheese and a big pot of tea. Then she packed them off to bed.

'What will you do tomorrow?' asked Vera as she was looking out some pyjamas for her visitor. 'Will you be going back home?'

'I can't go back there. I just want to get as far away as I can.'

'Is Cardiff far enough?'

'What would I do there?'

'Come with us. There may be some kind of job you can do at the theatre. It'll get you away from here and give you time to think.'

Vera and Lil went to sleep that night in the same bed snuggled up together like babes in the wood.

The next morning Lil was dressed up in some outgrown clothes courtesy of Vera's little sister. This time Vera explained the lack of clothes, blaming it on the wardrobe mistress who had taken away 'Jessie's' outdoor clothes by mistake. She made a good story of it telling about the distraught girl running about in her leotard and tights desperately looking for her going home gear, until Vera came to her rescue. Everyone laughed a lot and asked no more questions.

The stage manager arrived in his old banger, eagerly looking forward to the opportunity of being alone with Vera on the way to Cardiff and not concealing his annoyance and disappointment when he found he had another passenger. Lil was unceremoniously bundled into the back of the car where she was quite happy to stay. The sooner and faster she got away from Hull, the better. Vera went back to the house to say goodbye to her mother.

'I seem to recognise that young girl,' she said. 'What's her name?'

Vera grinned.

'Jessie' she said 'Jessie O'Malley.'

Her mother looked relieved.

'Oh I must be mistaken. She has a look of the little red headed girl that sang in the pantomime – do you remember – in Cinderella?'

'Of course I remember,' she said. 'Lily Marsden – but she was about three years younger.'

'Of course she was,' laughed Mrs Delaney. 'Silly of me.'

*

Maxine heard the police arrive. She heard her mother answer the door and she listened to Connie's side of the ensuing conversation.

'Lily Marsden? She was a pupil of my sister in law – but she was killed by a bomb at the end of the war!'

'Really? Oh well, we didn't know that.'

'No, she certainly hasn't been here I can promise you that – Yes, goodbye, Sorry I couldn't help you.'

Connie shut the door on the police and came to join Maxine.

'How extraordinary. It seems that Lily Marsden wasn't killed after all. It was her sister Janie, Remember the ugly one with glasses?'

'What did the police want?'

'It seems she has vanished into thin air. They were looking for her to tell her about her stepfather. He is dead apparently. They fished him out of the Humber.'

'How did he die? Did he drown?'

'Well, it seems, they think somebody shot him.'

*

Once in Cardiff, Vera arranged for Lil to get a job as a theatre cleaner. The company were to stay there for three weeks, so Lil could stay with them until the end of their short run. This meant she would have to find digs. Vera was staying with a well-known theatrical landlady who wouldn't give houseroom to anyone who wasn't a featured artist, let alone a skivvy. Lily found herself somewhere to stay. It was surprisingly easy. She studied the list posted at the stage door and rang the least expensive. She found herself a small but clean room on the poor side of town. Bronwen, the young mother who rented the flat was only a few years older than Lil and was grateful for the company as well as the extra money.

Lil was as happy as anyone could be under the circumstances. She had no wish to be a burden to Vera who had her own friends and had already done enough for her. Vera had been kinder to her than she had any right to expect, but the most unusual thing of all was Vera's lack of curiosity about her predicament. She guessed that Lil had run away from home, but she never asked any questions. Her friend was in trouble and it never occurred other to be anything but helpful.

In the end she was even more helpful than she would have thought possible. It was at the end of the second week in Cardiff, Lil was cleaning out no 2 dressing room when the stage manager called for her.

'It's a desperate situation, maybe you could help us out.'.

'If I can.'

'One of our chorus girls, Paddy Linford has sprained her ankle. Vera said maybe you could stand in for her till we get a replacement.'

Lil gasped.

'I'm told you are a trained dancer,' he went on.

'Yes, yes I am.' replied Lil boldly.

'We cannot get anyone down from London at such short notice. Can you come along and let us see what you can do.'

Again she felt the joy of using her body, her talent. She was way ahead of all the other girls in the chorus of the fairly low scale revue, but she played herself down. She knew from past experience how vicious girls could be to a clever clogs and although she picked up the steps quickly, she was clever enough not to be too proficient – just enough to impress the management without antagonising the rest of the chorus.

'You did well, young Jessie,' said the stage manager, 'In fact, the management would like to give you a short term contract as swing girl for the chorus. How'd you like that?'

'Smashing,' she breathed.

'You are a bit on the young side –how old are you?'

'Nearly fifteen,' she lied valiantly. It was not in his interest to disbelieve her.

'You look younger. You'll have to get permission from your parents of course.'

'Oh – I'm an orphan,' she said quickly.'

'I'm sorry about that. I'll give you the form and maybe you'll get your guardian to fill it in.'

'Yes, that would be fine,' said Lil quickly. Forgery had never been a problem for her in the past and it wouldn't do to start having scruples about it now. She knew Bronwen would oblige.

'You won't mind being away from home?'

'No I want to see the world. I'm bored with dreary old Cardiff.'

He looked her up and down.

'I really thought you were younger,' he said, 'You will also have to do the ironing and look after the props – any other little job that comes along.'

'I don't mind. I just love being in the theatre.'

She meant it. The theatre was the only place she really felt at home. She made up her mind to stay with the company, become as irreplaceable as it was possible to be and she constantly added to her duties as she went along. – Touching up the paint on the set, redoing props that were beginning to look a bit shabby, darning costumes and replacing sequins. Nobody asked her again how old she was, nobody asked her any questions at all. They took her for her looks and her talent just as she stood, and she wasn't about to volunteer any information.

She had already mastered her make-up and with a little help from falsies and greasepaint could just about manage to pass for fifteen.

When the three weeks finished at Cardiff, Lil, not wanting to be a burden to anyone hitched a lift to the next date and was amazed when she was given the money for her train fare.

She felt incredibly grateful for the kindness of the company in taking such good care of her. It made her even more determined to spend the rest of her life working in show business.

When she read in the paper about Bill Marsden's body having been found at the bottom of the Humber, presumably shot in a drunken brawl, she read the piece with interest as if it had nothing to do with her. It was Lil Marsden's concern, not that of Jessie O'Malley.

9.

'Maxine darling, now you are fourteen you can join the country club.'

Maxine was lying on the sofa, eating grapes from a paper bag and reading *'Love in a Cold Climate'* She didn't particularly want to be disturbed.

Connie Fletcher raised her voice.

'Maxine, did you hear me? I've put you down for the Meldrake Country Club. It would be good for you to play tennis during the holidays.'

'Oh wow. Yippee,' muttered Maxine.

She dipped her hand in the bag, bringing out the large bunch of purple grapes.

'Darling, don't be such a slouch. It would be good for you to have some exercise.'

'You know I hate games. I get plenty of exercise with my ballet class.' And Maxine suddenly became interested in how many grapes she could fit into her mouth at the same time.

'Tennis is much more than a game Maxine. It is a social asset.'

'Huh.'

If Maxine had a comment to make on her mother's last speech, she was unable to do so until she had successfully disposed of the grapes. Her mother, seizing her advantage went on.

'Mr Parkes is such a nice man and is very fond of young people.'

'Mr Parkes! Crikey that creep,' Maxine murmured automatically, her mouth full of pips. Her mother looked around for a receptacle and presented her with an ashtray. Maxine spat the pips out. Her mother looked away, pretending it hadn't happened.

'He likes to get them involved in the community spirit.'

Maxine decided she was now taking part in a film about ancient Rome and she held the bunch of grapes over her head and started to bite the grapes straight off the stem just as she had seen them do in the orgy scene.

'You ought to get to know some of our new neighbours, you never see any of the local people when you're at school all the time.'

Maxine put down the grapes and looked at her mother in astonishment.

'Local people? At the country club? Only the snobby ones – Doctors and lawyers and stuffy old business men – girls with big calves and old women with stringy legs.'

'A lot of University people are members – and officers from the RAF station. They're all members of the local community aren't they'

'And so is Snarly Stuffins. I bet he won't be there.'

'Maxine, you are just being silly. That old tramp wouldn't want to be member of the country club.'

'I bet he would. All they do at that rotten old club is drink all day long. Snarly Stuffins likes drinking better than anything else in the world.'

And Maxine resumed her tricks with the grapes.

Connie looked at her daughter and sighed. What had happened to her sweet little daughter? She had changed almost unrecognisably since the end of the war. There had been lots of changes to the Fletcher family. Irene had married Scot and was now living in Edinburgh. Ada was in Ponders End with her husband and small son; Aunt Paget had discovered an old boyfriend of hers who was a builder and looking for post war employment. He had done a great job on her cottage and she had moved back there. She had been glad to go. Life at the Laurels wasn't much fun now Tom was back and behaving more and more erratically. He'd hardly spoken a word to Maxine since he got back from Egypt.

Connie was happy with her garden and was into growing roses. Tom seemed to be happier away from the house that seemed to hold so many ghosts for him, but Maxine was a different person and Connie was worried.

Other people's daughters seemed to grow up by the time they were fourteen. Maxine delighted in playing the child. She was determined to pursue her absurd premise right to the better end.

'And what about the darling gypsies – they're not members are they? Maybe if they were, they'd feel more like staying in one place and not moving about all the time. And then there's Dan Thompson, the blacksmith. He's not a member either.'

Connie cast her eyes to heaven.

'You are being idiotic.'

'So you see, its not for the real community – its only for stuck up people like us.'

'Maxine darling, how can you possibly say we're stuck up? Your father and I have always been socialists. Even after the war when Mr Churchill had been so splendid – we stuck to our principles and voted against him.'

'Well, Snarly Stuffins is a Tory – he thinks Antony Eden would be a great leader – and he loves the little princesses too. And the gypsies, they're Tories as well. They really believe in private enterprise. I discussed the matter with them at some length.'

Connie sighed.

'I don't know how you can go near the nasty smelly creatures.'

'They're only filthy and smelly cos they keep moving about. They don't have baths and things; they don't have time to wash their clothes before they have to move on. Think how difficult it must be to dry your clothes in a tiny little caravan. It's not at all healthy, especially for those poor little children. I look at them sometimes and think, 'There but for the grace of God go I – except that I don't believe in God.'

And Maxine returned to her book.

Connie gave another sigh and prepared to leave the room.

'Anyway I hate tennis. I'm no good at it,' said Maxine

'All the more reason. Mr Parkes is a wonderful coach. Everybody adores him.'

'I bet. Muscle bound cretin. I think he's a creep.'

'I'll take you there this afternoon. You can have your first lesson directly after luncheon.'

*

'So this is your daughter Maxine,' Mr Parkes looked at her with a twinkle in his eye 'She is a bonny girl.'

Maxine scowled.

'We'll whip you into shape in no time,' he said, licking his lips.

Connie smiled into Mr Parkes' eyes. Maxine noted sourly how her mother behaved when Mr Parkes was around. They were all the same. All the women smiled a great deal and made their eyes flash, darting him coquettish glances and standing very straight to show off their busts to better advantage. Even as Maxine watched, her mother's breasts appeared to grow in size, their nipples straining almost vulgarly through her dress.

'I'll leave her with you Leslie,' she said with a girlish giggle.

'She'll be in good hands,' he promised. 'Run and get changed,' he added and gave Maxine a pat on the behind.

Feeling distinctly nauseous Maxine wandered reluctantly into the changing room. There were three girls in there heavily into gossip, but they stopped their chatter and looked at the new arrival.

Maxine returned their stares.

'I'm Maxine Fletcher,' she said.

'Oh yes, the ballet dancing show-off. We know all about you,' said one of them 'My mother says it's common to be in pantomime.'

'Well I'm not going to do any more pantomimes. I'm going to be a Shakespearean actress.'

The girl laughed derisively.

'And I'm going to be prime minister,' she said, 'I'm Betty, this is Pauline – And over there is Karen.'

They all turned and looked at her with ill-disguised hostility.

'So what are you doing here, Maxine Fletcher?'

'I'm supposed to have a tennis lesson. 'said Maxine putting on her white shorts.

'Who with?' asked Karen, teasing out her long brown curls between her fingers?

'Mr Parkes!'

The girls all giggled.

'Lucky you,' said Pauline, with envy.

'He's gorgeous,' giggled Betty.

'I expect he'll take you behind the pavilion.'

Maxine stopped tying the shoelaces on her tennis shoes.

'What do you mean?'

Betty opened her eyes and mouth wide.

'Don't you know?' she asked 'He does it with all the new girls.'

And the girls giggled again.

*

'Service.' cried Mr Parkes and delivered a ball over the net.

Maxine again made a desultory attempt to receive the ball, but it bounced on the ground beside her.

'Fletcher,' cried Mr Parkes, 'You are not paying attention. Keep your eye on the ball.'

Maxine shrugged and took up her position again on the court. Mr Parkes delivered another service.

Again she missed the shot and stood, her racket hanging loosely in her hand.

'Come on Fletcher, make a bit of an effort,' he shouted.

'Can't,' she shouted back, 'I'm too hot.'

He came up to the net to speak to her. 'Come here,' he said and she reluctantly obeyed.

'You're behaving like a sissy. I might have known I'd have trouble with you. All that cavorting about on stage makes you soft. You've got no backbone.'

'It's a damn sight better that running around in the heat with a stupid bat and ball,' she said.

Mr Parkes took a deep breath. 'There's no need to swear, Fletcher. Try serving to me again.' And he returned to his position.

Maxine picked up the ball, threw it in the air and took a swipe at it, missing it by inches.

'All right Fletcher, let's call it a day,' he shouted.

Maxine looked at him, hardly daring to believe her good luck.

'We've only just started.'

'Never mind,' he said sternly, 'It's time for us to have a little talk. Come with me.'

She followed him reluctantly as he led the way across the tennis courts to the back of the pavilion.

She saw that Betty and Karen had stopped their game and were watching their progress with great interest.

Mr Parkes sat himself down on the bench and addressed Maxine.

'Somebody ought to teach you a lesson. It's obvious your father can't,' he said.

And with that he took her and put her over his knee, administering several hearty smacks on the behind.

Maxine was astounded. No one had ever struck her before in her life.

She felt the stinging blows raining down on her backside and waited for him to stop.

After he finished, she still lay there across his knees, wondering what in hell was going on.

'Get up,' he said harshly, and breathing heavily. She scrambled to her feet, her bottom smarting, her face flushed and her eyes misty with tears.

'Next time I find you slacking, it'll be the tennis shoe for you miss,' he said.

'What the hell do you think you're playing at?' she said, still defiant, despite the tears that were running down her cheeks.

'Poor little girl,' he said and his voice had suddenly gone deeper.

She looked up at him. It wasn't just his voice that had changed; his face had turned red, his thick lips had swollen to twice their size and his eyeballs seemed about to pop out of his head. He put his arms round her and held her close. She stayed still in his grasp, listening to his heart thumping, not knowing how to react to this unexpected turn of events.

He put his hand on her backside.

'Did it hurt?'

'No,' she said pugnaciously.

He stroked her bottom again and as he did so, he let his finger slip into the crease between her buttocks. She felt herself go all wet between her legs and nearly died of embarrassment. With his other hand he grabbed her suddenly, roughly, around her mound and squeezed.

'You little darling. You're ready for me, aren't you?'

He said and she felt one of his fingers separate itself from the others and slip round the side of her pants in the secret place beneath her legs. She tried to pull herself away.

'I have to go to the lavatory,' she said but he held her even tighter and gave a sudden jerk, a huge exhalation of breath and his body juddered as if he was in the grasp of something outside himself. She was convinced he was going to have a heart attack and didn't know what she should do about it, trying to remember what she had been told at first aid classes. *Do you give them hot tea with sugar? Do you lie them on their back or their side?* her mind was racing. However, he still had her in his grip so she kept absolutely still and waited until his breath became more regular and he seemed to regain possession of himself. He loosened his grip on her at last and held her at arm's length. He was looking a little better now – his colour was more normal although his face had a strange crumpled look.

'You are a bad bad girl,' he said, 'You really know what's what, don't you? I've seen the way you show off your little body on stage. Fourteen years old? It's disgusting.'

And he thrust her away from him.

'You filthy pig,' she cried and kicked him on the shin as hard as she could and dashed away running as fast as she could into the pavilion. She glanced back once and saw him sitting on the bench, thoughtfully rubbing his shin.

She ran straight into the ladies and threw up.

'Just like my mother,' she thought.

After she had finished, she sat on the loo and tried to work out what had happened to her. She felt almost indescribably dirty. Mr Parkes was so repulsive. She thought of his thick lips and slack mouth, the way he had looked at her, his horrible fat sausage fingers touching her in her secret place – and yet for some reason it seemed it was all her fault. He had called her a bad girl. What did he mean? She felt sick although there was a part of her that was excited, somehow proud of the power she had over him. She heard the other girls come in, she heard their chatter, One of the tried the door of the loo.

'Bloody hell,' shouted the girl. 'Who's in there?'

But Maxine sat quiet and waited until they went.

Then she crept out of the loo and got into her clothes.

As she was about to sneak out, Betty came back in. She took one look at Maxine and giggled.

'I saw you go behind the pavilion,' she said, 'What did you think of Mr Parkes?'

Maxine hit out and slapped the girl hard on the face. The girl, taken by surprise, hit back. Maxine lifted her leg and kneed her in the stomach and ran out of the Pavilion, out of the Tennis Club She went to her secret café, across the road from the church, ordered a cherry soda. She sat down and waited for her heart to stop thumping, for the anger to subside before she went home.

'Did you have a nice lesson?' asked her mother.

*

Maxine went to bed that night early and relived the strange experience of the day, wondering whether in some way she had imagined it. As she did so, she realised that the wetness between her legs was there again and all too real. She turned over and buried her head in the pillow, crying for shame.

The next day, before her mother got up, she rang her aunt in Edinburgh and, swearing her to secrecy, asked to be invited to Edinburgh to spend the rest of the holidays there. Irene, discreet as ever, didn't ask any questions, knowing that Maxine would confide in her soon enough.

Later that morning, she heard the telephone ring and her mother's voice answering it.

'Maxine darling,' said Connie, 'Your aunt Irene rang would like you to visit her in Edinburgh for a week or two. I told her you wouldn't be interested. The weather is so lovely here and you are so enjoying your tennis lessons.'

Maxine tried not to look too eager.

'Actually, I'd quite like to go,' she said.

'To that awful windy place? You'd freeze to death.'

'I haven't seen Irene for ages – and you know how much I like Scot. It would be quite nice to have a change of scene,' she said.

Connie looked at her with pain in her eyes 'Well of course darling. I had thought we could do some things together during the holidays. But if you'd rather be with your aunt, and leave me here alone, I won't stand in your way.'

For once Maxine was not in the mood to give in to her mother's emotional blackmail.

'Thanks Mum,' she said and, giving her a kiss on the cheek, ran upstairs to start packing.

10.

The Hon. Marcus Cranleigh was sitting in his brother's rooms at Oxford reading from the local paper.

'*Starkers in Paradise.* That's the one for us,' he cried to his young brother who was at his desk working on his essay.

'What are you talking about?'

'The new touring revue at the Tivoli, One of those nudie girlie shows '*Starkers in Paradise*.' Thought it would be appropriate for you, obsessed as you are with other worldly pursuits.'

'Marcus, give it a rest. I'm trying to work. You said you'd belt up until I finished.'

His elder brother put his finger to his lips in an exaggerated gesture of compliance and turned back to the paper.

'My God, old Hobbs has done a review for it. I never expected him to know the meaning of the word prurient. It's amazing what this kind of show drags up from the subconscious.'

He folded his paper and came over to Philip, who put down his pen with a sigh.

'It really would be a good idea to see how the other half enjoys itself,' he said, 'For Christ's sake, when you're at Oxford you're supposed to have a good time. All you seem to do is write endless essays and do charity work.'

Philip laughed.

'What rubbish,' he said, 'I go to the theatre every single week in Oxford and manage to fit in most of the West End shows as well. I also belong to OUDS. What more do I need?'

'You need a spot of prurience' replied his brother 'For heaven's sake if you are really serious about being a vicar and fighting the sins of the flesh, you need to know a bit more about the enemy first – otherwise you'll be at no end of a disadvantage. Come on old chap, it's not often you get a change to paint the town with your big brother.'

When Marcus really put himself out he could be the most persuasive person on earth. His bright-eyed enthusiasm was infectious. He had been through the war, one of the youngest test pilots ever in the RAF and had afterwards returned to Oxford to finish his final year. Despite the difference in their ages, people often mistook Philip for the elder brother, so serious was he in countenance. whereas Marcus was as fresh faced and eager as a child. Marcus lived life to the full, and with his outstanding good looks, every door, sinful as well as soulful, was open to him.

Suddenly Philip packed up his books.

'Oh very well,' he said. 'Where do you want to go first?'

'Well, first of course to the pub for a few pints to get us in the mood and then on to see the first house of *Starkers in Paradise*. I suppose we'd better book. Tell you what, you ring them up while I nip out and see what I can arrange for some dinner afterwards.'

'Why the first house?'

'So we can sit through it again if its decent fun. I'm told these things are a great laugh.'

Half an hour later Philip lowered himself gingerly into Marcus's brand new foreign sports car designed by some German designer by the name of Ferdinand Porsche and imported into the country at enormous cost and not a little jiggery pokery. Philip felt it was pretty unpatriotic of Marcus to have a German motor car, as the war had only been over for a couple of years, but Marcus seemed to have no scruples about it.

'Poor devils,' he said. 'It's not their fault. Herr Porsche also designed the Volkswagen, you know and all I can say is if Adolph Hitler was the inspiration for a great motor car, we should be grateful that he did at least some good in the world.'

Philip didn't think Hitler's good points were a subject worth pursuing.

'Mm, Don't care what you say. It's damned uncomfortable. I prefer Dad's old Bentley any time.'

Marcus, since leaving Oxford, and realising that his future lay in managing the family estate in Northamptonshire, had spent much of his time working alongside his father, learning the business for which he had been destined since he was a tiny child. This left him plenty of time for his real passion, motorcars, and he was a regular competitor on the Racing circuits of Silverstone and Brands hatch. His wartime experiences had developed in him a taste for danger and he was a regular speed addict.

Philip could not be more different. Philip wanted to be a minister of the church. His passion, equal to his brother was what Marcus called 'interfering in peoples' lives. Marcus dreaded to think what would happen to the family home should Philip ever inherit. He would no doubt turn it into an orphanage or old peoples' home or even a hospital for legless sailors – just too horrendous to even think about. He did his best to broaden his young brother's mind, but so far, had not weakened his resolve in any way.

Variety shows in those few years after the war came in two kinds. The first kind was based on 'Soldiers in Skirts' which was a more respectable version of the kind of transvestite show popular with the forces in the Middle East. The second one was a down market copy of the famous *Windmill Theatre* in the West End of London. The Windmill Theatre with its celebrated nude showgirls had continued staunchly during the bombing no matter how hard pressed. Their slogan was 'We never closed' It was not long before there was a copycat show called *'We never clothed'* and managements hastily put together similar types of revue to go on the road and entertain the provinces. Oxford's local variety theatre and fleapit had been running the gamut of these sleazy entertainments.

Devotees would be excused for thinking that all female performers were either nude or men in disguise.

The two young men sat themselves in the fifth row of the stalls and prepared to mock. The front cloth was painted with fluffy clouds and pictures of improbable looking angels complete with wings and flimsy draperies and heavily made up faces winking saucily at the audience. Philip was alarmed to read the legend writ thereon *'Starlets in Paradise'.*

'You told me it was *Starkers in Paradise*' whispered Philip furiously to his brother. Marcus laughed, 'Did I? Silly mistake. What a fool I am' he said.

'No wonder the man laughed when I booked the seats.'

It boded well for hilarity. The show opened with a row of girls scantily dressed as angels in cheap muslin with cardboard wings and halos and high heeled tap shoes, doing a fairly ordinary routine to a remarkable timeless ditty called – naturally – *'Stars of Paradise'*

A comic with a check suit and a red nose followed this. The audience began to boo the second he appeared and carried on booing all through his act. The guys in the audience had come for one thing and one thing only – made fairly obvious from the shouts of *'Bring on the Girls'* that echoed from all parts of the house.

The first part of what they had been waiting for arrived number three on the bill.

Les girls, posing like Tableaux Vivantes – in the nude except for the occasional strategically positioned wisp of chiffon stood there in turn posing as the Empress Josephine, or Jane from the Daily Mirror as the announcer made bad jokes about each character. The girls had to keep perfectly still. If they moved an iota, the management would lose its licence. This meant that the stage area had to be kept warm and dust free, a shiver or a sneeze could mean instant dismissal for the culprit and be fatal for the show and its management. After the first lot of *'artistic posing'* the comic came back to cat calls and boos. Luckily, this time he had only to announce the *'spesh'*, a man who did miraculous things with long pieces of cane and a whole dinner service. The audience appeared to appreciate this hugely despite the fact that they were only waiting for the next lot of nudes to come on.

The chorus girls came on again to do the first act finale – another tap routine, but this time they were dressed in short blue dresses and pinafores, their hair in plaits and the tap shoes were shiny and red. They performed to the tune of *'Somewhere Over the Rainbow'* which was sung by a small red headed girl who belted out the chorus in lusty Judy Garland fashion.

Marcus nudged his brother.

'Talent!' was all he said and Philip agreed.

There was no drink allowed on the premises of the theatre, so during the interval Philip and Marcus went along to the pub next door.

'I wonder what that little girl was doing in a show like this. She must have been under age,' said Philip.

'They start young.' said his brother, handing him a pint of bitter.

When they got back to the theatre after the interval, they found that their seats had been taken by a couple of men in long raincoats. Philip was all for turfing them out, but Marcus just laughed.

'They do this all the time. As soon as someone in the front leaves their seat, the row behind climb over the seats – to get nearer to the girls. I should have remembered that. Never mind, come with me.'

Marcus led the way into the foyer and escorted Philip through a door marked private. Up a few stairs and down a short corridor there was another door marked 'Box A'.

'We should have done this earlier' he said 'No matter how lawless they might be, those yobboes would never dare to go through a door marked private.'

They sat there in the box just as the tireless chorus girls came on again, this time in long dresses and dancing to a famous Fred Astaire number that began *'Heaven I'm in Heaven'.*

'You must admit they stick to their theme,' remarked Marcus.

The red haired girl again took the vocal dressed up in a stiff sateen evening dress of a hideous apple green that fought with her red hair and pallid complexion. It made her look startlingly plain and showed up all the angles in her thin face. Her voice though was pure magic. It took on the smooth and delicate cadences of sophistication without any effort, just as it had taken on the brashness of Garland's full-throated singing in her last number. As she sang, she moved her body, her arms and shoulders swinging her legs effortlessly above her head and with the utmost grace, so that the ugliness of the dress was forgotten and one was only aware of the suppleness of the body beneath it.

'When we're out together dancing cheek to cheek,' she finished and a roar of approval came from the men out front.

Philip looked at Marcus in astonishment. Marcus shrugged his shoulders.

'The girl is good,' he said.

'She's brilliant,' said Philip. 'What is she doing in a show like this?'

'Probably eating well,' replied Marcus.

After this was a ventriloquist in private's uniform with a dummy dressed as a brigadier who he treated with utmost contempt and actually managed to raise laughter from the audience.

The show was really hotting up and the audience was enjoying itself. And now came the piece de resistance. Referring back to the Mount Olympus theme, each girl appeared dressed –or undressed – as a goddess and the compère introduced each one with a suggestive limerick.

Philip watched the show, impressed despite himself. He in fact admired the artistry of the girls and was prepared to admit that most of them looked better naked than they did in the cheap spangled costumes.

What he was unprepared for was the sight of the redhead, who appeared as Diana, with a bow and arrow and a plaster greyhound at her feet.

She was much skinnier than all the others and her skin was white as milk with an opalescent glow that made her look as if she was indeed carved out of marble. The piece of white chiffon that covered the lower part of her body in Victorian style prudery seemed an offence – almost a blasphemy. Against the soft silkiness of her skin, the delicate chiffon looked rough enough to make jagged red marks on her white body. Behind the gauze curtain that covered the front of the stage for the artistic poses, one could see a flash of flame red hair, the gash of her scarlet painted mouth and the pale rose pink areola of the nipple at the centre of each barely formed breast.

As the curtain fell on her tableau he glanced at his brother, only to find that Marcus was looking at him with every appearance of amusement.

'Fancy the little redhead? She's a bit on the young side I should say.'

'Its disgraceful,' replied Philip, 'putting a child of that age through something like that. Making her display herself like a prostitute.'

'Come on bro, how can you be so naive. Why do you think they take on a job lie this? To tout for trade! Of course they are all no better than they should be. I'll take you round to the stage door afterwards, you'll see what I mean!'

'I'd rather not.'

'All part of your education. I insist we pick up a couple of them and take them to supper. I lust after the big blonde; you can have the minute redhead.'

'Out to eat – after the show. That would be about ten o'clock. Nothing's open at that hour.'

Marcus looked at his brother and shook his head.

'What are brothers for?' he asked 'Have you ever known old Marcus not be able to find a decent glass of vino at any time of day or night?'

Philip was forced to admit that his brother was right.

'Just leave it to me, Sonny,' said Marcus.

11.

Jessie looked at the young man that had been designated her partner and was not impressed. Next to the dashing Marcus, he seemed pale, insipid – well – goofy.

'I've got landed with a twerp,' she thought to herself.

But as she rarely got invited out to supper she was determined she must enjoy the food at least.

Marcus took them to a nearby pub, which was full of students making the most of the little time left before last orders.

'I wasn't expecting to go to a public house,' remarked big blonde Helen.

'Wait and see' said Marcus and he led his party to a door marked private, up a staircase and into a small dining room above the main bar where he was greeted like an old friend by the landlord, Mr Moffat.

'Uncle Henry' cried Marcus to everyone's surprise and Philip's total astonishment.

Henry Moffat seemed happy to cater to him in every way, partly because of the full-blown beauty of Marcus's young lady, but more perhaps because of the flimsy white fiver that was waved in front of him.

'Well, nephew, good to see you' he said and turning to the rest of the small party. 'If the police arrive, you are members of the family, OK?'

Marcus laughed and gave him the five-pound note on account. Henry pocketed the note, and showed them to their seats, looking at the blonde Helen with salacious pleasure.

'I can do you oysters,' he said with a leer and a wink.

'Splendid' said Marcus.

'Then lamb cutlets with peas and potato croquettes and a bit of nice home made apple pie and custard to follow.'

'Peas out of a tin?'

'What else? Nothing but the best' laughed Moffat.

'That all right for you, girls?' asked Marcus.

'Divine' said Helen. Jessie nodded nervously.

'But first... some wine' he looked at the girls 'Champagne do for you?'

'Divine' said Helen again. Jessie nodded again.

'I presume you have a bottle tucked away,' he said to Moffat.

'I have . . . it's even cold. I must have guessed you were coming'

'What a hero' said Marcus patting the innkeeper on the back.

Inspired by the champagne, Helen and Marcus soon entered into a flirtatious conversation. Helen was a great laugher and Marcus's jokes kept her in a constant state of giggle. Jessie also laughed at Marcus's jokes, though she hardly understood them. Just to look at him made her laugh. The sparkle in his eyes, the creases in his cheeks, the flashing white teeth enchanted her. Philip watched her watching Marcus and felt a little sad, unable as he was to match Marcus's wit and charm.

Soon Marcus had his hand on Helen's knee and she started to wriggle.

Suddenly she announced that she had to go to the toilet.

'Me too,' said Marcus. 'You don't mind being left together for minute?' he asked.

Jessie watched him as he left the room, his hand on the back of Helen's neck.

Philip's heart sank as he watched them leave, he knew what they were about to do – and that offended his sense of propriety – but he also realised that he was to be left alone with this strange, scrawny little red headed person and engage her in conversation.

'Do you enjoy working in this show?'

Jessie looked briefly at him, as if not knowing to whom he was addressing his remark. Then she looked back at the door where Marcus had just left.

'Jessie' he said 'Is it fun doing this show every night?'

'Twice a night and two matinees' she said hardly raising her voice above a whisper.

'It must be hard work'

'I like workin'. It's what I like to do' she said and turned her eyes back to the door.

Philip tried again,

'You're from the North aren't you?'

At once a panic-stricken look passed across her face.

'Aye' she said cautiously.

'From whereabouts?'

'From... Manchester' she said improvising quickly.

'You have an unusual accent'

She laughed a lot at this. Her laugh was light and delicious and made Philip smile.

'It's you what's got the accent,' she said.

'Me?' Philip was astonished.

'Yes. George said so an all.'

'George?'

'Stage doorman,' she said. 'Don't you know him? Your brother knows 'im.'

'My brother knows everybody in the world,' laughed Philip.

'Anyway, George said you talked like a toff. That's an accent in't it?'

'No. On the contrary, it means I *don't* have an accent.' Philips blushed, feeling that he was being criticised.

'I don't mind it,' she said soothingly, 'It's quite nice really. Sort a cockney but with your voice coming through your nose.'

'Good grief,' he said and fell silent.

His silence seemed to encourage her to make an effort.

'What do you work at?' she asked.

'I'm reading Divinity.'

'You read, for a livin'?'

'Not exactly for a living.'

'What's Divinity?'

'Religion. I'm...going to be a parson.'

'Blurry 'ell.'

He laughed, he was used to this reaction though not in those exact words.

'Well, I think I might. I haven't decided yet. It will be time enough when I've finished at University.'

'Oh – you're still at school then. Like our Jamie...'

Suddenly her eyes filled with tears and she looked away. He proffered his handkerchief. She dabbed her eyes with it.

'Try blowing your nose,' he said.

'No! Not on that clean hankie,' she said and gave a little nervous laugh.

He thought it was time to change the subject.

'I enjoyed your performance in the show. I think you have a lot of talent.'

'I wish other folk thought so.'

'I have a friend in the OUDS who's doing a revue in London. Maybe he could get you a part in it.'

She looked at him pityingly.

'You don't get jobs like that,' she explained carefully. 'You've got to audition for them.'

'Right.' He took the admonition. 'Then maybe I could get you an audition. When will you be back in town?'

'Which town? I won't be coming back to Oxford. I go to Northampton next week.'

'I mean, when do you go back to London?'
'I'll be out of work after that. I don't know where I'll go'
'Look me up in London' he said impulsively.
'But you live in Oxford, don't you?'
'Only some of the time. I'll be in town in a couple of weeks'
He picked up a paper napkin and scribbled a telephone number.
'Fancy living in two places. I don't even live in one'
He could sense the tears weren't far away again and for some reason he desperately wanted to help this child. She was looking fixedly at the napkin.
'Put it in your purse'
'What... you mean... pinch the serviette?'
He laughed and, picking it up said,
'Give me your purse.'
She handed it him and he put the paper napkin inside.
She looked around to make sure nobody saw the precious napkin disappear into her handbag.
Philip put his hand over hers, marvelling at the small size of it
'Promise you'll ring'
At this moment Helen arrived back at the table looking flushed, followed shortly by Marcus who also looked a little dishevelled. His tie was loosely tied and he was putting on his jacket as he entered. Helen took out her compact and started powdering her nose. The food had arrived.
'Just in time,' said Marcus and gave his brother a wink. 'I'm famished.'

12.

Sunday train calls were everybody's idea of hell. Jessie's digs were in Cowley Road, some way out of the centre of Oxford, so she had to lug her suitcase all the way to the station. She had discovered that the amount of tender loving care offered in the business depended entirely on the generosity of the management. The producers of *Starlets in Paradise* did not provide anything that did not directly concern the show and the girls were obliged to carry their own clothes and personal possessions wherever they went. This may not have been such a big deal for those with their own flats in London, but a girl like Jess, with no fixed abode had to carry all her worldly goods with her.

Once on the train, the journey always seemed endless, stopping every few minutes for repairs to the rails, or whatever Railway employees did on Sundays to earn their overtime. One thing they seldom did was open the buffet. If your landlady was unaccommodating about making sandwiches the night before there was little chance of anything to eat until your arrival at the new digs in the next town. On Sundays there were positively no shops open of any kind and the chocolate slot machines on the stations had long been used up or vandalised. Some of the company survived on secret bottles of gin, but Jessie had long discovered from bitter experience that alcohol on an empty stomach made her terribly ill.

Jessie reminded herself that the journey from Oxford to Northampton would be mercifully short, but even on that journey there was a change that might entail an hour or two's wait on the draughty platform. The girls took it in their stride. They got pleasantly or unpleasantly pissed according to their dispositions, played giggly games of cards, piled into taxis at the station and finally arrived at the theatre to find out where they were going to sleep that night – and that week. The list of digs was posted up at the stage door, but those who had played the town before had usually phoned ahead and established their accommodation in advance. They would remove from their suitcases what would be required for the night and off they would go, usually meeting up at the stage door pub in the evening. Jessie was too young to join in these festivities and usually, once she found her digs, she'd go straight to bed after tea.

So this is what she was looking forward to when she heard the shriek of brakes and the low sports car drew up beside her. She stopped and looked inside and her heart starting pounding violently. The driver was Marcus.

'Hi Jess,' he said as if she were an old friend. 'Want a lift?'

Staggered by the surprise and dazzled by his beaming smile, she was unable to actually speak but nodded eagerly.

He took the suitcase from her and put it into the boot and opened the passenger door for her to climb in. She got into the car and giggled when she found she had to lie almost prone on the low seat. He turned the key in the lock and the engine started up.

After a while as Jess was simply enjoying the feeling of being in such a superior automobile, he said 'Well?'

He was looking at the road ahead. She felt able to talk to him when she didn't have to look into those wicked eyes.

'Well what?'

'Where to, stupid?' and he turned those eyes on her again.

As she didn't speak, being mesmerised by the sight of him. He started up the car.

'By the sight and the size of your suitcase I presume you are about to embark on a journey, so I'll take you to the station. OK?'

The eyes were turned on the road again so she found she could speak.

'Yes, the station. I have to catch the train to Northampton.'

'What a strange coincidence. I happen to be going to Northampton myself.'

'Why?'

'That is where I live.'

In her amazement she forgot her shyness and looked at him accusingly.

'I thought you lived in Oxford – or London.'

'All of those' he laughed, 'I'll take you all the way. Let's get this show on the road.'

He dropped her off at the station briefly so that she could tell the company manager she was making her own way.

''Ere don't get one of them cross country buses, darlin'. You'll still be travelling a week on Thursday.'

Jessie reassured him. 'A friend is giving me a lift,' she said.

He looked at her with some respect. He had not been aware that this red headed scrap of humanity had any friends outside the company, and when he caught a glimpse of her climbing into a shiny red Porsche he was duly impressed.

Marcus was a brilliant driver, but very very fast. Jessie realised that he was having fun, trying to frighten her, but she was determined not to let her fear show, so she put her foot down along with his and began to enjoy the sensation of speed.

His concentration was complete, and apart from the occasional blasphemy when lesser drivers hindered him, he never uttered a word.

'Time to pick up a sandwich' he said after only about fifteen minutes driving, and leaving her in the car, ran into a roadside café and came out with a couple of bacon sandwiches. They sat by the roadside on a fallen tree stump and ate their breakfast. Jessie was ravenous, the breakfast at her digs had been meagre to say the least and she had never been able to stomach food first thing in the morning. She ate the sandwich with enormous relish and concentration. Halfway through, she looked up and saw that he was watching her.

'You like to take life in big bites' he said.

'Sorry, I do eat a bit fast' she said, 'We all do in our family. If you don't eat fast you don't get nowt.'

'We don't have that problem in our family, but I take even bigger bites than you do.,' he said 'See I've finished already.'

'You've got a bigger mouth.'

'Bigger – but not so pretty' he laughed. Jessie blushed. He took her hand and pulled her up.

'Come on we must get on. I've got places to go, things to do.'

'This is Northampton,' he said and Jessie was startled to find the journey had passed so quickly. 'Where do you want me to drop you?'

'The Theatre. I have to find digs, they usually have a list up at the stage door.'

'Why don't you go to a hotel? Or even the Feathers. It's pretty decent I'm told.'

Jessie laughed.

'Do you think I'm made of money?' she said.

When they arrived at the stage door, Marcus got out of the car and collected her battered cardboard suitcase from the boot of his shiny new car.

'Something I want to know Jessie,' he said.

'What?'

'How old are you? I mean really?'

She giggled.

'Promise not to tell?'

'Cross my heart.'

'I'm fourteen, but I tell everyone I'm nearly sixteen, so don't tell on me, will you?'

'Why would I do that? Another question.'

'Yes?'

'Are you a virgin?'

Jessie blushed. She had never heard that word before unless it was surrounded by the words Blessed and Mary.

'You shouldn't talk like that,' she said.

Marcus laughed, 'I'm sorry. It was impertinent to ask. I was just interested to know whether you'd ever had a boyfriend'

'No' Jessie tried to make the blushes subside by pinching herself violently on the hand.

'You surprise me – a pretty little girl like you'

She tried to avoid the teasing look on his face.

'I've never had time,' she stammered

'All right young'un. I believe you'

He took her chin in his hand and studied her earnestly

'You're only a little girl still aren't you? But your beautiful eyes have grown up secrets. And that mouth, that is the mouth of a woman, warm, sensual.'

Jessie bit her lips and tried to look away.

He laughed and took his hand away.

'I can't wait to see you when the rest of you has caught up. May I see you again when you are all grown up?'

'Yes' she whispered.

'That's a date?'

'I promise'

'One more promise I'd like from you'

'What's that?'

'Before we meet again – try to get rid of that horrible accent.

13.

It was panto time in Richmond. Vera was playing Alice in *Dick Whittington*. Vera had persuaded the management to audition Jessie for the part of Puss, but although they found her talents impressive they decided she was too inexperienced in comedy. Instead they offered her the understudy and chorus.

'I'm back where I was when I was seven years old,' she grumbled.

Vera laughed, 'No, this is London,' she said, 'This is a job that really counts.'

'This in't London!' she protested. 'Where's Buckingham Palace? I've never seen the Houses of Parliament or Big Ben or the bloody Tower – any of them places.'

Vera, who hadn't seen them either, laughed a little patronisingly.

'London is a big place, you know. But being at Richmond is closer to Shaftesbury Avenue than Hull or Scunthorpe.'

'Shaftesbury Avenue?'

'Where all the big West End theatres are. We should take a trip there one day.'

Vera was living in a flat over a bakers shop in Putney High Street – a short bus ride from the Theatre and she offered a tiny box room to Jessie for a miniscule rent. Vera was prone to homesickness and the presence of someone from Hull comforted her. Jessie on the other hand, apart from occasionally wondering how little Jamie had fared, had only a kind of shuddering disgust for her hometown and relief that she had left it behind.

One evening Vera picked up the local paper and gave a delighted cry as she read the listings of pantomimes in the area.

'Sonnie Pitts!'

'What about him?'

'He's in Mother Goose at Wimbledon. We must go and see him,' she cried, 'I didn't think he ever played down south. He is famous for being a Northern comic.'

Vera rang him at the theatre and he was overjoyed to find that they were nearby.

It was a while before they could make it over to Wimbledon as they were doing three shows a day during the school holidays. However the schedule let up a bit during February and as the matinees did not coincide, the two girls took the trip over to Wimbledon to see their old friend.

Before the show they went to see him in his dressing room. Jessie was sad to see that some of the hidden fires that used to light up his eyes when he laughed had dissipated. He had always been dour, but now he looked old, tired, and full of anxiety. She felt a great ache for him. She would always be grateful for the friendship he had shown her in the old days.

*

After seeing the first half of the show, they understood his unhappiness. He had been used to gales of laughter coming from the audiences in Hull. Here the laughter was scattered and meagre. The audience just didn't seem to find him funny.

In the interval the girls sat on the steps outside the theatre with their ice-cream and wondered why. Vera tried to explain it.

'They have a different sense of humour down here. That must be it.'

But Jessie had another idea.

'They don't understand his accent. By the time they've worked out what he'd said, the joke's gone cold.'

'You mean because he speaks Northern?'

'Aye.'

'They used to tease me about my accent. I never knew I had one till I came down here.'

'It's nearly gone now,' said Jessie. 'You can't hardly tell. It's just things like – when you say one, it sounds like Won, instead of wun and you say chick*en* instead of chick*in*.'

Vera looked at her in astonishment. 'But that's the way you spell it.'

'Dun't seem to matter. That's what they say on wireless.'

'Then how is it you still talk the way you do?'

Jessie coloured, reluctant to tell Vera how much she practised whenever nobody was listening.

'I can't get up the nerve,' she said 'And I can't get my face into the right shape, you know, to talk through my nose.'

Vera looked at her in a confused kind of way.

'Well, the way I talk is good enough for me. As long as it can keep me working until I find my Prince Charming.'

'You want to get wed?'

'Don't you?'

'Well, only if its somebody I really want,'

Vera laughed 'I suppose you're a bit young for it yet'

'Well... I have met my Prince Charming! He's waiting until I'm all grown up.'

To Vera's astonishment Jessie's eyes took on a dreamy look

'He's the most beautiful man in the world – and he has lots of houses and a red sport car and he talks BBC.'

'Oh yes, and I'm a monkey's uncle.'

Jessie gave a secret smile. She knew that Marcus was the only man she would ever love, and was convinced that one day she would have him for her own. After all what is a prince on a white horse to one in a red Porsche?

'Anyway when I grow up I'll talk exactly like people on wireless.'

The bell went for the end of the interval and they trooped back into the theatre.

Sonnie was better now. His charm and his body language managed to overcome some of the audience's reluctance to laugh – and by the third part he was almost back to his normal self.

'It's hard,' he said when they went to see him afterwards, 'Folks are different down here. I don't want to do it down south any more. My place is up North with my own kind. Its too late for me to change my ways at my age.'

They didn't stay long. Sonnie had another show to do and a very short turn round. The two girls had to get back to Richmond for their own show. But before they left, he took Jessie to one side.

'You're a young lass,' he said. 'If you want to get on, and I know you can, you have to learn how to do it their way, talk like them, think like them. Take some lessons if you can afford it.'

Jessie nodded. She had to do something and she was beginning to get an idea. When she got back home after the show, she took out from her purse the carefully preserved paper napkin that Philip had given her all those months ago and she looked at the number he had written on it. Would he still remember her – and remember that he told her to call? She thought not. She did not dare to try. She shook her head and replaced the paper carefully.

The pantomime lasted way into March and Jessie got to play Puss a couple of times near the end of the run. The management were impressed and offered Jessie a job in Summer Season in the Isle of Wight.

This time she was allowed to do her own thing. She had a solo song and dance spot and took part in several of the sketches.

She worked hard and learned hard as she went along and gradually she began to be able to project herself in the sketches as well as in the song and dance items. As she grew more confident, her personality grow and flourished and before long she was the toast of Shanklin.

By thetime she returned to Putney in the following September 1948 she was brimming with self-confidence.

The day after her return She collected her pennies together along with her courage and rang the number.

14.

Philip answered the telephone on the third ring. Jess nearly panicked again at the strangeness of his voice. She loved the upper class accents of the BBC announcers and in the privacy of her room tried to emulate them, but Philip was even more *'pale blue'* than they were. She found it oddly intimidating and nearly hung up.

'Philip Cranleigh speaking' sounded to her like 'pheeleep crairnlay spaykeng' – and she put the information in her memory bank to work on later.

'Mr Cranleigh?' and as she spoke the name she heard the round 'a' sound and felt how clumsy it was by comparison with his elegant vowels.

'Yes,' his voice seemed a little cagey, 'Who is speaking?'

'I'm Jessie, Jessie O'Malley – do you remember? From *Starlets in Paradise* – We met at Oxford. You said I should call you when I was in London.'

'Good grief,' he said – and laughed, 'You took your time.'

'I've been working', she said.

'Good for you.'

There was a long pause and Jessie began to feel sorry she'd rung him.

'Hallo, have you gone?' she asked.

'Where are you living now?' he asked.

'Putney.'

'Maybe we could have tea together sometime'.

'Yes please,' she said, feeling cast down. Sometime meant never in her book. It was definitely a brush off, she thought, but before she had chance to do any further thinking he continued.

'Are you free this afternoon?'

She took a breath of relief.

'Yes, yes I am.'

'Putney, let me see. Do you know Fullers in the High Street?'

'I live just near there.'

'Why don't we meet about four thirty? Is that convenient for you?'

*

Vera was painting her toenails in the bathroom

'I'm going out to afternoon tea,' announced Jess, 'To Fullers.'

Vera looked up.

'They charge the earth there. I thought you were broke.'

Jessie felt a throb of fear – would he expect her to pay? Surely not. He was rich and anyway he had issued the invitation.

'I'm meeting a toff.'

'A toff – where did you meet a toff?'

'When I was on tour.'

Vera was struck by a sudden thought.

'Not your Prince Charming?'

'Bloody hell, no!'

The violence of this response set Vera laughing, but as usual she asked no questions. Just said *'Good luck'* and went back to painting her nails.'

'Can I go as I am?' asked Lil anxiously 'What should I wear?'

Vera looked at her young friend.

'What do you want to look like?' she replied, 'You should always dress for the part.'

Jessie was still a little girl despite her on stage sophistication. At fifteen she was still wearing little blouses and skirts and her face was scrubbed clean of makeup.

'I don't have any proper grown up clothes.'

'Well, nothing of mine will fit you that's for sure. You've got your own stage wardrobe, there must be something there that will do.'

'Yes,' she said thoughtfully. 'I'll see what I can find.'

*

Philip looked up from the table and tried not to gasp with shocked horror at this vision approaching him. She was wearing shiny red lipstick and a shiny red dress both equally scarlet and fighting for attention with her flaming red hair. The high-heeled shoes she was wearing seemed a size too big for her and she had to totter along with her knees slightly bent in order to keep them on her tiny feet.

The shoes had seemed perfectly all right on stage in the dinner party sketch proving once again how Dr Footlights can transcend all pain and discomfort.

Jessie saw Philip sitting there and was equally horrified.

She had built up a picture in her mind of the two young men who had been at the supper in Oxford and had forgotten how little they resembled each other. Marcus was like a picture from a woman's magazine illustration. Broad and fair with blue eyes and a square jaw. Philip seemed like an elongated caricature of his handsome brother. He was tall and thin with a high bony nose and narrow chin. His pale eyes with their sandy lashes seemed abnormally large, framed as they were in the big round spectacles and his thin fair hair was combed back over his high forehead. To Jess he did not resemble in the least her Prince Charming, but seemed – well – a bit – goofy to say the least.

Philip, still a little shell shocked, pulled himself together quickly and rose, pulling back a chair for her to sit. She waited until the chair hit the back of her knees before she sat – just one of the tricks she had learned in Shanklin during the dinner party sketch. She put her old leather handbag on the table in front of her.

'Shall I get rid of that for you?' said Philip, aware that people were watching and afraid that she might be embarrassed by the unwelcome attention she was causing.

He took the bag and placed it on the shelf under the table in front of her.

He seated himself opposite and in order to avoid seeing her gooey lips looked her straight into the eyes, feeling he should make some comment on her appearance to put her at ease. She had obviously gone to some trouble.

'You look…sort of grown up' was all he said.

Jessie laughed nervously and twiddled with the fork that was laid on the table in front of her. She didn't feel grown up at all. She felt young and stupid, even more so than when they last met in Oxford. His voice with its lah di dah rhythms inhibited her, made her feel embarrassed and inferior. To his horror she picked up the fork and started to polish it with her napkin.

He put her hand on hers.

'Would you like toasted teacake, scones and cream, or just cake maybe?'

She smiled nervously.

'What are you having?'

Philip's paused. During the past year he had become very much involved with theatre and theatre people and realised that the walnut cake he had in mind would not be considered a suitably healthy tea for a youthful and starving Thespian. He also realised that, coming from the North, tea meant something much more substantial to her than a slice of cake.

'On the other hand, you certainly don't have to watch your figure,' he said gallantly 'Perhaps you'd like something on toast, soft roes or a poached egg or – I know, what about Welsh Rarebit? They do an excellent one here.'

'What is it – I don't think I like rabbit.'

'No, its like cheese on toast, but much nicer and you can have it with a poached egg and anchovies.'

Her eyes began to sparkle even though she had no idea what anchovies were either.

'Smashin,' she said.

As she spoke he remembered the reason for his interest in this small person. Suddenly he knew why he had been prepared to renew acquaintance with her. He remembered the youthful vitality of her, the childlike eagerness and most of all, her startling talent. He felt he had to take care of that talent, make sure it was given a chance to blossom. He laughed and recklessly announced. 'And after that, we'll have scones and jam and cream – and perhaps even walnut cake!'

So what are your plans now?' he asked after she had devoured the Buck

Rarebit with little cries of joy and was anxiously awaiting the appearance of scones and cream.

'Nothing much. I'll have to see what comes along' she said.

'I'll have a word with my friend Jasper who is putting on a revue in the West End. There may be something you can do in that.'

'You mean chorus?'

'Well, yes I expect it would have to be. Most of the solo work is for actresses.'

'I've been doing my own turns in Shanklin and I did solos in Panto when I was seven years old.'

'But this would be the West End, people would see you.'

Jessie laughed.

'I thought that was the idea of being on stage,' she said.

'West End is different'.

'But they'd not see me in the chorus.'

Philip bit his lip. He couldn't bring himself to tell her that he saw no other future for her.

'Lots of people start that way,' he replied, 'whatever the job is, it's better than starving.'

But starving wasn't on the agenda as the scones arrived complete with thick cream and strawberry jam.

*

When he got home that evening he called up Jasper and praising her singing and her dancing to the hilt, managed to arrange an audition.

Despite all his misgivings he realised he wanted to see her again. She was dying to see the sights of London and he delighted in acting as a tourist guide so he suggested an excursion to the Big City in a few days time, thinking that teaching the little girl about his city would be a bit of fun.

And so it was. She was enraptured by the Tower of London, fascinated by its history cried over the fate of Anne Boleyn and Lady Jane Grey and shivered at the excesses of bloody Mary and was most especially interested in stories about the battles between Queen Elizabeth and Mary, Queen of Scots.

'She had red hair, like me,' she said, 'If I was a famous actress I could play the queen.'

Philip laughed at this. It was a strange ambition for a tiny childlike song and dance girl.

'I could be a famous actress,' she said indignantly, 'I'm not fully grown yet. You'll see.'

There was a kind of steely determination in her voice and Philip looked at her with a kind of respect. There was even more to this little girl than he had at first suspected. Her education was lacking in so many areas but her mind was so alive and so eager for knowledge. She asked questions continually, wanted to know the whys, the wherefores, who was who. They spent a happy day at the Tower of London and made a further arrangement to explore the sights of London the following week.

Their London dates became more and more regular – there was always something new to see. He began to lose his ultra serious air. She gave him vitality just as his classy manners began to rub off on her. She began to feel at home in the great metropolis. This is where she was meant to be.

He took her to see the two recent smash hit imports from America. *Oklahoma!* at Drury Lane and *Annie Get Your Gun* at the Coliseum and was interested in her comments. 'That Laurie was a bit of a drip,' she said, 'I'd rather play Ado Annie if I had the chance.'

Annie Oakley, however, was much more her style. She identified with the hoydenish Annie. After their visit to the Collie, the two of them skipped back to Covent Garden laughing and singing '*You cayunt git a mayun with a gun*' not caring about the passers by who smiled and pointed at them.

It was a pleasant evening and Philip suggested a walk around Covent Garden market before going home. When they arrived at the portico of St Paul's church in the Piazza, they sat on the steps.

'This always reminds me of Henry Higgins and Eliza Dolittle,' he remarked.

'Who are they?'

'Eliza Dolittle? She was a poor flower girl that Professor Higgins turned into a lady,'

'How did he do that?'

'By teaching her how to speak like one, dress like one, behave like one'

'Is that true?'

Philip laughed.

'No, it's only a play by George Bernard Shaw. He was interested in the way people judge each other by their accents.'

'Oh, I see,' she was quiet for a while as Philip watched her face in silence.

'Is that why you said I couldn't be an actress? Because of my accent?'

Philip knew that something important was happening, the child's mind was zapping in overdrive.

'It's just a play,' he said.

'Where can I see it?'

'I don't think it's on anywhere at the moment!'

'Oh.' She was downcast.

'I've got a copy of the text, if you're interested.'

'Yes, please, will you borrow it to me?'

Philip felt he was in some kind of avalanche – being driven along by the young girl. It was as if he couldn't see enough of her and she was giving him more and more opportunities for them to meet.

'Are you free tomorrow? Why don't you meet me tomorrow in Fullers and I'll bring along a copy of Pygmalion.'

'That's the name of the play? Pygmalion?'

'By George Bernard Shaw.'

'Yes I remember his name.'

When she came to meet him, it was to his surprise that she had already found herself a copy in a second hand bookshop. She launched into the attack straight away.

'I don't understand it,' she said, 'This Eliza doesn't speak English.'

'That is Shaw's way of showing how difficult it is to communicate when you have a cockney accent.'

'Or a Northern one?'

'No, not so much. Your vowels are much clearer. You are fairly easy to understand, once one gets into the swing of it.'

Finding a sympathetic listener. Jessie told him the story of her friend Sonnie Pitts and how difficult the audience found his accent.

'Oddly enough,' said Philip, 'you shouldn't worry so much about Sonnie Pitts. He is actually touring in a play at the moment. It's a North Country play and he is wonderful in it.'

'But that's why you said I couldn't do solos i'nt it?'

He admitted with some surprise that this was the case. That it was only her accent that set her apart. She had given up wearing the outré dresses and theatrical make up. Her clothes, though not expensive were simple, almost elegant and her make up was discretion itself.

'All right then' she said 'Teach me to speak the way you do.'

'I thought you said I had an accent.'

'I know better now. Other people – like the ones on the wireless – speak like you. I've got to learn it or I'll never be an actress. I'll never be able to play Queen Elizabeth.'

So the lessons commenced and Philip knew he had found his true vocation. He was enormously patient and he was sympathetic and helpful in many ways. He not only taught her how to speak, but how to dress and behave the way an actress should.

Jessie went to work in the chorus of Jasper's show. She was the lowest of the low chorus girl, but her confidence was burgeoning and she knew that sooner or later, with Philip's help, her circumstances would change.

15.

Maxine Fletcher gave one more despairing look into her mirror and sighed deeply. If she sucked in her cheeks, raised her head, lowered her lids and looked at herself out of focus, she could arrive at a face that almost pleased her. But to catch herself by accident with her chubby, childish face, her big round eyes, her limp fairish hair, gave her cause for the deepest depression. Apart from the colour of her eyes, she could find no resemblance at all to her idol, Vivien Leigh.

How is it that some girls became beanpoles at sixteen, whereas she simply became more Michelin shaped everyday. Her hair refused to curl, she could spend hours with the curling tongs, torturing it into spirals, only to have it fall out again in a limp shining flap within twenty minutes. Sometimes her mother would look at her with regret.

'You used to have such lovely ringlets' she would say, but Maxine remembered the agony she had been put through in order to achieve them. Her mother's relentless tugging at her head as she doused sections of hair in setting lotion, wrapped them in long thin rags and rolled them up into tight little screws; An operation that needed a whole, long, sleepless night to take effect. It was with great joy that she had graduated into plaits, leaving the ringlets as a painful memory.

At least she didn't have spots, but sometimes she would have traded her puppy fat for a whole crop of them. Girls with spots didn't get laughed at in the same way – or leered at by their friends' fathers.

She was terribly aware of people staring at her large breasts and snickering behind their hands. Boys wanted to touch her, rub against her, and when she protested, they shouted that she was a PT. She didn't know what a PT was and did not care to ask, but she knew it must be something quite disgusting and she, for no fault of her own, was one of them, and not quite nice to know.

The mothers of her friends stopped inviting her to stay with them during the holidays. The fathers of her friends tried to get her in to quiet corners. Lizzie Jenkins' father had even turned amateur photographer and requested her services as a model. Connie seemed quite flattered by his attention but as soon as Maxine found out it was not Art that prompted this request, she carefully avoided him after that.

Her only defence was to adopt a surly arrogant manner. From being a sunny outgoing kind of child, she turned herself into a disagreeable hermit hiding away and not talking to anyone if she could avoid it.

I don't care what they think of me, she told herself repeatedly. *Soon I shall get away from this town.*

She was determined to go to London to be an actress – a serous actress, not a song and dance person. All she had to do was to break it to her parents. It wouldn't be easy. Connie had been amazed and delighted to see that Maxine had become academically talented. Tom, who now spent his life in a wheelchair unable to speak, but was still treated as head of the house by his devoted wife, nodded enthusiastically when her exam results were read to him.

Maxine had no idea how it had happened. After years of dancing school and wandering through her schoolbooks with little enthusiasm, she found that she was easily out stripping all the girls in her class. This gave her an incentive to love her books and to advance even further,

'Your father is so thrilled with your progress,' Connie remarked one day, 'He has set his heart on your going to University.'

Maxine looked at her face again and grimaced. She pulled on a sweater and turned sideways to look at the effect. She hastily pulled it off again. There they were, those two monsters with the vulgar large nipples straining against the wool. She hunted out a baggy shirt and dragged it on. She shied away from the mirror, closing her eyes as she passed it and went down into the garden to search for her mother.

Connie Fletcher was in the garden cutting roses. Maxine shuddered as she saw her mother's hands operating the secateurs. Her mother had no idea how it hurt. She didn't realise that flowers had feelings just the same as everything else. She wouldn't dream of torturing an animal for instance, but Maxine had heard that flowers screamed when they were cut and in her imagination, she could hear them calling out in pain. She shut her eyes and ears to the image and approached her mother.

'Hello dear. Would you like to help me? We need some roses for the dinner party this evening.'

'Who's coming?'

'Leslie and Lotty Parkes.'

'Oh no.'

'Darling don't sulk. Why will you never speak to Mr Parkes? He's always so jolly and friendly. You were positively rude to him last time.'

'He's a sex maniac,' she mumbled.

'You shouldn't make silly jokes like that. Why it's almost slanderous.'

*

How could she possibly tell her mother, explain why she felt this way? How could she tell her what had happened the last time the Parkes came to dinner? How she kept managing to touch her bottom every time she passed him? Calling her a bad girl. How he sat next to her on the sofa and put his hand under her, wriggling his fingers and carrying on the conversation as if nothing was happening. She didn't know what to do. Just found the first excuse she could to move away. She didn't dare to say anything, because she knew, for some obscure reason that the whole thing was her fault and she would have to endure some fearful punishment for it.

She had managed to escape by offering to do the washing up. He followed her into the kitchen.

'I'll give you a hand,' he said jovially, giving her a hearty smack on the bum.

She grasped the big kitchen knife and shielded herself with it.

'If you ever lay a finger on me again, I'll kill you,' she said.

He looked hurt. She realised she was being melodramatic and put the knife down, a tactical error, she realised, as he moved in on her and continued.

'I didn't mean any harm, you silly little ninny. I know you like me I can tell. And you like me fooling around, don't you? Otherwise why would you ask for it?'

'I don't know what you mean.'

'Don't come the innocent with me' he whispered 'Now shut up and give me a kiss or I'll tell your mother.'

He put his hand on her left breast.

'Now, there's a pretty thing,' he said, rubbing her nipple.

His face had turned a brilliant red and his bulbous eyes bulged and watered.

'Why don't you take off that blouse?' he said in a hoarse whisper.

'Don't be silly,' she snapped and, pulling herself free. She walked out of the kitchen.

'Mummy, I've got a headache,' she said. 'I'm gong to bed.'

'Without doing the washing up? And Mr Parkes so kindly offered to help.'

'He can do it on his own,' and left the room.

She rushed to her room, feeling with disgust the familiar wetness and, getting a flannel and soap started washing and washing Mr Parkes from her body. She felt sick at the thought of him, but why was her body acting in this peculiar way. Maybe Mr Parkes was right, maybe she was asking for it – but how? What was it she was doing?

Since that time she had made sure that she would never be around when Mr Parkes came to visit.

*

Her mother was still regarding her with concern.

'Did you hear me? I hope you don't say things like that outside these four walls,' she said at last.

Maxine shut her mouth, refusing to speak.

'I don't understand you at all,' said Connie.

'I shall not be at home for dinner this evening'.

She went to the shed and took out her bicycle. She mounted and went into the village; She stopped at the sweet shop and ordered herself a Mars Bar and a cherry ice cream soda. She took the fizzing drink outside to a table on the pavement and began to suck it through the straw, breaking up the floating islands of ice cream and swirling the whole into a thick creamy mess.

She was halfway through when she felt his presence. Mr Parkes sat down on the seat opposite her and stared at her breasts.

'Well, well Fletcher,' he said after giving an appreciative whistle. 'You're looking bonny today,' and with a wink, he clicked his tongue at her.

Did the man never give up? She glared at him haughtily. Tis seemed to inflame him even more. His face reddened and his prominent eyes misted over.

'Out for a bike ride?' he asked.

'No I'm going canoeing,' she snapped back.

He laughed.

'Always a merry quip,' he said. 'What are you doing here?'

'I was enjoying myself until you turned up.'

'You are a very cheeky and provocative little girl,' he said with a leer.

'Will you please go away and leave me in peace.'

He laughed again.

'Oh come no, Maxine. After what we've been to each other, you treat me like this.'

'What are you talking about?'

'The afternoons behind the pavilion. You surely remember what *I* did to you.'

'One afternoon. And you did it with every girl in the tennis club.'

'You were always the best – no need to be jealous.'

She took a deep intake of breath and counted to ten.

'You are a disgusting old man, do you know that?'

His face turned from hot red to purple

'You little slut,' he said. 'Look at you. How can you deny that you want me? Look at the way your nipples stand up every time you see me. That's a sign that you're ready for me. And I daresay anything else in trousers.'

Unable to take anymore, she got to her feet.

'Listen Mr Parkes,' she said, 'I just want to say one more thing. If I even catch sight of you again I won't be responsible for my actions. I will kill you – and that's a promise.'

She got on her bike and rode away, conscious of his eyes upon her bottom as she rode down the street.

She spent the rest of the afternoon and the early evening in a cinema, hardly knowing what she saw. She kept breaking out in a hot sweat, thinking of Mr Parkes' pale bulging eyes looking at her in that peculiar way. She bought herself a bag of chocolate covered nuts, and crunched her way through them, which consoled her somewhat and kept her mind off the hunger which was beginning to make itself felt.

When she got home, she went straight to her attic room at the top of the house and got into bed with her books. Although she was two stories away she believed she could still hear the dinner party going on downstairs, could hear the loud and hearty tones of Mr Parkes and the girlish laughter of her mother and Mrs Parkes. She was now enormously hungry, but wild horses wouldn't have dragged her downstairs in case she bumped into her enemy. She lay flat and putting down her books, lay back, persuading herself she was relaxed and going to sleep.

Suddenly she sat up in bed as she heard her door stealthily open and close.

'Little Maxine,' it was, of course, Mr Parkes. 'Missed you all evening, why didn't you come in and see me.'

'Because you make me puke.'

He laughed delightedly.

'Methinks the lady doth protest too much,' he said – and without further ado leapt on top of her.

'Get off, you fool or I shall scream.'

He put his hand over her mouth. With the other hand she saw he was fumbling with his fly buttons.

'Come on little girl. You can't pretend you're a virgin. People talk you know. Everyone knows what a little whore you are.'

The voice, which had been carefully lowered to a whisper when he came in, began to get louder and Maxine could smell the wine and whisky on his breath. She realised he was out of control. She forced her mouth open against his hand and bit it hard, as hard as she could. He vainly tried to pull it away from her, but she still held on.

'You little bitch,' he shouted loudly and struck her across the face with his other hand.

She was forced to let go. But the effort had cooled his ardour a little and he looked at her now with anger.

She was glad. At last it seemed he had got the message.

'Leslie, where are you?'

Letty Parkes opened the door and came into the room. She took in the scene of her husband lying on the bed with Maxine, his flies open and his limp cock peeping out through the cloth of his trousers and she paled at the sight.

'Leslie, what's going on?' she gasped.

'This girl darling, she's crazy. I didn't know what hit me. She shouted to me to come in and say goodnight, and before I knew where I was she made a grab for my flies. Little slut.'

Mrs Parkes looked at Maxine with disgust.

'I don't know where you get it from. Your mother is such a nice lady – and your poor father an invalid. You are disgusting.'

'She needs a good spanking,' agreed Mr Parkes and Maxine was horrified to see him close one eye at her in a lecherous wink.

The old lecher had already got over his anger and was prepared to start all over again. She pulled the bedclothes over her head. There was no point in arguing. Mrs Parkes would believe anything her husband told her.

'Yes a damned good hiding, that's what you need my girl,' she said – and her small eyes gleamed with an emotion Maxine couldn't put her finger on – 'and if we weren't in your mother's house I would strongly suggest that Mr Parkes administer it to you. In fact I've a good mind to mention it to your poor father.'

'You sneaky old bitch, you know what kind of a man your husband is and you know my father wouldn't touch me.'

'Such language,' put in Mr Parkes and he shook his head at her with a twinkle in his eye. 'She's a bad bad girl.'

But Letty had got her dander up now and was keen to continue her tirade.

'It's no wonder you're such a spoiled little brat. Lack of parental control, that's the problem. Dancing and singing – kicking up your legs like a chorus girl. That's not way to bring up a child. Strict discipline is what is required.'

Mrs Parkes took her husband's arm and steered him out of harm's way.

'I shall not tell your mother about this,' she remarked as she pushed him out of the door. 'It would break her heart, especially with all her worries about your father. But you can be sure I shall warn other respectable people in the neighbourhood.'

At the door she turned and delivered her parting shot, 'You are a disgrace to our town,' she said.

Maxine buried her head under the bedclothes until she heard the door slam as they left the house.

16.

A couple of afternoons later Maxine was sitting at the dining room table, writing her essay on *Antony and Cleopatra* when Connie entered, looking extremely worried.

'Maxine darling. I've just had the strangest letter,' said Connie. 'Maybe you can tell me what it's all about?'

Maxine put down her fountain pen with a sigh, 'Oh Mummy, I'm trying to work.'

'Sorry darling, but I think this is important.'

'Ok. What is it?'

'It's a strange letter.'
'Who's it from?'
'Well, that's the point. It doesn't say.'
'You mean it's a poison pen letter?' she said eagerly, 'I thought they only happened in Agatha Christie.'

Maxine's levity upset Connie even more. She knitted her elegant brows in distress.

'It's just not funny, darling.'

Connie was twisting her pearl necklace between her fingers and her lips were so tight they had almost disappeared.

Maxine leaned back in her chair and crossed her arms.

'All right, then tell me what its all about.'

'No – I couldn't possibly – you'd better read it' and Connie thrust the letter at her and sat down on the edge of the chair opposite.

It was written on pink paper with violet ink

'Ugh, pukey,' said Maxine as she took it from her mother's hand.

When she gave it the first casual read through her first reaction was to laugh.

'It's just so silly,' she said. 'What does it mean?'

Dear Mrs Fletcher

I think you ought to know that your daughter Maxine is behaving very badly indeed. She should be warned to let other people's husbands alone or the consequences could be disastrous. I can only think she learned these lessons from her grandmother.
Yours sincerely,
A well-wisher.

'How dare she say rotten things about my grandma?'
'What makes you think it's a woman?' said Connie thoughtfully.
'She talks about husbands, doesn't she?' Then Maxine had a thought. 'Unless... oh yes. Just a minute. I can guess who it is. It's Mrs Parkes. Or even, possibly Mr Parkes.'

Connie shook her head.

'That is so ridiculous. Mr Parkes is a perfectly nice man. Why don't you like him?'

'He's as thick as two planks for a start,' said Maxine.

'That doesn't make him a villain.'

'All right' thought Maxine, 'It's own up time'.

But she still didn't have the courage to tell the whole truth.

'Mummy, I didn't want to tell you before but – Mr Parkes – he – touches me all the time.'

Connie laughed uneasily, 'You mean, he teases you? What happened to your sense of humour?'

'It's not a joke. He touches me in a yucky way. There's something wrong with him. He's a dirty old man.'

'And you're just a silly little girl. He wouldn't do anything to hurt you. It's probably just a bit of fun.'

'I don't find it fun,' snapped Maxine.

Connie didn't really want to discuss it any further. She stood up and pushed the chair under the table.

'Well he must think you enjoy it, or he wouldn't do it. You must have given him some encouragement?'

Maxine jumped to her feet and looked at her mother in horror.

'Mother, what are you saying? That you don't believe me? That you'd rather believe him? Or this filthy letter?' and she shook the letter in her mother's face.

Connie looked away, fiddling with her pearl necklace, not knowing what to say, not knowing what to think.

'No, no I believe you, of course. I didn't mean that. What I meant was – there must be some kind of misunderstanding.'

Maxine bit her lip and sighed. There was never any point arguing with her mother. She sat down and throwing the pink paper on to the table put her head in her hands.

Connie saw that the opposition had resigned and the tension in her shoulders relaxed a little.

'Anyway I'm sure he's got nothing to do with that nasty letter.'

Connie picked up the paper from the table and threw it into the fire.

Maxine leapt up again.

'Mum what are you doing? We should take it to the police.'

'What could they do? Anyway, if the police were involved, people would find out – and then it would be so beastly for you. No – better we forget about it. I wouldn't want your father to know. He is so proud of you. It would break his heart.'

'But I'm innocent. I haven't done anything bad. I promise you. You must believe me.'

'Of course I believe you,' she said and gave her daughter a hug.

'Just – please be careful,' she said, 'We don't want people to think you are the kind of girl who would – who would – have a baby before she was married.'

'Mother – what are you talking about?'

'You know what I mean.'

'No I don't! What about Ada? She was always having babies. You never worried about her?'

Connie smiled wanly.

'She wasn't my daughter,' she said gently.

The rest of the holidays went past in a dream of unhappiness. It was with great relief when they eventually came to an end.

*

'Maxine Fletcher, the head wants to see you.'

'Oh my God,' thought Maxine, 'What have I done now?'

This was the first day back at school. Already, it seemed she was in trouble.

She entered Mrs Fairfax's office and sat down as she was told. The head's first words had a familiar ring about them.

'I've just had the strangest letter. Making some serious accusations against you.'

'What kind of accusations?'

'I must say I find them rather confusing. I would hate to be disappointed in you. We have had such excellent academic results from you recently.'

Maxine bit her lip. She was beginning to feel guilty even though she had no idea what was going on.

'I've done nothing wrong as far as I know.'

'Then maybe you can explain this letter to me.'

'If you tell me what the accusations are I'll try to explain. Who is the letter from?'

'I would not normally take notice of anonymous letters, but this one is of an unusual nature.'

The headmistress went to her drawer and removed a pink missive from it.

Maxine's heart did a flip as she took in the familiar pink paper and violet ink.

'Would you care to read it for yourself? I'd rather not read it aloud. It is too distasteful', and the headmistress handed it over with her eyes averted from it as if it were just too disgusting for her eyes to see.

Maxine took it reluctantly and read.

It was in essence similar to the last one, but this time she was not only accused of attacking other women's husbands but also of *'unnatural practices.'*

She looked up from the letter at the cool watching eyes of the headmistress.

'I'm sorry, I don't understand. What are unnatural practices?' said Maxine, 'I don't know what unnatural practices are.'

'Well', said the head awkwardly, 'Spooning. I think she means. Kissing other girls.'

'But why would I do that?'

Why in fact would she kiss anyone? Her mother had never been exactly demonstrative and since she had lost Ada and her aunt she couldn't remember kissing anyone at all.

Except – except on stage. Her mind started racing. Being a tall girl she always played the male roles and had gallantly kissed her leading ladies, bending them backwards and closing her lips tight just like in the movies. It had never occurred to her that there may be anything wrong in kissing a woman. Nevertheless, she felt guiltier than ever. Maybe there was something wrong with her. Maybe she had an evil streak. Maybe it was the fault of her grandmother...

'I wondered if it was just one of the other girls who has a crush on you,' said Miss Fairfax. 'You realise I had to bring the matter up with you. I'm sure you understand that. And also I have to ask – is there any truth at all in this?'

'I have to be honest. I have kissed girls when I was playing the hero in plays – Like Robin Hood and Percy Blakeney. But that is only play-acting. It never occurred to me that there is anything wrong in that.'

'Thank you for that reassurance. I am satisfied that you have been unjustly accused and the least said about it the better. I will not in this instance trouble your parents with this. They have enough problems to bear.'

'However there is one thing more', and Mrs Fairfax took up her pen and wrote a word on a piece of paper, which she handed over to Maxine.

'Have you ever heard of this?' she asked.

Maxine looked at the one word written there. LESBIAN. She shook her head and handed the paper back.

'I suggest you go and look it up in the dictionary,' said Mrs Fairfax. 'It is something very wicked and one should be aware of it and not lay oneself open to temptation.'

And just like her mother, Mrs Fairfax took the letter and burned it along with the piece of paper with the wicked word written on it.

It was a brave gesture on her part. Maxine was aware that it was only her word against the letter writer's. By now Maxine was beginning to think she had quite enjoyed kissing Missy Langdon who had thick lips and had been her Maid Marion. She knew quite well that both the letters had come from the same source. Missy Langdon was a niece of Letty Parkes. It was difficult to believe that someone, even Letty, disliked her enough to want to destroy her, but there could be no other explanation. She was powerless to take any kind of action. The evidence had been destroyed. Nobody wanted to make a scandal.

After a few days of frustration, anguish and feeling sorry for herself, she decided she didn't care any more. She read avidly everything she could about lesbians. There was a book on her father's secret bookshelf called 'The Well of Loneliness'. She found it desperately sad, but decided that there was nothing in it for her. In the meantime why should she stay here in a town where nobody trusted her, where everyone believed she was a kind of scarlet woman? Who were these people anyway? None of them were as bright as she was. Even if she was morally bad, she was at least more intelligent than they were. All she had to do was get away from them. Get away from these narrow minded, filthy minded people, people who thought of nothing but sex and scandal.

'This is it,' thought Maxine, 'I've got to get out where people don't know me. They can hate me all they want when I'm no longer here, and once I've got away I'll never come back, never.'

17.

Mabel Duncan, assistant to the wardrobe mistress at the Olympic Theatre, yawned as she pushed open the door of the wardrobe room. It didn't occur to her to wonder why there was no key in the door as she was rarely in at this time and had never found it locked. However this morning she had come in especially early as the leading lady, Monica Le Vell – or Madame as she was generally known in the company – had complained about a tucker at the seam of one of her costumes.

No one had the nerve to tell her that the tucker was due to the couple of pounds she had put on during the run. Those vital couple of pounds made the contours of the dress just a little too snug around the hipline. Instead, Mabel had volunteered to let out a couple of seams and press them carefully so that the tucker would disappear and Monica would not be embarrassed. When Madame was embarrassed she became a termagant and nobody felt strong enough to cope with that kind of thing.

So Mabel was creeping into the theatre at the crack of dawn to do her secret alterations.

She closed the door behind her, glad to be in the familiar warmth. Dying for a cup of tea, she made straight for a table beside the fireplace where the gas ring was. Here a kettle bubbled away all during the show making endless cups of tea for the staff – and for any of the cast who happened to drop in for a fitting.

Before lighting the gas ring, she took down the box of matches from the over mantle and, bending down, turned the brass tap to release the gas and lit the old gas fire to give herself a spot of company. The fire leaped into life with a joyous pop. She stood up and rubbed her back. An ex dancer with the ballet, she had suffered a back injury some time go which had put paid to her career for ever. She didn't miss it in the least. She had worked hard all her life as a dancer and she found her new job relaxing. She enjoyed working on the costumes and spent happy hours at work embroidering, replacing pearl buttons on the cockney costumes, sewing sequins, bugle beads and feathers on the glamorous evening dresses – ironing, darning and generally keeping everything in order.

She watched the fire leap into life, the blue and yellow flames shooting upwards into the broken white elements, gradually turning them red. She held out her hands to the gentle flames, smiling as the warmth reached her fingertips. Though the old gas fire resembled a mouth full of broken teeth, it was efficient and soon the whole room would be suffused with warmth.

Mabel felt content. She couldn't imagine how she had ever thought for a moment that the slog of being a dancer was worth it. She had found her milieu, right here amongst the furs and satins and feathers. She loved the feeling of the strong but supple fabrics between her fingers. She loved the fact that they had to be taken care of. To be worn once only, then refurbished, washed or pressed again for the following night. They had to be carefully and strongly made for such over use. No delicate sewing here, that was for the couturier. As long as they didn't show from the front, it didn't matter how perfect the stitches wear. Accidents happened during the show, dresses got ripped on the way up and down the stairs, or catching on the furniture. Many a glamorous lady would be tacked together or even held together with safety pins by the end of the show. But to the audience, the actresses were always shining and perfect despite the underpinnings. Mabel found the magic of it, the divine deception of it, fascinating.

She took the box of matches over to the gas ring where the aluminium kettle with its little whistler with its black nipple resided. She always needed a cup of tea before starting work. She noticed something unusual, the cap had been removed and placed on the table and as she picked it up she could feel heat emanating from the kettle.

There was no way the gas ring could have been left on. The gas would have run out by now and the fire had lit without the need of a shilling in the metre. Someone had recently been making tea. She looked at the cups that were hanging on hooks just above the table and she saw that one of them contained a drop of liquid as if it had just been rinsed and left to dry. She felt it and it was warm to the touch. It had recently been used. Could it be a burglar? Her heart started pounding furiously, though her head told her it was hardly likely that a burglar would break in to the theatre and come all the way up the stone staircase to make himself a cup of tea. That would be ridiculous. What then? Terrifying thoughts flooded through her mind, escaped criminals, and murderers hiding out her in the wardrobe – at the very top of the theatre.

There were plenty of places to hide behind the racks and racks of costumes that surrounded the room. As she stood there, scanning the dress rails, trying to find a suspicious bulge, the door opened and Jessica's small red head peeped around it. The head quickly withdrew, but realising that she had been discovered, Jessica opened the door and revealed herself in her gaudy kimono, bearing a toothbrush in one hand and a washing bag in the other. She stood there and put her finger to her lips.

'Jess, what are you doing here?'

'Please don't tell on me,' she said.

Mabel looked at her open-mouthed.

'Have you got a man in here?' she said.

Jess laughed.

'A man. What would I want with a man?' she asked.

Mabel shrugged her shoulders and as she did so, became aware of the kettle, which she was clutching to her bosom. She lit the gas ring.

'I see you filled the kettle. Would you like another cup of tea?'

Jessica came over and planked herself on one of the two wooden chairs by the fire.

'Don't tell on me,' she said again.

'What are you doing here, how did you get in?'

'There weren't nowhere else to go. The train was cancelled cos of the bad weather.'

'But how did you get in?'

'If you know a place, you can always get in somehow.'

The only drawback to being a West End chorine was that when Philip was not around to chauffeur her, she had difficulty doing the journey back to Putney each night. So on several occasions she had camped out in the wardrobe. Like Mabel, she found it the warmest and possibly the most congenial place in the theatre and there was always a spare key above the lintel – due to a lost key panic several years before. Jess found it was not difficult to remain behind after the show and the theatre became her home for the night. She could make full use of all the facilities just as she had a couple of years before at the New Theatre, Hull.

She explained most of this to Mabel as they drank their tea and ate biscuits. Mabel was impressed, but apprehensive for her safety.

'You can't keep on doing this. I can't allow it. Surely we can find you a pied a terre,' she said.

Jess looked at her in total lack of comprehension.

'Somewhere to live here in the West End,' explained Mabel 'I don't know of anywhere at the moment, but I'm sure one of the girls could help you.'

Jess took a bite of her morning tea biscuit.

'They won't help me,' she said.

'Why's that?'

'They all hate me.'

'Are you sure of this?'

'Oh yes, I'm sure.'

Mabel looked at the girl, puzzled by her calm acceptance of this supposed hostility.

'Don't you mind?'

'No, I'm used to it,' she said tranquilly.

Mabel regarded the little girl with concern.

'You must be mistaken, what reason would they possibly have for hating you?'

'Well, I'm different to them. I have a funny accent and I'm little and scrawny. I've always been different.'

'But you are young. Wait a few years and you'll be a knockout. I promise you.'

Jess looked at her, at the kind worried face and was reminded of Janie. At the thought of her sister and of her loss, tears came to her eyes, her carefully preserved tough exterior crumbled and her body was racked with sobs. Mabel went over to the girl and putting her arms around her, held her until the crying creased.

At last Jess allowed herself the luxury of tears. She cried for Janie, for her brothers, for her stepfather but mostly for herself.

When the sobbing stopped Mabel produced a packet of Woodbines, poured her another cup of tea and the two sat together smoking a cosy cigarette by the flickering fire as Jess told her about her feelings of rejection; The way the other girls had treated her at Madame Renee's dancing school – in particular the girl – Miss Shirley Temple as she named her – who had despised her, treated her like dirt, spurned her cry for help. She had not yet the confidence to go in to particular details and still did not dare to confide about the death of her stepfather and the events leading up to her escape. Mabel knew there was more to come, but didn't press her. She just sat, smoked, made tea and listened. It was all that was required.

After Jess was all cried out and they had finished off a whole kettleful of tea, Mabel picked up her sewing again. But before she did so, she assured Jess that she would ask around on her behalf and find her somewhere to stay, here in Covent Garden.

Mabel was as good as her word. The very next day Jess was able to move into a flat in Maiden Lane with two other girls from the chorus who had been having trouble finding a third to help with the rent. They grudgingly allowed Jess to join them, making no secret of the fact that she was only there for her share of the rent and that she must know her place at the bottom of the pecking order.

The top bird of this particular tree was Linda, a sulky blonde who was proud of her position as second understudy to Monica le Vell. Madame's first understudy Fiona Cooper had a small but showy part, which she would have to relinquish if she had to take over from Madame. Linda would then step into Fiona's shows. In theory, if they both fell ill Linda would play the actual lead. This was such an unlikely situation that Linda, whose main energies were employed in trying to hook herself a rich husband, had not even bothered to learn the lines. The other girl in the flat was Gladys, a plain girl who doted on Linda, picking up after her, ironing her clothes, generally acting as dogsbody to her. In her turn Gladys expected Jessica to perform the same service for her in addition to cleaning the kitchen and bathroom and scrubbing all the floors.

The two of them mocked her accent whenever they could, ganged up on her and markedly avoided including her in any of their plans. Not that she was in the least interested. All she knew was that when the older girls were taken out to supper after the show there was always a price to pay. A price they paid without question – not having experienced anything else. The discussion of their escorts, their generosity and their prowess, was one of the main topics of conversation in the dressing room the next day.

But they had no idea of what she did after the show or how she spent her days. They might have been surprised by her excursions to the Ivy and the Caprice especially as Jess was never asked to sing for her supper. Jessica at the advanced age of sixteen was still a virgin. She never really wondered why Philip never attempted to make love to her. He would just plant a chaste kiss on her cheek at the end of the evening and go on his way. She accepted his friendship and appreciated his patronage, but never gave a thought to what he might want in return.

He was not her lover, he was her teacher, her Pygmalion and with him she practised constantly, not only the nuances of dialect but also the tone and pitch of her speaking voice. She sat quietly in the restaurants watching the way Philip used his knife, how he spoke to waiters. She watched the glamorous women who frequented such places and studied their mannerisms, their make up and the way they wore their clothes.

She learned but had not yet the confidence to try out her new voice except alone or in the privacy of Philip's flat in Lowndes Square. This was the flat he shared with his brother Marcus who, as far as Jess knew, had never been there. Marcus spent most of his nights at home in the country only using the flat as a hotel, crashing out when it was impossible to get home. For Marcus this was rare, he thought nothing of driving back home every night no matter how long the distance. Though she thought of him and dreamed of him constantly, Jessica was grateful that he was never there. She didn't want him to see her until she had tailored herself to be worthy of him.

18.

'Mummy, I want to talk to you,' said Maxine as she and her mother were cooking breakfast together. 'I've decided I don't want to go to University.'

'Not go to University? Don't be so tiresome dear; your father would be terribly disappointed. Pass me three eggs dear.'

'I'm going to be an actress.'

Her mother laughed.

'Really Maxine – you do have some silly ideas. I mean – just think of the boredom! I said three, Maxine.'

'It wouldn't be boring for me.'

'Of course it would, I should know. Saying the same thing at the same time every night. Changing your clothes half a dozen times every evening – Or even worse, dancing in the chorus line – being exactly the same as all the other girls. Do you want fried bread?'

'Oh Mummy, it isn't like that any more. Times have changed. No fried bread Mummy, you should know I have to watch my figure.'

'They can't have changed that much. Irene tells me that she saw Lily Marsden in some terrible tatty show that came to Edinburgh. In the nude she was, behaving like a prostitute, she said – calling herself Jessie Matthews or something. I mean she always was such a common little creature but Irene was fond of her and she was very upset. She went round afterwards to talk to her, but Lil refused to see her.'

Maxine shrugged. Nothing Lil Marsden did was of any interest to her.

'Well, I've no intention of turning into a prostitute, thank you mother – despite that anonymous letter. I'm going to be a real actress At Stratford upon Avon or the Old Vic.'

Connie sighed deeply.

'I hated every second of it. I'd never have gone in for it if it hadn't been for Maudie. She was so determined to go on the stage and made me audition with her. Poor old Maudie was so plain, she didn't stand a chance' and her mother gave a reminiscent laugh 'How many pieces of toast? She thought it was a good way to catch a husband you see 'Men are mad about actresses' that's what she used to say. But she had the most awful buck teeth, no one could possibly want her.'

'Looks aren't important these days mother. It's personality that counts – and brains – and talent – I've got those.'

'Well, I wouldn't be too sure about the personality darling. You just sit and sulk all the time, never say a word – and you always look so disagreeable. Toast?'

Maxine caught her breath and bit back an angry reply. It wouldn't do to antagonise her mother right at the moment. She wasn't disagreeable – she was cool and aloof – maybe a little distant perhaps, but then who wouldn't be with that crowd of idiots her parents went around with.

'Anyway I've decided. I'm going to London next week. I've got three auditions. And I'll have two pieces of toast please.'

For the first time in her life Maxine felt she had her mother's undivided attention. Connie put down the bread knife and faced her daughter.

'But how – when?'

'Heather and I wrote some letters last term to RADA and Guildhall and the Webber Douglas. We've both got auditions next week.'

Connie played with an unruly tendril of hair that was escaping form her neat chignon – a sure sign that she was losing her usual composure. She searched her mind for an objection – any objection.

'You're Higher School Certificate what about that?' she asked at last.

'It's a doddle – you know I've never had any trouble with exams. Anyway I'll only be gone for a week and I don't do the exams for another two months. I need a holiday, don't I?'

Connie considered this for a while.

'I suppose it wouldn't do any harm to get away for a bit. You're obviously not happy here. Mr Parkes was only saying last night how peaky you looked'

At the very mention of the name Maxine felt her confidence slipping away. From being vibrant, bright and decisive, she became fat and overblown – dirty. Her mother carried on regardless.

'You are quite wrong about him you now. He really does like you a lot. He's a caring sort of person. Why don't you get on with him?'

While Maxine watched her mother's mind drift away to a land where all was sweetness and honey, Maxine felt as if she herself was slumping into a sea of rancid custard. She gave a loud sigh to bring her mother's mind back to reality. Her mother, seeing her depression felt guilty thinking it was her fault.

'Well I suppose you could stay at Twickenham with your Aunt Beryl. I'll ask your father.'

'You mean I can go?'

'I'll ask your father.'

Maxine took a deep breath.

'You don't have to ask my father. I'm going whether he likes it or not.'

Connie shook her head and returned to her eggs, which were beginning to burn.

'I don't see how I can stop you.'

Maxine, having won some kind of victory, pressed her advantage.

'May I borrow your black dress? It makes me look slim and slinky.'

'Darling, young girls look so foolish in black.'

'Please mother...'and Maxine put on her sweetest little girl expression.

Connie looked at her daughter; she was a dear little girl after all when she wanted to be. She put her arms around her for a moment.

'Tell you what. We shall go into town tomorrow you and I and find something really suitable for you.'

Maxine grimaced. Her mother's idea of something suitable was not likely to coincide with hers. But at least she didn't say she'd make something for her. Maxine decided not to press her any further.

'So I can go?'

'Very well. I don't suppose it would do any harm.'

Connie thought again for a second 'Maybe we don't need to tell your father about the auditions. Just tell him you are going on holiday.'

She was struck by another thought 'I know – why don't I come with you? We could do some shopping -, see a few shows. It would be fun – just girls together. Besides I haven't seen your Aunt Beryl for ages.'

This was a set back Maxine hadn't even thought of. She thought again quickly.

'Actually Mummy. I've been invited to stay with Heather from school and there won't be room for you there. She's doing the auditions too you know.'

'Oh – really? How interesting. She should do so well. Such a pretty girl; that lovely slim figure and those blond curls. What a bonus curly hair can be.'

She gave a quick look at Maxine and added hastily

'Your hair's nice too of course – shiny. Nice and healthy. Thank goodness we never had it permed. Perms ruin hair you know.'

Now that she had got her own way, Maxine was content to listen to her mother ramble on.

'Poor Maudie Winchester had a perm. Her hair was a mass of frizz. It just stood out all over her head. We did laugh.'

'Did Maudie laugh too?'

'I expect she did. She always was a sport.'
'With those buck teeth she'd have to be I suppose.'

19.

Maxine dressed with care. She wasn't impressed at the result, Although the New Look was the rage at the moment, the dress her mother had chosen had a tight bodice, nipped in waist and a billowing skirt which emphasised her bust and hips, making her feel like an overblown green rose.

'No – more like a green balloon tied in the middle,' she muttered to herself furiously. Nevertheless, the full skirt that swirled around her calves had a nice feel, especially as it was filled out with net petticoats underneath. It was like the tutus she had always loved wearing, and it make her feel like dancing. She pulled back her hair and pinned the sides and top of it in a knot at the top of her head, leaving the underneath hair hanging down her back. Her sleek hair, drawn from her face, helped to show off her cheekbones and jaw line and took attention away from her chubby cheeks. She applied a little more green eye shadow to her lids, which were already heavy with grease and re-applied mascara. She tried a new shade of lipstick, admiring the effect of the dark red, which made her teeth look pearly white.

'Are you ready?' called Heather and she came into the room she shared with her friend.

Maxine couldn't suppress a pang of envy as she surveyed the slender figure and golden curls of her friend. Heather in her turn sighed as she looked at Maxine.

'Oh I do wish I had a bust,' she sighed, 'You look so sexy.'

'I'm not supposed to look sexy,' said Maxine 'I was hoping to look dramatic.'

Heather laughed, 'Ok dramatically sexy,' she said, 'How do I look?'

'Very pretty.'

'Oh how boring. Next to you I'm like a country bumpkin.'

'Well,' considered Maxine, 'you're not wearing much makeup. You don't look like an actress.'

'Oh dear,' said Heather, worried. 'Do you think I should put on more? I don't want them to think I'm provincial.'

'Heather, you look lovely,' said Maxine with a trace of regret. 'They'll be crazy if they don't want you.'

Their auditions did not coincide. Heather had to go to RADA and Maxine to the Webber Douglas. They wished each other good luck.

Maxine presented herself at the tiny theatre in Clareville Street and spoke to the Secretary who was sitting at a desk in the Foyer.

'I'm Maxine Fletcher.'

The secretary looked up. Maxine thought the women's face registered distaste. That n some way she disapproved of Maxine who asked...

'Is something the matter?'

Miss Pigeon pursed her lips over the prominent buckteeth. Maxine thought of poor Maudie Winchester.

'I don't know what you mean,' she said, a twitch appearing in her left eye.

'You are looking at me as if I were overdressed or something.'

Maxine's attitude took Miss Pigeon aback. It was not usual for applicants to be so direct. She spoke out in defence.

'You are wearing too much make-up,' she said.

'It's the fashion,' replied Maxine, 'or maybe you hadn't heard.'

Maxine was furious. She hadn't come here to be criticised by this ugly old trout.

Miss Pigeon's eyes shot sparks of anger.

'Come along Miss Fletcher. We're waiting for you.'

Maxine felt she did a pretty good audition. The people out there in the dark seemed kind and friendly, and she felt her rendering of Cleopatra's death speech was excellent. It gave her an opportunity to use her deep voice and flash her green-shadowed eyes.

For her comedy piece, she chose Shaw's Cleopatra, which she believed showed a kind of ingenuity on her part. She was able to perform this in her high, light voice, – the one that she'd copied from children's programmes on the BBC, although it came as a shock when they laughed. No one had ever laughed at her before – and at first, she resented it, until she realised that laughter was not a bad thing when one is playing comedy. She began to enjoy herself, to time her delivery, adjust to the laughs, and as she did so the laughter increased in volume and quantity.

She felt exhilarated as if she were having a wonderfully funny conversation with the people out there. She was sorry when the speech came to an end, but happy to hear the spontaneous applause that came from the people in the dark. She got through the improvisations, sang her song, did her dance. However, singing and dancing was not why she was there. She had no interest in musical theatre. The Old Vic or the Royal Shakespeare – that was where she intended to spend the premier part of her career.

'Thank you Miss Fletcher,' said a kindly voice and she gave a curtsey and left the stage.

Miss Pigeon was waiting.

'We'll be in touch Miss Fletcher,' she said.

'When?'

'Within a week I should think. Have you applied for any other Academy?'

'RADA of course.'

'Of course.'

'And the Guildhall.'

Miss Pigeon pursed her lips and looked at Maxine speculatively.

'I see – you'll go to one of those I suppose. If you get in?'

'Well yes,' said Maxine confidently, 'I feel I am more suited to the academic syllabus. I came here because my teacher suggested it.'

'I'll do you a favour,' said Miss Pigeon surprisingly, 'Stick to comedy – musical comedy's your forte. The classics just aren't for you.'

Maxine was indignant.

'Thank you very much for your opinion,' she said, angrily, 'As it happens I think that Musical Comedy is a load of rubbish,'

'I see,' said Miss Pigeon, and Maxine left – her cheeks burning with anger.

Maxine didn't do well at her RADA audition. For some reason, she had lost her nerve, and during her Shakespeare, she dried several times. In the Shaw, there were no laughs forthcoming and by the time she had finished she felt utterly demoralised.

Maxine and Heather arrived together for their auditions at the Guildhall. Heather was getting into her stride and beginning to enjoy herself. Maxine, on the other hand, was plunged into the deepest gloom. She performed efficiently, but her spark had deserted her.

'How did it go?' asked Heather.

Maxine grimaced, 'I didn't do very well – how about you?'

Heather confessed, 'I have absolutely no idea. I'm just relieved it is all over.'

The two girls retired to Lyons corner house and ate Welsh rarebit and ice cream with chocolate sauce.

*

The following week a letter arrived from RADA. They were quite polite, almost encouraging but suggested Maxine was a little young yet and wasn't ready for training. They suggested that she should take another audition for PARADA the preparatory school. Maxine was disappointed; a whole year at PARADA and then another three years at RADA? Why she'd be in her dotage before she even started her career. She had fully expected to be winning Oscars by the time she was twenty.

Next, there came a letter from the Guildhall. They were awfully sorry, but all the places were filled. They also felt she was a little immature and suggested that she take the audition again the following year. The letter from the Webber Douglas came last.

This girl is obviously very talented, especially in the field of comedy, but though her stage presence and appearance is unusually excellent, we do not feel she has the right temperament for the theatre. Perhaps she should wait until next year and try again. By this time she may have learned a little humility and her attitude may have improved.

By the same post came a letter from Heather, saying she had accepted the chance to go to PARADA.

Her mother handed the letters other as they came, but didn't utter a word. Maxine read them silently full of impotent anger against herself. She had behaved stupidly, getting uppity with that ugly secretary. Obviously, Miss Pigeon had been telling tales. She cursed all buck-toothed women.

Maxine took the three letters and the one from Heather, and after tearing them into tiny pieces; she threw them in the fire. Her acting career was over

'Mother,' she said later, 'I've decided to go to University after all.'

'Oh darling, I'm so glad,' she said, 'I was worried about your leaving home and going to London. Your father is not a well man, as you know. I think you would e happier if you stayed at home – for a while at least,'

'At home – you can't mean Hull University. I want to go to a proper one,' she wailed.

'Leave it for a while darling,' said her mother. 'Give it another year at least before you go out of town.'

20.

When the phone rang, Linda was still in bed, sleeping after a late night and Fiona still hadn't returned to base. Jessie went to the phone in the hall, taking a pencil with her to jot down any messages, not expecting a call for herself at this time in the morning. Vern Jones, the company manager was on the line asking for Linda.

'I'm sorry she's not here at the moment, she must have – er – gone out to the shops,' she said unconvincingly.

'What you mean is, she's still in bed. Well get that lazy tart up and tell her to get to the theatre instantly.'

'Why, what's happened?'

'Madame Monica has the flu and is also off sick. Linda is second understudy so she's going to have to go on. We need to rehearse as soon as possible.'

'Do you think she's up to it? Does she know the lines?' she asked, amazed at her temerity, but knowing that Linda had not exactly put her heart and soul into the understudy rehearsals. He was too frazzled to notice.

'She's fuckin' better know the fuckin' lines or learn them fuckin' quick or we'll have to fuckin' cancel. Mr Black would not be pleased.'

'I'll try to find her and get the message to her somehow,' said Jessie. She put the phone down and rushed to her room.

She sat for a moment on her bed. Then she picked up the photo of Janie she always kept on her dressing table. Janie looked out of the picture through her big round glasses and Jess knew that she was telling her something – urging her on. Without stopping to think any further, she went to the cupboard and took out the grey suit she had bought recently. Her friendship with Philip brought her many advantages, one of which was that she never had to spend any money on food, but could spend her entire salary after she had paid the rent, on clothes. She had bought the suit in a Harrods sale and, although it did not fit her as precisely as she would have wished, she enlisted the assistance of Mabel, who cut and tucked and sewed until it was perfect. The suit was a pearl grey with a tightly fitting jacket and along narrow skirt. With it she wore a violet blouse and matching kid gloves that accentuated the unusual colour of her eyes. She put on her new pair of dove grey high heeled shoes, and to complete her ensemble, she pinned across her shoulder her most treasured acquisition, a fox fur.

*

She picked up her bag, dropped the photograph of Janie inside it for luck and prepared to leave. As she opened the door a bleary Linda appeared on the stairs.

'Was that the phone?' she said.

'Yes it was for me. I have to go and meet a friend.'

'At this time in the morning?'

'It's almost eleven,' laughed Jessie. 'So long' and she flung out of the door before Linda could ask any further questions.

So far she had behaved on impulse almost as if possessed, as if Janie was truly driving her on. As she hailed a taxi, she began to panic.

What was she doing? What was her next step? But by now it was too late to turn back. She put all negative thoughts from her and let her other self take over – the lady. The Eliza Dolittle transformed into a duchess or what was even more difficult – a West End actress, poised and confident. The little girl from Paradise Street was firmly pushed away – she no longer existed.

She instructed the driver to take her, not to the stage door, but to the front of house where the porter was already on duty. She smiled graciously at him as he rushed to open the taxi door and she made her way to Mr Black's office.

She swept past the secretary who rose from her desk to attend to her.

'Mr Black is expecting me,' she said and she waltzed through the big double doors. She posed at the doorway to collect her breath and also to allow Mr Black, who was sitting at his big oak desk to have a good view of the vision she presented. He rose to his feet instantly and indicated one of the low comfortable chairs that were arranged around his office.

'Good morning Mr Black,' she said extending her gloved hand graciously, and, ignoring the chair, perched on his big empty desk.

'Good morning Miss...'

'Jessica. Jessica Sherwood. Surely you remember me. People don't usually forget me so easily.'

Mr Black looked slightly embarrassed. He was unsure of his ground but covered himself quickly with gallantry.

'Of course not. Who could forget somebody as lovely as you?' he said gallantly.

'Well Mr Black. I have come here to tell you that your troubles are over.'

'My troubles?'

Jessica wasted no time in getting down to basics. She was worried that any minute Linda would appear on the scene and give her away.

'I believe darling Monica has succumbed to the influenza and I have come to offer myself as substitute.'

'We have an understudy.'

'Fiona is also off sick as you know – and I have reason to believe that the second understudy, though a charming girl I'm sure, has hardly the class or the intelligence to play a leading role.'

Any sting of bitchery her remarks might have had was covered by a bewitching smile as she looked down at him.

Taken aback, yet oddly intrigued. He was not used to being looked down upon and got to his feet.

'I see,' he said, 'But it's quite a heavy role, what makes you think you can learn it in time?'

'I know it already.'

He lifted his eyebrow at her, wondering how it could be possible. Before he had time to enquire Jessica broke in.

'May I show you? Please sit.'

He fell back into his chair, and Jessica flung off her fox fur and whipped off her coat and skirt revealing practise dress underneath and launched into the first part of the show. Mr Black watched her, stunned, as she went through it, singing all the songs, dancing the dances, and for good measure doing all the parts, male and female. Mr Black let her continue for a good fifteen minutes before stopping her.

'Stop stop. I believe you. Please don't exhaust yourself.'

Jessica perched herself back on the desk and waited with beating heart.

Mr Black pursed his lips and putting his elbows on the desk, pressed his forefingers together, surveying her. He saw that her sophistication was a front, he suspected that she was much younger than she appeared. He guessed that she was a chancer, but her cheek impressed him as did her talent, her style and her class. Eventually, after what seemed like hours, he spoke,

'The piano player is in the green room or somewhere waiting for something to happen. Let's look for him. I can hardly call in the whole orchestra at this stage, but we can work out some keys for you.'

'I can sing in any key you want,' she boasted.

'I'm sure you can,' he laughed. 'How on earth did you manage to learn all that?'

She realised it was time to own up.

'I attended the rehearsals.'

'I never saw you there.'

'Oh you did Mr Black. Don't you recognise me at all? You just said you'd never forget anyone as lovely as me,' she said with a grin.

'You do look familiar of course – but I can't quite put my finger on it.'

Jessica used her old voice for the very last time.

'Don't you remember young Jessie O'Malley?' she asked.

'Oh my God,' cried Mr Black, 'I'd never have guessed it, never in a million years. What happened to your awful accent?'

'Excuse me, it was not awful,' she said boldly, 'just different.'

'I do beg your pardon,' he said.

'Do I still go on tonight?'

Mr Black shook his head in bewilderment.

'Let's go and have a word with the pianist,' he said.

Jessie joined Joe Tully, the piano player on stage. Mr Black, Vern Jones and Gervaise, the director watched from the stalls as Jessie and George worked for an hour or more, checking all the keys.

She was then taken through all the dance routines with the choreographer. She knew Jessie of old and was perfectly content that she would be able to handle them all with ease.

It wasn't until they were taking a well-earned break with coffee and sandwiches that a furious Linda arrived on the scene.

'What the fuck is going on?' she said.

'It's Ok,' said Vern. 'Monica is off, but we have sorted out the problem. We couldn't get hold of you earlier – you were still in bed. So Miss Sherwood is going to go on for Monica this evening.'

'Miss Sherwood? Fuck Miss Sherwood. I am the understudy, not little Jessie O'Malley from god knows what dung heap.'

'You should have been there when I called.'

'I was there. I was,' she shouted. 'This little snake in the grass took the call. After all I've done for you.'

She turned to the assembled company

'I took her in when she was destitute. The rotten little bitch.' She spat the words at her.

Jessica's self satisfied smile angered her even further and Linda would have attacked her physically if Vern hadn't seen the murderous look in her eyes and held her in a half Nelson.

Gervaise intervened.

'Let us not fight about it now, we have work to do. Jessie will go on for Monica and you'll have to stand in for Fiona. Do you know the lines?'

'Of course I know it. I know it all.'

Gervaise looked dubious. But there was nobody else who was even mildly competent and he spent the rest of the day he spent working with Linda, convinced that Jessie would be more than competent playing the lead.

21.

As soon as she had a chance Jessica rang Philip and told him about her good fortune.

'But how on earth did it happen?'

She hesitated to tell him about her deception. After all, he had nearly been a vicar and she didn't think he would approve of lying.

'They were going to cancel the show because Linda didn't know the part. I just happened to be there at the time and they were really worried. So I just showed them I could do it. They were really grateful.'

'My god, you've got a nerve,' he said.

'I don't know how I managed it,' she said smugly, 'It just sort of happened. Something made me do it. Something inside me just said 'go on girl, this is your chance. So I took it.'

Philip didn't want to continue with this, he was afraid he might worry her before the big night so he just said,

'Good luck Jess. I'll be there rooting for you – and we'll have a celebratory dinner afterwards.'

She sat in Monica's dressing room nervous but feeling completely confident. She had all the important people on her side – the orchestra, the choreographer and director. It was only the rest of the cast that were doubting her ability and secretly hoping that she would not succeed. Mabel had been entrusted with dressing the new girl and had been busy at work making over the costumes that could be made to fit her and finding alternatives for those that couldn't.

No one wanted to say anything to Jessica but all were aware that some of the chorus were gunning for her. She was an upstart, and most of them had worked with Linda for a long time and had feelings of loyalty towards her.

Jessica kept thinking of Linda's furious face but kept putting the thought from her. She looked at Janie's picture that she had propped up against the mirror and told her 'I'll think about it tomorrow'.

*

The evening passed in a kind of dream. Mr Black had come on stage before the show and told the audience that she would be a new star in the making. He made a good story about the star and the understudies all falling ill at the same time. He ensured that the audience was on her side from the beginning and when at the end he went on stage again and brought her forward for an extra bow, the theatre erupted. Afterwards he told her that she could play the role as long as Monica was ill, but she must be prepared to go back to the chorus as soon as the leading leady returned to the show.

*

Philip was delighted at her progress and secretly thrilled to think that he had had a part in encouraging this talent to fruition.

'You were really good,' he said, but did not hesitate to criticise her for things that she could do better, and after the show, they went back to Knightsbridge and ran through the whole thing once more in preparation for the following night's performance.

He also brought up another problem that had been worrying him.

'I'm thinking of Linda, didn't she have something to say about your taking over what should have been her opportunity?'

'Oh you know these people, they are only in the business to catch the men. She doesn't have any real ambition.'

'Nevertheless. You have to share a flat with her. It may not be too comfortable for a while. She won't like you very much.'

'She doesn't anyway,' she muttered, but not for the first time she was dismayed at what she had done, or rather how other people were going to react to it.

'You'll have to face her tonight.'

'Oh God,' she said, 'I didn't think of that.'

'Would you rather go back to Putney tonight? I'll drive you there if you like.'

For a moment she thought longingly of Vera's unquestioning acceptance of her. It was a comforting thought, but she wanted to be on the spot for early rehearsals the next day. So she turned down his kind offer.

'If things get too bad perhaps you'll ring me up?'
'Yes of course I will.'

It was late when they got back to Maiden lane and she was very sleepy. He kissed her quickly on the cheek and opened the door for her.

'Goodnight – star! You are definitely on your way,' he said.

She blinked at him dozily and went up the wooden stairs.

*

Sure enough, the call came before nine o'clock the next day and Philip raced round to Maiden Lane. He found her sitting glumly on the pavement outside the house, still in her best suit which was beginning to look a little crumpled.

'I can't stay there. I've left.'

'But where are your things?'

'I have no things anymore. They're all in pieces. Those bitches have gone through everything, broken my radio, took away my sheets and cut all my clothes to ribbons, all my clothes. All I have is what I'm wearing.'

'How did you sleep, without sheets?'

'I was too tired to do anything but fall asleep in front of the gas fire. They left the rug. It belonged to Miss Castang. Trouble is the shilling ran out in the middle of the night and I couldn't find another one.'

Philip reached out and touched her hand. His kindness was too much, the tears started to run down her face, right there in the middle of Maiden Lane. He put a comradely arm around her.

'Look,' he said, 'let's get out of here.' And as he spoke a friendly cab came trundling down the road.

'Well, would you believe it?' he said and he hailed the cab and bundled her into it. She was still weeping and he offered her the clean white handkerchief from his top pocket.

'Ta,' she said. 'You in't 'alf good to me.'

Philip laughed as she lapsed into her northern speech patterns.

'Oh but Philip they've destroyed all my clothes – and my wireless. What can I do?'

'I'll get you a new one,' he promised. 'And we'll find you some clothes.'

'No, I can't let you buy my clothes.'

'All right, you can pay me back later when you are earning a hundred pounds a week. In the meantime you need things to put on. You can't go around naked now, can you?'

She gave a watery smile. 'That's how you first saw me,' she said.

Philip flushed a little with embarrassment. He preferred to forget *Starkers in Paradise*. It was a long time ago and Jess had come a long way since then.

'Actually it's as well to get rid of those things,' he said. 'We can get you some new ones to suit your star status. Let's have breakfast first and then we'll go shopping.'

'But where will I live?'

'I'll think of something,' he said.

He took her back to his flat in Lowndes Square and after lending her a dressing gown, he had all her clothes washed and cleaned by the laundry service. They had breakfast sent up by the restaurant below and afterwards she sat back in his huge bathtub covered in bubbles and thought how easy and delightful life would be if one was rich.

Then, ignoring any protests she may have left, he took her shopping.

Left to herself she would have gone to a bargain basement at C & A or Harrods sale if there had been one but Philip wouldn't have known how to handle these and he took her to Knightsbridge where she sampled the delights of sitting in an antique chair in a richly carpeted boutique whilst some girl who was her shape and size tried on dress after dress until Jessie – and Philip – decided which one she should put on her precious back. Then the fitter and dressmaker would enter and small adjustments recommended, a tuck here, the armhole maybe a trifle too large, the skirt a quarter of an inch too long and out would come the pins and the dressmaker's chalk.

Jessie revelled in the attention and surprised herself by not resenting or feeling embarrassed in the least that Philip was footing the bill. He was enjoying it so much, so excited and delighted to be dressing her up like a living doll, considering it all part of her education. He knew just how to charm the salesladies in little boutiques around Knightsbridge and Jessie was into the kind of life she had never even dreamed could exist. Her confidence blossomed; she felt she could conquer the world. Neither mentioned the fact, but her accent and her way of speaking had changed yet again in the last twenty-four hours. She was Eliza Dolittle at the ball, the Pygmalion legend had again come to fruition.

After lunch they returned to Lowndes Square and were delighted to find all the parcels awaiting them. However Jessie still had other worries on her mind.

'It's been lovely, this morning,' she said, 'But I should really have spent the time looking for some digs.'

'I've been thinking of that and I have a plan. Tell me if you think it would be all right for you.'

'If it's your idea I'm sure it'll be all right. I owe you everything. You do know how grateful I am, don't you?'

'It's been a pleasure,' he said gallantly, 'Now for the plan. For the moment you can stay here.'

'Here? In this flat? Where will you go?'

He laughed. She would never think for a second that he was suggesting they live together.

'I can move into my parents' town house just round the corner. It will be no problem. You don't really have time to worry about anything at the moment, not while you have the show to think of.'

'Won't people talk? I don't want them to think I'm a kept woman.'

He laughed, 'I don't suppose so. We often have friends to stay here. Anyway none of the neighbours would dare to think ill of us. We are the landlords here after all.'

The matter was out of her hands. All she wanted now was to concentrate on the evening's performance.

That night she was better in the role, having taken on board all Philip's notes. The following night she was better still.

The night after that she was back in the chorus.

As soon as she heard of the new girl's success, Madame's health improved by leaps and bounds and she was happily back in harness.

Jessie was not so happy. Linda made no secret of what had happened and regaled the girls with her own highly exaggerated version. The girls rallied around Linda, the martyr and Jessica was sent to Coventry from that moment. She had never had much to say to them in the past, so she was able to ignore their silence and, without a word, cleaned off the obscenities that were scrawled on her mirror, but the persecution did not stop there. Her costumes were interfered with, her clothes would be found in dishevelled heaps on the floor. Again she said nothing, just picked them up and straightened them.

Then one day she was about to apply her stick of number five to her face and found, just in the nick of time, that a pin had been inserted into the tube. This really scared her and she ran to Mabel, asking for her advice. Mabel, though disapproving of what she had done, thought the girls had gone too far and talked the wardrobe mistress into letting Jessica change in the wardrobe until things settled down. This didn't stop the girls from trying to trip her up on the stairs, but it meant she could change in peace and quiet.

She had been dressing there for about a month when she had a surprising visitor. It was her erstwhile room mate, Fiona.

'Jessica,' she said, holding out her hand, 'I don't care what the other girls think. You were wonderful in Madame's part,' she looked around and lowered her voice to a whisper

'Better than Madame herself.'

'I'm not saying what you did was right,' she went on, 'But I don't know what would have happened if Linda had gone on. They would have taken the show off and we'd all be out of work. You did us a favour.'

Fiona had had enough of Linda and her constant demands and was secretly happy about her come-uppance. She braved the hostility of the other girls to change her allegiance but the other girls soon followed suit and equilibrium was restored.

The show had only a couple more months to run. In its place there was to be another revue written and produced by the same team. This time Jess did not have to change in the wardrobe – or in the chorus room. This time she had her own dressing room and a part – small, but significant and written especially for her.

22.

Maxine slipped into the white cable sweater she had bought that day at Marks and Spencer. All the other students were wearing them and she had felt wrong not having one of her own. She surveyed the effect in the mirror and thought it looked cheap. She turned sideway on and felt sick at the sight of her huge breasts with the ever erect nipples sticking out. The white jumper accentuated them. She pulled off the jumper and got out a book to read.

'Aren't you going to the College dance this evening?' asked Connie.

'No I'm bored with all those people. They are all so old!'

'How can they be old? They are students.'

'Yes they are – apart from the ones that are children,' she snapped back.

It didn't take long for Maxine to realise that Hull University was not for her. It was the other students that really upset her. The war had been over now for five years but National service was still in operation and many of the male students were there on a Further Education Training Grant. They were very grown up, for the most part working class and came straight from living a tough army life. She felt they treated her with contempt. They laughed at her when she talked of her Mummy and Daddy and vied with each other in their attempts to get her into bed.

Neither was she impressed with the female of the species who seemed, by contrast, incredibly young. The pretty girls read *Woman's Own* and talked of nothing but clothes make up and '*fellas*', and the academically inclined girls were completely disinterested in how they looked and were mostly thick set, bespectacled, hairy and spotty. The fumbling attempts of the younger men to get in to her pants were as boring and infuriating as those of their elders.

She had expected University to be a place where people of kindred spirits could get together and talk the night away. Talking was something none of them seemed to be interested in. She was in despair of ever being taken seriously, ever being treated as a normal human being. Of courses she wanted boy friends, what girl of her age wouldn't? But Maxine was beginning to think that sex was the only thing that anyone cared about and it was something that left her cold. But there were times when in her sleep she dreamed she was riding a horse, faster and faster, harder and harder and she would wake with an almost unbearable itch and flutter in the womb and a sudden wetness that frightened her. Sometimes in her dream the horses face turned into that of Mr Parkes and the familiar shame enveloped her.

Dear Sir,

I wonder if it would be possible for me to try again for a place at your Academy. When I auditioned for you last year, you seemed to think I was suitable for musical comedy, but at the time I was insistent that a more academic approach would suit me better. Having spent half a year at University College I think you were correct in your assessment of my abilities. I would like to try again. May I audition for you once more?
Yours sincerely,

Maxine Fletcher

Dear Miss Fletcher,

JD has asked me to tell you that he remembers you vividly from your last audition and that there is no need for him to see you again. He thinks you do have certain ability for singing and dancing as well as a true comedy talent and that you should concentrate on the lighter fields of the profession. I have pleasure in offering you a place starting September.
Signed: Adelaide Pigeon.

P.S We do not care to call it an Academy. We prefer to use the word School.

She quickly wrote off her acceptance of the place and posted it before telling her parents. It was with the gravest foreboding that she approached her mother and father who were drinking their coffee in the breakfast room.
'I've decided to go to Drama College after all,' she said.
Her mother looked at her reproachfully
'You do seem to change your mind a lot.'
'I've been offered a place at the Webber Douglas,' she said.
'The one that turned you down because you were too uppity?' said Connie.
'They've changed their minds as well,' she snapped.
Her mother looked at her reproachfully.
'Just as you were getting on so well at University.'
Maxine almost exploded.
'What! You must be mad. I hate it and it hates me. How could you think I was getting on well? Have you seen me smiling a lot? Haven't you noticed how miserable I've been?'
Connie replied in her patronising, soothing voice that made Maxine want to throw a bucket of water over her.
'You do exaggerate darling. Leslie Parkes plays golf with your professor and some of the lecturers. They all think you're a bright girl. Your father was so pleased and proud, weren't Tom?'
Tom gave a faint smile as he often did when directly approached. Then almost as if he was embarrassed by being appealed to, he abruptly stood, walked over to the window and stared looking out over the lawn.'
'Why is it always Leslie Parkes? Why should he be the oracle that shapes my life?'
Connie smiled enchantingly with a shrug of the shoulders.

'Anyway I have decided. Have written back to accept the place they offered. If you don't want to pay the fees I'll try for a scholarship.'

'That was little rash of you. Nevertheless, we must ask your father.'

The both turned to Tom who was gazing blankly out of the window.

'Maxine wants to go to London to drama school.'

'Kicking up her legs?' he asked.

'That's about it,' said Connie.

Maxine went over to him and put her arms around his neck. He stiffened instantly at her touch, almost leaning backwards in an effort to keep away from her, but she was determined to make him understand.

'No Daddy, this is a proper drama school where you do Shakespeare and stuff. The kind of thing you really adore.'

The blank look lasted for a second or two, and then he smiled.

'Yes, good good,' he said.

'So you have no objection. Daddy?'

'No I don't think so,' he said and he patted her absent-mindedly on the shoulder and putting her away from him, returned to his chair.

Maxine could see Connie biting her lip and could tell that her mother had expected one of his uncontrollable bursts of rage and she had been looking forward to saying, *'Now look what you've done'.*

None of this was forthcoming, so she sighed heavily.

'Well, if your father says so.'

Maxine felt she must show her gratitude.

'Would you like me to read to you again?' she asked him.

'I prefer the way Connie reads to me,' he said, turning his loving blue eyes on his beautiful wife, 'Maxine puts too much expression in it.'

'So I'm not required,' said Maxine, hurt at the slight to her acting ability, but she laughed and kissed him forgivingly on the top of his head. He seized her and sat her upon his knee.

Maxine gave him a quick hug and released herself carefully. It was too late for him to start treating her like a little girl.

*

She felt as if a burden had been lifted from her as she took out her bicycle and made her way to the village to her favourite popshop. She knew that the two-tone car was following her. Mr Parkes seemed to have some kind of tracking device. How did he know where she would be at any given time? She sent up a prayer of relief that soon she would be free of his nauseating presence.

As usual, she ordered her favourite cherry soda with an ice cream float, and as usual, he came and sat opposite her.

He looked her up and down in the special way he had which made her feel she smelled bad.

She swirled her long spoon around in her drink, watching the ice-cream melt.

'Still a child,' he said and he laughed.

He had a laugh that made her toes curl with distaste. A wheezy laugh that seemed to come from somewhere in his stomach. It was the kind of laugh she associated with Fagin or Uriah Heep. A laugh with no joy in it – *heh heh heh! heh heh heh!*

'Yes, still a child,' she replied through tight lips.

'Don't you think its time you stopped behaving like a schoolgirl?' he asked.

'I shall do that when people stop treating me like one,' she said silkily. 'And that's not likely to happen until I get away from this God forsaken town.'

He looked at her sharply.

'You are going away?'

'Yes, very soon. I'm going to Drama School in London.'

'You'll hate it there,' he said. 'They're very unfriendly down South.'

'Unfriendly? All the better. Better than my so-called friends up here.'

Mr Parkes laughed again, a little uneasily.

'We're all very fond of you. And you're doing so well at University.'

'No I'm not,' she said, 'And do you know why?'

He shook his head.

'Because all those sex obsessed ex-soldier boys remind me too much of you!'

The laugh came again and this time Maxine realised what it was that made it so unpleasant. There was no enjoyment in it. He laughed because he was nervous. This man who ruined her life was actually afraid of her – and she understood now that his attempts at domination had a kind of desperation about them.

Now she laughed, and her laugh was pure joy.

'I'm going now,' she said. 'You can have my ice cream soda. It is paid for.'

She thrust her drink across the table. It splashed up and made a sloppy cream and red stain on his cricket club tie and his clean white shirt. This made her laugh even more.

She went to the door, and turned to look at him where he sat and she was pleased and interested to note that for once, his eyes were focussed higher up than usual, on her face.

She treated him to her best smile.

'I despise you laughing boy,' she said sweetly and went out, slamming the door behind her as the sound *'heh heh heh'* of his nervous laugh followed her.

*

She went home, singing. Her heart was lighter than it had been for many along time. The thought that she was soon to leave all this behind; that she had a different kind of future; that she was about to embark on an adventure, gave her spirits an enormous lift.

During that summer, her puppy fat began to dissolve as if by magic. Her health and her disposition improved. B the time September came round, her hair was shining, her complexion was clear and rosy, her body was perfectly toned. She had blossomed into the confident beauty that she always hoped she was going to be.

23.

Philip had accompanied Jessica to the first night party in the upstairs room at the Ivy where the daily papers were to be delivered as soon as they came out. The cast and crew had donned their glad rags, collected their nearest and dearest and were all there to eat, drink and celebrate their success. It was not an unalloyed joyous occasion however, as the verdict of the audience had to be endorsed by the critics. Monica Le Vell was putting a brave face on it, drinking her champagne and laughing loudly, but she was, quite rightly, apprehensive. She knew what a hit her young rival had been and that it was a possibility that Jessica would figure prominently in the notices.

But when the papers finally arrived at 3.30 a.m., it was worse even than she expected. Jessica Sherwood had wiped the floor with her.

There was even a bitchy article in one of the cheap papers, which must have been prepared in advance:

"***Chorus girl sparkles in her first principal role***. *Once Monica le Vell's understudy, Jessica Sherwood stepped in at a moment's notice when Our Monica was victim to the flu. As a result of her success in the role, the producers* *have introduced into this edition of the Follies several sketches that have been tailored to the youngster's individual personality. She stops the show every time she appears. Monica le Vell must rue the day she succumbed to the influenza..."*

When rehearsals started Monica had noticed that Gervaise, the director was impressed by Jessica's talent and had instructed Jasper to write extra material for the young actress. On seeing how Jessica handled his work Jasper wrote her in even more and her once tiny part grew and grew until it was in danger of taking over the entire show. Monica looked on helplessly. She had a reputation for being a good trouper, for encouraging new talent. She also was objective enough to see what an asset Jessica was to the show and that using her talent would serve to keep the show running and the whole company in work indefinitely.

Her apprehensions were well founded. On the opening night the press took Jessica Sherwood to its heart and she became the West Ends newest and brightest discovery, queues formed at the box office and Monica had to accept that she no longer was the public's number one darling.

'Why are you crying Jess? This is your big moment?'

Jessica was standing outside the room in the corridor, her shoulders shaking with sobs. Philip, who had followed her out, took her by the shoulders.

'What is it, Jess?'

Unable to speak, Jessica allowed him to put his arms around her and she sobbed quietly against his shoulder. He took out his handkerchief and wiped away the tears that still came thick and fast. He realised he had never seen her cry before.

'Please tell me, what's wrong?'

But Jessica just shook her head and cried all the more. He held her quietly until the paroxysms ceased.

'Shall I take you home?' he asked.

'No,' she said violently, 'I want to enjoy the party.'

Philip laughed.

'Then you'd better tidy yourself up a bit,' he said, 'You look somewhat dishevelled to say the least.'

'I don't care. I don't care any more what people think of me. I want them to see me as I am.'

'My sweet girl. You will never be the same again, now. You are a star. You are a person with responsibilities to others. You owe it to the world to look your best at all times. Never forget that.'

She gave a hefty sniff and blew her nose.

'You are always so right, so wise,' she said and was able to laugh a little.

'I do what I can,' he said and made a little grimace that made her laugh again.

'Come downstairs,' he suggested. 'Maybe one of the kind waiters will give us a cup of their emergency coffee.'

The restaurant was deserted. The chairs had been put up on the tables ready for the cleaners who were due to arrive at 6.am. Philip took down a couple of the heavy chairs and ordered her to sit.

'Should we be here?' she said, looking around anxiously.

'Certainly. Until somebody comes along and tells us we can't.'

He left her there for a moment as he went to the kitchen in search of coffee. He came back, triumphantly carrying a couple of cups.

'They always have coffee brewing up when there's an all night party going on,' he explained, happy to see that she was looking almost her old self. Just a faint flush on her face indicated the recent burst of emotion.

He put the cups on the table. 'It's black I'm afraid,' he said. 'Now tell me why you cried.'

Already she was beginning to recover her usual spirits. He could see as she sipped the bitter coffee that her young complexion was already almost back to normal from the onslaught of weeping.

'Happiness in a way. In another . . . you wouldn't understand.'

'Try me.'

'They will never know it's me.'

'Who?'

'All those people who hated me, who despised me. They will never know that she turned into Jessica Sherwood – who had all those nice things said about her.'

'What about your family? There must be somebody you can get in touch with.'

She shook her head. There was no way she could tell anyone, even Philip about them. She often thought of little Jamie and wondered what had happened to him. The thought of her stepfather came back to haunt her, sometimes in the middle of the night. She was glad he was dead, but was afraid to find out how it had happened. When she had first started work she had vowed to put a little money aside for Jamie – maybe he would be able to get some kind of education, but she had soon found that she needed every penny she had in order to keep herself alive. She knew that her elder brothers were both working – maybe by now Jamie was too. Since her fortunes had changed she had not even thought of sending money to them.

'They were all killed in the blitz except Janie, my sister – and then she was killed by a doodle bug.'

At the thought of Janie, the tears started again. But the sudden appearance of a young waiter on his way home prevented her.

'Excuse me. You are Jessica Sherwood, aren't you?'

She smiled graciously. 'Yes, I am,' she said.

'I heard you were brilliant in the show tonight.'

Jessica smiled again.

'Thank you.'

The boy paused for a second, then in a rush said, 'May I have your autograph?' and he pulled from his duffle coat pocket a well-filled autograph book.

'I'm not supposed to do this,' he said, 'so don't tell, will you?'

'Absolutely not,' promised Philip.

As she took the book, Jessica gave a laugh of pure joy as she noticed the name of Jessie Matthews on the adjacent page.

Philip laughed too. 'The very first of many,' he said.

'Am I really the first? Will you put that please?'

'What is your name?'

'Marcel.' And she wrote: '*To Marcel, the first of all, with love, Jessica Sherwood.*'

And she wrote it on the page adjacent to the autograph of Jessie Matthews.

Critically acclaimed musical comedy actress, Jessica Sherwood celebrates her wildly successful appearance in the Olympic Gaieties with budding impresario, the Hon Philip Cranleigh. Is there romance in the air? The aristocratic pair insist that they are 'just good friends'

And for once, this was the case. 'Just good friends' was what they remained. Jessica revelled in her success. Never in her young life had she been paid that kind of attention and Philip watched her progress with propriety amusement. He was so proud of her and quite contentedly accepted the fact that his protégée's time would now be taken up by boundless other admirers. He escorted her to functions and was always on hand to build her up whenever she began to feel insecure, which became less and less often. It was rare now that she lapsed into her old voice. She no longer had to think before she spoke and having discovered the power of her voice, she used it even when speaking to herself. Both she and Philip knew now that she was capable of independence and this suited them both. Philip felt his work had been accomplished, his ugly duckling had been successfully metamorphosed into a swan and he started looking around for something else to occupy his mind. His beloved sister Melissa was about to start her first term at the Webber Douglas in the autumn and he was looking forward to having her around.

What Philip did not know was that Jessica's thoughts turned continually to another member of his family, the man who had given her a lift all those years ago in Northampton and his words to her

'Let me see you again when you are all grown up.'

His final admonition about her accent had been suitably adhered to and accomplished. The accent had disappeared. She felt, and hardly dared hope that now she would be worthy of Marcus and she racked her brains to find a way in she could bump into him – as if by chance.

*

Jessica had news.

'I've found it!' she cried. 'The perfect flat. Now you can be rid of me at last!'

She had been increasingly aware that her presence in the Lowndes Square apartment was becoming more and more inconvenient for Philip. He couldn't live in his parents' house forever. So she had recently spent much time with estate agents. Philip had asked to accompany her, but she said, 'No this is something I must do on my own'. However, being a very young, female person meant that she was not able to take out a mortgage on her own account and if Philip hadn't intervened she would have told them what to do with their mortgage. Instead, on his insistence, she allowed him to be her sponsor on the required papers.

The flat was in Ebury Street, small but compact and she fell deeply in love with it on sight. It was perfect for a single person, even though the rooms were small, the bedroom only just big enough to contain the large double bed she bought to furnish it.

'A single bed looks sort of pathetic,' she said seriously, much to Philip's amusement.

Furnishing the flat became the centre of her life. She had acquired a taste for the kind of antique furniture that filled the Lowndes Square apartment and she haunted the salerooms, happily bidding at auctions and signing autographs for the other punters who often found her of more interest than the goods they were aiming for.

Although refusing point blank to let Philip have any part of choosing the décor, she didn't object when he gently talked her out of her mistakes, as he compensated for his interference by wholeheartedly approving her good taste.

After a couple of months' hard work, she was ready to move in and all that was necessary was to get the water heater to be set in operation. The afternoon before this was to happen, she was taking a leisurely bath in the Lowndes Square apartment when she heard the front door slam.

'Who's that?' She knew it wouldn't be Philip, who never dropped in without ringing her first.

She doubted that anyone could get through the security system, but she still felt alarmed that it might be an intruder. Always one to meet a problem head on, she vacated the bath, wrapped herself in a big bath towed, armed herself with a bath brush and marched boldly and bare footedly into the sitting room to find out what was going on.

The man, warming his backside at the open fire and drinking whisky was the one person in the world she was most longing to see.

Marcus smiled and looked at her with a quizzical expression.

'I know I haven't come to the wrong place. The setting is correct –only the dramatis personae is rather more interesting than I expected. Where's my kid brother?'

'He's at the house,' she stammered. 'He doesn't live here at the moment.'

'And you would be –?'

'Jessica. Jessica Sherwood' and forgetting she was holding the bath brush, held out her hand.

'And I am Marcus Cranleigh. Don't bother to shake hands,' he said, 'the result might be disastrous. I gather you were in the bath when I came in.'

'You gather correctly.'

'So – I don't mean to be rude, but what are you doing here? Has my brother suddenly become a landlord? Or are you just here for the bath? No don't bother to answer that. Allow me to think the worst. It's bound to be more interesting than the naked truth' he gave a cheeky grin 'If you'll pardon the somewhat indiscreet expression.'

Jessica wrapped the towel even more firmly around herself. She was disconcerted by the fact that Marcus didn't recognise her and couldn't decide whether or not it was a compliment. He didn't even show any interest when she mentioned her name – the name constantly bandied around in the national press. This was hurtful and disconcerting. She was used to being recognised wherever she went.

'I think I'd better get dressed,' she said.

'Oh must you?' and his lazy eyes sparkled with admiration. 'I think you look pretty nice the way you are.'

'Nevertheless I think it would be wise.'

'Have a drink first.' He moved to the drinks cupboard and taking out another glass, poured another drink and freshened his own.

'Soda?' he asked.

'Why don't you make yourself at home?' she remarked with heavy irony.

'It may have escaped your notice,' he said, 'But I am actually at home. What I need to know is what you are doing here. Are you my brother's bit of fluff?'

'Don't be so vulgar,' she said, losing in her embarrassment her hard won sophistication. She bit her tongue, realising she might be giving herself away. She was not wrong.

'Hang on,' he said and he looked her in the face, searchingly, 'It's all coming back to me now. Those eyes'

'Nice to know you've managed to raise yours above my neckline,' she retorted tartly.

'Don't I know you from somewhere?'

'Do you really not remember me?'

'Yes, yes I do,' he said slowly, 'I get the feeling I'd remember you better if you let that towel slip.'

She could feel a blush covering her entire body. She had forgotten for just a moment how he had first seen her. He snapped his fingers in triumph.

'You're the little girl from the nudie show. Am I right?'

'That's right. You told me to look you up when I grew up.'

'It seems I saved you the trouble. Well, well well. Old Philip. He's a dark horse and no mistake. You've turned out rather well.'

As he spoke he took her by the shoulder and looked directly into her eyes. She felt the warmth of his fingers shoot through her body like an electric shock.

'I really must go and get dressed,' she said.

'Yes, do,' he let her go, 'Why don't I take you out to lunch?'

'In the middle of the afternoon?'

'You know me. I can get a meal and a decent bottle of wine any time of the day or night. What do you say?'

'What could she say but 'Yes please.'

She felt the sheer sexual power of him surrounding her like a blast of warm air. She felt hot and had an irresistible urge to drop the towel – to say *'take me, forget lunch'.*

*

During the meal at a small Soho dining room, the Maitre D' who seemed to understand the situation left them alone. They exchanged long looks as they devoured the oysters. Jessica had by now got used to the slippery slimy things and was even able to give a decent impersonation of enjoyment and she licked her lips and kept her eyes on Marcus as he watched her flickering tongue.

She was enveloped in a wave of euphoria, of incredible lightness like something with no gravity, something not of this planet. But none of this interfered with her appetite and she devoured all the delights he ordered to be set in front of her. After the oysters came the most succulent chateaubriand, along with a bottle of the best wine that Baron Philippe de Rothschild could offer, finishing with crepes Suzettes and champagne. It was with a wrench that she tore herself away to go to work and she arrived at the theatre, ever so slightly drunk and still in a state of euphoria. She was amazed that nobody appeared to notice and treated her in the same way as usual. Now she knew beyond all doubt that she was superior to her colleagues. She had just had lunch with the most glamorous man in the world. It was a pity that he had sworn her to the utmost secrecy. She was dying to tell somebody her joy, but Marcus had been insistent that it must remain a secret. It was important that Philip must not hear of their meeting. Too often Philip had had his nose put out of joint by his elder brother and Marcus was anxious that it should not happen again. Philip came to pick her up after the show, she complained of a headache. As usual he treated her chivalrously, recommended aspirin and hot milk and drove her back to the apartment where Marcus was waiting for her.

24.

'I have a bottle of something jolly for us,' said Marcus.

The champagne bottle was nestling in an ice bucket near the bed. On a tray on the bedside table were two glasses and a crystal dish of Beluga in crushed ice sitting in a silver dish with its own silver spoon.

'You must be starving,' he said as he spooned some of the fish eggs into her mouth.

'You'll make me fat as a house,' she protested.

'Feed me,' he demanded, and putting his lips close to hers, he licked the caviar from her mouth with his tongue. She opened her mouth, wanting to devour him along with the caviar.

Abruptly he left her and poured a single glass of wine.

'From now on we eat from the same spoon, drink from the same glass,' he said, and taking a mouthful of the champagne, he emptied it between her eager lips before he kissed her.

His kiss made her know beyond all doubt that this was what she had been living for. She purred like a small sleek cat as he fondled and stroked her and undressed her carefully and slowly, kissing every part of her trembling body. Her loins burned for him and the wetness came pouring from her.

'Please, please,' she gasped, not even really knowing what it was she was asking for. At last he gently pushed open her legs and inserted his hardness into her body. She gasped with the shock of the sudden pain, but it didn't last long. Within seconds she was moving with him, feeling wave upon wave of dizzy sensations, until the final shock of her orgasm coursed through her body over and over again, leaving her weak and spent. He rolled away from her. She made a little cry of protest as she felt him go and then she laid there, her arms behind her head, warm, drowsy and full of well being. He got up and sat himself down on the side of the bed.

His face had a strange – almost angry expression.

She sat up. 'What is it?' she asked.

'I didn't expect you to still be a virgin.'

Her shock at hearing this word, which was not in common parlance even in the chorus dressing room was intensified by the bitterness with which he spat it out.

She tried to laugh if off, but he had made her feel young and stupid. His attitude had changed towards her. No longer the romantic Lothario, he seemed troubled, ill at ease.

'I've never done it before,' she admitted.
'Why didn't you say something – stop me?'
'Why should I?'
'Because – you deserve something better. I'm sorry, I thought that you and my brother... that you were just a—'
'You thought I was a tart?'
'No, no of course not. But most girls these days are – well – experienced – Especially those in the theatre. How did you manage to survive Starkers in Paradise?'

She tried to reassure him.

'It's only because I've always been too busy. Please don't worry about Philip. He's just a friend.'

'Yes, I see that now. Even so. I would rather you didn't...'

Jessica lifted herself on to her elbows and looked up at him.

'Didn't what?'

He took her by the shoulders and looked hard into her face.

'I have to ask you understand. I'm not like Philip – not a serious kind of person. This cannot grow into anything; do you understand? Please believe me.'

She shrugged, scared by the look in his eyes. He went on.

'I thought it was just a bit of fun, for you and for me. You didn't protest. You just let me.'

'I wanted you to...' she said, and the tears welled up in her eyes.

'I didn't mean to hurt you,' said Marcus and he turned his head away. 'I didn't realise you were such a child.'

She wanted to reassure him, he looked so devastated. She sat up, and taking his face in her hands, gently turned his face towards her.

'Please don't worry about me – or about Philip. I told you, he's just a friend.'

Marcus rose and walked away from her. She sat there on the bed, watching him.

At last he turned and spoke,

'Now look here, old girl. You have to understand that there can never be any question of anything serious between us. I swear if I'd known I'd never have – I can only apologise for what I did.' He turned and came over to her. 'Will you forgive me?'

She smiled a shaky smile. 'I do understand, I do.'

'There is something else – I want you to promise me something.'

'Anything.'

'Don't ever let Philip know that we have been together.'

'Why? He is bound to find out if you come to the flat.'

He turned away with a sigh.

She knew she sounded like a little girl. She realised she was pleading and it hurt her pride, but she had to say it:

'We can be together again, can't we?'

At the woebegone look in her face, he laughed and kissed her on the forehead.

'You're such a little thing,' he said. 'All right, but let it be our secret.'

She knew she mustn't protest further, and he gave an encouraging smile.

'It's more fun that way isn't it? Our secret love affair.'

She nodded.

'Promise?'

'I promise,' she said, crossing her fingers. Secret for the moment, she thought to herself, *then – we shall see.*

'I'm moving out of here tomorrow,' she said aloud. 'I can't keep Philip out of his apartment for ever. I have already found a flat.'

'That solves a lot of problems,' he said, smiling.

'Then we can be – loving friends,' she said, stroking his face.

She felt she was now well in charge of the situation.

His face cleared immediately. He was let off the hook.

'I'm so glad', he said. 'One can never be sure. I don't want to sound conceited, but you do see, if one is going to be a lord one day ridiculous as it is – one does get pursued by all the debs in town – not to mention their awful mothers.'

'Of course one does', she said, 'but I'm not a deb and even if my mother were alive, she wouldn't even have heard of you.'

He gave a relieved laugh.

'Of course not. You're a decent little soul. You'd never expect... well of course not. Come on, let's have another drink.'

'Yes, good idea,' she cried, but as he turned away to pour the champagne, she looked at his back and narrowed her eyes speculatively. She knew now what she had to do.

Now it was Jessica who had to take control.

She felt she was irresistible; she was strong, stronger than he. She put her arms around his bare back and ran her hands over the soft fair hair that covered his chest. His back straightened as he felt her soft touch and she allowed her hands to drop to the other, silky hairs below.

As she stroked and caressed him, he turned to face her, delight and astonishment on his face. She stroked his member, which had become strangely limp after their embarrassing conversation.

'Poor old chap needs a drink,' she said, and taking the glass of wine, she poured it over him, then, kneeling before him, she licked him dry. He responded instantly, his penis leaping up again, as strong and solid as before, and she gently guided him home to the place where he belonged.

25.

The din was deafening in the Green Room as the eager students greeted each other after the vacation.

Maxine felt shy, but excited, not able to follow any of the conversations but certain emphatic words and phrases spilled out loud and clear.

'Too divine – Darling – Larry Olivier – So wretched – darling – and Gielgud – Madly exciting – darling –Ashcroft and Scofield – too thrilling darling – deadly boring – and What about Diana Wynyard!'

*

She didn't have the courage to join in until she had learned the vocabulary and mastered the cadences of their voices – both of which were different from any she'd ever heard before.

'Are you a new Bug too?' said a clear cut voice in her left ear. The voice belonged to an attractive face with a smile that stretched from ear to ear, the possessor of more teeth than one would have thought possible in a human being. The girl, tall and abnormally slender, dressed like something out of Vogue, her warm honey brown hair spilled over her shoulders in a riot of curls.

The twinkling amber eyes sparkled, reflecting Maxine's own excitement. When Maxine nodded, the girl put both hands over her ears and jerked her head in the direction of the door. Maxine followed her out into the relative quiet of the corridor.

'I'm Melissa Cranleigh,' said the girl, holding out her hand 'What's your name?'

'Maxine – Maxine Fletcher.'

'I knew you'd have a pretty name,' said the girl, 'I saw you standing there, looking so distinguished. Adore your hair. How do you get it so shiny?'

Maxine laughed and shook her head, showing off the glossy blondness of her long straight hair. She wanted to return the compliment couldn't quite find the confidence.

'God what a racket – almost like being back at school,' said Melissa, 'I'd forgotten about the noise. I believe we are registering in pairs. I hope my pair will be you.'

Maxine felt extraordinarily happy at being singled out by this stunning young person.

The two girls looked about them, drawn together by their companionable newness.

'Most of the new bugs have come straight from school. Makes me feel quite old,' laughed Melissa, 'I've already done a training course. What about you?'

'I was at University for a year.'

'Gosh you must be an intelligent one. Lucky you. I went to model school It was appalling, the girls were rivetingly stupid Are you ambitious?' she asked all in one breath.

Maxine stopped to think

'Of course,' she said, 'Otherwise there would be no point in being here, would there?'

'Oh yes', laughed Melissa, 'A lot of these are debs. They treat it as a finishing school. I'm not interested in all that stuff. I'm gong to be an actress – in musical comedy. That's what I really want to do.'

'Melissa Cranleigh, Maxine Fletcher,' Miss Pigeon, the tight lipped secretary called out their names, 'Come to registry please'

The two girls looked at each other. Already their names were being linked. It seemed like an omen for the next two years.

Their reception by Miss Pigeon was quite different. Maxine had forced her face into a friendly smile and was rewarded with a frosty one. On the contrary Melissa was greeted like a princess.

'How are you dear?' said Miss Pigeon, 'it is such a delight to have you here. I know you'll do well.'

'Thank you. I hope I will', replied Melissa with a dazzling smile and as Miss Pigeon was preparing the registration form, she turned and made a silly face at Maxine, making her giggle and causing Miss Pigeon to lookup at her sharply.

'That Miss Pigeon really hates me,' said Maxine when they got out into the corridor again, 'She looks at me as if I was a bluebottle or something. What did you do to make her so friendly?'

Melissa gave a rueful laugh.

'It was what my fathers and grandfathers did.'

'Sorry?'

'I'll get it over with. I am a Hon!'

'What – I don't understand.'

'By some freak I was born daughter to a peer of the realm. It impresses some people.'

'It impresses me,' laughed Maxine.

'Well don't let it, for God's sake. Promise me you'll instantly forget what I just said.'

'Difficult,' she replied, 'I've never met a Hon before.'

At this moment, there was a commotion coming from the green room and the two girls went to see what was happening. A hatch had flown open revealing a small man in brown overalls, a tea urn and dishes of rock cakes and pastry buns with strips of coconut on top. Maxine took a rock cake, the other buns looked too much like ground rice chizzicks. Melissa had a cup of tea without milk or sugar.

'Aren't you having a bun?'

'Daren't,' replied the other, 'I need to watch my waistline. I have a madly distressing tendency to put on weight. Don't you have to diet at all?'

Maxine shook her head and looked at the slender silhouette of her friend. Apart from the proudly erect bosom there wasn't an ounce of flesh on her person.

As they stood there, one of the older students came over. She was dressed in what appeared to be the unofficial uniform of the establishment. Rolled up blue jeans, an emerald green cross over blouse, high heeled sling back shoes, a pony tail, heavy green eye shadow and a ludicrously long cigarette holder held between somewhat dirty paws, resplendent with fingernails with chipped red varnish.

'Love your clothes darling,' drawled the girl to Melissa, 'Where do you shop – Harrods?'

Melissa blushed slightly at the condescension the girl's tone.

'Dior,' she said sweetly and turned away to wink at Maxine.

Later, when all the preliminaries had been dealt with, timetables copied and parts distributed, Melissa and Maxine agreed to go for coffee at the

Chanticleer Café just down the road from the school. The place was full of screaming students and there was no place to sit.

Melissa shouted above the din.

'Let's get out of here.'

Back in Gloucester Road, they sought the sanctuary of the Hereford Arms, a quiet old-fashioned pub on the corner of Clareville Street.

'Phew,' said Melissa, 'I expect we'll get used to it.'

'They may calm down later when they've all done their hello darlings,' suggested Maxine, 'I can't believe they can go on like this for the whole term.'

Neither had spent much time in pubs and didn't know what to ask for.

'We could have whisky and soda,' suggested Melissa. 'That's quite a smart drink to have.'

So they sat there, sipping their drinks, pretending to be sophisticated, and giggling occasionally.

'You told old Pigeon toes that you were staying at a hostel. Can that be true?'

Maxine grimaced at the question

'The Mary Considine Hostel for Young Ladies,'

'Mary who? Who was Mary Considine?'

'A Victorian philanthropist of some kind who spent her time saving fallen women.'

'Who was she saving them for?' giggled Melissa, already feeling no pain after her large whisky.'

'She put them all in this hostel and reformed them – pretty viciously I think.'

Melissa's mouth dropped open in awe

'How absolutely ghastly.'

'Excruciating.' agreed Maxine and went on to explain further

'I've only been there a couple of days so far, but I don't think I can put up with it much longer. It's like living in a convent.'

'Tell me more. It sounds wonderful, I love it, I love it.'

'Right. For a start – breakfast finishes FINISHES at eight thirty in the morning. Fried eggs, hard in the middle, black frills round the edges and swimming in grease. Cold baked beans on soggy toast, then more cold burnt toast and margarine and stewed tea.'

'My dear – your waistline! You don't eat it of course!'

'I try not to. I leave it lying on the plate. Then somebody comes round and asks if I'm feeling ill. They think it's evil to waste food – and dieting is a crime – total vanity.'

'I didn't know such places exist. It's like something out of Dickens.'

'Then there's the ten o'clock curfew,' went on Maxine, enjoying Melissa's rapt interest. 'We have to get permission from our parents if we are out for the evening and there's any chance that we won't get back in time.'

'Do you get locked out if you don't make the curfew?'

'I presume so. I haven't tried it yet.'

'What about boyfriends?'

'No such thing. Except on Saturdays when they are allowed to come to tea.'

'Visiting time at the Scrubs!'

'At eleven o'clock in the evening the electricity is switched off at the mains. No light, no heat, no hot water. You can't study. There's nothing for it but to go to sleep – or die.'

'You've got to get away from there.'

'Then there are the signs up all over *Do not leave rings in the bath* That's supposed to be a joke by the way.'

'Oh ha ha.'

'Exactly. Then there's *leave the bathroom the way you would wish to find it!*'

'With a bath full of Gerard Philippe!'

'Wow, yes – Don't you adore him?'

'He's my idol!'

'Me too!'

They smiled at each other.

'Obviously you can't stay there,' said Melissa at last. 'Why don't you come and stay with me?'

'I thought you said you lived with your parents in Knightsbridge.'

'No that was just to placate old Pigeon toes. The flat belongs to my two brothers. It's absolutely huge and Philip is the only one who spends time there and he's out a lot. He worries about me on my own so he would be really happy if he saw I had a responsible sort of friend like you.'

'I'm not sure I like being a responsible person.'

'How about it?'

Maxine had to think for a minute. She was tempted.

'It depends on the cost really. I'm on a grant you know.'

'There you are you see? A thoroughly responsible answer. It won't cost anything and we'll go halves on the food – that is the stuff we don't nick from the fridge. Think about it. First I'll arrange for you to meet my wonderful brothers.'

*

Drama School gave Maxine a whole new perspective on life. From despising her shape, she learned to love and appreciate her body, to look upon it as a very useful and efficient piece of equipment to use in her career.

She basked in Melissa's honest admiration of her. Something she had never experienced before. It was so good to meet someone who genuinely seemed to like her – to be impressed by her.

Melissa was the best friend a girl could have. There was not a trace of envy or rivalry within her nature. With her encyclopaedic knowledge of fashion and make up, she helped Maxine to choose her clothes. – To make use of her assets. She was even persuaded to wear the white jumper, which somehow didn't look so cheap and tarty anymore.

'It's so sexy.' Melissa cried and Maxine realised that his was a word that could be a compliment rather than a kind of sneer.

Melissa had rhapsodised about her brothers, both of whom she worshipped in different ways. Marcus, who was the heir to the title and family fortune, was the most ravishing, exciting man in the entire world. He was a rally driver whose passion was racing cars and racy women in almost equal measure. Melissa built up such a picture of this dashing creature that Maxine imagined him as a sort of cross between Gerard Philippe and Clark Gable.

She also had boundless admiration for her other brother, Philip, who may not be as dashing as Marcus but was clever and good and wise. He had recently given up his ambition to become a priest and was working with a West End Theatre impresario, intending one day to start his own production company.

'You'll have no trouble getting work then,' said Maxine

'Don't be too sure. Nepotism doesn't run in our family,' laughed Melissa 'But you'll have no problem getting work Max, what with your face and figure.'

'And my talent?'

'I shouldn't worry too much about that. Philip says there are a million girls with talent – but few have the LOOK. That's what you have!'

*

Marcus came to pick up his sister one day in his flashy red sports car and took them both for a drink at the Grenadier pub in Knightsbridge. To her infinite sadness, she did not share her friend's admiration for her big brother. Marcus was big and well built and with his fair complexion and blonde hair, he could have been mistaken for a Nordic god – but Maxine found there was something repellent about him. Maybe it was his heady lidded, light coloured eyes with their pale lashes and his fleshy sensual mouth that gave him a dissolute air and also reminded her vividly of Mr Parkes, the enemy she had left behind in Hull. The way he looked at her, boldly undressing and assessing her, brought back all her adolescent feelings of insecurity and distrust.

'*He thinks he's God's gift to womankind,*' she thought to herself.

'Isn't he gorgeous?' asked Melissa. 'And he really admires you. He said you were very sexy and had great breasts!'

Maxine smiled without replying, but she shuddered inwardly.

After this disappointment she dreaded meeting Philip. According to Melissa he was a vastly superior person but sounded to Maxine like a pompous bore.

This time she was agreeably surprised. The two brothers could have come from a different planet. Philip's kindness and sensitivity shone out from his long thin face. His voice, despite its pronounced Oxford timbre, was gentle and his large eyes sparkled with intelligence and humour from behind his horn-rimmed spectacles. Like his sister, he was warm and friendly and made Maxine feel secure and admired. She had not known that she could find that kind of friendship from a man and she knew instantly that they would become soul mates.

'Philip knows everybody in the West End.' boasted Melissa 'have you heard of Jessica Sherwood? The musical comedy star! He takes her out regularly. People say she's his mistress.'

'Sherwood? I used to live in Sherwood Park!'

'How blissful! You are lucky to live in a place with such a pretty name.'

'It gave me strange ideas. I always thought I was Robin Hood. It was a huge shock to my system when I grew breasts and turned into Maid Marion.'

'Someday I'm going to play Robin Hood and be a world famous principal boy,' said Melissa.

'I thought you wanted to be Peter Pan.'

'That too' and she laughed.

26.

Melissa lost no time in getting Maxine ensconced in Lowndes Square. 'How brilliant to have a room all to myself. You can't imagine what hell it was sharing at the hostel.'

Melissa was a little disappointed

'You don't need to be all alone, there are two beds in my room.'

'But this means we can both have a bit of privacy when we need it.'

Melissa, having been brought up in a close and loving family, found it difficult to understand – privacy was something she had never had and never wanted, but she respected Maxine's wishes and gave in gracefully. happy that she had found a congenial flatmate.

After Maxine had moved in Philip took them both out to L'escargot for lunch in the hope that Jessica might join them. It was not often young Drama students got the chance to meet real working actors and Philip thought it would be a treat for them. He rang her number; for once she was there.

'Hello Jess, Philip.'

'Oh hello darling I haven't seen you for ages.'

Jessica had been so busy rehearsing, meeting press and posing for photographs that every minute of spare time was precious and was being spent with Marcus or thinking of Marcus or waiting for him to call. He was not the most careful or reliable of lovers, but when he did turn up she felt it was worth every minute of waiting. Her main regret was that she didn't see Philip so often; after all, she owed everything to him.

'Did you hear that my young sister is in town?'

Jessica couldn't remember who had told her, was it Philip or Marcus. She decided she ought to keep a diary to check who said what in case she made a terrible mistake.

'Yes, I think you told me she was coming when I was living in your flat. I was quite sorry that I had to move out before she came. I was looking forward to meeting her.'

'Well now's your chance. We're having lunch at L'escargot tomorrow and I wondered whether you would join us. If you can't make lunch, maybe you could have an aperitif with us or even just join us for coffee. How does that sound?'

'Oh that would be lovely,' Marcus was at Silverstone the next day, so there was no danger she would miss him. 'I look forward to it. About one o'clock? I haven't been to L'escargot for ages. I miss the ancient waiters.'

It was not a place much beloved of Marcus. He had crossed swords with the famous grumpy waiters and had decided to eschew the place for ever more.

She didn't know the full story but determined to ask Philip.

Jessica dressed herself beautifully for the meeting. She wanted all members of the Cranleigh family to approve of her, and so she went to a special effort for the young girl. Jessica laughed. Philip spoke of Melissa as if she were a child but she must be just about the same age as Jessica herself. Would they be friends? she thought. It would be nice, She still had only one real girl friend in the world and that was the ever-faithful Mabel Dear Mabel – who reminded her so much of Janie.

Melissa, Maxine and Philip arrived a little early and Philip ordered a bottle of champagne. They were sitting at the inner end of the room and a couple of times Philip looked towards the door to see that familiar figure arriving, but he remembered Jessica's eager voice on the telephone, as if she would be really looking forward to the occasion.

He reassured himself and turned his attention to the menu.

During Philip's discussion with the waiter about what were the choices of the day, Maxine suddenly leaned over to Melissa and said, 'Who is that wonderful looking woman.'

'Where?' said Melissa looking round the room.

'NO no, by the door.'

'But where? I can't see anybody.'

Maxine looked back at the door.

'She was there I swear it.'

Philip had finished his conversation with the waiter and picked up on the conversation.

'What are you talking about?'

'There was this woman at the door. Wonderful she was with bright red hair and wearing a violet suit. Sounds awful I know, but it was remarkably effective. Everyone turned round to look.'

Philip looked puzzled.

'Sounds like Jessica. I don't know any other redhead who would wear purple. I wonder where she went.'

'Well, I'm going to the loo, see if she's in there,' said Melissa getting to her feet.

She returned within a minute or so.

'No signs,' she said.

'Well it's a mystery,' said Philip. 'She was really looking forward to meeting you Mel.'

The waiter came over to their table.

'Excuse me, sir – Mr Cranleigh?'

'Yes.'

'There's a telephone call for you. Will you follow me?'

So the waiter led Philip away to the telephone in the hall.

'I really think I've seen a ghost,' said Maxine, 'It was awfully strange. One minute she was there and then she wasn't.'

'It must have been some mistake,' said Melissa perusing the menu,' Do you like snails?'

Philip arrived back, looking disappointed.

'That was Jessica,' he said, 'She can't make it –something to do with a photograph session. She said she might make coffee, but couldn't promise anything.'

*

Jessica was still trembling when she came out of the telephone booth and fell into the taxi. It had been such a shock seeing Maxine sitting there with Phil. She hadn't set eyes on her since that glimpse she had of her looking through the lace curtains at The Laurels. Someone as hostile as Maxine could give her away, could tell the press that her she was not an upper class young woman but a dirty little girl from the Hull fish docks – and a possible murder suspect.

One day, when her position in the theatre was completely established, it might be possible to let them in on the secret. But for the moment it was important that Marcus should not find out. He seemed very fond of her still but had never broached the subject of marriage. He would be even less inclined to marry her if he knew the truth.

'Where to Miss Sherwood?'

Despite her feelings of panic, she smiled. It never ceased to give her pleasure to be recognised by the people around town Recognised as Jessica Sherwood, though, not as Lil Marsden. Lil Marsden didn't exist. Except in the eyes of Maxine Fletcher. There had been no sign of recognition in the other girl's face but maybe even now she would be regaling Philip and his snobby sister with stories about the dirty little girl from Paradise Street.

She must keep her secret until she felt thoroughly established in the theatre. In a way she had Maxine to thank for her current good fortune. She had been one of the steps along the way. If Maxine hadn't turned her away from The Laurels she might never have come to London, never become a star. But even so Maxine had treated her meanly and one day she would get her own back. At the moment she couldn't think how, but somehow she must get control of her erstwhile enemy. She must also find out how much Maxine knew about her past – about Bill's murder. Having made up her mind on this she told the driver to take her to her destination. Her hastily arranged appointment with Raymond to have her hair done.

27.

'I'm madly bored with being a virgin,' grumbled Melissa. 'It is a little shaming when we are the sexiest girls in the whole school.'

At the Webber D virgins were in the minority – despite the youth of the students most had managed to lose their virginal status by the end of the first term, if not before.

'Yes. It's definitely a liability,' sighed Maxine. 'It's – getting it over with, that's the problem.'

They both had boyfriends. Maxine was constantly escorted by Philip he was a dear kind and affection man but there had never been any question of actual love making between them.

Melissa had captured the attention of Jarvis Leeson, a big dark Australian whose favours had been sought by many of the girls – hardly surprising as at least half of the young men had little interest in making out with the female sex and had already paired off with each other.

Jarvis fell for Melissa like a ton of bricks and was suffering agonies of frustration because she couldn't quite bring herself to sleep with him. Having kept her virginity for so long, she didn't know how to break the ice and from sheer habit pulled away from every time he made the attempt.

'I find it so hard to actually – do it. It seems so madly inelegant – doesn't it – do admit!'

Maxine did admit.

'There's only one thing to do,' decided Melissa. 'Let's do it together.'

'What, me and you?' Maxine remembered her erstwhile reputation as laid out by the anonymous letter received at school.

'Don't be silly, darling,' laughed Melissa. 'We're obviously not *lesbians!*

What I mean is we both do it at the same time!'

'With different people?'

'Yes, just think how gleeful my Jarvis will be – and Philip. Marcus says the only thing wrong with Philip is that he doesn't get his end away often enough.'

'OK. If you're game, so am I.' They shook hands on it.

'By the way,' added Melissa. 'What is it that lesbians *do*?

Maxine laughed and shook her head.

'I don't know. I've never really thought about it.'

'I mean I know what queer men do, it's sort of obvious,' she said with a shudder. 'But women – I mean they don't have the right...apparatus. Do you think they just kiss each other?'

'A bit of cuddling – and stroking perhaps.'

'Mm, that might be nice,' nodded Melissa. 'OK. Well let's get this over with first, then maybe we can explore other possibilities.'

And the two of them dissolved into giggles.

*

'Philip,' said Maxine as they were eating spaghetti at Dino's, 'do you like me?'

Philip looked at her from behind his big spectacles and gave a quick laugh.'

'You are my girl,' he said. 'Of course I like you.'

He put his hand on hers, and for one long moment they looked into each other's faces.

'There's nothing worse than cold spaghetti,' he said and went back to his food.

'Why have you never tried to seduce me?'

Philip was in the middle of winding a long strand of spaghetti on to his fork. He stopped in mid twist.

'What an extraordinary question'

'Have you never thought of it?'

'I think of it quite often' he admitted.

'Then, why not?'

Philip considered for a while.

'I suppose it's because I – never considered it a possibility. Not yet away.'

'Why not?'

'Well, I suppose it's because – this sounds terribly old fashioned – I respect you, your purity, your virginity.'

He looked down at his plate and continued his twirl.

She watched him with narrowed eyes for a while before she replied.

'But that sort of thing doesn't matter any more.'

'Doesn't it?'

'Everybody does it nowadays. Even you – don't you?'

'Er – no, not a lot' he smiled.

She felt it was time to broach s subject that had been worrying her for some time.

'What about that actress, Jessica Sherwood? Everyone says she's your mistress.'

She was happy to note the somewhat startled look that crossed his face.

'Jessica? God no! She's just a kid. We are good chums that's all.'

'A kid? How old is this kid?'

'Well,' he laughed, 'About the same age as you, I suppose.'

'So I'm a kid am I?'

Philip put down his spoon and fork.

'Let me just say I've known her since she was a kid and still think of her like that. There's never been anything like that between us. I just act as her. . Escort when one is required.'

Maxine looked keenly at Philip.

'You're not one are you?'

'One what?' he asked suspiciously.

'A virgin.'

Philip laughed uneasily. 'Don't be silly.'

'So who have you had? I'm broad minded, you can tell me. Prostitutes?'

'I have once, I'm sorry to say. But – Wendy Humble behind the barn, that was my first real experience – on my fifteenth birthday.'

'Wendy Humble, who was she?'

'Oh a strapping wench – the grocer's daughter and the local tart. She'd already had the rest of the village population and Marcus dared me to have a go. I was almost pulverised with fright, but I couldn't welsh on a dare. It was hardly an Oscar winning performance. Afterwards I felt really guilty – she was a sweet generous girl and I should never have used her in such a cavalier fashion. So stricken was my conscience that I told my parents I wanted to marry her.'

Maxine laughed. '*Marry* her? What did they say?'

'They recommended I should wait a while until we were both old enough to know our own minds.'

'Very sensible.'

'Yes – I was enormously relieved. Though a kindly soul, she wasn't all that attractive.'

'So what happened next?'

'We considered ourselves engaged for a while until the following year she threw me over for the blacksmith. They got married, quite hastily and produced three chunky kids in quick succession. They are now living happily ever after'

He joined in her laughter and he covered her hand with his as it lay on the table

This made Maxine almost forget the job unhand. She gently pulled her hand away.

'What else? Any further revelations?'

'Not a lot actually. I soon came to realise that nobody is put in the world simply for other peoples' convenience. That realisation put me off casual relationships for good. So that is why I like to take things slowly'

'Oh come on, you dear old fashioned thing. Melissa and I are considered freaks at school because we are still virgins.

That wasn't quite true, the fact was they had never dared to own up to it. They allowed the rest of the school to think they were vastly experienced and were greatly envied as a result.

'It's so embarrassing' she added.

Philip shrugged slightly and with a gentle smile, continued eating. Maxine took a deep breath

'So, let's do it! Tonight!'

Philip swallowed and pushed his half eaten plate of spaghetti to one side.

'Darling, do you know what you are saying? Apart from anything else, the mechanics would be madly complicated.'

'What do you mean?'

'For a start –Where? In the back row of the cinema? In the back of my car? In some sleazy hotel room in Kings Cross?'

Maxine was shocked at the idea

'Of course not! Is that what other people do?'

'I'm afraid so. We could hardly do it at the flat. It's just not convenient. What would we say to Melissa?'

Now Maxine had the bit between her teeth. She had made a vow to Melissa that they should both divest themselves of the undesirable commodity that very evening.

Maxine crossed her fingers. 'She won't know,' she said.

'She might suspect. This is my kid sister you're talking about. Big brothers are supposed to set a good example'

'I wouldn't want to do anything to upset your darling sister. You don't have to tell her'

'It seems so cold blooded!'

Maxine tossed her head.

'I've made up my mind. If you don't want me I can easily find somebody else,' she said boldly.

He knew she didn't mean it, but he also knew that she meant business. He said no more, paid the bill for their hardly touched spaghetti, and after buying a bottle of wine, walked back with her from South Kensington back to Knightsbridge. Melissa was already there with Jarvis sharing a bottle of wine.

As he poured the last few drops of wine into the glasses, Melissa was beginning to yawn, giving meaning looks at Max, who was finding it difficult to make the required move. Philip opened his bottle and filled all the glasses.

'Well I don't know about you' said Melissa 'but I have work to do. Jarvis, would you come and hear my lines?' and she left the room 'And I wanted a word or two with you about Chekhov'

He needed to no urging. Didn't even say 'Chekhov who?' as he was wont to do.

'Yeah, Chekhov, bonzer – anything I can do to help!' he replied following her eagerly.

Maxine and Philip sat quietly for a while, not speaking, slowly drinking their wine. Now the time had come they were finding it difficult to make a move.

Philip cleared his throat.

'Maxie – I don't think....'

'Be quiet Philip.'

'It doesn't seem right with Melissa in the next room'

'If we go to bed she won't be in the next room any more – will she?'

'Are you absolutely sure this is what you want?'

'Yes. Come on, let's go.'

He looked at her, shaking his head slightly.

'Pull me up' she ordered and she stretched out her arms to him.

Philip crossed over to her and took her hands and kissed them on the backs and then turned them over and kissed her palms.

She purred like a cat and he pulled her to her feet, kissing her quickly on the mouth

'OK, bossy boots. Have it your way,' he said.

And she led him into her room.

28.

Next morning, it was a relief to Melissa and Maxine that Philip had to leave early for an appointment in the West End. They didn't know how Philip would have reacted to Jarvis at the breakfast table.

The three of them sat round the kitchen and ate rice crispies, toast and marmalade and drank instant coffee. They laughed a lot; a little hysterical now the ordeal was over. Maxine and Melissa made silly jokes, conscious that each was wondering how it went.

They eventually made their way to Clareville Street still giggling until the exigencies of dance classes and rehearsals effectively put it out of their minds. But not for long.

'Isn't it AWFUL?' said Melissa to Maxine as soon as they broke for lunch.

Maxine nodded and they picked up their books and made for the Hereford Arms where they had a favourite corner table for gossiping. Melissa waited until they had served themselves with potato crisps and half pints of mild, then exploded into conversation.

'I've never felt such an idiot before' she said. 'Ever since I was three, people have been telling me to keep my knees together – and now THIS!'

Maxine nodded and laughed.

'I feel so sort of empty,' said Melissa 'And sore!'

Maxine didn't feel sore. She felt warm, cosy and loved.

'It's all so... madly messy. Those awful squelching noises – and the smell!!' Melissa went on 'Why in the world do people enjoy it so much. What's all the fuss about?'

Maxine shook her head.

'You are quiet,' said Melissa 'Did it hurt?'

'A bit,' said Maxine.

Melissa persisted in her interrogation.

'How did it feel? Tell me, was it as bad for you?'

Maxine took a deep breath.

'I think I'm in love with your brother,' she said.

*

It was true. Even though their sexual encounter had not exactly made the earth move for either of them – Philip was a little gentle, too concerned about hurting her, about making her feel relaxed and contented, she loved the feeling of him inside her, filling the gap she never knew she had. When he withdrew she ached for his return, but he was not ready for her a second time and she had no idea how to make him rise again. He was too sensitive to her possible embarrassment to show her what to do, or even to help him to an erection.

'I'm sorry,' he kept saying and she took him in her arms like a baby. She felt protective, like a mother with a newborn child. She wanted to love him and hold him.

All through the morning, the thought of his warmth surrounding her. It started deep inside and spread through her whole body.

'Did you have an orgasm?' asked Melissa, 'I didn't.'

Maxine smiled secretly. She had no idea what an orgasm was, but she wasn't about to let on.

Melissa took the secret smile for assent.

'Lucky old you. I'm really pleased it's worked out for the two of you. Philip doesn't fool around, you know. He's a really good person.'

'Yes, he is.'

'Now I'm starving!' said Melissa 'It certainly makes you hungry. Shall I get more crisps?'

'We could go to the ABC and have a Welsh rarebit or something evil like that.'

'Yes why not. To hell with the diet. Today we must celebrate'

Poached eggs on toast having been demolished –

'We must go to Doctor Corvin,' said Melissa.

'Who?'

'The contraceptive doctor. To get Dutch caps fitted – so we don't get pregnant.'

Maxine had a flood of panic 'Is that possible?'

For some reason the thought had never crossed her mind.

Melissa laughed.

'You are so naïve sometimes. What did they teach you at your Yorkshire seminary?'

'Latin and Algebra. They didn't believe in sex.'

'Anyway I don't think there's anything to worry about. They say it never happens the first time anyway'

'Are you sure you know what you're talking about?'

She laughed again.

'Not really. But that's all the more reason to visit Dr Corvin,' she said. 'I'll make the appointments.'

*

The doctor's receptionist was friendly, beautiful and elegantly dressed enough to have figured on the pages of Harper's Bazaar or Vogue, Copies of which were piled up on the small tables scattered around the small waiting room. She was shown to one of the expensive looking red leather armchairs and offered a cup of coffee and the latest copy of 'The Tatler'. She found the Tatler disappointing, full of pictures and stories of people she didn't know although she was thrilled to see a picture of Melissa's brother Marcus seated inside his Ferrari with what she thought of as his cheesy grin smiling out at her. 'He really fancies himself,' she said to herself. 'Not like my darling Philip.'

She laid the Tatler aside and picked up a copy of 'Vogue' and was interested to find underneath it a copy of 'The Heiress' a magazine aimed at teenage girls emerging into puberty. 'Do girls that young come in here for contraceptives?' she thought to herself.

She had been early for the appointment and she was called into the surgery at the exact time arranged.

Maxine found the whole business scary. Dr Corvin a small man with protruding teeth, a heavy foreign accent and a Savile Row suit, was kind enough, but although as a dancer, she had been used to talking about her outer body, she had never had the inclination to discuss her innards. She was not looking forward to the experience.

She lay on his couch, bereft of her lower garments and shivering slightly from the cold.

'I can tell you are not used to people touching you down there' he said 'Don't be afraid.'

After the examination, he told her everything was fine and that he had measured her for the contraceptive. He showed her how to use it. Explained how to apply the contraceptive jelly and how to use the introducer, putting one foot on a chair in order to clear the way, and to make sure the cap was firmly in place by hooking it with two fingers. Then he told her to practise the routine while he watched.

As she followed the instructions she began to feel faint. 'You don't touch yourself very often, do you?' he asked

She shook her head.

When he had finished. he told her to sit down.

'Describe your orgasm,' he said.

She looked at him blankly.

'Very well' he said 'It has been described to me as a kind of fluttering like a flock of birds in your womb, getting stronger, wave upon wave until you feel you can't bear it any more. It takes over your body and your mind. For a moment you almost lose consciousness. Then there is a release, and you feel exhausted, but content'

Maxine nodded 'I expect that's about it,' she said.

If this was an orgasm it was not what had happened with Philip, but to her horror, what the doctor had described in his cool clinical way was similar to the sensation she remembered from dreams about Leslie Parkes.

This thought distressed her so much that she almost didn't see Marcus's red Ferrari outside the doctor's surgery. There was a woman sitting beside him. Maxine could see her red hair, her violet coloured coat and hat and the silver fox fur thrown casually over her shoulder. She had seen the girl before – but couldn't remember exactly when. As she passed them slowly, she saw they were kissing. A lovers' kiss deep and long. Melissa had always told her how Marcus avoided any kind of involvement. He certainly didn't seem to be avoiding this one.

Marcus looked up and saw her and then quickly looked away as if he didn't want to be seen or acknowledged. The girl emerged from the car and Marcus put his foot on the gas pedal and drove noisily away. The girl looked after him until he disappeared from view and then entered the surgery of Dr Corvin.

When Maxine got home, she tucked the equipment at the bottom of her undies drawer and there it remained. Maxine could not bring herself to perform the necessary functions without remembering the doctor's words or her emotions over the dreaded Mr Parkes.

She realised that her friendship with Philip was not dependent on sex. That however romantically she was in love with him, he wasn't the one who could set her body on fire. Maybe she should just give passion a miss. It could be something that was not for her.

29.

'The test was positive, Miss Sherwood,' said Dr Corvin with a jovial smile. 'You are going to be a mother.'

'Thank you,' she said, and her heart was beating so hard she thought he must surely be aware of it.

'Is this good news or bad' he said and got ready a suitable expression for whatever her reply was to be.

'I have a boyfriend,' she said.

'Yes of course. Otherwise—' The doctor stopped and looked at her quizzically.

For three weeks now she had been pushing the thought of pregnancy resolutely out of her mind. Her personal publicity, the fact that the press had fallen in love with her, meant that her position within Mr Black's company was getting stronger by the day. On Philip's suggestion, he had commissioned a well-known writer to construct a show around her. Already, again with Philip's help she had started work on some of the numbers he had written and she realised that this was her big chance. She had ignored her late period, her feelings of nausea when she awoke each morning. Her will power and concentration overcame any apprehension she might be harbouring. But now she had to face the truth. How would she tell Marcus? And even more uneasily she wondered how to tell Philip. As far as the world was concerned, Philip was her escort and the secret of her affair with Marcus was well kept.

The current show had at least four months to run, she would be able to handle that she was convinced – and the new show would take at least a year before it was ready to be presented.

'After all' she thought to herself, 'I can learn the lines and practise the songs even when I can't dance any more.'

'Marcus will make a wonderful father,' she thought. 'What a beautiful baby we shall have – and what a lucky one, born into such privilege.'

She was still crazily in love with Marcus and the fact that the child she was bearing might one day inherit a title filled her with such pride. The girl who was once Lil Marsden, the dirty little girl who had ruffled the feathers of that snobbish Maxine would be mother to a lord. It hardly bore thinking of.

Dr Corvin cut into her thoughts.

'Tell me about your fiancé, Miss Sherwood. Will he be pleased? Is he a nice man?'

Jessica gave a happy laugh 'He's wonderful' she cried.

'Good, good' the doctor leaned forward in his chair and resting his elbows on the desk and putting his two forefingers together under his chin, lowered his voice.

'If you should wish for a termination. I might be able to help. I have a colleague who is a specialist in such things.'

Jessica knew that many of the girls she worked with had endured abortions. Some of them treated it as casually as a cold in the head. On the other hand, her friend Gladys, who had been to a less than reputable woman, had suffered enormously and her chances of future motherhood had been reduced considerably.

'Isn't that against the law?'

The doctor smiled.

'Sometimes laws are not sensible'

'But surely it is dangerous'

'Not in the least, except to the doctor who performs it. You would have to keep all knowledge to yourself'

'I see'

'I'll give you his number just in case. Obviously I must not arrange the appointment for you'

Jessica took the card that he tossed on to the desk

'No one must know where you got the number,' he said.

'Thank you. I doubt if I'll be using it, but thank you'

'In that case, I expect to see you in two weeks. I shall make the necessary arrangements for ante natal care'

Her mind was already made up. The baby was what she wanted – what she needed to make up for all the love and kindness she had missed as a child.

The fact that Marcus had a title was almost too good to be true.

'That'll show them' she said to herself she said as she sank into the back of her taxi.

Show who? Who was she trying to impress? Her family had long disappeared from her life and she was glad to be rid of them. Only little Jamie occasionally entered her thoughts and she wondered what had happened to him. But she had no desire to see him or any of the rest of them. She was no longer Lil Marsden; she was Jessica Sherwood – a different person entirely.

No matter how she tried to convince herself of this, she kept on remembering that awful night when Bill had turned up and destroyed the happiness of the whole family.

It wasn't as if they would miss her over much. Having lived through the war, her brothers had got used to the idea of people just coming and going – sometimes disappearing forever.

Maybe when she was totally secure in her profession she would be able to own up about her past, but she wasn't ready for that yet. She imagined the look on Maxine's face when she was introduced to the future Lady Cranleigh. Maxine – yes it would be worthwhile impressing that bitch!

First of all she must break the news to Marcus.

*

'I went to see Dr Corvin today.'

Philip immediately looked concerned.

'Are you not well?' he asked

She laughed 'No, but I went to see him about.. . 'suddenly, idiotically she couldn't say the word. 'So that I don't get pregnant'

'You mean contraception? He's a contraceptive doctor?'

'I expect he does other things as well. But yes, that is why I went. I'm sorry I stupidly couldn't think of the word' and she laughed nervously.

'I'm not surprised. Why did you want to do something like that?'

'Well – Melissa – she thought it was a good idea. She told me about him'

Philip's eyes, usually so open and honest, narrowed a little

'You told her – about us?'

'Well naturally, she's my friend'

'And she's my sister. I don't like the idea of that.'

'Why not?'

'It changes things.'

'How? I don't want to get pregnant, do I?'

'Why not?'

'Well of course I don't. I don't expect to have to give up my career before I get started.'

'Your career?'

'Yes. My career as an actress.'

Why was he being so obtuse?

He offered a cigarette from his case and taking one for himself, he lit them both with his gold Dunlop lighter. He blew out a puff of smoke.

'Don't you want to get married, have children?'

'Of course I don't. I've got a career'.

'It's a very hard life. Do you think you are ready for it?'

'I will be when I've finished at the Webber D.'

'I don't like to think of you in the middle of all that rough and tumble'

'But what about your friend Jessica. You didn't worry about her, did you?'

'No. She's tough, she can cope. Anyway she would never have any trouble getting work, she is amazingly talented.'

'And I'm not? You've never even seen me on stage.'

He took her hand tenderly.

'Darling you are the most beautiful girl I've ever seen. As a movie star or in musical comedy you would be a knockout. But you are not going to be cast as a dramatic actress. You are, well, just too beautiful'

'That is ridiculous'

'No, it will be difficult for you to get people to take you seriously. Not until you are a great deal older anyway.'

'And you think your precious Jessica has more chance than I of doing serious work? What has she done besides musical comedy?'

'I'm sorry you never met her, if you did you would understand. She has an interesting face. She has personality. She's tough. She's elegant but not – well not obviously sexy. The theatre holds nothing but heartbreak for a girl like you.'

'Oh not that old song again. Well I'm sorry to disappoint you or disillusion you, but I am going to be a serious actress even if I don't get any leading roles until I'*m* old – about thirty five or something. So in the meantime I'll play all the little juves until I get old enough to do the proper stuff. I'll think about having children once I'm established.'

'You may change your mind when you get out in the big wide world.'

'Why are you so keen on children anyway?'

Philip looked away before replying. 'I've always wanted children.'

'Then you'd better find go and find someone to have one with.'

Philip gave a short laugh and stubbed out his cigarette.

'Are we having a lovers' tiff do you think?' he said holding out his arms. She took a step back.

'I have always thought of you as a good friend,' she said.

'And?'

'But I couldn't have anything to do with someone who obviously had so little regard for what I want to do with my life.'

'Maxine I'm sorry. I just want to take care of you, that's all.'

'Well forget that. I've been looked after all my life. It's time for me take care of myself – and I want to chose my own way of doing it. If I come a cropper at least it will be a result of what I wanted. Do you understand me?'

Philip shook his head. He was at a loss.

'So you just go and faff around your bloody Jessica. Maybe she'll give you a baby. It might take after its supremely talented mother – and its pompous bloody vicar of a father. All right?'

Philip shrugged his shoulders, lost for words

'I shall move out of here tomorrow. I'm sorry about Melissa but I can't stay here with you.'

He turned to leave.

'By the way, I brought you this. I thought you'd be interested'

He took a magazine out of his briefcase.

'I don't suppose you will be after all, but you may like to look at it nevertheless.'

'What is it?'

'Just a big spread on Jessica. Thought it might amuse you.'

He threw the magazine down on the coffee table and, closing his briefcase, left the room.

Melissa was aghast when she heard the news and agreed with Maxine that Philip had behaved in an abominable fashion. She wasted no time in telling him that she also had been to Dr Corvin. On seeing the shock on his face, she compounded the felony by telling him about the pact she had made with Maxine.

'How do you feel being the subject of an experiment?' she said. 'You should have felt flattered that my sexy friend, who could have any man she wanted, should have chosen you, should have trusted you to relieve her of her virginity. And all you can do is insult her.'

'By wanting her as my wife?' he said feebly.

'Certainly. She is going to be an actress. She doesn't want to be messing about with nappies and feeding bottles – *ugh* how disgusting. You should be ashamed of yourself.'

Philip shook his head.

'Well she's talking of leaving here. You must stop her.'

'Of course I will. She is my friend. If anyone should go it ought to be you.'

'I won't go as far as that. I'll just keep out of the way.'

'I should hope you will,' snapped Melissa.

Left to herself Maxine picked up the magazine left there by Philip. She turned to the page that Philip had mentioned bore a picture of Jessica. 'I want to see why she should be encouraged in her career while I'm just thought of as good enough to marry.'

What she saw set her heart thumping. The violet eyes that looked up at her from the magazine were only too familiar. Dirty little Lil Marsden calling herself Jessica Sherwood – how dare she use the name of our street.

Maxine knew now that this was also the face in the Escargot. The girl in the violet dress – and – the girl who was kissing Marcus so passionately in the red sports car

Fascinated she read the article. It seemed Jessica was a daughter of one of the noblest families in the land. 'They didn't approve of my being an actress and cut me off without a penny. I had to make my own way in the world.'

Maxine laughed bitterly. At least she doesn't give Philip any credit for her success. Daughter of a noble family indeed. She thought of the day she met her in Paradise Street, ragged and barefoot. One day she was going to tell the world that not only was the famous star a scrubby little urchin from the wrong side of Hull, but also – she could be a murderess.

Maxine didn't even tell Melissa about her findings. 'There will come a time she said to herself, when I can speak out. But not yet – I must chose my moment.'

30.

Jessica dressed herself sensibly in a pair of pale green cashmere slacks and matching jersey. She put on her long camel coast and picked up a scarf to wrap around her head.

She sat in her brand new sports care that Philip had decided was important for her image and she drove up to Brands Hatch.

She caught up with Marcus as he was preparing himself for the race.

'Marcus!'

He greeted her with a warm smile.

'What are you doing here?'

Jessica snuggled up to him

'I missed you' 'Oh you sweet thing. I miss you too' he kissed her lovingly.

'How did you ever get the time out of your busy schedule to come and see me?'

'I made the time,' she laughed and he hugged her again.

'Oh I'm sorry' he said 'I've put oil over your beautiful coat.'

'Never mind'

'That is an unusually cavalier attitude my darling'

'Well, you see. I need to talk to you – seriously'

'Oh no. That sounds ominous' he looked at her with comic apprehension.

'No, not really. It's very sweet, but it is important' and she gave him her sweetest smile, her confidence began to dwindle as she saw an alien look come into his face. Apprehension, disbelief as if he knew what she was going to tell him.

'We can't talk now' he said hastily 'I'm just about to enter the.'

Suddenly the words burst out almost of their own accord.

'We're going to have a baby'

Disbelieving she saw his anger rise. His eye blazed. She had never seen him angry and it scared her. He gripped her shoulders hard.

'I hope this is a joke'

'Well no. Isn't it wonderful?' she asked limply, by this time not able to convince herself.

'So what do you intend to do about it?'

'Me do something. It is our baby'

'No, no it isn't. Remember I said No commitment.'

'But surely—'

'No please. I do not wish to continue this conversation. I'll give you the money to get rid of it and then that will be the end of it. In fact it's probably time we split up.'

Jessica drew back. The look in his eyes did not bode well for her. He really seemed to mean what he said.

'You haven't had time to think about it. Won't your parents be pleased to have an heir to the title?'

'The title. So, that's your little game is it? Does little Jessie have ambitions above her station?'

'No, no I never thought of it before'

'Well I'm sorry. I'm afraid, far from being pleased, my parents would be horrified. They have other plans for their daughter in law. I told you. I told you right from the beginning that there could be no commitment.'

Her tears started to spill over. He relented a little and pulled her to him, smiling encouragingly'

'Come on old girl. Be sensible. I know several good doctors who will do the job. I'll write you a cheque as soon as the race is over. I can't think about it right now'

He kissed her hurriedly and went off to climb into his racing vehicle.

As she waited for the race to begin, thoughts were scampering through her mind at an alarming rate. She looked at the card that Dr. Corvin had given her, tore it up into pieces and let the pieces fall to the ground. It just wasn't possible. Already she had begun to think of the child as a person, there was no question of losing it.

'Don't worry little Hon' she said 'we'll get that Daddy of yours to make an honest woman of your mother.' and she gently patted the not yet visible bump on her tummy 'But I wont' think of that now' she added with a giggle 'I'll think of it tomorrow'

She was there when it happened. She watched as the car ran over the edge. She saw it crash into the other dead car. She saw it burst into flames. The attendants ran out to drag the body of Marcus from the car. She knew it was too late. She knew he was dead.

She also knew that although she felt no emotion at all, she could not trust herself to drive her car back to town. She calmly arranged for her car to be picked up later and she booked a taxi to take her all the way back to London.

One back in her apartment she called the theatre to say she was unwell and to alert the understudy. She retired to her bedroom to lie down and try to get her thoughts together.

31.

When Jess heard the doorbell, she jumped up. For one wild moment she thought it was Marcus who had forgotten his key – That the whole tragic business has been a dream. But it was Philip, standing on the threshold white and shaking.

'Please forgive me for barging in like this. I thought you would be at the theatre, and then I saw your light. I needed to talk to someone'

She helped him in and sat him down on a chair.

'Have you got a drink?' he asked.

She went over to the drinks cupboard and poured him a generous whisky. He drank it down in one gulp.

'I shouldn't burden you with my troubles.'

'Don't be silly. What's the matter?' she asked.

'My brother – an accident – in his car.'

Jessica felt as if an ice cold hand had gripped her heart- The cold spreading to her head and to her feet. She tried to control her voice.

'Marcus?'

'I suppose we should have been prepared for something like this, but he was – he'd always been so – lucky!'

Suddenly, she didn't want to hear what she knew he was going to say. She wanted to stop him saying it. She took his glass and went over to the drinks cupboard. She poured him another hearty glass. She took out another glass for herself, and then thought better of it. She needed all her faculties, working and in good order, to cope with what she knew was about to happen. Instead she took a slug out of his glass and brought it over to him. He was sitting with ashen face, just gazing into the distance. She put the drink in his hand. He took it and thanked her automatically. She sat down opposite him and composed herself to listen.

'Racing is dangerous I knew, but I didn't believe that it could happen, that he could actually...die.'

Jessica felt a wave of anger – how dare he take over her unhappiness. Marcus' death was her tragedy, not his. Sometimes she forgot that Marcus and Philip were brothers. The only time she had ever seen them together was at that first meeting.

'But how?'

'The car crashed. The car he was driving. At the race track'

'There's no doubt?'

'No. none' Philip nodded. His frozen calm had broken now. His eyes were streaming with tears.

'I am so sorry' she said through stiff lips.

Jessica poured another drink for him and a small one for herself. She didn't feel like crying. Marcus was gone. She saw with an awful vividness the car as it burst into flames in front of her eyes. His death was something she had never dared to think about, and yet, in some strange way, she knew it was inevitable.

'There can be no doubt. He couldn't survive a crash like that. The car was shattered, it burst into flames…It's taken me a while to believe it…I've been wandering about, trying to understand. Trying to make myself believe that it really could happen.'

Jessica took him in her arms and stroked his head.

'I can't expect you to understand what Marcus meant to me,' he murmured. 'He was such a special kind of person.'

Jessica smiled silently and went on stroking his head. Her brain was pinning. There was only one thing that could possibly occupy her mind at the moment and that was the child she was carrying. It seemed that it was all that was left of him. It must be allowed to live.

Philip was weeping copiously now. She held him tightly in her arms and allowed him to sob his heart out. All the time her head was spinning with thoughts, with ideas.

As the sobs subsided, she led him, like a lamb into her bedroom and persuaded him to lie down on the bed. She lay down beside him and, almost as if she were in a dream, she opened the buttons of his shirt and slipped her hand inside it. She had a slight feeling of revulsion as she did so, her hand was so used o the feel of Marcus and she searched in vain for the silky hair that covered him. She had expected Philip to feel the same, but the difference was so great, his body so smooth – almost hairless, she felt cheated. He kept very still and she could feel the pounding of his heart. She knew now that she had to go on. He allowed her to remove his shirt and vest, and then her fingers started – almost of their own accord to unbutton his trousers.

'What are you doing, Jess?' he murmured

'Just leave everything to me' she whispered 'I'll make you fell better'

Like a small child he lay, looking up at her, his astonishment mingling with the pain in his large blue eyes. She tugged down his rousers and saw his limp cock lying there, soft and lifeless.

She took it between her hands and massaged it gently, then more vigorously as it continued to lay inert in her grasp. She was startled, remembering how Marcus had leapt into life at a single touch from her little hand. She knew now what she was doing and it made her surprised at herself – though not ashamed.

She bent over him and placed her lips around his prick and licked it gently with her tongue. After a while she was rewarded by a tiny twitch as it came briefly to life and then died again.

'What's the matter with you?' she whispered furiously in her frustration.

Two huge tears appeared in his eyes and rolled down his cheeks – a sob racked his thin body.

She took him again into her arms and pressed her naked body hard against his, murmuring little words of endearment, willing him to come to life.

'I'm sorry, Jess' he said at last and he fell into a deep exhausted sleep.

She stood up and went over to the dressing table, studying herself in the looking glass. She looked as lovely as ever. Her body was slender and firm and her skin still had the silken sheen it had worn before. The pain had not yet reached her face – the pain that was postponing its arrival until the vital work had been completed. She ran her hands up and down her slender hips, feeling the warm sensuality of her flesh, and putting her hand between her legs, felt the wetness there. Her face, flushed and lips swollen with desire, looked more beautiful than ever before. She fought against relieving herself of the burden of desire. She thought of the tiny creature living within her body. She must do her duty. Somehow she had to make this man make love to her.

She went back to the bad and lay down beside him. He turned and clutched her as if she were a teddy bear. She hugged him back, and like two babes in the wood, they fell asleep.

An hour later, she wakened as she felt something stiff and hard between them. Gently she climbed on top of him and inserted the now erect penis into her body. She moved her hips from side to side, willing him to come. After a minute or two she was rewarded by a small spurt of sperm into her body and she lay down beside him for a while, exhausted. He had not opened his eyes, or made one movement to suggest that he know what was happening. She rose from the bed, leaving him lying there like a dead body, and after running herself a generously perfumed bath, got into the hot steaming water and tried to clean his sperm from inside her body.

This would be the last, the only time, she vowed. She had done her duty by the baby. The child and the heir to the earldom were safe, but nothing more would contaminate that precious seed of Marcus that was growing within her.

When she came out of the bathroom, Philip had woken up and put on his clothes. He was sitting fully dressed in the armchair, his head in his hands. He looked up as she approached, but wouldn't meet her eyes.

'Jess, forgive me,' he said.

She thought he was referring to his lack of potency and reassured him.

'Please don't worry' she said lightly 'No one could expect anything more in the circumstances'

'How could I have been so selfish?'

She touched his hand reassuringly 'Don't worry'

'It was the shock. I just lost my head when you were being so kind tome. I never wanted to take advantage of you. I wanted to respect you – always.'

Jessica could hardly believe her ears. He was apologising for seducing her.

Philip slipped down off the chair on to his knees. He grasped her hands.

'Oh Jess. I know you must be disgusted by what happened. You are so young and don't realise the wrong I've done you'

'Philip dear, please don't worry about it. You were distraught. How could I refuse you anything at such a time?'

'You don't understand my dear. What we did was wrong. Suppose you got ...pregnant'

Despite herself Jessica started to laugh. It was hysterical laughter born out of misery and her sudden relief. He held her close

'Hush my dear you mustn't. It's been a great shock to you' Jessica loved Philip more at that moment than she could have thought possible. The tears came to her eyes.

After Philip left, she picked up the snapshot of Marcus that she kept under her pillow and she kissed it.

'Your son will be just fine' she said.

And then the misery of her loss was brought home to her and she wept the bitter tears she had been storing up until her work was accomplished.

Act Three:

Curtain Up

1.

Maxine found she was not strong enough to lift the teapot. As she tried to pour the tea, she found her hand shaking so much that the tea splashed out all over the tablecloth.

Tears welled up in her eyes. The first tears she had shed for her father since she had received her mother's call – she had not even cried when she saw him lying there waxen and still in his coffin. It was not her father who lay there, and she regarded the body with the kind of impersonal interest that she would bestow on a carved image. It was the simple, everyday act of pouring a cup of tea that showed her inner turmoil.

She put the teapot down with a thump and as she did so she felt a kindly hand on her shoulder.

'Bereavement is a terrible thing. I understand. I've been through it myself recently. I lost my dear Letitia last year'

Maxine turned to look at Leslie Parkes in amazement. She had never thought of Letty as being short for Letitia. It gave Mrs Parkes a whole new perspective. Maxine's heart gave a jump of guilty joy at the demise of her enemy. She had always known it was Letty who had written the poison pen letters, who had tried to destroy her, just as she had always known that no one would ever believe it. She assembled her features into an expression of suitable solemnity.

'I'm so sorry,' she said 'I didn't know.'

'I miss her,' said Mr Parkes and, as the final shock to her system, she noticed his eyes filling with tears.

The short conversation and its revelations restored Maxine's equilibrium and she was able to continue with her task. When she had finished pouring the tea 'I'm sorry' she said again as she saw his eyes still upon her.

Her hands full of cups of tea, she nodded to him and turned to walk away – only to feel his hand on her buttocks. Speechless with anger, she stepped back as sharply as she could, grinding her stiletto into his foot and cracking his knuckles against the wall. He gave a strangled shout and she turned and was satisfied to see his face contorted with pain, 'Sorry' she said, and she felt a whole lot better.

After the funeral, they all went back to the Laurels and Maxine was able to meet and talk freely with the mourners.

She was pleased to see her Aunt Irene looking dignified and brave, but making no effort to hide her inner sorrow. Maxine had a pang of regret at the change in her. The aquiline features had somehow blunted and her body thickened from lack of exercise. As head of a girls' school in Greenock, she was no longer as physically active as before. Scot, her husband stayed by her side, always within touching distance of her. His grief at the loss of his friend was almost as palpable as her own.

By contrast Connie looked beautiful and elegant in her plain black dress and was as sociable as ever, smiling graciously, acting the hostess as if this was an ordinary party. There was not a trace of the despair she must be feeling. Leslie Parkes danced attendance on her as usual, and Maxine watched him out of the corner of her eye as her mother blushed and giggled at his attention.

Maxine was sad that Irene was unable to stay. She had taken the time off near the end of term to come to the funeral. She was unable to take longer as the girls were in the middle of their exams. Scot too was rushing back north to his job as chief accountant for the local rope works. It seemed Connie would be on her own so Maxine decided she must miss the last few weeks at the Webber D and stay with her for a while. She had never been back for longer than a weekend since she first shook the dust of Hull from her feet. She felt like a complete stranger – it was not the town that had changed, but she was now a different person. She spent her days going on long walks, retracing the footsteps of her childhood, which seemed now to have happened to somebody else.

Connie was still handling herself well. The fact that she was alone and also the presence of her actress daughter made her popular with neighbours and friends and the house was hardly ever free of visitors.

A couple of days before Maxine left to go back to London she received a letter from Melissa, enclosing a press cutting.

Actress marries aristocrat. Jessica Sherwood, famous revue star is to marry Philip, son of Lord and Lady Belize. The wedding will take place quietly owing to the recent tragic death of their elder son Marcus.

Dearest Maxine, What about this? Who would ever believe that Philip would turn out to be such a rat? If it had been darling Marcus – well – he was always a naughty boy. I was longing to have you as a sister in law, but it seems that wretched slut was actually pregnant. Jessica Sherwood isn't even her real name. Do you know what her real name is? Lillian Marsden – would you believe? The thought that she will be Lady Belize one day makes me sick. I don't know what the parents were thinking of to allow it. I'm still feeling so sad about poor sweet Marcus. I'm afraid he was always my favourite brother – even more so, now. Please call me. I'll be here for you if you need loving care, so come back soon.

Reading the letter Maxine had the same feeling of unreality as she had looking at her father's dead body. It just didn't seem possible that her lover and friend, Philip should betray her like this. That he should actually have married the woman that had been the bane of her life. They had been in love in a gentle kind of way. He had accepted the fact that she wouldn't marry him until she had established her career. She had claimed that marriage was a pointless exercise unless it was to provide a home for children. He seemed to have taken her at her word.

There was something puzzling her at the back of her mind, but she couldn't quite bring it to the surface.

Maxine went out for a walk to clear her head. As she walked down the lane, the same lane that Ada had taken her when they used to go to church together. She thought of Ada and her multiple pregnancies and wondered idly what had happened to all those babies that she had produced and never seen again. Ada was now happily living with her husband and child in Ponders End, a suburb of London. Although Maxine had the address, it had never occurred to her to look them up. Her life had become too full. Every minute of her days in London was taken up with some kind of activity. In addition to her curriculum, she was taking extra classes in singing and dancing. Her evenings were spent learning lines, visits to theatres and cinemas, but mainly talking, talking to Melissa, her fellow students – and to Philip. There came a pang of despair as she realised that they may never be the same to each other as before.

As the familiar mud track neared its end, Maxine saw that it had been turned into concrete road and that there were houses being built all down one side. It made her sad to think that her countryside, the country lanes, the fields and secret hiding places were all being turned into one vast housing estate.

The town centre was gradually rebuilding itself, but most of it was still just a huge bomb site. The bombing had taken the heart out of the town. Although she remembered little of the town before the blitz, the sight of it now depressed her and she could hardly wait to get back to Kensington where life was a little more gracious.

She thought of how dreadful it must have been for her father who had been so used to living in happier, more salubrious surroundings, to have to die in the town so damaged and defeated by war. She began to understand the causes of his madness; the distress and anxiety that had led to the fatal stroke and his untimely death.

She walked down the concrete road, missing the feeling of squelching mud beneath her shoes. The concrete was cold and hard like the grey unforgiving light of the north east coast. As she emerged from the lane she became aware of the brand new sporty MG that was standing in the road, waiting for her.

'Hiya,' said Mr Parkes emerging from the car and opening the door. 'Want a lift?'

'No thank you.'

'Please. I saw you walking down the road and waited specially for you. I was hoping you would come and have a drink with me.'

'I don't go into pubs – not round here anyway.'

'Who said anything about pubs? I have wine at home. I do need to talk to you; to explain a few things.'

She looked closely at his face. He did look kind. His eyes earnestly begged her to be nice to him. He was like a big Labrador puppy – bouncy and full of affection. She made up her mind.

'Very well,' she said. 'It would be nice to talk – like adults.'

'Exactly' and he helped her into the passenger seat as carefully as if she was Queen Victoria and he was John Brown.

It was not a long drive, but Mr Parkes was keen to show off his new acquisition – his new MG. so he took the long way round, whizzing down the lane, taking the corners at a lick. Maxine wondered idly whether Letty had forbidden him this little luxury in the past and now he was enjoying it as a child might enjoy a forbidden toy. His childish delight made her warm to him a little and she was grateful that his concentration on driving helped to keep his hands off her knees and on the wheel. Eventually, by various circuitous routes they arrived. The house, the familiar square edifice, set back from the road and surrounded by a well-kept garden, seemed strangely bleak and empty. When they went into the large bay windowed drawing room, there was something missing; something that had always been there in the past.

'I got rid of all the plants when Letitia died' he said 'She had green fingers. They just took one look at me and died'

She laughed. Suddenly Letty had become Letitia – was this more dignified for a dead person?

'I don't care for indoor plants all that much' she replied 'I especially dislike cut flowers; they make me so uncomfortable, being asked to give up their lives just to decorate our houses. I think they should be left alone with space to grow, to germinate and be free!

'I do so agree' he said 'Would you like red wine? I have a rather good bottle already opened. Rather good stuff. If you want white I can open a bottle for you. Or would you prefer something shorter?' he was anxious to please.

'Red is fine' she said and he poured it for her and handed her the glass.

She took the glass from him and looked around, wondering where to sit.

'Let's not stay in here,' he said. 'I find it depressing. We'll take the wine into my study.'

He picked up the bottle and led the way.

The study was obviously where he lived. Two big comfortable chairs covered in brown leather, one of which bore his imprint. There was a desk, some books, a daybed and a television.

'Do you have a T.V set?' he asked.

'My mother has. I don't have time to watch in London.'

He waited for her to take one of the big chairs, then sat himself down and sipped his wine.

'It must be really lonely for you down South.'

'No, no it's not. I like it.'

'Better than here?'

'Yes. I feel much lonelier here.'

Despite herself, she could feel the tears welling up. She did feel lonely. She was homesick for London. London was home. Since she had been living there she realised that she had been lonely all her life.

'Please, please don't cry,' he said. 'You must miss your father.'

'Yes, yes I do' but it was impossible to explain how she missed him; Impossible to explain that she had been missing him since she was six years old. His illness had changed him into a different person. She meant no more to him than a pet pony kept out in the yard. The father she missed was the one who took her in his arms and sat her on his knee when she was six years old, not the stranger who couldn't bear to touch her – hardly even to speak to her since he had come back from the war.

She couldn't explain this to him. She was ashamed of crying, especially ashamed of crying in from of him – her enemy, who strangely enough seemed to have become her friend. He got up and came towards here, and kneeling before her, wrapped his arms around her. She leant against, sobbing. After the sobs had subsided a little, he stood up and pulled her to her feet.

She could never have believed that such a thing could happen, but she found herself with him on the day bed, both of them wrestling to tear off each other's clothes. They hardly waited until they were naked before he entered her and pumped his seed into her body. As he did so she felt the orgasmic waves travelling though her body as if she was alive with electricity. She came; it seemed like for an hour. He stayed inside her until the spasms had ended and then he slipped off her, but still held her in his arms, stroking her, murmuring to her.

As he held her close his fingers started feeling her back, making long sweeps down across her back and buttocks, she felt herself squirm each time he came near to the centre of her until eventually he slipped his hand between her legs from behind and thrust fingers into the space between 'Good girl' he breathed 'You're ready for me again' She wasn't listening to what he said, she just wanted to feel his enlarged penis inside her filling up the gap, making her complete. This time the orgasms came more gently, she felt as if she had known this man all her life, that he was the closest, most loving person she had ever known. After it was over he rolled away from her and she fell into an exhausted sleep, deep and dreamless. By the time she woke the daylight had almost gone. He lay besides her dozing. She tried to work out what had happened and why she felt so contented. She remembered his arms around her, his body latched to hers. She reached for him again, wanting more. He woke at her touch and laughed at her eagerness.

Always wanting more' he said 'Just like your mother'

It was as if someone had poured a bucket of cold water over her. She pulled away from him. All desire vanished.

'My mother?' she asked, and she edged herself off the bed.

He sat up, looked at her and laughed – the laugh she had always hated 'heh heh heh'

'Connie – she's a right little goer, just like you'

She turned to look at him, not knowing what to say or what to do.

'I always knew you were a little scrubber just like your mother' he said 'Right from the world go. You and your toffee nose arrogance. You're no better than you should be. Just a fat little slut.'

The words slut and scrubber washed over her, but 'fat' was the one that got her.

Her passion frustrated, she was overtaken by a blind rage. Without even stopping to think, she grabbed a heavy lamp that was on the bedside table and with strength almost amounting to the superhuman brought it crashing down on his head.

He sank back on the cushions a drop of blood trickling down from the injury on his head.

She regarded his prone body with horror and disgust. Even inert as he was, the mocking eyes shut; she was revolted by his body. The black hair on his chest, the thick trunk-like thighs, and the fat, limp penis, everything about him was alien and distasteful what had she been doing? A moment's madness had led her into this situation.

She pondered whether to leave him to recover on his own, or whether to try and rouse him. She picked up her clothes and her shoulder bag from the floor and went to the downstairs cloakroom where she washed herself thoroughly at the sink, replaced her clothes and sorted out her makeup. She noticed dispassionately that she was looking rather well.

When she returned to the study, she saw that Parkes appeared to be sleeping. She held her compact mirror in front of his mouth and checked that he was breathing. She went back to the cloakroom and after soaking a flannel in cold water, applied it to the small wound on his head. As she did so, he opened his eyes.

'What happened?'

'I hit you,' she said.

'What on earth for?'

'You said I was fat.'

'Are you going now?' he asked as she slung her bag over her shoulder.

'Yes.'

'You can see yourself out,' he said.

She briefly wondered what had happened to his early chivalry/; But she provided the answer as soon as she asked herself the question. He would be anything, do anything to get his way. She was ashamed and yet at the same time she gloried in her shame.

2.

She let herself out of the house and walked down his garden path with a jaunty step. As she clicked the garden gate, she saw his next door neighbour Mrs Sopwith clipping her hedge. The hedge was in no need of trimming. It was obviously just an excuse. Mrs Sopwith was lying in wait.

'Good evening Mrs Sopwith. What a lovely day it's been' Maxine cried and it gave her a spark of elation to see the shocked expression on the old weather-beaten face as if she knew exactly what the girl had been up to. Now the whole village would know she had been seen leaving the house of Leslie Parkes.

'Private tennis lessons, no doubt' she would sniff to her W.I. cronies 'And we all know what that means.'

But it didn't matter to her any more what people thought of her. She'd grown up now and wouldn't let them hurt her ever again. One of the good parts about growing up is that one hears all the rumours and gossip flying around. Mr Parkes and his pupils were a common talking point amongst his neighbours. The sadness was that in all probability Connie was a subject for gossip just as grandmother Renton had been before her.

'Obviously' thought Maxine *'I come from a family of whores – how exciting. Perhaps a better word would be courtesans, that had a better ring to it'*

No wonder the family was despised in respectable circles. What a joke! And what a relief not to have to care, not to have to live amongst those petty minded people. Now at last she knew what sex was all about. *'Next time I see Philip I shall know exactly what to do'* she thought.

Then she remembered Melissa's letter. So Philip was lost to her was he? Not now she was a scarlet woman he wasn't. She decided there and then that from now on she would just go out and get what she wanted and the devil take the rest. She wanted Philip and she would have him sooner or later.

Connie was waiting for Maxine at the window. When Irene left, the family had moved down to the ground floor – more convenient for Jim, who might fall down the long flight of stairs. Maxine was staying in the basement with Aunt Paget who was still caring for the house and catering to Connie's needs. But the two floors in which Maxine had spent her childhood had been let to a Professor and his wife. They were intelligent and civilised and good friends to Connie. The two ladies lunched together frequently and together tended the garden which was too big for one person. Maxine saw her mother's face at the window of what had been Irene's office. She looked pale and tired, but dignified, distinguished. It was impossible to imagine her romping with Leslie Parkes but then it was impossible to imagine Maxine doing the same thing. Both scenarios made the mind boggle.

Her mother looked up and smiled at Maxine as she came through the door. Connie had been waiting anxiously for her. She had come to rely on her daughter's company since Jim's death and was dreading her departure. Plans were racing though her head as to how she could manage to keep her at home.

'Would you like some tea darling?'

she asked, jumping to her feet with a coquettish twirl.

'Why is she trying to flirt with me?' thought Maxine, and she looked at her mother in a new light. Connie had always flirted with everyone. Nothing wrong about that; it was a charming trait. But all her daughter could see now was the vision of Connie in bed with Mr Parkes. Her head started to whirl and she had an almost irresistible desire to smack her mother across the face. Suddenly she was a rival. They had shared a lover. She hated and despised her mother – a woman twice her age -for falling into the same trap of sex. With an effort of will she controlled her violent impulse and gave her mother a charming smile instead.

'Have you something a bit stronger?'

'Sherry, gin, scotch? We have quite a selection; left over from the funeral. I know what you would like – how about a whisky and soda?'

Maxine nodded and Connie went to the sideboard and started to pour the drinks.

'You were a long time' she said.

'I met somebody'

Connie turned with a smile 'Who...who did you meet?'

'Your friend, Mr Parkes'

Connie's smile remained frozen to her face.

'Mr Parkes, you persist in calling him Mr. He has a name you know. Why don't you call him Leslie?'

'Because that would assume a non-existent degree of intimacy between us. I call him Mr Parkes because he is a turd'

Connie laughed – a note of hysteria in her voice.

'He has always been so kind to me' she said 'He misses Letitia a lot'

Maxine smiled. Letitia again! The name Letty had disappeared along with her body at the crematorium.

'I daresay he does,' was all she said 'What's for dinner? I'm starving,'

That night when she was lying asleep, she heard her mother come into her room. She had never done that even when Maxine was a child and terrified of the dark. Maxine was even more startLed when Connie pulled back the covers and climbed in beside her. She tried to keep her breathing even, tried not to let on that she was awake.

'Maxie' whispered Connie 'Are you awake?'

Maxine nearly giggled at the stupid question. She remained still even when Connie put her arms around her. Connie had not held her since she was a small child. 'We are not a kissing family' she would say with pride. Maxine felt cold with embarrassment, unable to respond in any way to the call for comfort that her mother was hoping for. She just held her breath and kept still until she felt able to release herself as if turning in her sleep. She felt sick. She remembered that it was in this bed that Parkes had first tried to seduce her. She must get away from here... and soon. She must go back immediately to the life she knew and enjoyed. Her roots must disappear one way or another. She remembered how Jessica had re invented herself. If the dirty girl could do it, so could she.

Despite Connie's protests, Maxine packed up her belongings the next morning.

'You don't have to go back to that terrible life. 'said Connie 'Why don't you stay here. You could go to the University and finish your degree. Your father left some money for you to do that'

Maxine looked into her mother's face. She knew now that she actually hated her, always had. The woman who had nearly ruined her life.

'Why did you always made me wear green?' she asked suddenly.

'Darling, what are you talking about? Green was always your favourite colour. I never made you do anything, never in your whole life. You have always made your own decisions'

Maxine smiled and shook her head.

'Please, stay with me' pleaded Connie 'Just for a little while.

'I have to work. Rehearsals start again on Tuesday. I'm playing the lead.'

Her mother came with her to the station and saw her into the Yorkshire Pullman.

Maxine mounted the train, greeted by a steward in his burgundy waistcoat and bow tie. He settled her at a table for two by the window. Connie sat opposite her.

'You don't have to wait,' she said to her mother.

'Will you be all right?'

'Of course I will. Please go. There is nothing worse than waiting for a train to leave'

'Have you got plenty of magazines?'

'You have bought me all that I could possibly need.'

She laid the magazines down on the table and picked up the menu.

'If you're sure'

'Yes, I'm sure. Please leave me now' and Maxine stood up to encourage her to go.

Connie reluctantly got to her feet and wriggled out from behind the table. Then suddenly she leaned over and hugged her daughter.

'Take care' she said 'Come again soon'

As they stood close Maxine looked over her mother's head and realised how tiny and frail she was – something she had never noticed before. She gave Connie a kiss on the cheek and held her for a polite moment before extricating herself and escorting the older woman to the door of the compartment and helped her down the steep step on to the platform. Then leaving her mother on the platform, she got quickly back into the train and, shutting the door, leaned over the open window and kissed her mother again, quickly on the forehead.

'Please don't hang about. I'm going to sit down now' she said and she went back to her seat.

She settled herself down, picking up one of the glossy magazines her mother had bought her, but at the sound of a knocking on the window, she looked up and saw her mother's face, peering at her through the window. Tears were pouring down her face. Maxine raised herself from her seat, wanting suddenly to rush out and comfort her, but at that moment the train started to move and Connie was left there on the platform.

3.

'Is anybody sitting here?' said the tall young man.

Maxine looked up, her face wet with the tears she had shed without knowing it. She gave a pallid smile and shook her head.

The young man sat down opposite her, shaking away his straight dark auburn hair which hung down over his forehead.

'I'm sorry' he said, concerned when he saw the tears 'Are you in some kind of trouble?'

Maxine laughed unsteadily and looked for a tissue to wipe the wetness from her face.

The young man pulled out a clean white handkerchief from his top pocket. She smiled her thanks and wiped her face.

'Sorry, it's just… saying goodbye,' she said.

The young man smiled back at her. He had nice teeth, shiny white, slightly uneven. His face had a look of health, thin, tanned with a glow under his skin.

'I'm Stan Harvey' he said 'Are you going all the way to London?'

'Yes' she replied' My name is Maxine, Maxine Fletcher'

They shook hands, his hand was smooth and warm, comforting.

'May I buy you a drink?' he asked

'I was going to have wine with my dinner'

'Then say no more. I know just the thing. Do you mind if I order?'

Maxine agreed. Intrigued by his self possession.

He called the steward and ordered a bottle of champagne.

'Is this some kind of celebration?'

'Yes' said Stan 'A Celebration of our meeting'

Maxine giggled. She had never been so propositioned. It was doing her ego a power of good. The young man looked at her with denim blue eyes. He was quite obviously smitten by her appearance.

'You are very beautiful' he said, and he looked at her as if she was something especially good to eat. 'I don't like to see someone as beautiful as you in such distress. Who was it you were saying goodbye to? A lover?'

'My mother,' she replied, 'And my life here in this town.'

When the champagne arrived, he took the bottle from the waiter and insisted on pouring it himself. He poured it carefully and perfectly, all the time looking into her face. He passed one of the glasses over to her.

'Here's to our meeting' he said.

Maxine drank the wine quickly and he poured her another one, smiling the while

Despite there were still food shortages, the Yorkshire Pullman provided an excellent dinner – managing to provide wonderful meals without sacrificing rations. A grapefruit cocktail, followed by fried strips of plaice, roast venison, fruit parfait, biscuits and cheese. They had finished the champagne by the time the fish had been consumed, so they went on to have a decent burgundy to accompany the venison. By the time she arrived at Peterborough, Maxine was feeling no pain.

She had not felt such an affinity with a man since Philip. It was as if he were an elder brother who had made the same journey through life as she had. He too had left Yorkshire at an early age to live in the great metropolis and he too was always amazed how totally different life was south of Watford. As Maxine saw the stations slip past from Brough to Grantham to Peterborough, she felt herself changing into the London person she had become. For some reason she felt obliged to confide in him. To her own secret amazement, she told the whole story of her dealings with Leslie Parkes and her mother and her new determination to become a scarlet woman. She realised she was drunk, but then so was he. They were well into a folie a deux.

'Have you ever done it in the toilet?' he asked suddenly.

'No' she giggled

'Then you go along there and I'll join you in a short time. I'll knock three times on the door and you can let me in'

Maxine, giggling irresistibly, made her way down the rocking train to the door marked Toilet. She shut herself in and still giggling, slipped off her panties and waited for his knock.

She stood by the wash basin as he squeezed past her and sat on the lavatory seat and tried, with fumbling fingers to unbutton his flies. She pushed his hands aside and did it for him, setting free his slender but lively prick. He pulled her down to him, to straddle him as he sat and she helped him to insert himself into her body. It was hardly a successful seduction as he came almost immediately and neither of them could concentrate for laughing. Afterwards, she dismounted and they tidied each other, fastening buttons and adjusting their clothes. Maxine left first and, still laughing manoeuvred her way back to the seat where she sat heavily, still helpless with laughter. She laughed even more when he came back trying desperately hard to look dignified and took his place opposite her. The steward arrived with the coffee pot and poured them another cup of coffee. She thought he looked at them with disgust, so she gave him a bewitching smile and was disappointed to see he didn't respond.

'I expect you come from Hull' she said to his solemn face and Stan again burst into paroxysms of laughter.

'No I come from Solihull' replied the waiter.

'Near enough' said Stan.

Stan took out his wallet when the bill came and, though he raised his eyebrows at her as if about to refuse her offer to half the bill, she didn't offer, just smiled at him sweetly.

'So this is what it's like being a bitch' she thought to herself 'I like it'

He left a huge tip for the steward.

'This is on the company,' he said. 'Expenses'.

'I don't even know what your company is,' said Maxine. 'It's amazing how little I know about you even though you seem like an old friend.'

'Perhaps it's as well,' he said. 'I don't suppose we shall ever meet again.'

'Ships that pass in the night,' she said.

'Ships that collide in the night! Anyway I've enjoyed meeting you. Scarlet woman.'

'Me too – but just tell me, what kind of business are you in?'

'I'm an agent,' he said. 'I work for a theatrical agency.'

4.

Philip was delighted when Jessica told him she was pregnant and immediately started wedding plans. There was a problem that had to be resolved.

'I'm aware that your real name is not Jessica Sherwood,' he said. 'You would have to give your real name.'

Jessica had a cold fear running over her.

'That is impossible,' she said. 'I couldn't give my real name.'

'I guessed as much. What is your real name – Jessica Brown isn't it?'

She laughed uneasily.

'Not even Jessica,' she said, 'I'm just an out and out fraud.'

'That doesn't matter. What I'm saying is that you can't use a false name on the marriage certificate.'

'But I'm a different person now.'

He laughed.

'Not really, under all that glamour you are still the same little tyke I saw in 'Starkers in Paradise'. I think I fell in love with you right then. I said as much to Marcus but he just made fun of me.'

The mention of Marcus made them quiet for a while as each had their own thoughts of him.

'Anyway, we'll have to sort that out. We'll keep everything as quiet as we can. The family will understand that we don't want to interrupt the mourning for the death of Marcus. We'll tell them afterwards. They will understand if I tell them you were pregnant. They wouldn't want a celebration.'

'I suppose not'.

'They are good people', he said, 'But what about your people? Your parents? You never speak of them.'

'My mother and my father are both dead.'

'Brothers and sisters?'

Jessica paused. She had no wish to bring her brothers into her life.

'Only my sister Janie and she was killed by a doodlc bug.'

'You poor kid. You are alone in the world. Have you no friends who know about your background?'

'There is Vera – but I don't know where she is'. Jessica had no wish to meet up with anyone from the past, no matter how kind they may have been.

'Just Mabel the wardrobe mistress.'

'Perfect, she can be a witness – but nobody else? You must have friends from school.'

'No it was only always Janie and me,' she said firmly.

'Ok well, my friend Robert Morrison I can trust him with my life – and with yours when he has finished writing a script for you – We only need two witnesses, so we chould be OK.'

'A script for me. That is exciting. What is it about?'

'Don't worry about it now. We have to think about our wedding.'

'How can we keep it quiet – you being a Hon. Surely people know you.'

'Only as brother of Marcus. He was such a dominant personality. Nobody would think of me twice. The old man, my father is still alive so I'm not likely to come into the title or anything.'

'You have never mentioned your father.'

'He had a stroke a couple of years ago. They said it was just a matter of time but he's still going strong. Not speaking too well or all that mobile. He'll probably last for ever. And I am happy living my private life in the meantime. 'And tonight we shall go out to the Caprice for dinner and celebrate our engagement'

The wedding took place at Chelsea Register Office. Quiet but hilarious. The official began by meeting them and introducing himself and he seemed like an ordinary normal person but as soon as he started the marriage ceremony he put on a macabre psalm- like voice which got the four of them into hysterics.

Aterwards they all trouped to the Pheasantry club where a sumptuous dinner was laid on for them, even though Jessica was beginning to feel queasy and had to leave the party.

The baby although it was officially premature was big, lusty and perfect just like his father. Philip was so proud to be a dad and never seemed to suspect that anything was wrong. At this time Jess found that she was even fonder of Philip than she had realised. The relationship changed subtly once they were married. She loved the child, named him Jason and even breastfed him for a couple of months as Mabel said it was the way to regain her figure. As soon as she began to get rid of the baby weight a Norland nanny was hired to take over the business of looking after baby Jason.

To her relief, Phil's parents were happy to welcome her into the family and quite understood that they didn't want any fuss in the wake of Marcus's death. In fact Philip's mother who prided herself on being psychic had decided that the child was a reincarnation of her dead son and became a totally doting grandmother.

Jessie was in the nursery watching the Nanny bathe her son when Philip came barging into the room – he kissed his naked, wet son and took his wife by her shoulders

'Exciting news,' he said.

'What ?' she had never seen him so elated about anything except for the child.

'Come into theoffice,' he said 'And I'll show you something.'

He took her into his newly furbished office, sat her down and produced a thick script.

'What is this?' she asked.

'It's the play – Roger has finished it. A part you would give your eye tooth to play.'

'Tell me about it.'

'Don't you want to read it?'

'No I want you to tell me about it.'

'Right. It is about two powerful women.'

'Two?'

Yes, but you have the bigger part. You will be Elizabeth the first.'

'You 're joking! She has always been my heroine.'

'You have the strength, the power. It would be so good for people to see you in a non musical role.'

For a moment Jessica was speechless, then she flung her arms around her husband.

'Oh Philip you are wonderful.'

'Don't get over excited. Liz is the leading character but the story is of two queens Elizabeth and Mary Queen of Scots.'

'They never met.'

'No they never did and they don't in the play, but their lives are played out in tandem..'

'But who is the other woman?'

'She's a queen too. Mary Queen of Scots.'

'I don't like the idea of there being two queens.'

'They never meet. The two stories run side by side but they never actually meet. You get her head chopped off and you have a dramatic speech to bring down the curtain at the end. You will be outstanding in the role.'

'You sure I'll be good enough.'

'I'm putting my money on it.'

'What?'

'I shall produce. That is how much faith I have in you.'

Jessica took the script to her room and found herself getting excited about it. The part of the red haired passionate woman suited her down to the ground. Maybe there were two queens, but Elizabeth certainly had the edge. She owned the chopping block.'

'What do you think?' he said when she eventually returned.

'I have to do it. How did Roger know so much about me? It is as if he wrote it especially for me.'

'He did, I told you so. But he has always wanted to write about the Virgin Queen. When he met you, he knew you would be the one.'

'And you have the rights?'

'Naturally.'

She gave him a hug.

'Thank you so much. I'll do the best I can.'

Philip was excited by the project, knowing Jess as well as he did, he knew that her preoccupation as wife and mother would not last for ever and she would need something to occupy her so he immediately got himself to work hiring his creative staff and setting up casting the rest of the actors.

5.

Maxine picked up the phone.

'Maxine Fletcher?'

'Yes.'

The voice was strangely familiar but she couldn't for the life of her think where she'd heard it before. However the two words proclaimed the fact that the speaker was from the North of England. For a moment she had a bad feeling that it might be her old enemy Mr Parkes who had caught up with her somehow. The person she never wanted to see again.

'Why didn't you tell me you were a thespian?'

'What? sorry, but I don't.'

'Remember me – Stan – the Yorkshire Pullman.'

'Good heavens, how did you find me?'

'I was looking through Spotlight and there you were. So why didn't you tell me?'

'I guess that after you said you were an agent I felt a bit embarrassed.'

'No need I've forgotten about the incident in the toilet.'

She could feel the blush rising to her cheeks. She had been trying to forget the way she had behaved on that journey. She also felt a kind of twitch which also brought back the memory. She was actually getting aroused. How ridiculous. There was a long pause as she tried to think of something to say.

'How are you?' she said at last. He laughed.

'I'm well – and I have some interesting news for you.'

'For me?'

'Yes, as your agent. I gather you are not yet represented?'

'Not exclusively.'

'Then maybe you'll accept me as your representative in the possibility I have for you.'

There was another pause.

'Why do you keep going silent on me?' he asked

'I'm sitting down.'

'I don't believe you have trouble doing two things at once.' He laughed again.

'Any way nothing is set in stone, but your presence has been requested at a reading of a certain play. Would you dye your hair? Would that be a problem?'

'What colour?'

'Strawberry blonde – you are nearly there already.'

She glanced at the mirror – an auburn rinse on her blonde curls would not be difficult.

'You've gone silent again.'

'I'm thinking about it.'

'Don't you want to know what the part is?'

She gasped a yes – still not totally in control of her breathing.

'Mary Queen of Scots.'

She stopped breathing again. The Queen of Scots had always been one of her favourite characters. It was a story of a passionate woman who came to a sad end. Stan realised she had once again lost the power of speech and continued.

'Don't get too excited. It's only an audition so far, but I believe the producer knows you. He spoke very highly of you. Can't you guess?'

'I don't know any producers except the ones I've worked for in rep and on tour. Let me think. Geldberg? Smithson? – Geoffrey Williamson?'

'I see you've run the gamut of class two production companies.'

'They were very nice'.

'Yes, I'm sure they were. Who wouldn't be nice to a pretty girl like you? No this is a real live West end producer and he asked specially to see you.'

Maxine was at a loss.

'I give up.'

'Philip Cranleigh.'

How odd, she hadn't heard from Philip since she left the Webber D. And had even lost track of his sister who was slogging away in weekly Rep somewhere – in the Isle of Wight when last heard.

Maxine was beginning to regain the ability to breathe and even to speak. The sound of Philip's name was reassuring.

'I didn't know he had gone into production.'

'Convenient for you perhaps – one of your old boyfriends?'

This man was full of curiosity about her life – is this how agents always behave? Does she have to confide in him with everything?

'What is the play about?'

'I haven't read the script, but it is about Mary Queen of Scots and her meeting with the virgin queen.'

'Everyone knows they never met.'

'This is a play dear – the product of somebody's information. Obviously you are not playing the Virgin.'

'I told you I've given up the Scarlet Woman thing.'

'Sorry to hear that,' he said, 'I thought it was fun.'

'I just wish you'd shut up about it,' she said. 'Who is playing the virgin?'

'That is classified information,' he said. 'But I assure you it's hardly type casting.'

'You refuse to tell me?'

'Not allowed – actually I don't actually know. I just suspect.'

'Can you not at least reveal your suspicions?'

'Shut up Madam Temptress. I would never work again if I did.'

6.

She had every single word under her belt and was researching the life of Mary every second she could spare. But there had to come a time when she was going to meet up with Jessica face to face for a read through and it was to take place in the Olympic theatre where the play was to open in five weeks' time. She had hoped that Stan would be able to escort her, but he had to be in Manchester to follow one of his clients in a starring role.

So this was the day she had to face her enemy. She arrived much too early and went to the coffee shop next door to the theatre to have coffee and get her head around the idea of meeting the much dreaded Jessica –hoping against hope that she didn't address her as Lil. Memories of the white fur coat invaded her consciousness and she could smell in her mind the acrid aroma of burning fur when she had tried to erase 'the dirty girl' from her life. Now she was to meet her again – with a difference. Not only was Jessica a huge Theatre star but also she was married to the man Max had thought of with such fondness in the past.

She sat over her coffee trying the restrain the thumping of her heart telling herself it was caused by the caffeine rather than her fears. The rehearsals without Jessica had gone well and she had every reason to feel pleased with herself. But now – the crunch had come. She tried to occupy herself as she often did observing the other people in the coffee house. There was a skinny young man in a t shirt proclaiming '*I have the body of a god!*' She wondered which god it was and if when he turned around the shirt would read '*and the brain of an idiot*'. She made herself laugh, and then tried to think of what he would be like in bed. She made a quick decision and returned to brooding over her impending meeting with the girl she had hated for over twenty years.

She was actually scared even with the role safely under her belt and the full approval of the great director, she was still very nervous of meeting the rest of the cast and of course the star – something that filled her with apprehension. Would Jessica remember the time when Max had turned her away when she was in desperate trouble?

She arrived at the front of house and made her way to the auditorium. To her horror as she entered the back of the stalls, she noticed that a table had been erected on the stage and the entire cast and technical staff were sitting there.

Someone said, 'How nice of you to turn up.'

And the whole group stopped their talking and turned to look at her, watching as she made her way through the house and the stage manager went to the top of the small staircase on the right hand side indicating to her the way to get up on the stage.

'Good to see you,' said Lazlo.

'Am I late?'

'We started without you. I hope you don't mind,' said Lazlo.

'I am so sorry, I thought the call was half past ten.'

'Never mind dear,' said Jessica, 'Your understudy read in for you'

'She was very good,' said the stage manager.

'She was brilliant actually,' and Jessica laughed.

Philip was there and looking worried.

'We changed the call last night,' he said, 'didn't the stage manager call you?'

'Yes I did,' said the girl,' I left a message at your answering service.'

'I think several people did. I rang too,' said Jessica. 'I left a message for you. Welcoming you to the company.'

Philip shook his head 'You really should check your messages,' he said.

'Oh Philip darling, don't be unkind to the poor girl,' said Jessica, 'she's not used to our West End ways.'

'Well maybe we should pick it up where we left off,' said Lazlo.

'I've never been late before in my life,' said Maxine, 'I am so sorry.'

Lazlo looked at his watch.

'We've wasted enough time,' he said. 'For goodness sake let's get on with it.' And he turned to Maxine, 'Don't worry I'm just happy to see you.'

'Yes, thank you for turning up,' said Jessica.

The reading began again half way through act one.

Maxine was left feeling guilty and nervous. She hadn't checked her message service the night before, she had been too busy working on her lines and reading up about her character from all the available books she could find in her local library.

Ten O'clock was an unusual hour to be called and she was so used to the rigid discipline of the Rep where the time was short and every second had to be accounted for. Now she would be rehearsing for the whole six weeks. She felt ready even now – didn't believe she could get better in six weeks. Jessica was next to illiterate and not the best reader in the planet but she had Philip at her side to help her.

Rehearsals continued – she was very seldom called at the same time as Jessica, but the damage had been done to her confidence.

7.

After a couple of weeks, the two queens were called on the same day and Maxine was shocked to find that Jessica was still on the book.

'Doesn't it worry you, being still on the book at this stage?' she asked – and could have bitten her tongue immediately after the words left her lips.

'I haven't had your advantages of weekly rep. I prefer to let the reality of the character slowly develop itself into my head.,' said Jess and she turned to Lazlo,

'It must be so useful for you to have such a competent actress.'

'Maxine is a great deal more than competent,' he said.

Jessica laughed.

'Oh dear Lazlo – you just haven't got used to my sense of humour,' she said 'Maxine and I are old friends. We have known each other since we were children haven't we?'

'At my Aunt's dancing school that's all.'

'Yes you always made me feel so welcome.' Jessica smiled wolfishly.

'You were so talented in those days,' said Maxine with a smile.

By this time the initial red shampoo had begun to wear out and it was time to do it again. Lazlo suggested she should have a permanent job done by the company hair dresser.

Jessica was not happy. She called for assistance from Mabel who was working in the wardrobe and costume department.

'Why does she have to have red hair like mine? I am always the one with red hair.'

'It suits her,' said Mabel, 'But I agree it's a shame. Her blonde hair is so pretty. But Lazlo wants her to be red.'

Jessica took her complaint to Lazlo who was always kind and polite with her.

'I should be the one with red hair,' said Jessica. 'The Virgin Queen, was famous for her red hair – just like me.'

'So was Mary, they were cousins. It will be a different red from yours anyway. Mary was a tall girl like Maxine. Nobody is likely to get you missed up.

'I should hope not. Are we getting a voice coach in?'

'Why?'

'Mary wasn't a North country girl was she?'

'Who Mary? – no Scots or maybe French.'

'Then why is she using a northern accent?'

'No I'm not,' said Maxine.

Jessica turned back to Lazlo.

'It sounded to me like she was using her natural Hull accent! But you were saying 'won' instead of one. And 'uz' instead of us. Sorry Maxie darling no offence intended.'

'None taken, Jessica darling. I'm quite proud of my Northern accent. I didn't have your advantages with a convenient Professor Higgins to teach me.'

Lazlo was feeling that the amusement caused by the 'joking' rivalry was getting a bit tiresome so he suggested they should take themselves off to the coffee shop to get together over the play.

They ordered themselves a pot of tea and toasted teacakes. Jessica started dissecting the character of Mary almost immediately.

'She was just a Scottish whore, wasn't she? Her husband got killed and immediately she married someone else. She was always tangled with men.'

Maxine was horrified to hear herself saying -

'Just like you. One brother dies, you grab the other.'

'What do you mean?'

'Nothing really – I believe Philip had a brother? I met him briefly. Big, arrogant – thought he was God's gift to women.'

'Not at all, he was a great person.'

'Yes I saw you with him . You were visiting Dr Corvin, the gynaecologist.

273

I wondered why at the time. just hate the idea of you deceiving such a good kind man like Philip. It's not everyone that would take on someone else's child.'

'What do you mean?'

'I saw you with Marcus – you were at Dr Corvin's. Not difficult to guess why you were there. What you had been doing and who with.'

'I have no idea what you are talking about. You must be mistaken.'

'But it's true isn't it? No one goes to Dr Corvin for a wounded knee.'

'That's just a guess. Anyway you seem to know all about Dr Corvin yourself.'

'Yes I went there. Philip- sent me to see him. He gave me a contraceptive device. He only does that kind of stuff. Pregnancy and gyno probs.'

'Philip – he sent you?'

'Yes he recommended the Doctor to me.'

'Did you fuck my husband?'

'We made love.'

'That can't be true. Philip doesn't do things like that.'

'Really? Then you are admitting that Jason is not his progeny?'

'You are a bitch.'

'You are a whore. Giving yourself to the highest bidder. Lady Cranleigh? Lady fucking muck. Lady Lil Marsden Muck'.

'If you say a word of this to Philip I'll kill you.'

'Do you know – Jessica. I believe you. Your secret is safe with me.'

'So how are you two girls getting on?' said Philip as he joined them at their table.

'Terrific,' said Maxine.

'Isn't it fun learning about these two women? Fascinating!'

'Fascinating,' said Jessica.

'Fascinating,' said Maxine.

'Good – so was the discussion useful? Talking is such a good thing. Maybe if those two Queens had met and talked they could have resolved all their problems.'

'Somehow I doubt it,' said Max.

'In that I am in total agreement with you,' said Jessica, showing her teeth in a wolfish smile.

'Well there you are you see,' said Philip. 'You are agreeing about something. It bodes well for the future of the production.'

The two women smiled and nodded their heads.

8.

'Pop into my office tomorrow Maxie. I need to have words with you.'
What on earth Was Stan after? He wasn't always so peremptory.
'When do you require the pleasure of my presence your Majesty?' she was trying to make the occasion less formal.
'It's not a joke. It's a serious matter. Make it 10.30.'
'On a Sunday morning? Our day off.'
'I have things to do later in the day.'
'But ten thirty and I'm so tired.'
'Well if you don't turn up tomorrow you may get a chance to rest.'
'What?'
You'll have no reason to be tired.'
'Are you trying to tell me they want to sack me from the show?'
'We'll speak tomorrow.'
That night Maxine didn't get a wink of sleep. She had thought rehearsals were going rather well. She knew her lines and her moves – more than the rest of them did. They were most of them still on the book, still stumbling through their roles. She couldn't understand what was matter with actors these days – no discipline. Her anger at that state of affairs kept her awake most of the night and she presented herself at Stan's office next day bleary eyed and really tired.

She arrived on the dot of ten twenty-nine. He arrived at ten thirty-five.
She didn't say anything, just looked at her watch.
'All right madam, don't narrow your lips at me,' he said.
She gave a comical shrug.
'Will you sit here on the sofa?' he said.
'The casting couch?' she asked.
'Just sit,' he said and he perched himself on his office chair.
She sat on the sofa with ill grace.
'You are trying to look down on me,' she said, still trying to joke.
'I need to get a good look at you,' he said.
'So what's it all about?
'Some complaints have been made about your behaviour in rehearsals.'
'What? That makes no sense. If you think I've been coming in late again. It was only the once and it ws all Jessica's fault.'
He sighed.
'You must get over this antagonism to Jessica. Nobody else has a problem

with her. She is one of the most popular ladies in the business.'

'Huh, nobody has known her as long as I have.'

'That is as maybe. But you are hardly as high in the popularity stakes.'

Maxine shrugged. 'I'm not in the business to be popular.'

'Then that is a problem. You really should be a little more careful. Actors have ways of destroying those who are dismissive of them. They can ruin your performance in ways you will never understand.'

'It's very kind of you Stanley to take such trouble over me but I have never kow towed to anyone in my life and I'm not about to start now.'

'Then you may just find you are out of a job. Amy is learning your part – right now as we speak.'

'What?'

'You say Jessica has something against you? Well if she has, she is capable of influencing everyone in her favour. She has Philip of course, Lazlo would have to be on her side and the cast and stage management people adore her. You cannot afford to lose this job and I can't afford to have you lose it. If you lose your job you lose your agent. Understand?'

Maxine struggled to her feet.

'Is that it?'

'Sit down Maxine, I'm not done yet.'

'Having another go at me are you?'

'Just sit there and shut the fuck up.'

She sat reluctantly and waited for him to speak.

'Elmore Greenberg the film director will be coming to the show at some point – probably incognito. Jessica is up for the part of Queen Elizabeth in his new picture. There could be a part for you if he takes a fancy to you.'

'Jessica would have no authority over him surely.'

'She could put the kibosh on your performance if she felt like it. Not only that, she could give you a bad reference – and so could Philip – he's on her side, remember. So better be on your best behaviour. Hollywood is where you belong. Bear that in mind.'

'Yes of course.'

'So it would be greatly to your advantage if you could make friends with Jessica. Just for the run of the play. It won't be possible if Jessica goes to Hollywood. So it may only be for a month or so.'

Stan's mention of Philip being on the side of Jessica hit her really hard. She decided to confide in him a little.

'It makes me feel sad. There was a time when I loved Philip. Still do, rather. I was so upset when I saw him with Jessica someone I have always disliked. It is so unfair that they got together. It is depressing.'

Stan's face softened a little at the news.

'I'm sorry, I didn't realise that. But even so, it is important that you put all this behind you.'

'I thought you were my friend I thought you'd understand.'

'Just try to make friends with Jessica and the rest will follow. I have to insist on this.'

Maxine got to her feet.

'I've had enough,' she said, 'I don't think I need to be bullied by you Stan. You have no right to choose my friends for me.'

'Maxine I am your agent. I don't give a flying fuck about you and your little squabbles. All I'm interested in is what you can do for me. You owed me that much. I took you as a client when you were a mere novice at the game. I took the chance to gamble with you. Not for the sake of your pretty face but for the sake of my bank balance. Now please go home and think about it. I have a meeting with an important client.'

'More important than me?'

'If the cap fits. Off you go and learn how to behave.'

Maxine left the office almost crying with anger. No one had ever taken her to task before in that forthright style. She was full of resentment and hate for him.'

Still fuming, she went to the nearest coffee shop in Soho and ordered herself a Capuccino.'

'Hello Maxie.'

Maxine's scowl turned to a smile as she saw Mabel drinking coffee. She enjoyed the company of Mabel the wardrobe mistress. She was her only friend within the company. Mabel was sensible, had no axe to grind and she actually liked Maxine not caring about the nastiness that surrounded her from the rest of the company.

'Hello Mabel,' she said. 'How nice to see you.'

'Would you come and join me?' Mabel asked.

'That would be good.'

'You seem a bit disturbed.'

'Just had a row with my agent.'

'The gorgeous Stan?'

'Gorgeous or not. He seems to hate me.'

'I'm sure that's not true – otherwise he wouldn't be your agent.'

'Really?'

'Well of course. It is important for people to get along with each other, isn't it?'

To Maxine this was a sore point. Was she going to get a telling off from Mabel as well.

'You are having a go at me? – about me and Jessica?'

'Is that what the row was about?'

'We usually get on so well. It's Jessica that's the problem.'

'No not really. I know you and Jess don't exactly see eye to eye and it is disturbing for the rest of the company.'

'It doesn't interfere with my performance.'

'I'm afraid it does. It worries the whole company. They would all work much better if they thought the two leading ladies could get on together. You know they call you Miss High and Mighty, don't you? It's so unfair. I know you are a really nice person.'

'Didn't Mary and Elizabeth hate each other?'

'As you know they never met, but they were cousins and really had loving feelings towards each other, which made it even more difficult for Elizabeth to order Mary's execution. She was heartbroken.'

'Really? At the moment she is playing it aggressive and blood thirsty.'

'You've got to win her over in real life Maxine. Please try. You must know that she has had a hard life. You've got to admire her pluck.'

9.

Maxine rang Stan. She spoke to his Ansa phone.

'I'm thinking about it' was the message she left.

Much to her surprise, when she arrived at the theatre the following day Jessica approached her with a smile.

'Hello Maxine. How are you this morning?'

'I'm well. Are you?'

'yes.'

There was a pause as they surveyed each other – wondering how to start. Maxine took the first step.

'Look Lil Jessica. We are going to have to work together,' she said.

Jessica shook her head. 'We are supposed to be rivals.'

'Well yes, but that doesn't mean we don't like each other. It's good for the play to be enemies, but not good for the show.'

'Of course you have so much more about theatre after your years in Rep – while I've only been a big star in the West End. How should I know?' said Jessica with her wolfish smile.

'As a matter of fact you are probably speaking the truth.'. Said Maxine.

'It was a joke,'

'Yes of course, but slogging away in rep is a good learning curve.'

'They taught you to use clichés too.'

'Yes.' laughed Maxine.

'Anyway slogging away in shows is pretty rough too.'

'Physically.'

Jessica was indignant.

'I have to use my brain too,' she said.

'Yes I can tell. Physical prowess is not enough. You do need brains and ruthlessness.'

Jessica looked at Max who had a humorous glint in her eyes

Jessica laughed, 'Ok and I'll forget the time you refused to let me in when I was desperate.'

'And I'll try to forget how you usurped me in Irene's class getting all that best parts sucking up to the star to get an extra bit I'll try to forget that'.

'Mm Seems like a fairly uneasy truce to me.'

'Uneasy, but necessary. We'll just forget these things for the run of the play'.

'Shake hands?'

'OK.'

'We've got to be good when Elmore Greenberg comes. He's a big Hollywood director who is making a movie all about Elizabeth. I'm up for the part. I'll put in a word for you.'

'I can't see that happening – despite our new friendship.'

'.There might be a small bit you can play.'

'Thank you Jess. I appreciate it.'

As soon as she had a break Maxine went to the stage door telephone.

'Stan?'

'What is it Max?'

'There's this film person coming to see the show.'.

'Yes, don't worry. I have told him of your enormous talent.'

'Don't be sarcastic.'

'And he'll be aware of your presence although he is mainly here to see

Jessica. They need a box office name for the role of Liz.'

'She's hardly box office in America, is she?'

'You'd be surprised. She s done a couple of movies that impressed the yanks no end and she has a really good Elizabethan name. Can't get better than Sherwood'.

'She stole that name from me. It's the name of our street in Hull. Where my aunt's dancing school was. That's where she got the name.'

'How amusing,' he laughed.

'Glad you think so. Anyway it's hardly Elizabethan.'

'Well it has Robin Hood connotations. Americans don't know the difference.'

'All right then, what about Fletcher? Arrow maker?'

'Ok but you are not up for Elizabeth. That role is what they need the Englishness for. Still maybe there is a small role – I'll do my best for you. Hollywood is where you belong'.

'Ah think I should mention it. Jessica says she'll put in a word for me.'

'So you've made it up?'

'Briefly. Jessica had to say that to make peace but she is bound to stop me getting a part. She does really hate me – always has. One day I'll tell you all about her. I'll just say that when we met – as children – she spat at me and left liquorice all over my white fur coat.'

'You had a white fur coat?' he laughed again.

'It's not something to laugh at. It was not a pleasant meeting.'

'I can imagine hardly propitious.'

'We've hated each other ever since and she's been a real pain during our rehearsals. Making me late etc Remember?'

'She was the culprit? You didn't say.'

'She said she's left a message on my voicemail to say the theatre had changed the time. She did but I was drinking coffee next door to the theatre getting nervous and waiting for the call at 10.30. When I got there they had started without me. My understudy had been reading in. They said she was very good.'

'That must have pleased you.'

'You're laughing again.'

'Amy Jenks – she is so talented'.

'Well thanks a lot for that. Not exactly queen like.'

'Not talented and beautiful and intelligent like you my love She doesn't have your elegance but she is a great gel.'

'Of course she's one of yours isn't she?'

'Yes once I got you I filled up the rest with all my people. So you see I have to thank you for that. We are all in this business together. We have to help each other.'

10.

Her new friend Jessica invited her into her dressing room for coffee one morning. And a friendly chat. Maxine soon became aware of their class difference when she saw Jessica's dressing room. It was like a hotel suite and had been newly decorated for her. She had a shower room with WC, a tiny kitchen, a small television room with a day bed and in the spacious main room there were huge wardrobes, cupboards, a cocktail cabinet, radiogram and two easy chairs. Maxine had lived in smaller and less well-appointed apartments and felt a little resentful. Hers was a smallish room situated on the first floor upstairs from the stage. There was just enough space for a wardrobe with a full length mirror, a mirrored dressing table with a wooden chair and an armchair.

However, she reined in her resentment and it turned out to be a pleasant visit. They found they could laugh together as long as they carefully avoided any subjects of dissension. The relationship was working rather well. Suddenly from the worst of enemies, they had turned into the best of friends.

Rehearsals carried on without any problems and the first night audience were ecstatic. Obviously the critics were bound not to like it. Each one commented on the fact that Jessica had never appeared in a straight role before and were patronising in their faint praise. 'Newcomer' Maxine Fletcher came out quite well but again there was nothing overwhelming in plaudits for either the play or the performers. However, the audiences were enthusiastic and the show sold well – booking up to three months in advance. Philip was happy, feeling that he might actually get back most of the money he had ploughed into it.

They had been running a couple of weeks when there was a knock on the door – and Mabel came in with Maxine's newly washed and ironed petticoats that went under the farthingale.

She seemed worried.

'What's wrong?'

'Well nothing really. It's just that it is tonight the movie man is here'

'That's pretty exciting. How is our star?'

'Shaking like a leaf,' she said. 'I suppose we shouldn't have told her but nobody realised she would get so nervous.'

'Mm well I guess we shall all have to support her in every way possible. It would be great for her and launch her into an entirely new career in Hollywood.'

(and get her out of my hair – the further away the better) she thought.

Maxine called on Jessica in her palatial Dressing room suite. Jessica was lying on her daybed with an icepack on her head and a glass of champagne in her hand.

'I came to wish you luck,' said Maxine. 'It's a big night for you. Are you drinking Alcohol?'

'No, love, its only champagne. I need it to settle my nerves.'

'You can use the nerves without resorting to alcohol.'

Jessica laughed bitterly,

Maxine continued,

'Listen Jess. Not only are you great in the part, but everyone is rooting for you.'

'I can only be grateful it is Saturday night and I can get some rest tomorrow. He won't let me know about the part till Monday'.

'Well Ok, just give me that glass and get yourself together. The nerves will be helpful to you. We were always taught to use nerves to our advantage.'

Jess allowed Max to take the drink from her and Maxine gave her some breathing exercises and helped her with her nerves. Jessica had a ballet barre in her dressing room and Maxine encouraged her to make use of it to stretch her legs and body. She had stopped shaking and seemed her old confident and autocratic self again,

'Thanks Max,' she said as she did her plies.

Max had found the whole routine working with Jessica exhausting and she went back to her dressing room following her own advice to re energise herself to perform that evening. She didn't have facilities that Jessica had so she did a few deep breaths and Mabel came in to do up her costume,

'You worked wonders Maxine, you're a star,' she said. 'Madam is quite composed now. She will win through.'

The show went exceptionally well that evening and there were roars of applause at the end – even one or two of the audience got to their feet.

Maxine was happy – now it seemed that Jessica would get to Hollywood and out of Maxine's hair. She went back to her room and took off the Mary wig and costume and put on her dressing gown – it was an oriental silken garment with a large Chinese dragon on the back – an opening night present from her new friend Jessica.

She sat in her armchair and lit a cigarette to relax. It was a ritual she enjoyed before removing her make-up and getting into her street clothes.

She was feeling tired, it had been an exhausting night – usually after the show the adrenaline was still running and she wanted to get to the Buckstone actors club and join the rest of the cast in general high jinks, but tonight the emotional energy in trying to reassure Jessica had worn her out.. She was almost nodding off when there was a sudden commotion and a banging on her door.

The door flew open and Jessica stormed in followed by Philip.

'You bitch,' she shouted, 'How did you do it? I always knew you were a double crossing cow. What about that wishing me well and bolstering me up when you were working on your own dirty little plans?'

Jessica advanced on Maxine and would have punched her if Philip had not held her back. She squirmed in his hold.

'I'm sorry, I don't know what you are talking about.'

'Tell that to the fucking Marines lady. You and Stan had it all worked out didn't you? Planning my destruction in front of… Bitch! Bitch! Bitch!'

Maxine was dumbfounded. She had intended to go and congratulate Jess on her performance – she had been brilliant. The nerves had added an extra dimension to her performance.

Philip held Jessica tightly in his arms. Mabel came in and the two of them took Jessica who was still kicking and screaming.

'She'll need a sedative,' said Philip as they went out – 'Get George to call the doctor – urgently.'

After they had gone there was a knock on the door.

'Are you decent?' said Stan.

'Well I'm not naked.'

'Are you able to receive a visitor?'

'Oh dear, not really. Hang on a minute.'

And she tried ineffectively to put a splodge of Crowe's Cremine on her face to try and remove the makeup.

'Don't be too long. This is important. It doesn't really matter what you look like.'

'Oh all right,' she said, 'bring the visitor in.'

Stan and Philip came in followed by a middle aged man – short in stature and about as wide as he was long. He reminded her of pictures of John Bull. But this image was dissolved when she heard his powerful American accent.

'It's a real privilege to meet you Miss Fletcher. I enjoyed your performance'

'Thank you.'

'Maxine, this is Elmore Greenberg'.

Maxine was so dumbstruck she practically curtsied.

'I have to tell you that you are the person I am looking for.'

'Oh er – good.'

'I loved your Mary, but I think you'll be even better as Elizabeth'

'Elizabeth, but that...'

'I've arranged to have your things packed' said Stan hastily

'and I am so happy that you will be able to accompany me to LA on Monday'

'Monday – LA – I'm sorry. I don't quite understand. '

'Elmore is offering you the role of Elizabeth in his picture and I have accepted'

'Well it's a bit difficult, I'm in a play.'

'I apologise for the short notice.'

'Don't worry about the play,' put in Stan.

'Yes your producer tells me your understudy is well rehearsed so the play will not suffer.'

He looked at his watch.

'Forgive me, I have work to do tonight. But I will see you Monday. The plane goes at midday – your seat is booked in first class.'

Maxine felt she had to protest.

'I don't know the role. It's Jessica's part. I don't know the lines.'

Elmore laughed.

'My film is a different story. The script will be with you when you get home tonight so you can peruse it in advance. I look forward to seeing you Monday.'

. 'But Jessica was...'

'She'll be OK,' put in Stan quickly. 'She'll be very pleased for you.'

Stan took Elmore to the door. They shook hands and Elmore left.

After Elmore had left they were silent, just listening to Jessie still screaming and cursing in the distance. After a while Philip came in and went over to where Maxine was slumped in her arm chair and kissed her on the cheek.

'Congratulations. Jessica is Ok now,' he said and hastily left.

Finally, Maxine recovered her voice.

'Stan what's happening.'

Stan laughed, he was perched on her dressing table and looking as if he was a cat in front of a big bowl of cream.

'Elmore has a big idea. You are to be his new star.'

'I don't believe it. How can I be ready?'

Stan took Maxine home in a cab.

'When did you get to hear about this?'

'I sat next to him – for some reason he confided in me. He told me that Jessica Sherwood was only a song and dance girl. That he needed real actors. And then when you came on he said 'That's the one' and he gave his secretary who was on his other side to get a script to you asap. He asked me for the address and of course I gave it to him.'

Maxine sighed heavily. She still couldn't understand what was happening and what it might entail.

'Oh and by the way, don't worry honey. I shall be with you on the plane on Monday as your personal manager. OK?'

'Yes fine,' she replied.

'You never know,' he grinned, 'we may even join the mile-high club.'

11.

Jessica recovered her equilibrium. She never suffered too long and she found she didn't miss the theatre at all. After the play finished its run, she retired to Philip's country house and concentrated on being a wife and mother. Her memories of that Christmas at Sonnie's farm had been the happiest time of her life and to live in a country house was something she had always longed for.

She had become a regular Lady Bountiful presiding over the Women's Institute and the Young Conservatives. Her child Jason was four years old and growing into a handsome little boy with a close resemblance to his natural father. They had fun together acting out scenes, dancing and singing. He was obviously destined for the theatre and Jessica got her ration of performing without ever having to leave the house.

They were playing happily together when there was a knock at the door.

'Enter,' said Jessica and Jane came in looking a little flushed.

Jane was Mabel's daughter and had moved in to look after the little boy when his mother was in the theatre. When the show closed down, she never went away, staying to help with all the Parish work as well as taking care of Jason when necessary.

'There's a gentleman to see you,' she said.

'Oh no. You know I don't wish to see anybody. This is my special time with Jason.'

'He is very insistent.'

'Ok how boring. What kind of a gentleman is he?'

'Well, he's not exactly a gentleman if you know what I mean – but good looking and very attractive.'

'Mm,' said Jessica, 'a handsome gentleman. Obviously made an impression on you.'

'Not arf,' said Jane with a giggle.

'Did he say what he wanted?'

'He said he had important things to tell you. Things you ought to know about.'

Jessica gave a sigh and hugged her little boy.

'OK wheel him in.'

The man that came in made Jessica shudder with the resemblance – he was the living image of her stepfather Bill. Tall, handsome with black curly hair and eyes the colour of an August sky. But without the pallor Bill had when he came out of prison. This man looked as if he spent his life out of doors.

'Hello – Madame – Milady – Jessica – Lilian – recognise me?'

'It can't be…Jack…is it?'

He smiled flashing his white teeth.

'Jack it is. Big brother Jack.'

'You look a lot like your father.'

'Hardly a good thing.'

'I didn't say you resembled his personality.'

'I should hope not. He was a monster. The world should be glad to get rid.'

Jane gasped and giggled at the same time.

'Oh my God. Jane – Please leave us.'

'Will you be all right?'

'Course I will. Take Jason please.'

Jane took the child's hand. He complained bitterly, losing his precious time with his Mummy.

'Jason darling – we can play later – maybe we'll go to the Park – to the swings?'

Jack opened the door for them, with a charming smile, and closed it behind them.

'Didn't know you had parks in the country,' said Jack.

'Yes we have our very own park and children's playground. We built it for the village children so that Jason could play with them. Jason loves the swings.'

'He's a nice looking boy. Very fair. Resembles his Dad?'

'Yes.'

Rather at a loss about what to say, Jessica indicated one of the comfy leather chairs.

'Why don't you sit down?'

Jack sat and arranged the cushions – making himself completely at home.

'Well sister you done pretty well for yourself. Who would have thought it. But you always wanted to live in the Country.'

'We had a good time on the farm didn't we? That Christmas – don't you remember Jack?'

'Yes, it was memories like that that kept me sane in the nick.'

'Oh, you went to prison?'

'I got ten years, even though it was self defence. The old bastard, he would have killed me if I hadn't got him first.'

'And Michael – he was with you wasn't he? Did he go to prison too?'

'Borstal – had a bad time. Got into drugs.'

'Oh my God, how awful'

. 'Couldn't cope – killed himself. Wasn't strong enough. They were pretty rough in there.'

'And Jamie?'

'Oh never see him. Got toffee nosed – took his mother's name – went to University and is a professor now. Professor O'Malley at Oxford.'

'Oxford? That's where I first met my husband.'

'Yes, he did all right. Too posh to have owt to do wi'me.'

'So what about you? You seem to be OK.'

'Ah'm the only honest person in the family. Even kept my own name. Didn't have a bad time in nick. Got to work in the garden – made it my business to learn all I could about the job – studied and got qualifications.'

'That's very good.'

'Sounds good dunnit? Except that I can't get a job. Not with my record.'

'That's terrible . It doesn't mean you'd go around killing people.'
'Exactly.'
'So what are you going to do?'
'Well I thought maybe my kid sister would be pleased to see me. So I tracked you down. New name and everything Done well.'
'Yes I guess so.'

He got up and went over to the French widow looking out over the meadow beyond.

She watched him carefully, wondering what he had in mind.

He turned back to her.

'Do many people know you used to be Lil Marsden?'
'Very few but they are discreet. I'm lucky that way.'

Jack stretched his arms above his head as if he was bringing blood to his brain.

'Well it would be good to keep it that way wouldn't it?'
'Of course.'

There was a long silence as they looked at each other. He was smiling a gentle smile – full of charm. She was beginning to suspect his intentions but unsure what he required from her.

'Erm I take it this is a form of blackmail,' she said at last.

He looked as if she had struck him across the face.

'That's not a nice thing to say,' he said.
'All right then what are you wanting?'
'Just a chance. You got a large estate – you could do with a man like me.'
'My husband is responsible for hiring people.'
'But I bet you can twist him round your little finger.

He turned away from her and went back to gazing out of the window.

'I just feel it would be a shame if the press – for instance – got hold of the story. It's a good one. The aristocratic Lady Cranleigh or – Jessica Sherwood the famous musical comedy star is really little Lil Marsden from Hull who was involved in a murder and ran away. I expect the police would like a word with you too.'

Jessica's confidence was beginning to crumble. Jack went over to her and put his arms around her, his cheek against hers.

'But that's not going to happen is it? I am a very good gardener.'

12.

Maxine was lying by her swimming pool outside her house in Laurel Canyon and she was bored. She hadn't been in the studio for three months. Her roles had been getting smaller and it was nearing the end of her contract. She was a little scared about what would happen to her but she was rather glad it might be all over. She had been in Hollywood nearly twenty years and had never really enjoyed herself. She could never get to play the leading lady. Pretty as she was, she didn't have the allure required for a movie star, nor was she able to join in any Casting Couch activities. Her very Englishness played against her, and she had learned to develop a protective reserve since her schoolgirl experiences and this precluded her from getting the starring roles. She sighed heavily and sipped her mojito. Happily the telephone rang and she leaped out of her daybed and rushed indoors to answer it.

'Hello light of my life,' said Stan.

Bad news obviously, she thought. it was always bad news when he spoke to her with affection.

'Bad news? 'She asked, not caring one way or the other.

'Why would you think that?'

'Because you are trying to soften me up to prepare me for the worst'.

'Mmm I see. Okay. What do you think I'm going to tell you? Have a guess.'

'Oh really, you are impossible. Just spit it out Stan.'

'No, I'm interested in what you are going to say. What you think the bad news might be?'

'All right,' she sighed, 'they are terminating my contract.'

'Nearly right.'

'Oh come on Stan, what do you mean?'

'*You* are terminating your contract.'

'Oh I see, and why am I doing this?'

'Because you know you are approaching a difficult age.'

'You are telling me I'm middle aged? '

He laughed.

'Approaching middle age. You must have noticed that Hollywood tends to forget women when they are over forty.'

'Mmm I'm too old for movies. Is that what you are trying to tell me?'

'Hollywood's tastes have changed. When Elmore died the writing was on the wall. He was always your champion.'

'Well I can tell you, Hollywood has definitely lost its attraction for me.'

'That's the ticket. So I did the right thing. You've got to get out before you get the push or get sidelined.'

'Mm I see. Hang on a minute.'

She got up from her telephone chair and wandered over to the table. She took a cigarette out of the alabaster box and lit it with the table lighter.

Stan was shouting over the phone

'Where are you – are you still there?'

She laughed and shouted back 'I'm here, just getting a cigarette'

'I have more news. The reason I rang. I have another project for you.'

Maxine sat herself down again and took a puff of her cigarette.'

'I'm listening,' she said.

'Do you ever get homesick?'

'For England? Or for the Theatre?'

'Both,' he said.

'There's a part for me?'

'Yes.'

'A middle aged lady?'

'Not at all. Young, vibrant and sexy.'

'You're kidding.'

'Not at all.'

'You just told me I'm too old for Hollywood.'

'Not exactly. Anyway you can easily be thirty.'

'Really?'

'From a distance.'

'Gee thanks Stanley.'

'And what is more, they are thinking of using a lovely new young man to play opposite you.'

'A lovely young man – how young?'

'27 but can easily play 30 or over.'

'From a distance?'

'Ha ha, Yes he's well built. Looks mature. But he's very sexy – so watch it.'

'Oh come on Stan. I'm no cougar.'

'You haven't seen him yet'.

'I'll be fine'.

There was a moment's silence. Maxine took a long puff of her cigarette and enjoyed the feeling of the smoke filling her lungs waiting to see what Stan would say next.

Eventually he spoke.
'Not that I would be jealous or anything.'
'I should hope not,' she said. 'We've been divorced for seven years.'
'My god so we have. Can't be that long surely.'
'Yes it is.'
'Doesn't time fly when you're enjoying yourself.'
Maxine laughed. She always laughed when she was talking to Stan.
'I see you haven't lost any of your charm,' she said.
'Thank you.'
'Do you know, said Maxine. You were my first real lover.'
'On the Yorkshire Pullman?'
'Yes'.
'And the mile high club.'
She laughed.
'That was even more uncomfortable,' she said with feeling.
'How do you fancy a repeat performance?'
'At our age?'
'Why not?'
'The Pullman or the mile high?'
'Well I reckon it could be both. You'll be visiting your poor aged mother, won't you?'
'My Poor aged mother! Connie ran the gamut of central casting when she was here. She's the baby snatcher in the family. Maybe she'll get it together with your young man – what's his name?'
'Jay Leonard.'
She gave the name a little consideration.
'Mm not bad,' she replied.
'Anyway, I've said yes to the job,' said Stan.
'Without asking me?'
'Yes wanna fight about it?'
'Course not darling Stan. You always know how your bread is buttered.'
'With you my pet – my star and soul mate.'
'Yes – but what about that trophy wife of yours. Mrs Precious Stepford. Still cooking and cleaning for you?'
'No out o f my life. Too boring for words.'
Maxine laughed. 'What did I tell you?'
'Dearest Maxine, you said I'd be bored to tears.'
'Exactly.'

'Well my tears are falling – tears of relief. Such a relief to lose her.'
'How did you manage it?'
'She's divorcing me. I struck her apparently.'
'Apparently? Domestic violence? Can't approve of that.'
'I merely patted her backside.'
'Did you have a motive?'
'She was boring me. I thought it would break up the tedium.'
'Did it?'
'Nothing could.'
'So you are looking on me to provide some amusement again.'
'You always do. Funny – we always get on better when we are not married.'
'Thank you. Enough of this gay badinage. Tell me of the play.'
'It's an up to date private lives. Divorced but still in love. That's why I thought of you.'
'Flannel again?'
'Ok doll. I've arrange to have your traps packed. They are coming on Tuesday so get yourself ready for moving. You'll need to get some make up stuff. No more Mr Factor for you. You'll have to put on your own pollyfiller.'
'I do get a bit bored of these unkind jokes.'
'Can't think what you mean.'
'Too old for Hollywood; 30 at a distance, pollyfiller. What I had to go through all those years. What a happy divorce that was.'
'Thanks for the memory.'

Maxine hung up the phone. Another adventure was on the way. Boredom had flown out of the window. 'Look out London. Maxie's back!'

13.

The First Night party was going well. The stage was filled with happy excited people, all talking, none listening – a typical theatrical get together. Everyone was feeling optimistic, the general thought was that the production was working really well and could run for over a year.

Maxine turned her back on the chattering crowd and strolled downstage to the footlights.

It had been a long time since she had looked upon her favourite view. To stand on a stage and look at the empty fully lit auditorium was a privilege enjoyed by few. A sight never enjoyed by an audience and only rarely by the actors.

Empty plush seats – a wave of shimmering crimson in the soft light of the chandeliers, reached row upon row right to the back of the auditorium. Above them, the sweep of the dress circle, circle and gallery, three graceful curved balconies upon which sported chubby golden cupids, holding in their dimpled hands the painted garlands of ribbons and flowers chasing each other around the azure fascias of each one.

High above, flying across the ornately painted ceiling the carousing gods and goddesses of Mount Olympus, for whom the theatre was named. The colours had been restored to their Edwardian richness, pinks, blues and purples with a glittering highlight of gilt, which brought the Olympic guardians into sharp relief. And in the centre of the ceiling amidst the roistering Olympians was a giant crystal chandelier, which cast its diamond light into every corner.

There were eight boxes altogether, four on each side of the proscenium arch. Maxine had sat in each of them at different times during rehearsals, just as she had occupied seats all over the house, judging the sound, the sightlines, checking on all the technical details that allow the audience to see, to hear, to enjoy, to understand what was going on in that brightly lit rectangle in front of them. There was a royal crest above one of the boxes proving that Royalty had appeared on several occasions during the theatre's two hundred years run.

During the run of the Two Queens Maxine had grown to know and love every nook and corner of the Olympic. She knew about the startling contrast between the front of house and the utilitarian bleakness backstage. The golden and crimson lushness of the public rooms, bars, foyer seemed somehow overblown when you went backstage and saw the plain stone steps, the painted wooden doors. Everything totally functional, utilitarian, but the strong smells of make up paint and size, the wear and tear of generations of actors, dancers, singers and musicians had left their stamp and created a strong essence of humanity of a living breathing community.

She knew that at the top of the building, there was a huge wardrobe room where the costumes were stored, ironed and repaired. Even when empty, this room had a faintly musty aroma of old clothes, sweat, cleaning fluid and starch.

On the other side of the top floor corridor was the chorus dressing room with its row of double sided dressing tables down the centre, clothes rails around the walls and the all pervading ghostly smell of wet white, grease paint and Johnson's baby powder. In addition, mirrors –mirrors everywhere so that each member of the chorus was able to check the tiniest detail of their costume, make up and – most important of all, posture, before they went on.

On the floor below was a collection of almost identical small square rooms, used by small part players and understudies. Originally intended for single or at most double occupancy they had contained a dress rail running down one wall with shoe racks beneath and a dressing table with a large mirror surrounded by naked light bulbs. But recently many of these had been joined together by a connecting door, as due to economy measures, the casts got smaller, the parts larger and the actors more demanding of amenities such as lavatories, showers and storage space for their costumes and personal effects. Even so, they retained an essence, something of the character of those actors who had occupied them during the years.

*

She was feeling so happy to be here and remembered the day they came to rehearse in the theatre for the first time.

'Morning Bert,' she said to the stage door keeper.

'Nice to have you back Miss Fletcher,' he said.

It was strange to be back in that very same theatre. At the time she had been an also-ran to Jessica Sherwood who was the star name. Now she had come back with her name above the title. She could see the posters with a huge picture of her face and the words Maxine Fletcher in *Days of Grace*, underneath the list of actors with their headshots ending with And Jay Leonard. Larger than the others, but not as big as hers. She was a Hollywood star and was the reason most people would come to see the show. It was good to see old Bert was still there – twenty years older but looking exactly as he did all that time ago. He always looked like an old man. Maybe he was born old she thought to herself. She was also occupying the star dressing room. She remembered when she had visited Jessica and been so impressed by the luxury of it.

Bert handed her the key and she walked along the corridor feeling full of excitement as if she was going home after a long absence. Funny that this theatre where she played for only a short time seemed more like home to her than her parents' home in Hull. Everything that happened to her before she left for Drama School had been erased from her memory. The theatre was her whole life.

The dressing room was just as impressive as before – except for the smell of paint. It made her laugh that they had decorated the dressing room especially for her.

They had been rehearsing Days of Grace for four weeks already and at last they were to play it through on stage. She had met Jay Leonard, the young man who was to play Roger – Grace's husband He was a big blonde man so not her type and she thought he was a trifle arrogant – but then he was a young person and certainly very attractive and attentive to her. He indulged in the kind of badinage that Stan always used as if he was afraid to seem overawed by her. They made friends quickly and indulged in banter making their own jokes, laughing a lot.

They had both learned their lines well in advance of rehearsals but on one occasion a dispute broke out between them. It was a line Jay insisted Maxine had got wrong.

'The line is '*come in to see me.*'

'That is what I said,'

'No you said '*Come up and see me*'. Like Mae West.'

'Then that must be right. I always learn my lines perfectly.'

'Bollocks – you improvise all the time.'

'I do not. Anyway it means the same thing.'

Maxine reached for her copy of the play which was on a nearby chair. At the same time Jay reached for his and they collided. They laughed and both picked up their scripts.

As they straightened up they came face to face and suddenly they found it impossible to look away.

After a while, they carried on with the rehearsal and when they were dismissed they left together, not exchanging a word but almost automatically walking together to the flat Maxine had rented in Covent Garden .There was no denying their overwhelming attraction for each other.

14.

Maxine inserted her key into the door and paused a little, anticipating that frisson of excitement she felt every time she entered her dressing room.

As she took the step inside, she pressed all three of the light switches that were lined up beside ther door and flooded the room with light. The bulbs that surrounded the drssing room mirror reacted and communicated with the full length looking glasses on the wardrobe doors – so that everywhere there was Maxine. She could see herself reflected over and over and by turning her head this way and that she could view herself from every possible angle.

She felt happy. The reflection of her perfect face framed by the straight flaxen hair pleased her.

'Do I really look this good or am I just accustomed to my face?'

Cue for song – and as she hummed to herself, she slipped out of her cashmere wrap and left it carelessly bundled up at one end of the dressing table. Anthea would be along later to pick it up. She had already laid out the costumes – lovely – washed and ironed after every performance by the wardrobe department and there were fesh flowers in the heavy crystal vases that had been a first night present from someone she couldn't remember who.

She glanced at the letters that lay inside their slit envelopes.

Anthea was allowed to open any letters that came to the theatre and to edit them for abusive content. Although Maxine had fan letters by the hundred there were always one or two that really objected to her and were vociferous in their hatred. The bad letters were usually to the effect that Maxine had deserted her native country for Hollywood and then when she didnt exactly set Hollywood on fire, came back with her tail between her legs. None of this was true of course. She had finally given into her homesickness for London and most particularly the London Theatre where she felt she truly belonged and was happy again.

She glanced at the mail. There was onl y one that Anthea had singled out for her to read before the show and this one hadn't been opened. It hadn't even been posted but delivered by hand.

Maxine looked at the rather too perfect handwriting on the front and smiled. It was from Jay, her co star. It was a greetings card of the Rokeby Venus and on the inside was scrawled the words *'I love you'* a hundred times and at the bottom was *PTO*. She turned over to the back of the card on which was written in big letters *'I adore you'* and underneath in smaller hand *P.S I love you. This is how I imagine you look when you think nobody is there.'*

She looked again at the voluptuous figure. It ws awfully silly, but it made her laugh and she felt warm, bathed in his affection. Eighteen years her junior – but on stage he had looks culture and sophistication way behond his years and an audience would never guess at the disparity of their ages.

The boy came bursting into her dressing room as Maxine was making up for the evening's performance. He came up behind her and kneeling at her side pressed his cheek against hers. She looked at the two faces reflected in the mirror and silently despaired. His fresh faced youth made her feel old, she did not enjoy the experience. He on the other hand was delighted by it.

'Don't we look good together?' he said.

'What are you so excited about?' she asked in order to change the subject.

He got up and taking up a positioning the centre of the room.

'Look at me,' he said, 'I'm going to do a twirl.'

She laughed as he pirouetted.

'New clothes,' she said.

And indeed he was resplendent in crackly new jeans and a shirt which still bore the fold marks of newness!

'My agent has signed the contract for the new series!' he cried.

'Wonderful.'

'This is my TV breakthrough,' he cried. 'I'm going to make lots of money.' And he started to sing *Baby I'm a rich man, Baby I'm a rich man.*

'Ok. You're gonna be a rich man on TV.'

'And in real life. A long contract and lots a money. *Money money money.*'

'Make up your mind. Beatles or Abba? Not both at the same time.'

'Well they do say it's going to be a kind of sequel to *Upstairs Downstairs.*'

'Sounds good.'

'You probably don't remember *Upstairs Downstairs* you would have been in America.'

'We did get it over there,' she said. 'But I even remember the *Forsyte Saga.* That was the first of these Edwardian series. Before you were born probably.'

He tightened his lips. He hated references to their disparate ages.

'I remember the Forsytes,' he said, 'I used to watch it with my mother. I was in love with Susan Hampshire.'

'OK,' she said.

'So I shall take you out to dinner to celebrate,' he said.

'But surely you would rather celebrate with someone of your own age?' she laughed, 'I'm old enough to be your mother.'

As soon as she said it, she knew that it was a mistake. His usually happy laughing face turned into a positive mask of anger and his light green eyes flashed.

'You would go and spoil everything,' he said – and he turned abruptly on his heel and went out slamming the door.

Maxine looked again at her forty year old face in the glass.

Why should this vibrantly attractive young man chose her to fall in love with? Despite his sophistication he was really still a child, with a child's enthusiasms and a child's temper.

She carried on with her make up knowing what would happen next.

She was right. Jay came back happy mood completely restored.

'I've booked the table,' he said. 'You don't have to get poshed up, it's a jeans and t shirt place.'

'As long as it's not one of those streaking places where you have to take your things off,' she said.

'Where have you been my lovely?' he laughed, 'nakedness is out of fashion, people don't strip off in public any more.'

'You mean not this week?'

He cast his eyes to heaven at her ignorance.

'You've gotta keep up with the trend,' he said 'But tonight is going to be something special.'

'Why?'

'Surprise,' he said.

The dinner was good and a great deal of wine was drunk before Jay came up with the surprise.

He reached into his jeans pocket and came out with a little box which he handed to her with a wide smile.

Her heart sank a little as she guessed what the box contained. She opened it and there was a ring. A heart-shaped sapphire surrounded by small diamonds.

'Why have you given me this?' she asked.

'Well it's pretty obvious isn't it? It's an engagement ring.'

'My sweet boy. You are supposed to ask me a question first.'

He was dashed.

'I thought this was a good way of doing it. You do want to marry me don't you?'

She paused not knowing what to say?

She was afraid to mention age again. She certainly loved him and hated to let him down.

'Darling boy', she said at last, 'I know I should say this is so sudden and that is exactly what I'm going to say – this is so sudden.'

'We are in love – and that's what people do when they are in love. They get married.'

She paused, trying to think what to say.

'Can we just think about it for a little while? Yes I do love you and we do get on well together.'

'So why not then?'

'I have an idea. You could move in with me for a few days a week and see what happens. How about that?'

'You will wear the ring though? It cost me a lot of money I don't want to waste it.'

This made her laugh and after a while he joined in and they ended up drunk and helpless.

He moved in with her the next day – and Maxine wore the ring on her right hand. She was a little ashamed that he had spent his TV money on her, but at least it was a tangible thing something that would never lose its value.

They were ecstatically happy and on the evenings they slept together they were in perfect unison. Stan stood aside and watched the progression of the affair with a cynical smile on his face.

'So you didn't heed my warning,' he said to Maxine.

'I am in love,' she said, 'You can't argue with that'

15.

'Maxine, I'd like you to meet my mother,' remarked Jason as they lit their post coital cigarettes.

As he spoke, Maxine, as if in a waking nightmare, suddenly remembered again the age of her young lover.

It hadn't mattered in the play – the eighteen year age gap. On stage they seemed to be the same age. Nor had it hadn't mattered when they became lovers, it was accepted within the company; They were lovers in the play, they could be lovers in real life. Even when she felt she might be pregnant they had both rejoiced at the idea. Both only children, they had been hoping to know that there would be a family. She had to confess she was a little relieved when it was a false alarm.

However, she hadn't reckoned on a Mother. A Mother who could easily be the same age as her.

'What is she like – your mother?'

He laughed. 'Oh she's all right really.'

This sounded ominous. Mothers are supposed to be wonderful or infuriating – beautiful, motherly, whatever – not 'all right really.'

'Is there something you're not telling me?'

'Some people find her a bit – intimidating. She's inclined to be a bit of a snob. Upper crust – you know.'

Maxine didn't know. Her only experience of the English upper crust had been many years ago.

'She will love you though. She used to be an actress herself many years ago.'

'Why has she not been to the play?'

'No, not yet, she has lots of good works to do in the country. She will be coming soon I think.'

Maxine was dying to ask her name, realising she had probably heard of her – maybe even worked with her in the old days, But somehow she didn't want to talk to the boy about anything in the past. He knew roughly how old she was – she didn't actually elucidate – like lady Bracknell she believed that telling her age seemed calculating and she tried so hard not to mention too many of the things in her past. It was necessary for her to forget the age gap or at least make it seem normal.

She put out her cigarette, slipped into her robe. She turned away from him and went towards the bathroom for a shower.

'Was it something I said?' he laughed.

She turned to look at him. He was so beautiful. His tow coloured hair falling over his forehead, his eyes full of eagerness and mischief. His appearance had not entranced her until she got to know him. At the beginning, she had been enraptured by his charm, his wit and his intelligence. Although he seemed to have no inkling about his spectacular appearance, he had the confidence that comes with it. He delighted in putting their faces together in the mirror – to compare them. It always made her feel ancient.

'We look perfect together', he often said.

'I just wish I could be younger for you.'

'Age is so unimportant. Ann Hathaway was older than Shakespeare.'

'Second best bed,' she laughed, and he kissed her into silence.

'Maxine darling, I want you to meet my mother.'

Maxine got up from her dressing table to greet him and as she did so, another presence entered the room, bringing with her the familiar scent of 'Femme'.

The diminutive creature was dressed in sable from head to foot like something out of Dr Zhivago and was wearing the biggest shades that covered most of her face. Maxine held out a hand which the lady seemed not to see. She merely nodded acknowledgement.

Under her huge fur hat, Maxine could just see the wings of hair which held a touch – a shadow of red. The tiny figure made Maxie feel like a giant or overgrown schoolgirl and yet the exquisite creature was probably not much older than she was.

Even though her face and body was almost totally hidden, there was something very familiar about her. Maxine decided to play dumb.

'Jay tells me you were an actress,' she said. 'What was your acting name?'

The creature laughed. 'You can't remember?' she said and Maxine looked at her sharply seeking the signs of irony in her face. It was half covered by a pair of enormous shades, but she could discern the hint of a smile – a slight twitch of the dimpled cheek.

'I am Jessica Sherwood,' she said, and removed the dark glasses.

Maxine found herself looking into the eyes – the deep violent eyes that filled her with a kind of fear. She had known those eyes before – ever since when she was six years old. Jay's Mother was no stranger.

'How enchanting to see you again Maxine,' she said and turning to her son she said,

'You knew Maxine when you were four years old.'

'Yes? Well now I know her much better.'

'Of course, nothing like being in a show together to develop a friendship.'

'It's more than a friendship,' he protested.

Jessica gave her remembered wolfish smile.

'Of course it is darling,' she said and turning to Maxine, gave her a conspiratorial wink.

'We must get together and talk about old times,' she said, 'Come to tea on Sunday – that is your day off isn't it?'

'Good idea,' said Jay. 'We are having a read through of the TV script that afternoon – so you can get together and have a good old chinwag – about *me*!'

Maxine could not think of a reason to turn down the invitation, and anyway it would be good to see Philip after all this time – so it was arranged that Jessica's driver would pick her up and take her to their country house.

16.

The driver that came ringing at Maxine's doorbell that Sunday was hardly the kind of person she expected. He was in his late forties or early fifties with touches of grey in his curly black hair – and was simply the most gorgeous man she had ever seen and this was a women who had spent a lot of time in la la land hobnobbing with the likes of Paul Newman and Robert Redford but her driver – or rather Jessica's driver – was something else. He treated her with great respect, opened the door for her, helped her into the Mercedes and made sure she was quite comfortable before he shut her in. Once in the car she noticed that from her seat in the back she could see his face in the driver's mirror and she could feast her eyes on his amazing good looks. He was unusually bronzed for a Brit and had the flashing white teeth that spoke of expensive dentistry. She was dazzled by his bright blue eyes fringed with jet black lashes and longed to brush back the lock of curly black hair that seemed to fall over his forehead of its own volution.

They sat in silence for most of the journey eventually she urgently wanted him to speak.

'Has anyone ever told you that you look like... Tony Curtis?' she asked.
He laughed.
'Yes, they 'ave, but A'm taller and better loooking,' he said.
She was as started by his accent as she was by his response.
'You are from Hull?'
'Aye that I am,' he replied, 'just like you. I don't expect there's many famous film stars that come from Hull.'
'No, not a lot,' she replied. 'Plenty of them in theatre over here.'
'Don't know much about theatre,' he said. 'I've seen nearly all the films though. It was the pictures that kept me going.'
'Going? Where was this?'
She never heard any reply as he took a corner a little recklessly and rather fast.
'Hang on,' he said, as he turned into the long drive leading up to Jessica's house.

Jessica met Maxine at the door to her drawing room. She indicated a small tea table and guided her to a comfortable leather chair.
'So lovely to see you after all this time. I hope Jack behaved himself on the journey.'
'He was very quiet. We didn't talk much'.

'So good that you are back. Were you rather bored with Hollywood?'
Maxine laughed.
'I think perhaps Hollywood was bored with me.'
'Well maybe they were afraid of you. You've always had aggressive tendencies.'
'No Jessica – that was a joke. They were still offering me work. But the play seemed a better bet and I was homesick.'
'Sorry about the divorce. Stan was such a nice man.'
'That's Ok we are still best friends.'

Jessica pour tea from a silver teapot into pretty china cups. She concentrated on her task, not looking at Maxine.

'Nevertheless, it must seem strange for you to play opposite a man young enough to be your son.'
'Are you offended by that Jessica?'
Jessica gives a silvery laugh.
`Of course, not. Milk or lemon?'
'Whatever is most convenient. I don't mind what you put in my tea – except perhaps cyanide.'
'Haha. You always had a great sense of humour, Maxine.'
'Yes?'
'That is at least one thing that hasn't changed about you,' remarked Jessica, handing out a cup of tea.
'I'm happy about that.'
'I mean we all get older, don't we?' said Jessica with a smile. 'My hair is turning grey.'
'It doesn't show at all,' Maxine replied.
'Your hair looks so good,' said Jessica. 'The colour really looks natural.'
'It is natural.'
'Of course it is… Cake?'
'We just don't have grey hair in our family.'
'Very sensible,' smiled Jessica.

Maxine smiled back. It was seldom she really wanted to strike somebody. But today would not be a good idea.

'Do you take sugar? No of course you don't you have to look after your figure.'
'Yes I fear so.'
'Otherwise other people might stop looking after it. How about some carrot cake?'

'Yes please – it looks delicious.'

'Not all that worried about your weight then Maxine?'

'I like to have an occasional treat.'

'So I've heard.'

Jessica handed a slice of cake to Maxine. As she did so there was a kerfuffle at the door and a very young and very pregnant woman entered.

'Why Molly, hello dear. How lovely to see you.'

'You said Maxine Fletcher would be here and of course I had to meet her.'

'Of course. Come in and have a good look at her.'

'Maxine, this is Molly – my niece' and she looked fondly at the girl. 'Sit down dear, take the weight off your feet. How is the bump?'

'My good friend the bump? Doing fine. Hoping one day to meet his Daddy.'

'We cannot expect miracles. Just live in hope. Some cake?'

'Shouldn't really, but yes please.' She turned to Maxine. 'My future mother in law always has excellent cake. Good family to be a member of.'

There was a silence as Maxine tried to digest the previous remark. Maybe she heard it wrong – ot maybe there was another child nobody had mentioned.

'I'll think about it later,' she said to herself. She felt it was up to her to make some conversation.

'Will Philip be coming today? I thought he might be here.'

'Oh he doesn't do tea. He is in London. Reading scripts. He likes to do that on Sundays when everybody else in the business is playing golf.'

'Tell him I'm sorry to miss him – maybe some other time.'

She turned to Molly. 'When is your baby due?'

'About a week ago', – she laughed. 'He's in no hurry to come out'.

'Having too good a time in there,' put in Jessica.

'It is a boy then?' asked Maxine.

'Yes I'm convinced.'

'What are you calling him?'

'After my second cousin, Marcus – who died when he was a young man.'

'I remember him,' said Maxine, 'he was Philip's brother'.

'Yes,' said Molly. 'We want to preserve his memory. They tell me he was such a wonderful man. So brave and so handsome. I wish I'd been able to meet him. He died before I was born.'

Maxine wondered whether Jessica remembered a converstion they had all those years ago and she noticed the slight tightening of Jessica's lips. Oh yes, she remembered all right.

'Yes I met him once,' said Maxine. 'He was so unlike Philip. Strange how two brothers can be so different.'

Molly hoisted herself to her feet.

'Oh Golly, got to fly, going to the movies with Sandra. She will be so jealous when I tell her I've met Maxine Fletcher.'

'You should have brought her here.'

'You kidding? She'd be impossible. I want to be the one to boast about meeting the big movie star.'

With a flurry of activity, hugs and kisses with Jessica, she left the room.

'Nice girl,' said Maxine.

'Yes I couldn't have a better daughter in law.'

'She's engaged to ...?'

'Jason, they have been engaged since they were six years old.'

Maxine's conversational talents just gave up on her. She saw Jessica's smile and considered it unbearably smug. She felt it was imortant that she get away from here. From what she regarded as an kind of artificial richness. It made her unconfortable and when she looked at what she thought of as 'Lady Muck' in front of her all she could see in her mind was the little ragged girl with no shoes. The one who had destroyed her white fur coat. After an uncomfortable silence she drank her tea in one slurp. She looked at her watch.

'Oh my goodness what's the time? I think I should go.'

'Must you,' Jessica said mechanically, but she stood up anyway to say goodbye.

'*I'm surprised she doesn't take a bow*,' thought Maxine. '*Now her act is over and her dirty work is done.*'

'Yes afraid so.'

'I'll call Jack so he can come and pick you up.'

'That is the man who brought me here?'

'Yes.'

'You don't have to trouble him. I can catch a train.'

'There are no trains near here,' said Jessica.

'No, there is a station. I saw it as we were driving in. Five minutes away.'

'It's closed.'

'It didn't look closed.'

'Better you get Jack to drive you. He was so happy to bring you here. Very impressed with your movies. He is a great movie fan.'

'But that's ridiculous, we hardly spoke. I sat in the back.'

'Then next time you must sit next to him in the front and have a proper conversation. I think you'll find it interesting.'

17.

Jack arrived with the Mercedes and stood there in front of the car waiting for Maxine who went to get in the back seats.

'What's matter with yer,' laughed Jack and with his broad charming smile, he opened the front door for her. 'Too posh to sit next t' me?'

She laughed. 'Of course not.'

He smiled again and gave her an exaggerated bow as he helped her in to the passenger seat.

She got in the car and felt around for the safety belt.

He got into the driver's seat.

'What's up?'

'I can't find the safety belt.'

He laughed again.

'We're in country madam. We don't bother with them things.'

'Oh, I see.'

He fired up the car and proceeded down the drive into the road.

'So you're the famous Maxine Fletcher.'

'Not all that famous.'

'I've always wanted to meet an 'ollywood film star.'

'Well now you know, we are no different from anybody else.'

'Still impressed.'

'Well don't be. After all you work for the most famous musical comedy star.'

'No, she's just me sister!'

'Your sister? I didn't know…'

'She probably dunt brag about me much,' he laughed.

She was trying to digest this information and there were a few moments of complete silence.

'You're not bad looking really,' he said at last and he put his hand on her knee – as if by mistake.'

This remark was a bit surprising but she replied jokily as she pushed his hand away.

'I'm glad you approve'.

'Damn right I do. Bit of a sex pot I shouldn't wonder – nymphomaniac I think they call them.'

She was startled by his remark and felt he was definitely out of order.

'Not in the least'.

His next remark was even more surprising.

'Then I reckon you're a proper P.T.'

'I beg your pardon. What?'

'Prick Teaser. Oh now I see, you are a bit put out by that.'

She tried to make light of it.

'Well it was a little unexpected.'

'Its true though intit?'

'Well no it isn't.'

'Good – I knew you fancied me. How about having a bit of sex with me?'

'No – certainly not. I don't know you.'

'I don't suppose that stops people like you from having a bit. Actresses are famous for it. All of show business are sex mad – especially Hollywood' and his left hand returned to her knee – and again she brushed him off.

'Sorry Jack. Will you please drop me at the nearest station.'

'No.'

'Please. I don't like this kind of convrsation. And I don't appreciate being touched like that.'

'Well sorry. I can't talk the way you do Mrs Toffee nose.'

'Toffee nose?'

'The kind of person who cares for nobody but themselves'.

'I don't know what you are talking about.'

'You look down on people like us.'

'No, that's not true. I don't look down on anybody.'

'What about my sister? She told me you were mean to her when she was in trouble.'

Maxine cast her eyes to heaven. This old story coming back again.

'I didn't know she was in trouble.'

'She ran away and left me to take the rap. I got landed in prison. Ok she was a bitch, but she came to you for help and you turned her away.'

'It had nothing to do with me'.

'You've just forgotten haven't you?' he said – and without taking his eyes off the road, he unzipped his fly. Keeping his right hand on the wheel he put his left hand behind her neck.

She shouted, *'Get off me.'*

He pulled her head down onto his lap holding it down with his elbow.

'Suck me bitch', he said 'you know you want to'.

'You are entirely mistaken,' she tried to say, but her voice was muffled.

Instead she bit his thigh as hard as she could and dug her finger nails into him..

The next thing she knew, she was in hospital. Having lights shone in her eyes.

18.

'What is your phone number?' asked the doctor.

'Mind your own business'.

The doctor laughed

'Ok, what did you have for breakfast?'

'What day is it?'

'Sunday'

'Then I would have had eggs, bacon, fried tomatoes and mushrooms. With toast and marmalade'.

'But this morning – did you have that? Can you remember having that?'

'Erm. Why should I remember?'

The doctor shook his head and sat down beside the hospital bed.

'You have been in a car accident and probably have concussion. We need to know if you can remember anything about today.'

'Ok my phone number is.... I can't remember. I'm feeling really tired. Leave me alone. I want to go to sleep.'

The doctor laughed.

'Sorry that just isn't allowed. You have to remember something before you go to sleep.'

'What if I just make something up?'

'Pointless. Lets concentrate on the phone number.'

A nurse came in.

'The gentleman's here,' she said.

'That's good. He's bound to help.'

He turned to Maxine.

'This is the man who saved your life. He may be able to help you. I will come back and see you later.'

With an earnest worried air Jack came into the ward accompanied by a giggling and obviously infatuated nurse.

'How are you Maxie?' he said caressingly.

She looked at him, for a moment not knowing who he was.,

'It's Jack – remember me?' he said. 'You got a nasty bump on your head dint you?'

And somehow the familiar accent from her childhood gave her a warm comfortable feeling.

He sat on the chair beside her bed.

'Does it hurt very much?' he said. 'It must have been a nasty bump. What are they doing for you?'

'Nothing much. It doesn't really hurt at all. But they keep on asking me silly questions and flashing lights in my eyes.'

'What sort of questions?'

'My telephone number – what I had for breakfast.'

'Not about the accident?'

'No, they seem to know all about that.'

'I told 'em what happened. They just want to check that you've not been concussed.'

'How did it happen?'

Jack got up and walked round to the other side of the bed.

'I was giving you a lift home We was in a narow lane and some barmy driver came straight at us. I had to swerve to avoid him and crashed into a tree. You hit your head on the windscreen cos you hadn't fastened your safety belt.'

'That was a bit silly of me.'

'I shoulda checked after you came out of the toilet'.

'I went to the loo? In a service station?'

'Yes.'

'I don't remember any of that.'

'It in't important. All you need to remember is your phone number.'

She tried to check him out.

'Can't you tell them what it is?'

He laughed. 'That's cheatin, you got to remember it yourself.'

'You don't know it, do you?'

'Course I do. My sister gave it to me before I picked you up.'

Maxine became sleepy again. The nurse got her to her feet and she and Jack walked her around the ward.

'Mebbe you should go now. Get a cup of tea,' said the nurse, 'you've had a bit of a shock yourself.'

'Don't worry about me. This lass is more important than me.'

'Everybody's important,' she said.

After Jack left the doctor came back and like a quick flashes of light she started remembering things one at a time.. Her phone number,her breakfast and the teaparty with Jessica – but none of what happened and nothing to do with the drive home with Jack. It was enough for the doctors and although it was considered advisable that she should stay in for the night. She was to be released early the next morning.

Jay came in to see her. He hugged her as best he could as she was lying in bed and she did not rise to meet him. She was not keen to enter into an embrace with him. She was remembering pregnant Molly.

'Darling I was so worried when I heard about the accident. My mother called and told me you were staying the night with her. She didn't want to worry me. So I had a dismal evening here on my own watching TV. Then she rang me this morning and told me the poor old Mercedes got a bit knocked about and so did you. Thank goodness Jack was there to help.'

'He helped?'

'Oh yes. He carried you all the way to the AA telephone box and phoned for an ambulance. I'd never realised he was a heroic type. Mum was so chuffed that he was a hero.'

'Yes I suppose she must be'.

Maxine listened to the story and had a great desire to think it over on her own. It somehow didn't make sense to her. She didn't encourage Jay to stay longer – saying she was still sleepy after her accident.

Maxine's understudy went on that night. Despite the vestiges of memory she had discovered, the doctor at the hospital had decided she should rest. She was happy to stay in bed. She needed sleep and she needed to think – in that order.

19.

It was a shock next morning when Stanley arrived with the early edition of the Evening Standard under his arm.

'What have you been saying to the press?'

'Nothing.'

'Then what's this about your childhood sweetheart. The one that rescued you from a burning car.'

'No that was Jack.'

'Your childhood sweetheart?'

'Certainly not. I'd only just met him. He was driving me back from Jessica's house. I had been there for tea. I remember it perfectly – just can't remember the drive home.

'Well apparently you did something stupid, forgot to shut the door properly after you went to the loo at the service station and you were about to fall out of the car and he saved you and the car crashed into another vehicle. You hit your head on the windscreen. He carried you all the way to the AA phone box and called an ambulance.'

'Why did he have to carry me? What about the people in the other car? Couldn't they have driven me to the phonebooth? Or were they totalled as well?'

'He didn't mention that apparently. I suppose it just drove off'

'What kind of car was it. Did he say that?'

Stanley laughed.

'It was a mini.'

'Great – and it withstood a collision with a Mercedes?'

'The story varies as to which paper you read. He seems a bit of a romancer and then the tabloids put their own twist on the story.'

'Romancer – that is a strange way to describe it.'

'Talking of Romance. I think we had better try and kill those ridiculous rumours. It was bad enough you having a toyboy – and now the childhood sweetheart story is not a good one.'

'And you think people believe it?'

'Of course they do. Who is this bloke anhyway? He comes from Hull – it does make sense that you should have known him.'

'I know I didn't.'

Maxine didn't want to reveal his name just yet. She had to try and deal with the rumours before the wretched man invented more stories.

*

A week later, when the press were hanging around outside her flat and calling her incessantly on the phone she cut off her public number and rang Jessica on her private line.

'Jessica I want to speak to your brother Jack.'

'He's not here at the moment he said he had a meeting. Can't think what about.'

'The bloody press of course. Talking about his childhood sweetheart – that is me.'

'That's ridiculous,' laughed Jessica, 'Why would he say something like that? There was talk of somebody writing a book about his life.'

'Haven't you seen the red tops?'

'I dont read that kind of rubbish.'

'Well its time you did. They are calling him my childhood sweetheart and they are saying that he rescued me from a burning car and carried me to the hospital single handed'

Jessic 's voice took on a tone of pride in her brother's achievements.'

'Did he really do that?' she asked.

'No I think he really didn't do that – I can't swear to anything of course I was concussed.'

'Oh it must have been how he damaged the Mercedes. I wondered how that happened'.

'Well now I am wondering too. I don't believe his story but I don't have another one to replace it. I believe he is taking advantage of the situation – what ever it is. But its a bit annoy ing for me.'

'Well at least they are giving Jay a rest. Your toy boy as they call him.'

'Aha so you do read the Redtops.'

'No I receive everything about him from Romeike and Curtis . They send me all the press cuttings.'

20.

Beautiful movie star Maxine Fletcher's latest squeeze was her co star Jay Leonard – the son of millionaire theatrical impresario Philip Cranleigh. She has now gone down market and returned to her humble roots in Hull becoming reacquainted with her childhood sweetheart Jack Marsden. A handsome war hero who saved her from a burning car a couple of weeks ago. Which one will she choose?

Philip came into the breakfast room waving a copy of the *Daily News* – a local paper that he very rarely bothered to read. His head was still involved heavily in Show Business and rarely read any of the national or local scandal sheets.

But this story had got everywhere. . Mocked up pictures of Maxine flanked by her two supposed lovers . The toy boy that was Jay and the childhood swettheart – Jack.

'What's all this stuff about Maxine and your driver? It doesn't seem her style at all. It was pretty strange her getting involved with our boy. But that's just showbusiness. Often happen when people play love scenes together. Its just a phase. Doesn't usually last after the play is finished – often a long time before that. I could never understand why he didn't get married to Molly. Such a sweet girl.'

Philip was mostly worried about the family and the scandal that was being banding around the Upper Classes, discussed amongst all the upmarket families in the area.

'Why did Maxine have to do this? She has never been a publicity hungry person before. Why has she suddenly started doing this? I find it disappointing. And to involve our own son in the business.'

'You shouldn't taken notice of the press darling. You must know by now they are a class on their own. They just say whateve they like.

'Jason has always been a bit of a rebel. Calling the chauffeur Uncle Jack as if he was a member of the family. That's OK I'm not complaining about that, but peope might think Maxine is just obsessed with the men in our family.'

'Wait till they hear about your invovement with her.'

'God yes, that might be possible.'

Despite the fact that her life was now in a comfortable settled state Jessica found herself getting a little jealous of all the publicity Maxine was getting. – especially as both of the gentlemen involved were closely related to her. She was getting afraid that the story of Maxine and Philip would be the next to hit the press. Another of her menfolk.

'I think the Maxine thing is all a misunderstanding darling. Molly is Jason's fiancee and I'm sure they'll work it all out between them.'

'Yes We need to give the little boy a proper status as the heir to the estate.'

'So nice for your parents to have a little boy to play with. They are worried about his legitimacy too I believe.'

Philip gave a wry laugh.

'I think they gave up worrying about that when Marcus was killed. He was the one intended to inherit. Anyway I doubt if there will be much to inherit by the time Jason's baby is old enough.'

21.

Shortly after her discussion with Stanley, Maxine woke up suddenly gasping for air. A terrifying feeling that she was dying. But it was her mental activity winding up and she was finally remembering the whole scenario of events that happened before the accident. Her memories were clearing bit by bit and she was feeling the experience all over again. She got on the phone to Stanley who was n his office.

'Stanley help me. I've remembered what happened. Its so horrible I can hardly believe it.'

'Tell me.'

'No, not on the phone. Please come over so we can talk… and bring gin.'

'Oh my God – that bad?'

'Worse.'

'I'll be there. I have work to do this morning, make a few calls but I'll come as soon as I can.'

'Are calls more important than me?'

'Who knows honey? See you soon' and he hung up.

*

Maxine was ridiculously angry with Stan for not immediately rushing to her assistance. But she paced her flat, remembering little by little had happened and what had caused the crash. Her childhood sweet heart indeed. A Monster.

The doorbell rang at last. She had paced the floor about thirty times and she still felt ridiculously angry with Stan for not coming straight away. She rushed to the door, flung it open and despite her resentment, she flung herself into Stan's arms.

'I brought tonic as well and some pretzels. Have you got ice and some glasses?'

'Yes of course and lemon's in the fridge. But let me tell you—'

'Let's calm down and pour a drink. I'll get the mixings. Don't fash yourself – just sit down.'

'I can't sit down and want to fash myself.'

'There's no way I can listen to you if you are marching about like that. Sit sit.'

Sighing heavily Maxine perched hersel on the edge of a chair and began to repeat the stuff she had just remembered.

'He was trying to get me to give him a blow job.'
'What? You said he was a complete stranger.'
'Yes he was – well more or less.'
'So the sweetheart story is not all rubbish.'
'Shut up Stan, of course it was rubbish.'
'But you were in the car.'
'He was Jessica's driver. He was driving me home from her house.'
'So he did this while he was driving?'
'He pulled my head down on to his lap – his flies were undone. I bit him.'
'Hard?'
'Yes, and I kicked him and dug my nails into him.'
Stan shuddered at the thought.
'Ouch. So if he was just a driver. Why were you sitting beside him?'
'He asked me if I was too posh to sit next to him. I said of course not.'
'You are so stupid.'
'I don't like hurting people.'
'Mm. you managed to hurt me a lot.'
'Did I really? I never knew.'
'You didn't ask. Anyway, We are not talking about us. We are talking about this monster.'

Maxine looked at Stan with new eyes. They had both been too proud to admit their heartbreak.She had no idea he had felt so deeply about their separation.'

'I hope you hurt him bad.'
'Must have done – he crashed into a mini.'

Despite the importance of the situation, this made them laugh together. Suddenly friendlier than they had been for years.

Stan took a long slurp of his g and t looking at her closely, he said.
'Please for give me if I ask you an impertinent question.'
'Living with you I got used to it.'
'Are you sure you really remembering all this? You are not making it up? Imagining what happened?'

She jumped to her feet furious that he should doubt her for a second.
'You think I'm a liar?'

She raised her hand against him. He stood and took hold of her threatening hand and sat her down again, putting her glass in her hand.

'No need to beat me up as well,' he said, 'Calm down. The problem is – everyone seems to think he's such a splendid chap.'

She took a hit from the glass and put it on the table.

'He is very good looking,' she said thoughtfully, 'I thought he was stunning when I first met him.'

'You fancied him?'

'For about five minutes.'

'But not now?'

'You've got to be joking.'

She put her head in her hands.

'I just don't know what to do next.'

'You should go to the police. Report sexual harassment.'

'Report him? Who would believe me?'

'Yes its not easy to believe I must admit. Even I had doubts at first. But surely the cops would belive you.'

'Come off it Stan. I am a woman remember? Women are expected to put up with that kind of thing. My account would not be acceptable or believable. A man that good looking!. How would I turn him down?'

'Even though he was a stranger?'

'Yes, Even though I had never met him before that day. I didn't even know Jessica had a brother.'

'What? Jessica's brother? You didn't tell me that. So you must have known him before. You said you and Jess were at school together.'

Her childhood snobbishness came back and was appalled at the idea.

'Certainly not school. The Marsdens and I did not attend the same kind of school.'

'I beg Milady's pardon.'

'She only came to my Aunt's dance classes. She had talent and my aunt gave her training for nothing.'

'So you were not all children together.'

'Of course not.'

'And yet you were having tea with Jessica at her house. Why the sudden friendship?'

'Jessica is Jay's mother.'

Stan's mouth opened and looked as if it would never go back to normal.

'You missed that bit out.'

'Sorry, it has sort of lost its importance.'

'What, they wouldn't even dare use that story in Hollywood. The plot is so thick it would never get through the projector.'

Maxine was wringing her hands. She was back on her feet and began pacing again. Stanley took her shoulder in both hands and settled her down on the chair

'Shut up and drink your gin, he said,' I'll think of something. That bastard must not be allowed to get away with this.'

22.

'Maxine, I have more news for you. Shall I come over?'

'Of course Stan if you have anything to tell me, she said, 'I'm going crazy about these stupid rumours.'

'I'll bring gin again, this time you will really need it.'

He seemed to arrive almost immediately and although he seemed to be bursting with news, he first of all arranged Maxine on the sofa and made sure theywere both sitting down with drinks in their hands before he began. Maxine could never understand why he never just burst in with news just as she would but always felt he had to delay even the most urgent of information. He began with a typically enigmatic remark.

'Ok Dollface,' he began,' what a remarkably muddled up life you do lead'.

'What do you mean?'

'Well last month you were in love with a child – the one who has suddenly become a Daddy.'

'Oh has he really? He didn't mention anything about it to me. Mind you, he totally believed Jack's childhood sweeetheart story and he was behaving like a jealous lover. When I told him it wasn't true he accused me of playing the field. I told him to fuck off .Luckily his mother called him home – I guess because of the impending birth. He is quite simply out of my life now. I hope he marries little Molly.'

Stan gave big sigh.

'Have you finished?

'Sorry. He just pissed me off.'

'Well any way in your own special way you have usurped my other little bit of startling information.'

'There's more?'

'Yes something even more dramatic.'

'OK then.'

'Are you sitting comfortably?'

'Oh hurry up for Heaven's sake.'

'OK I'll start again. OK?'

'Yes yes yes.'

Last month you were in love with a child who has become a Daddy and now your are supposedly having an affair with a *murderer.*'

'What?'

She jumped to her feet.

'Tis true. I've been making a few enquiries and find that Jack Marsden did time for killing his own father. Shot him, then dumped the body into the Humber.'

Maxine sat heavily down on the sofa.

'Wow, that's frightening.'

'Sorry to tell you so abruptly. But I don't know of any other way.'

'My God he could have murdered me. Why did he do this – to his father?'

Stan shook his head.

'I don't know anything more. But I think as he has already done time people will be less inclined to believe his stories. We can safely go ahead with the prosecution.'

'Not yet though.'

'Why not. I should have thought the sooner the better.'

'We don't know the whole story. It seems a bit like hitting a man when he's down.'

'Come on – he behaved like a beast'

'Yes I know but...'

'But what?'

'If he's only just out of prison.'

'Not just – he's been hanging around for some time. Been trying to get work as a model.'

'A model?'

'Well you said he was pretty.'

Maxine's mind was whirling about. She was finding it difficult to sort out her thoughts. To express what she was feeling.

'Come on Maxine,' said Stan. 'Let's go and get a nice cheap pub lunch. I bet you are not eating enough.'

*

Safely ensconced in a corner seat in the local pub. Maxine felt she had anoither question that was preying on her mind.'

'Okay let me into your mind a little. What is worrying you?' asked Stan

'Was Jessica around when this happened? This ... murder?'

'Yes, I wasn't going to tell you, but since you asked. She did a runner when the police came calling and left Jack to take the rap for it. The police caught up with him. The girl known as Lily Marsden just disappeared. Somehow she became reborn as Jessica Sherwood a famous actress.'

'Do you want Shepherd's pie or fish and chips?'

Maxine was not interested in food at this moment in time.

'I'm not hungry.'

'Yes you are. Shepherd's pie then..'

He went off to order food at the bar. Maxine just sat there knocked all of a heap.

'Have you told anybody about this:?'

'Lord no. You are the only one I've told – and I wanted to keep Jessica's name out of this. After all, she is married to a friend of mine. How would this sort of thing affect people like the Cranleighs?'

'Darling Philip. I wonder if he knows her past history.'

'And anyway I cannot let the redtops know that Maxine Fletcher has been consorting with an assassin.'

'But I'm not consorting. I hardly know him.'

'You were driving with him. Had a motor accident in the car with him.'

'I was just a passenger.'

'Riding shotgun with a professional chauffeur – and an assassin?'

'Dont go on about guns again.'

'I did have one rather scary thought about Jessica,' said Stan after a while.

'Yes I am probably having the same scarey thought too,' said Maxine.

'Supposing Jessica did the shooting and he just hid the body.'

'Yes OK, but where would she get a gun? She was only about thirteen years old.'

'Of course Maxie. Do you actually think she is capable of killing somebody?'

'I felt pretty near to it when I heard about Jack's fairy stories and then remembered what he did.'

'But you didn't have a gun.'

23.

A furious Jessica arrived at Maxine's flat.

Maxine looked at her through the window in her door and saw this tiny redheaded fury She opened the door, suspecting trouble, but she decided she would have to face it.

Jessica burst through the door and stormed into the flat.

'Nice to see you,' said Maxine. 'Won't you sit down?'

'I don't need to sit down with what I have to say.'

'Okay, then, we'll stand,' said Maxine. 'How about a drink?'

Jess's violet eyes flashed pure hatred at her. Maxine had a quick thought: *Maybe she did do the killing after all.*

'Wouldn't you feel better if you sat down? Something is obviously worrying you.'

'I've just had a visit from your ex husband.'

'Stan... yes.'

'You told him what happened with Bill – Jack's father.'

'No I didn't tell him, I didn't know about it. He told me.'

Jessica looked at her wondering whether or not to believe what she said. Maxine took her hand.

'I am so sorry I didnt help you when you were in trouble.'

'You weren't to know,' she replied grudgingly.

Maxine indicated an easy chair and Jessica sat. She put her head in her hands. She was obviously deeply distressed.

'Help me Maxine. Surely this time you won't turn me away. It's all your fault.'

'*My* fault?'

'I'm talking about your little flirtation with my brother = you have put the whole family at risk.'

'What are you talking about?'

'It is disgraceful what you are doing to poor Jack, hasn't he suffered enough? Telling lies about his sexual interference with you.'

'But it was true, he behaved like a monster.'

'Even if he did, you must have encouraged him. He is in a vulnerable state.'

'That really doesn't excuse him.'

'You encouraged him.'

'I didn't.'

'I saw how you fancied him.. I could see the way you looked at him when he came to pick you up.'

'You weren't even there. You were in your drawing room.'

'I was watching, through the window. You got into the front seat. You wouldn't normally have done that. But I saw it, you gave him your little girl act. And then you accused him of molestation and made him crash the car.'

'Jessica – dear – I'm afraid what I said was true. He did molest me. He tried to make me...'

'Of course he didn't – that was your story to discredit my family. You've always hated the Marsdens. Ever since you were a little girl you've hated us for being poor and because I spoiled your stupid white fur coat. What were you doing with a thing like that anyway. It wasn't even cold. I survived the winter even though I hadn't any shoes. And there were you pretending to be Shirley Temple.'

'And you were pretending to be Jessie Matthews.'

There was a long pause.

'OK,' said Jessica.

'Are you remembering?'

'Yes – I really was Jessie Matthews in those days. Were you Shirley Temple?'

'No I was never Shirley Temple. I hated her with her silly dlimples. My ridiculous costume was all my mother's idea.'

'At least you had a mother.'

'Yes – but she felt she had to control everything I did. She forced me to do things I didn't want and tried to make me believe it was all my idea.'

'I noticed that. It was because you always acted like a good little girl . You never made any real decision on your own. You let everyone bully you. Even that awful mongsewer with his big stick. Vile man.'

'Is that why you left the ballet school?'

'You mean you noticed? You actually noticed I'd gone?'

'Well of course – you were the star of the class. Even though he treated you badly, he knew you had real talent. Is that why you left him?'

'I left because I lost the only person I ever really cared about. The only one who ever cared for me. My sister Janey. I had from Janey the thing that you have always had from everybody. She cared about me and looked after me.'

Jessica's fury had turned into self pity. She was very near to tears.

Maxine didn't say anything, she just poured out a whisky and handed her the glass. Jessica took a big sip and the tears subsided.

Maxine risked another question.

'Does Philip know anything about this?'

'No. I'd rather not worry him. I didn't tell you before but Philip is not well. He has a heart problem and any shock might just kill him.'

'Oh darling. I am so sorry. He is such a lovely person.'

'Yes I am aware you thought a lot of him. He told me you had been an item – briefly.'

'I would like to see him. Would that be all right?'

'Of course. You can find him in his office. He spends a lot of time there at the moment. Making sure the business is in good order – that we will be all right – in case.'

Jessica was near to tears again. Maxine knelt beside her and put her arms around her. A geture she would never have expected in her life.'

The two women hugged each other as if they were the dearest of friends instead of the worst of enemies.

24.

Maxine went to see Philip . His secretary let her into his office without any hesitation. He had been sitting behind his desk but he rose with difficulty when Maxine entered the room. His face lit up with delight at seeing her. She went to him and gave him a hug. When he sat down again, she could tell that the effort had been exhausting. His face lost the glow it had when he first saw her and he was very thin and very pale – like an old man.

'Maxine – how nice of you to come and see me. Beautiful Movie Queen. I always knew you would be a star.. I guessed it when you turned me down.'

'That was a difficult thing to do.'

'That is how I knew how you would make it. Such bravery deserves reward. Oh dear that sounds terribly conceited. But I was in love with you,you know – and I was rich.'

'You married lovely Jessica instead.'

'Yes I did, and I was always fond of her, but there was a kind of family problem that had to be solved.'

'A family matter? I'm sorry.'

'Maxine I do have to tell somebody. Its a secret I've been keeping for such a long time, but you seem connected with our in so many ways.'

'Philip, Are you sure about this?'

'Absolutely. You probably realised, knowing Jason so well, that his parentage could be in question.'

'You always knew this.'

'I was not stupid. Jessica was pregnant and Marcus was killed. I knew what had to happen.'

'So you knew all along – but you didn't tell Jessica...?'

'No. Somehow I couldn't tell her. She has no idea that I always knew. Maybe that is a mistake. It left her open to blackmail.'

'Are you talking about that vile brother of hers? He was blackmailing her?'

'Yes of course – and I knew about that too. I know it's not a good thing to say to you at the moment. He's not really such a bad man. He is a romantic – not really in touch with real life. He was locked away for quite a long time.'

'He wasn't very decent to me.'

'Yes, I know and I'm sorry. But the fact that you, a famous movie star, actually consented to even talk to him was enough to make him believe you were in love with him and wouldn't object to what he did.'

'Philip, I'm sorry, but there is no way I can condone his behaviour. There is absolutely no excuse for him.'

Philip sighed.

'Yes you are right of course... but you do realise that if he feels we are going to get him into trouble, he is capable about telling about Jessica's involvement in the murder. If he is publicly attacked he may incriminate her. She did – after all – run away from the police. We have got to keep his mouth shut. Please explain this to Stan, will you?'

'To tell him to shut up? Yes I'll talk to him.'

Philip smiled. Already his colour was almost back to normal. This had obviously been preying on his mind. He looked better already.

'I suppose Jessica has told you that my time is limited?'

'Yes she is finding it difficult to cope with it.'

'Listen to me Max. I know you've never been actual friends, but there is no reason why you shouldn't be. You compliment each other. Together you can conquer the world. Why not start a company or something together. She has strength and you have charm. That is what made The Queens such a strong play.'

'I see.'

'So I have said the same to Jess. It is the dearest wish of my heart that you two should be friends. It will help me to leave you both without distress. Will you try?'

Of course she said yes and of course she didn't really mean it. Not when the smell of that burning fur assailed her nostrils whenever she was subject to stress.

25.

Maxine left Phillip's office, her mind in a whirl. She popped into Gerry's club in shaftesbury Avenue to share a gin and tonic with a couple of early thespian drinkers – but she couldn't get the face of Philip out of her mind. The sick man she had cared for, who wanted to make sure there would be no scandal in his family and wanted to protect his wife. She made the decision to intervene for his sake, finished her drink qickly and rushed around to Charing Cross to find Stan and tell him to lay off Jack. It was unusual for her to go round to his office without calling first, but she felt the matter had urgency.

She took the lift up to the first floor to the door marked Stanley Harvey Ltd. She knocked once and opened the door to his outer office.

She was amazed to note that his outer ofice was no longer the fairly ramshackle place that she was used to. It wa clean, tidy and instead of the usual client photos – it had brightly coloured pictures.

She took a glance at one of them and to her horror saw that it was a picture of puppies in a basket.. As she stood there looking at them and feeling a little nauseous, the inner door opened and a young woman came out slightly staggering on five inch heels.

At first she assumed it was an actress, one of Stan's clients, but that supposition didn't last long. The girl was blond with curls very neatly organised. She was wearing neat little blue jacket over a blouse tied at the neck with a bow, and stud earrings. It was as if she was aiming to be a clone of Margaret Thatcher.

The young woman looked at Maine and smiled in a professional kind of way.

'Is there something I can do for you? You'd probly like a cup of tea?'

The voice didn't match the appearance.

She had a high pitched childish voce with a pronounced American accent.

'Er yes, OK. I'm Maxine Fletcher'

'Yes I know,' said the girl.

'Your face is very familiar,' said Maxine

The girl laughed. 'Of course it is,' she said. 'I'll get you some tea.'

She moved around to the table on which resided a small kettle and sone tea things. As she did Maxine couldn't help noticing her stomach which was unusually protuberant. The girl caught her glance and patted her tummy. Maxine's eyes followed the trajectory of the hand and realised by the slightly swollen tummy that the young women was pregnant.

'What is the matter with everhyone these days?' thought Max. *'Everyone seems to be pregnant. Hope it's not catching.'*

Suddenly the fact dawned on her.

'Why it's Precious, isn't it? What are you doing here?'

'I'm Stanley's wife,' she said.

'But... I thought you were divorced.'

The girl laughed.

'I did think about it, but then Junior started to arrive and I thought 'He needs a poppa, so I hopped on a Jumbo and came to help darling Stanley in his office.'

'Well that is so sweet, Precious,' said Maxine – and realised in that moment that she had been secretly hoping to renew marital acquaintanceship with Stanley. She looked at this cute girl and remembered Stanley's secretary, plain, horsefaced, bespectacled and quite brilliant.

'And Mildred ... where did she—?'

'She retired.'

'Well what a surprise,' said Max, 'Stan never told me.'

'He's only just found out,' laughed the girl and handed Max a cup of tea. 'Wanna cookie?'

'No thank you. I would like to talk to Stan. It is an urgent matter.'

'Yes, it always was.'

Precious spoke on the intercom 'Maxine Fletcher to see you. She says its urgent.'

She took the cup of tea from Maxine and escorted her into Stan's office, placing the cup of tea on his desk.

'Would you like a cup of?' she asked Stan.

He refused.

'I've had enough tea to launch three hundred lifeboats,' he said. Precious left the office, leaving the door ajar. Maxine slammed it shut.

'OK Mr Stepford what's going on.'

He shrugged.'Search me.'

'You told me you were divorced.'

'No', he said, 'I told you she was out of my life and she was. No apparently she's back in it.'

'Its not fair.'

'What dyou mean?'

'Well – I need you.'

'Don't be so silly. You are not interested in me. You only like toy boys and murderers.'

He laughed. She was not in the mood for jokes.

'You rotten shit. I could hit you.'

'OK have a go. A little S and M never harmed anybody. Maxine sit down and stop walking about, it makes me tired. Sit down and tell me why you are here – without calling. It must be urgent.'

'I never thought of you as a daddy.'

'Netither did I. But I think I might enjoy it'

'But will you enjoy living with that idiotic Stepford woman?'

He paused for thought.

'We came to some arrangement on my last trip to LA. Fool that I am.'

'But you said you couldn't stand her. You won't be happy.'

'Mmm probably not. But I guess I'm lumbered. We'll just have to see what happens. I'm prepared for anything.'

Maxine gave up and sat down.

'Ive come to tell you to lay off Jack,' she said.

'Yes, Ive been thinking about Jack. He came to see me this morning. He is very charming.'

'Im glad you think so.'

'I'm not paying him a compliment. I'm not fooled by spurious charm. But he is so good looking you can't help but be taken in when you are actually talking to him. I understand your fascination.'

Her indignation forced her to her feet again.'

'That so called fascination lasted about ten minutes.'

'Will you please sit down and we can discuss the matter without hysteria.'

She reluctantly took her seat again.

'Yes Ok. I spoke to Philip just now. He thought it was unfair to ask you to do something to help a man that had been such a bastard. He called me as soon as you left him. I made a few phone calls and I've got him an interview with *Spectacular Films* the film company downstairs. Mrs Stepford took them his pictures.'

'He already had pictures?'

'Sure – all over the News of the World, remember? He is extremely photogenic – the red tops loved him – you must have noticed. He brought a whole lot of copies with him.'

'So he was using me to make himself a career.'

'Why do you think he sold them that story? I gathered he didn't seriously want to be your childhood sweetheart.'

Maxine gasped. 'I feel used.'

'We are all using each other. It's what life is about. You used me. I used you.'

She considered this.

'I hate the idea of being used by a villain.'

'I shall be using him. You must admit he got his punishment, served his time. It's good to give him a chance to rehabilitate himself. He has a great face. A middle aged model.'

'But what he did to me.'

'That was horrible but I sort of understand. He had been incarcerated for much of his life. When he went into quod it was probably fashionable to treat women roughly. He didn't have the chance to learn how to be a new man.'

'It is still unfair to let him off when he did that to me.'

'But prosecuting him would cause heartache to so many other people you care about. Philip, Jessica and your lover Jason. They would all suffer if he spoke out. He did threaten it in a gentle off hand sort of way.'

'So we give in to blackmail?'

'It's your choice Max. Just think of the consequences.'

26.

There came a time when Philip could no longer manage the jounrey to London each day and decided to bring his work home. Jessica to her secret surprise was delighted and eager to spend time with him. She had found there was an ususpected side to her. When Philip became ill she quite suddenly realised how much he had meant to her His constant presence and supportiveness had never been obvious. He always played himself down – years of playing second string to his brother Marcus had become a habit.

She turned herself into a carer – in spite of the Doctor's advice she would not hear of him being transfered to an expensive hospital – would rather look after him, read to him his beloved novels and plays. She took care of him with great tenderness as she had with Jason when he was a tiny child. Now Jason was out of her care with his own son. Philip was taking his place in her heart, just as Jason was the only person who had ever managed to take the place of her sister Janey. The only person she had ever trulyloved. She recognised her infatuation with Marcus was just that but she blessed him for being the progenitor of her beloved child.

Now Philip was her child, and she took care of him. But she was possessive, now she hd found him she wanted to spend every minute of every day with him. And she resented any moment he was with other people. She realised it was true love at last and she knew that it was not going to go on for ever. That he was on the way out and she feared what her life would be like without him.

She loved his smile his happiness at when she talked to him of the past. When she brought his meals to him .They listed to the radio and watched TV together and she had moments of jealousy every time Maxine appeared on screen.

She was determined that he would have happiness at the end of his life so when he asked if he could see Maxine, she was hurt and jealous and yet didn't want to deny him anything. Max had rung him frequently but Jessica always answered the telephone. She was afraid that people might come and depress him. She wanted to keep him and be with him every second of the life he had left. especially when very near the end he took permanently to his bed.

'He wants to see you,' said Jessica.

Maxine got a thrill of satisfaction. She had been wondering about Philip but Jess was always rather close and was not about to say much.

However this time she was to be allowed to see him at home.

But she had one worry

'Don't let Jack come and pick me up. I can find my way on my own,' she said.

'Jack is no longer with us.'

Maxine's heart gave a thump, a thrill of excitement.

'You mean he's dead?'

'No he's just disappeared. Found somebody else to scrounge off. I think your ex-husband. Stan has managed to get him some modelling work. Anyway you can get the train and we have a contract with the taxi firm so they will pick you up. Much simpler.

'OK I'll be there.'

Maxine was only allowed 10 minutes with her former lover. Philip was sinking fast, unable to speak much but there was one remark that lingered in her mind. He asked her to lean close to him and he almost whispered in her ear.

'Don't tell Jess that I knew... about Marcus.'

'Someone else might tell her.'

'You are the only person who knows. Promise me.'

Maxine had no choice but to promise.

When she arrived home she was alarmed to find that the house was surrounded by masses of people – some with tape recorders and some with cameras. Fearing the worst she dodged out and went into the local hostelry where her cleaning lady had a second job working behind the bar. Norah greeted here with a smile.

'Did you get the flowers?' she asked. 'I would have waited in for them but they were short staffed here and thought I'd better get my skates on.'

'No I didn't get any flowers. All I got were a whole bunch of press people milling around the house. I didn't get anywhere near my flat. I just did a runner and came here to see if you knew what was going on.'

'Are you sure they wanted to see you?'

'Well who else would it be? Unless there was a disaster of some kind, there is nobody living there who would be plagued by the press. But I haven't given out my address to anyone and I don't think Stan would either.'

Norah suddenly clapped her hand over her mouth.

'Oh my God, *NO*.'

'What's the matter?'

'It's all my fault?'

'How can it be all your fault?'

'The delivery man from the flower shop rang me, said he had some red roses for you but the rain had washed away the address on the label.'

'So you gave it to them?'

'Of course. They said the roses were from Jack Milner.'

'OK. But when was the rain?'

'I was busy, didn't look out the window. Oh I'm so stupid.'

Maxine tried to reassure the woman, but she was furious and she rang Stan.

'OK I'll sort it out and get rid of the bastards. Can you stay where you are for an hour or so?'

'How will you do that?'

'I'll let them know you've gone somewhere – John O'Groats or somewhere far enough away'.

'How can you get that news to them?'

'Easy I'll get Precious on to it.'

'Precious, what can she do?'

'She can call them and say Maxine has been seen boarding a train at Kings Cross. They have all sorts of informants. In the meantime, I'll book you into a nice hotel – far away – on the Isle of Wight – give you a false name.'

'What would that be?'

'Oh I dunno – erm Helen P... Barker.'

'Why Helen Barker?'

'Helen Parker was a girl I ws in love with at Kindergarten. But she might object if you used her real name. Helen Barker sounds good.'

'But how can I pretend to be somebody I'm not?'

'Don't be daft. I thought you were an actress. You do it all the time.'

'Yes I suppose so. Hadn't thought of doing it in real life.'

She was beginning to find the idea intriguing.'

'Hey but what about my passport?'

'For the Isle of Wight? That is a joke isn't it.'

27.

Stan had booked her as Helen Barker into a very pleasant hotel in Sandown. She loved the Island with its medieval cottages and tourist-friendly people. After settling herself in, she took her book with her down to the dining room in order to have her evening meal before going to her room and getting some sleep. She was feeling pretty tired, but she reckoned John Irving's book *Hotel New Hampshire* her favourite author, would amuse her and help her to relax more than her other likely one *Gorky Park* which she would rather read in the daytime.

She had finished her main course and awaiting her chocolate mousse when a young woman approached her.

'Excuse me,' she said. 'You are Mrs Barker?'

Maxine, suddenly confused. For the moment, then remembered who she was supposed to be.

Maxine laughed. 'Well, yes, of course I am.'

'Well I'm Janice Barker. Isn't that a coincidence?'

'Not really. I don't suppose it's a very unusual name.'

'It's not so usual in Hull I think. That is where I come from.'

'But I detect an Australian accent?'

'Mum and Dad emigrated there when I was a kid.'

In spite of herself Maxine was intrigued. ,

'Good to meet you,' she said 'I'm from Yorkshire myself.'

'Oh really? Do you mind if I sit with you? I'm here on my own and I feel embarrassed a girl on her own, people look at me strangely – know what I mean?'

Maxine felt she couldn't refuse. Janice sat down opposite her.

She was pretty with long dark hair curled and with the front strands taken to the back of her head and tied with a ribbon. She wore rimless glasses and a wide friendly smile. She was dresed rather like an office worker in a narrow skirt and a shirt with a jumper pulled over it.

'You are so kind and so understanding', she said. 'What are you reading?'

'Its the latest John Irving. 'Hotel New Hampshire'.'

'I love his books,' enthused Janice.

'Have you read the one about Garp?'

'Oh. Yes, His characters are so well drawn. And he's so handsome.'

'Yes, I suppose he is. I never thought about it.'

'Oh I did. He reminds me of that man in all the ads for electric shavers'. What's his name? Jack Miller?'

Maxine was impressed, but beginning to feel a little uneasy.

'You know his name? The man in the advertlsements? That is unusual.'

'I'm interested in names. Especially of famous people who come from Hull. His real name is Marsden, but he changed it for professional reasons.'

'Yes, I see.'

The girl gave a chuckle.

'Just like you. You are not Helen Barker are you? My mother was called Helen Barker.'

'And you are...' she whispered the name, 'Maxine Fletcher?'

Maxine gave a quick look around the room to make sure nobody was watching.

Maxine saw no point in denying it.

'Don't tell anybody, I beg you.'

'Of course I won't. I am so thrilled to meet you,' said the girl. 'I'm a great fan of yours.'

Maxine smiled and thanked her and went back to *Hotel New Hampshire*. But the girl persisted.

'Oh you are so kind,' said Janice 'Wait till I tell me friends in Scunthorpe. I believe you come from Yorkshire? Just across the water.'

'Not Hull then? you deceived me.'

'We are all in the deception business I guess.'

Maxine found herself enjoying the young girl's company – someone who seemed so happy to be with her. Het confidence had taken a tumble ever since the accident in the car. She was bored with all the reporters and photographers who plagued here with questions about her relationship with her 'Childhood Sweetheart' but here was a nice young girl who just wanted to be with her.

'I was sorry about your accident,' said Janice. 'The word went around that you had messed up your face and were practically unrecognisable.'

'No, it was just my head that was messed up. I still don't remember anything about it.'

'It must have been nice though to be with that lovely man, Jack. Your childhood sweetheart?'

'No – he was a stranger.'

'How do you know, you said you don't remember anything'

'I would hardly forget a childhood sweetheart – not it was just the accident I don't remember.'

'It was so romantic. Coming all the way from Hollywood to be with your sweetheart. Is that why you returned?'

'No, there were no films I was interested.'

That was her rehearsed line. She must never admit she jumped before she was pushed.

'But you were still filming. There's one of yours on at the local cinema – a new one.'

'I made it three years ago. It takes that long to edit and distribute it.'

Just then Maxine saw the girl's hand move in a strange way.

'What is that book you are reading?' she said.

'Erm, it's *Animal Farm*.'

'How interesting, may I have a look at it?'

Maxine grabbed hold of the book and found it was just a cover for a small recording device.

'Who are you?'

'I'm just a fan.'

'Bollocks. What paper are you from?'

Maxine grabbed the tape recorder and pulled out the tape.

'I have no wish to discuss my life with the Daily Star,' she said.

'Don't be rude. It's The Evening News,' said the girl.

'Right. Can you leave me now? Please?'

'Just tell me about Jack. He's so attractive.'

'No no no. I'm leaving now. Goodbye.'

*

It was only nine thirty, but she decided to go to bed with her book.

It was still early evening when the banging started.

There was a knock on the door. Thinking it was room service, she opened the door and there was a flash. Blinded by the flash she took a step back and Janice bounced into the room.

'Oh sorry I must have the wrong room. Mine is next door'.

'Now you are talking to me as if I was an idiot. Nobody knocks at their own door.'

The girl laughed.

'Please leave my room,' said Maxine

'I'm not dangerous, just enthusiastic.'

'I shall call security.'

'Just give me a quote.'

'Ok, here's one. *Fuck off*.'

And Janice turned and left, laughing. 'I'll definitely quote you on that,' she said.

But it was not the end.

The banging started on the wall from the room next door. And carried on all through the night.

She rang Stan.

'Bloody girl's destroying my life here. Do you know her Janice Barker?'

Stanley told her to wait while he made some enquiries. She hung on to the phone tapping her foot impatiently. She wanted some answers and she wanted them quickly.

Stan came back on the phone.

'Must have been Denise Ranger. Does she look like a very young nerd – maybe a librarian – with glasses – not very convincing Australian accent?'

'Yes, that's the one.'

'Oh she's a menace. Gossip writer. Always goes out in disguise.'

'I'm out of love with the Isle of Wight.'

'Then come right back. I'm afraid your friend Philip is sinking fast. He won't last the week.

*

Jessica was tired. It was emotionally draining looking after her husband. He was hardly awake. She read to him his favourite books, for some reason he loved Dickens – bored her to tears, but she carried on with it for his sake.

He seemed to be totally insensible. In fact the doctors told her that though he seemed to be in a coma he could actually hear everything she said and did – so she talked to him at length about their life together. She reminded him of Oxford where they had met. The shows she had done, how she had been thrown out of her digs, the actresses who hated her and yet she got the better of them and became a star. She told of their lovely little boy Jason and stories about him when he was a child and how he was funny and tough and very affectionate to them both. She talked about his little baby son and his happiness with Molly who was such a good girl. And all the while she held his cold thin hand.

Then one day he opened his eyes gave her a beautiful smile and it was all over.

The funeral was cold. Funerals usually are. It was not a happy affair. Unlike most Show business funerals it was rather solemn, Maxine felt sorry thinking that Philip would have liked a little fun. But it was nice to see his sister... again after all those yeats.

Everyone seemed amazed that she had looked after Philip so well, that she had sacrificed herself to take care of the man she loved.

28.

A few months after the funeral Maxine had a call from Jessica.

'Can we meet, do you think? I would like it if we could.'

Maxine tried to hide her astonishment.

'Erm yes of course that would be nice.

'We could have tea in Town somewhere.'

'You don 't want me to come to your house?'

'No I spend a lot of time in Town hese days. I find the house very dpressing without Philip'.

Maxine made a sympathetic sound.

'Yes I understand. Would you like to go to Fullers?'

Jessica gve a shudder Fullers was where she had met Philip in the old days.

'No, rather not. Fortnum's Fountain?'

'So the meeting was arranged. Maxine, for some reason she couldnt completely explain really dressed up for this occasion. Suddenly she wanted to impress Jessica. On the other hand Jessica was also deciding to be impressive. And the two of them looked like a couple of royal princesses and were met with astonished stares by the people having their quiet tea in the famous Picadilly venue. The waitress rushed around tried to sit them in the centre where their presence could be a good advertisement for the cafe, but they opted for a quietish corner instead. They felt this was an important occasion and wanted to make sure they would be able to concentrate.

They settled themselves down and ordered tea. At first the converstion remained general.They discussed shows and movies they had seen. Then finally, Maxine let the conversation remain general until she couldn't hold out any longer and needed to talk about soemthing that was always on her mind.

'So what has happened to Jack?'

She was surprised by the expression on Jessica's face.

'What's wrong? Is he in prison or something?'

'You mean, you don't know?

'Know what?'

'He is really famous.'

Still being my sweetheart?'

This made Jessica laugh.

'No my dear you are a thing of he past. He is the flavour of the month

335

now – and apparently he's very good at it.'

'What? ... How?'

'You must know what has happened to him. All through your ex husband. I thought he would have told you.'

'No, he may be my agent but we are hardly attached at the hip. I know Stan was trying to get him a job modelling thought it might keep him out of my hair.'

'That bit of it worked well.'

'Stan said he's got quite a good face for modelling.'

'Obviously – his face pops up all over the place. Maxine where have you been?'

'New Zealand. I just had to escape. Stan's wife was driving me spare. She is the stupidest thing the world has ever invented.'

Jessica laughed.

'Not quite the stupidest. An idiotic TV producer took a fancy to that face and gave him a job in a soap. Have you heard of *Generations*?'

'Well of course, who hasn't. But the only one I really know about is Coronation Street.'

'*Generations* is only three times a week at 6.30.'

'My step brother is in every episode.'

'What as?'

'A loveable rogue – a criminal of course. Everyone's in love with him. The press follows him around. I'm a bit surprised they haven't been on to you.'

'Stan keeps then all out of my hair. When I came off the plane I was met by a couple of boring and unattractive gangsters. Who follow me wherever I go.'

'Bodyguards?'

'Not much actual body work involved. As I said they are all of them dull dull dull. If I was interested in football or motor cars or mortgages I could hold a conversation. As it is I put up with their presence and only talk to friends. I see my old friends when I go to the theatre or the cinema which I do most nights. They are fun and Ok – and discreet. The press never gets a chance. It was so horrible before.'

'Well I guess they can't be that interested in you any more. You had your fifteen minutes of fame when you were Jack's childhood sweetheart. Now your star is waning and Jack's is rising.'

'You can belittle me as much as you like Jessica. I'm not missing the fame. I'd already had all I'll ever need of notoriety and Jack only made it worse.

Do you ever see him?'

'No he's disappeared out of my life completely. He doesn't want to know me or Jay any more. I expect he'll be back with his tail between his legs if he gets chucked out of the soap. Just a matter of time I guess – he'll be on the scrounge again.'

'So you no longer have any information about him except what's in the papers?'

'No, but Jack has been in touch with my little brother. Jamie, he really is my brother. He is a professor at Oxford. Professor James O'Malley – sounds good eh?'

'I remember him a little red haired boy with glasses. He doesn't bear any resemblance to Jack.'

'Jack is no actual relation to us. His father maried my mother and got lumbered with her three children. Janie was useful. She could look after us and also made some money working on uniforms at the factory.'

'He didn't marry again then afer your mother died?'

'He had a series of girlfriends, some them were OK, most of them hated the children, they weren't very kind to us.' We got a lot of battering from them.'

Jessica gave out this information with a smile – as if it were something trivial. But Maxine was shocked.

'My life would have seemed like heaven to you.'

'It was ok. I'm sort of grateful for it. I think it made me more capable of sorting my life out. And your aunt Irene was wonderful. So kind.'

'She wanted us to be friends.'

'Unlikely at the time. How is she now?'

'Not too good I believe. Scot had a stroke and he had a bad medical condition so they are thinking of moving back to the Laurels. So that My mother can keep him company while Irene is working. She intends to start up the school again.'

'She's working? She must be a bit old.'

'Not too old. In her sixties I guess.'

'I suppose she has to do something.'

'What fun. I'd love to do that'

'Really?'

'I've been through a lot, Maxine. I want to pass a bit on to younger people.'

Maxine had an idea.

'I have to go up there to see them soon. Its ages since I've seen my Mother.. Why do nt you come with me? I know Irene would be delighted to meet you again. It would do you good to get away for a while.'

29.

The telephone rang in Maxine's apartment. It was her mother Connie. This was unusual. Since Maxine had come back from Hollywood Connie had been strangely absent. She had adored being in California with sunshine and many handsome men to squire her. The citizens of East Yorkshire were no comparison to those of Hollywood in her eyes.

But after she went back to Hull she seemed to turn religious. Religion had never interested her before, though she had expected Maxine to go to Cottingham Church twice every Sunday. Her daughter had also been encouraged to join the Anglican Young Peoples Association which was not without advantages – all the best looking boys were members.

However, now Connie seemed to be taking it seriously, going to Church at least three times every Sunday and spending much time with the local population, involving herself in all the social and charitable events. Maxine was glad she had something to occupy her. She still felt guilty about that day at Paragon Station when Connie had so wanted her to stay at home. What would have happened if she, Maxine, had remained in East Yorkshire? Probably married some fish merchant instead of meeting Stanley and taken up her career. Did they still have fish merchants in Hull any more? If not there would be some young boring businessman to marry and she would have joined her mother at the Women's Institute. Maxine shuddered at the thought;

She turned her attention to what her mother was saying in a strange birdlike voice – totally unlike her lazy way of talking.

'Hello darling,' she trilled, 'I'm so happy.'

This was odd. Usually she only rang when she had something to complain about. Somebody's misbehaviour within the W.I. or children being noisy outside in the street.

'So, what's happened?' said Maxine. 'Oh I hope its good news.'

'The best,' said Connie, 'I'm getting married.'

Maxine struggled to get her breath back in order to reply.

'Well, that's nice,' said Maxine after a pause, 'is it someone I know?'

'How could it be? You don't know anybody any more these days,' said her mother slightly huffily but continued with the good news. 'I met him at St Mary's.'

'St Mary's, Cottingham?'

Well that figured, it wasn't a bad place. Very friendly, old and pictursque, High Church so it had lots of singing and the staff wore pretty cossacks.

'Are those choirboys still irresistible?' asked Maxine, rememberng their adorable faces and filthy minds.

Connie paused for a second, obviously giving the choirboys some thought.

'It was love at first sight,' she said, 'It might seem a bit sudden to you, but then you haven't been in contact with me recently.'

'Sorry, I've been a bit busy. But yes, that all sounds good. As long as you are happy.'

'Oh I am and I think you'll like him. He's a nice boy.'

Maxine laughed. *'Boy?'* she asked.

'Erm yes, he's younger than me. But that's all right, isn't it?'

'Yes of course, although my affair with a younger man didn't exactly end in happiness. But then he was an awful lot younger than me. Eighteen years! much too much.'

There was a long pause and Maxine puffed at her cigarette.

'But it would have been a kind of theatrical romance, wasn't it? People always havig affairs with each other – and getting divorced just like you. Nothing really means anything.'

'It doesn't count on tour you mean?' laughed Maxine.

'Different for us more... ordinary people.'

'Yes of course. We're at it like knives – as the landlady said.'

Connie didn't reply, obviously not familiar with the allusion.

Maxine, worried by the silence asked her if there was something wrong. Connie made a sighing noise.

'Erm...'

'What is it Connie?'.

'It's a bit more than eighteen years.'

'Oh I see. How old is he?

What connie mumbled was not easy to hear.

'Sorry I didn't quite catch that. What did you say?'

She could hear Connie taking a breath plucking up her courage.

'Rick is twenty seven,' said Connie.

It was Maxine's turn totake a breath. She stubbed out her cigarette and made an effort to keep her voice steady.

'I see,' she said slowly. 'Well, yes, that is quite young. You could be his grandmother.'

'That's a mean thing to say.'

'Simply the truth. Are you sure about this?'

'Yes, I am. Thisis the real thing. I've never felt like this before. About anyone.'

'Even my father?'

'Well I loved him of course, but this is something quite different. It's as if it was meant to be.'

'MM, I always think that, evey time.'

'Please be happy for me.'

'I'm just thinking of him,' she said carefully. 'He might want children one day – and you will get old and you may be infirm.- will he be able to cope with that?'

'Yes, he says he wants to look after me.'

Although her mother was just a voice Maxine could hear the soppy smile on her face. She put down the phone, It was just too much for her. She felt shocked. This boy – whoever he is – could be her son. She could hear Connie at the other end of the phone saying Hello hello where are you, but somehow she couldn't think of anything to say. She waited until Connie hung up, and she rang Stan.

'My mother has finally flipped her lid,' she said.

'Oh what now?'

'She's getting married.'

'Good for her.'

'To a boy of twenty seven.'

Stan laughed.

'Toy Boys run in your family. Seems they don't run fast enough.'

'Shut up Stan, this is a disaster.'

'Oh come on let the old girl have a bit of fun in her life. A young man of 27 is ideal for a woman in her seventies.'

'An affair is one thing. She shouldn't be allowed to actually marry him. She says it's all his idea.'

'Ok Remember your toy boy proposed – even though he was engaged to someone else.'

'Don't rub it in.'

'It's true though young men are romantic like that.'
Maxine hung up the phone.

*

She worried about the situation for two whole weeks. Then she had another call from her mother.

'I've broken off with Rick.'

'Oh I'm sorry about that.'

'No you're not, you thought I was being stupid.'

'Just a little unwise.'

'Anyway I have found someone more suitable.'

'You mean you are still getting married, but to an older man?'

'Yes that's it. Someone I have always admired. You know, for being a real man's man.'

'Sorry I don't know what that means.'

'He plays golf and drinks pints. He takes care of things. I've never been good at that. And he's older than I am. So you'll be pleased.'

'No but as long as you and he get on well together.'

'We do, we always have.'

'Do I know this wonderful person?'

'Yes I think you met him when you were here but you never remember anyting about Hull any more.'

'Try me.'

'Leslie Parkes.' She brought that out with a burst of triumph.

Maxine's gorge arose, but she managed to swallow the vomit that was rising in her throat.

'Honestly Mother. You just rushed in to marry anybody.'

'Leslie is not anybody, he's an old friend. He and Letty were very close to us in the past – all the time when your father was alive. We used to have dinner with them regularly. But Letty died and so did Tom. Since then we've been rather close. You can hardly say I've rushed into it.'

'But how could you change your mind like that? You were so happy about getting married to Rick.'

'You complained about that too. You just don't want me to be happy. Just because your life has been a mess.'

Maxine was so incensed by this remark she remained silent.

'The wedding is on the 25th – I hope you'll be there. Bring Stanley if you are still talking to him. I don't know why you didn't hang on to him. He was at least a Yorkshire man.'

'He will probably be busy.'

Then she had an amusing thought.

'Is it all right if I bring someone else? Someone famous?'

'A man?'

'No a famous musical comedy star. Jessica Sherwood.'

Connie gave a swift intake of breath. Jessica Sherwood was a favourite of hers and the rest of the Women's Institute crowd. Leslie and Lettie had really been impressed with her in some of the shows they had seen together. This would really make the wedding go with a swing, she thought.

Maxine was grinning. Her mother had no idea who Jessica Sherwood was or had been in the past. Her daughter couldn't wait to give her the news.

30.

'Your new stepfather is very attractive,' said Jessica after she had been made at home and was well settled in to the Laurels. She was having tea with Maxine when she made the remarked that shocked Maxine to the core.

'Leslie Parkes? He's a real shit.'

Jessica laughed.

'He's very good looking.'

'He is? I never noticed. Maybe I've known him too long.'

'Why yes. He reminds me a little of Jack'.

It was the first time Maxine had noticed the reemblance. Of course, Jack was exactly the same type of arrogant man as Leslie Parkes. No wonder she had been wary of him. It was some kind of heavenly punishment, she felt, that she had been molested unpleasantly by two of the same kind of man. She thought wiith a sigh of sweet, kindly Philip and the sardonic but gentlemanly Stan – both now out of reach.

Jason – he had seemed different – but then his generation had changed the status of men and they were supposed to act with respect to women. But he could have grown up to be a Leslie or Jack or like his natural father, Philip's brother Marcus to whom he had a strong resemblance.

Her supposed affair with Jack had really put the kibosh on her relationship with Jason. He had believed every word his Uncle Jack said. Maybe it was because he needed an excuse to finish their affair so he could marry Molly. It was just as well, he could never catch up with Maxine and her longer experience of life.

On the other hand would he have married Molly without Jack's intervention? How much of the situation had been manipulated by Jessica. She had pushed her on to Jack sugesting he gave her a lift home, telling her there were no trains.

As she thought of these things, she looked at Jessica. Her face seemed small and mean and Maxine was reminded of the barefoot urchin who had spoiled her coat. The smell of the burning fur filled her nostrils again and she thought that despite their recent companionship, they could never really be friends.

Jessica in her turn looked at Maxine and remembered her fair beauty '*She still looks like a big blonde doll*' she thought and she too remembered the white fur coat and the anger she felt at not being allowed to touch this perfect little Shirley Temple. How she had been given a stinging blow on the ear just because she had touched the coat and was being threatened with a proper beating from her step father when she got home and he heard what had happened. Luckily the German bombers saved her from that terrible punishment The whole family was rescued from the cellar where they had gone to escape the air raid.

As the two women looked at each other, critical but carefully hiding their antagonism.

Connie burst in on them.'

'Guess who's here. Your Aunt Irene.' She turned to Jessica.

'Maxine used to have dancing lessons from her. She trained at Sadlers Welles.'

'Yes I know,' said Jessica.

'Maxine must have told you.'

'I took dancing lessons too.'

'You did? Oh I suppose you must have. You danced very well in all the shows we saw you in. But Irene's lessons were very special .'

'Yes I know. Irene was kind enough to take me along with Maxine.

'How strange – I don't rememberyou. I would have remembered that wonderful red hair'

Connie stopped. Jessica looked at her with amusement.

'Are you sure you don't remember me?'

Connie looked at Jessica closely and everything began to fall into focus.

Connie sat down suddenly.

'My God, yes I do – the red hair, the violet eyes. It's not *possible!*'
Jessica laughed.
'It certainly is. I am the person once known as Lily Marsden.'
'The one that murdered her father?'
'No that wasn't me. I never murdered anyone in my life.'
'Neither did I,' said Maxine, 'but there's always a first time for everything.'
Jessica gave her a glance. 'I reckon you are right,' she said with a laugh.

31.

Maxine was sitting in the drawing room, reading her book when Leslie entered. She immediately stood up and tried to leave the room. Leslie intercepted her at the door and grabbed her round the waist putting his hands around her buttocks.

She threw him off.

'You belong to my mother,' she said. 'Leave me alone.'

'I don't belong to anyone,' he said.

'You are a sexual pervert – how dare you marry my mother. It is positively obscene.'

He gave her a beaming smile. It was as if being called a sexual pervert was a thing he treatedd as a compliment.

'I rescued her from that awful little money grubbing child. You should be grateful to me.'

'Gratitude is hardly the word.'

'Well, now I'm your Dad you'll have to obey me,' he said. 'Otherwise you know what'll happen to you. I know how to treat naughty little girls, don't I?'

'You filthy bastard!'

'Joking joking. You never did have a sense of humour. I bet your friend will be more friendly with me.'

'You mean Jessica?'

'Yes I like red heads. Passionate, not like icy cold big blondes.'

'Leave her alone. Her beloved husband has just died. She is trying to get over the pain.'

'In that case leave her to Leslie, she'll be needing a bit of fun.'

'Certainly not. She needs sympathy and understanding.'

'No, sex is a good cure. She would enjoy it. Like Connie when your father popped his clogs?'

'What are you saying?'

'It never stopped her, did it? She was always ready for a bit of *how's your father*.'

With all her strength Maxine struck him across the face with such force that knocked him back into his chair.

'You are a loathsome pig and you just can't stop lying. Can you?'

He rubbed his face which had a red streak across it.

'You see, you can be passionate when you need to be. Proves how much you love me.'

Maxine went out slamming the door.

She got out of the room only to meet her mother coming in to see her new husband. She felt she ought to stop her mother seeing him in his dishevelled state.

'Oh mum where did you put my tennis racquet, she said. 'I can't find it.'

'It's in your room'

'Whereabouts is it? I didn't see it.'

'Honestly Maxine you must be blind. Let me get it for you.'

Maxine escorted Connie to her room and kept her there as long as possible. But eventually they had to return to the drawing room.

Leslie was still sitting, down a with his hand over the red mark on his face.

'What happened to your face?'

'Maxine did it.'

'Maxine – how?'

'We were practising the tango, she sort of tripped me up and I fell against the corner of the sideboard.'

'Oh Maxine you should be more careful.'

Leslie gave a laugh and winked at Maxine.

'She needs a good spanking,' he said.

Connie laughed

'That is what you used to say when she was little.'

'Yes, she hasn't changed a bit, has she?' and he gave Maxine a wink.

'Don't blame her, she grew up without a father. '

'Will you stop talking about me as if I'm not here'.

Maxine was clenching her fists, ready for a fight when the phone rang.

'It's for you Maxine,' said Connie and she handed her the handset. She excused herself and left the room as soon as she heard Stan's voice. He had surprising news.

'Precious has gone back to America,' he said.
'Oh Bully for you,' she said.
'Bullier than that, she took the babe.'
'Oh no.'
'She said he wasn't mine after all.'
'I didn't think he could be,' remarked Maxine,' there was no resemblance.'
'Exactly. Anyway the birth father has claimed him.'
'Well that's a shame.'
'No. Not really, I never did warm to him.'
'Not a pretty child,' she said.
'Just a noisy blob,' he said. 'Anyway, he's out of my life now.'
There was a silence as both of them wondered what this might mean. Eventually he spoke again.
'I'm paying a quick visit to my folks in Beverley.'
'Oh good.'
'May I take you out to dinner?' he asked.
'Do you think you can stand it?' she asked.
'I think so, you don't eat much.'
'I mean can you bear my company?'
'Oh yes, I can put up with you…'
'Mm. As long as it's just for a couple of hours,' said Maxine.
'Nothing permanent,' he replied.
'God no,' she said.
'See you at sevenish?'

32.

Jessica was feeling content. It was so peaceful at the Laurels. Despite the fact that she had longed for a country house all her life, she was glad to get away from Cranleigh. Without Philip it seemed cold and lonely.

She thought it was more appropriate for Jason to take over the house, to get used to being Lord of the Manor before he was called upon to do so when the old Lord finally died. Jessica always had to work hard to stay on top of local society but both Jason and Molly had grown up to riches and would have no trouble keeping the status quo.

In the same way, she was Ok playing the doting grandma, but she was not the type to become a kind of spare nanny.

Jay had been embarrassed when she told him that she was the same age as his lover. He hardly spoke to her any more, but then he was involved in his new little son and his pretty wife. She wasn't too upset about this. He had grown up into a person she didn't really recognise.

'How quickly young people can recover from an unfortunate love affair' she thought and wondered how things would have turned out if she hadn't manipulated her menfolk She hadn't expected Jack to manhandle Maxine, but it made her giggle a bit when she brought the picture of Maxine's humiliation to her mind.

She was beginning to formulate a plan for herself. Ever since Irene had returned from the services she had been looking for her star pupil and was delighted to see her again.

Jessica enjoyed her admiration and was hoping she might stay at the Laurels forever, to help Irene in her work, teaching what she knew to a class of young hopefuls.

She enjoyed meeting Alastair who was disabled and unable to work, but was still cheerful and fun to talk to. He was so in love with his elegant wife and despite his stroke, was still enjoying his life with her.

Jessica had a longing to get back to the happy days of her childhood and at the same time teach other young people the way she had been helped by the wonderful woman. Jessica was used to working for herself and it was a joy for her to use her talent with an audience of people.

She sat there in the garden and gently dozed. Maxine and Connie had gone off to visit Tom's grave. Connie needed somehow to ask his permission for her marriage to Leslie and wanted Maxine to be with her as an unwilling witness.

Jessica was pleased they had gone. Although she was happy to be here with Irene she found the presence of Maxine and her mother most uncomfortable. Not only because of the way they had treated her in the past, but their constant arguments over every little thing. They were fond of each other, but Maxine was hardly polite to Leslie, her stepfather to be. She was actually aggressive and rude to him. He just laughed at her. Jessica found this charming and was soon over by his charm.

He was in her thoughts as he came into the garden.

'Hello Red,' he said. 'Left you alone at last?'

She explained to him where they others had gone, and invited him to sit down.

He sat in a garden chair opposite her and laughed into her eyes.

Leslie was looking at her in a way that spoke of his admiration for her and she was enjoying that. She realised she had missed the voice of Philip and the jokes they had shared.

'You are looking well,' she said. 'You have a tan, suits you.'

'Well thank you. Such a compliment from a famous actress. I am honoured to be in your presence.'

This made her laugh.

'Maxine is much more famous than me.'

'Movie business,' he said, 'you are a real star. I have seen you in so many shows. *Why should we dance?* was my favourite. You were stunning. Lettie and I went to see it.' And as he mentioned his late wife, his eyes filled with tears. 'She died twenty years ago,' he said. 'But I still miss her as you must be missing your Philip. Was he good to you?'

She smiled.

'The best,' she said.

'He must have been good for you to give up your stupendous career.'

'All I ever really wanted to be was a lady of the manor. I'd always longed to have a country house. But the country house is empty without him.'

His tear filled eyes showed his pity of her, but Jessica was not tearful. Her tears had been shed.

'You are a brave girl,' he said.

Jessica smiled to herself.

Brave was a word she often applied to herself, but he didn't know the half of it. She felt tempted to confide in him, but just in time, she realised that although confiding in strangers was usually a good idea, in this case it could be disastrous. She must not let him into her life – her heart and her soul. But in spite of this, she knew that he would somehow find how to worm his way into her body. The body that had been starved of physical love since the death of Marcus, the only man she had loved as a woman, as a sexual being.

He seemed receptive to her mood. He loved the fact that she was not going to cry over her widowhood. Instead he took her face into her hands.

'Such a tiny creature you are,' he said and he kissed her.

*

When Connie and her daughter returned, Maxine noticed that Jessica was looking bright eyed and rosy cheeked.

'You're looking well,' she remarked, 'quite pink in the face.

'I've er – been sitting in the sun,' she said, but Maxine was not satisfied with the explanation.

'Jessica what have you been doing?' she asked.

Jessica became a little redder and turned her face away.

'While we were away you were left with Leslie – surely you haven't...'

'Maxine, you are not my keeper. You have to right to criticise me.'

'I have every right. Connie is my mother and I want her to be happy.'

'Connie doesn't mind – he told me so.'

'The man is a rat – of course she'd mind.'

'No apparently not. It's going to be an open marriage. Connie has her little Ricky and Leslie can have whoever he wants.'

'Open marriage? They haven't even got married yet. You'd think he'd wait until after the honeymoon.'

33.

Connie had decided to make herself a suitable wedding dress and that kept her busy so Jessica and Leslie were able to carry on their affair in peace. Leslie would arrive in the morning, they would all have lunch together and Connie would retire to her sewing room. Maxine tried desperately to keep the lovers occupied, engage them in conversation but they would always manage to escape to Jessica's bedroom.

Then one day Jessica borrowed a pair of Connie's scissors and took them to her room. Connie missed them and, instead of going to find her another pair, Maxine suggested she should go and get them from Jessica's room. Never one to hang about when she needed something, Connie wasted no time and went up to Jess's room while Leslie was in there with her.

When Connie came back, she seemed a little disturbed, but totally in control.

'Everything all right up here?' asked Maxine, hiding her glee but ready to sympathise.

'Yes, I thought Leslie had gone, but here he was with Jessica. They seemed to be getting on very well together. I don't know what he'd think of her if he knew she was a murderess.'

'Oh, they were having a good time? What were they doing?'

'I don't think you want to know.'

'Oh I do.' replied Maxine with feeling.

'I know how prudish you are. They were... holding each other.'

'You mean they were having sex?'

Connie tutted and cast her eyes to heaven.

'Why do you have to be so vulgar?'

'Sorry Mum. So they were just having conversation? Holding each other?'

'All right darling. They were fucking.'

'Oh... I see.'

'I was quite surprised in your friend Maxine. She has only just lost her husband. She's just a Hessle Road slut after all.'

'You were not surprised about Leslie?'

'No of course not,' she laughed. 'He's a man.'

'Oh my God. That is unbelievable.'

Connie went on laughing at her daughter's amazed expression.'

'Where have you been all your life?' she said.

'All men aren't like that,' said Maxine.

'How do you know?' replied Connie. 'Do you believe everything they tell you?'

Maxine had another anxious thought.

'You're not still going to marry him?'

'Of course. We are engaged. The wedding is all planned. I've almost finished my dress. It's looking really good by the way. I think you'll be pleased.'

'But Leslie is unreliable where women are concerned.'

'Oh come on darling, don't be so naive'

'You cannot marry a man like that.'

'Maxine why are you always trying to spoil my happiness? I remember how you went away and left me after your father died. All on my own while you were travelling all over the country having a wonderful time.'

'I was in Rep. I was working.'

Connie gave a kind of snort. She had never really considered acting work. It was just what some lucky people did to pass the time.

'You enjoyed being in Hollywood?' said Maxine.

'Yes, there's another thing. You left Hollywood just as I was having a really nice time. We all had to come back to London – on a whim.'

Maxine had never admitted before that leaving Hollywood wasn't her idea. That Stanley had said she should go before she was pushed.

She explained it to her mother, who came up with a knock out sentence.

'There must be parts for middle aged actresses. Chars and bag women. Things like that.'

'Can you see me as a bag woman?'

Connie looked her gorgeous daughter up and down. The idea made them both burst into laughter.

'Mother I am not yet in my dotage'.

'You're no spring chicken do admit. You won't see forty again.'

'What age would that make you?'

'I was a mere infant when I married your father,' she said with a laugh.

'A child bride,' said Maxine and they both dissolved into laughter.

'Actually darling, I am being very practical. I can't live in this big house on my own. I can go and live with him. His house is smaller and he has a housekeeper.'

'You'll sell this place?'

'Yes, unless you or Irene wants to take it on. But you hate it here.'

'I used to hate the people here but I don't know anybody any more. So it is not relevant. I would like to give the matter some thought.'

'There is no rush. But I think Irene might find it too much on her own – having to look after Scottie.'

'Oh yes, poor Alastair. So sad.'

'Men don't last. Not like us. They had a war to get through. Nobody knows how much they had to put up with.'

'Yes everyone except Leslie.'

Maxine had meant this as a slur. Connie refused to take it that way.

'Yes, you see. I'm so lucky have a man to look after me. A man who is still fit and healthy'

'Not fit and healthy enough to go into the army was he?'

'He was in a reserved occupation.'

'The Home Guard?'

'Don't be cheeky. It was secret war work.'

'Oh MI5? I expect he thinks of himself as James Bond. Typical.'

34.

How could people have changed so much? thought Maxine. Was it just because of the Bridge? When she was young East Yorkshire had been a country on its own – having little communication with the southern counties and the other side of the Pennines. The huge Humber estuary was the cut off point and Hull and District was a world of its own. To get away involved a long train journey.

Now the Hullensians had become very much the same as all the rest of England. She noticed the subtle changes in their voices. The northern accent had settled down into its own version of RP.

She felt the difference personally. The people that had treated her with disdain when she was a girl now were friendly, was it just because she was with the famous musical comedy star Jessica Sherwood. Nobody knew yet that she had once been Lil Marsden the girl from the fish docks. It would be interesting to know what would happen if the press got hold of the story. Would she be more of a celebrity or would she be castigated? Maxine smiled to herself at the thought that it might happen.

Maxine's TV appearances were just taken for granted. The Telly was something that happened in people's own homes. She was just another neighbour. No longer the girl that had gone wrong, the girl who had gone off to be 'an actress' something very near to being a prostitute in their eyes.

Television was not impressive, except in the case of Jack who was a real local hero.

Maxine had never appeared in any episodes of Generations. Stanley was keen not to expose her to the soap. As for the movies, they didn't mean anything any more. But what they did remember was Jessica Sherwood the musical comedy star. The rich people would take the theatre trip to London on the train and others would go on coach parties to see the big musicals. They would be big events in their lives.

*

The wedding party was going well. Connie was looking beautiful in cream. And she smiled a lot being a perfect hostess. Leslie spent most of the afternoon sussing out all the women, dispensing winks and lip licks at them. Maxine just felt sick at the sight of him but Jessica thought he was funny. She had spent her early life with brutish men and didn't think anything of his strange behaviour.

Ada turned up to help out at the wedding. She was pleased to do so, she was alone in Ponders End these days and was not very happy Her husband had died of war wounds twelve years after the event. Too late to get compensation and he was too young for her to get a windows pension, so she was forced to go out cleaning to make enough money for her and her twin daughters. Now Mavis and Sheila had grown up into beautiful girls and moved out of the family home to start their own lives.

She was lonely and bored and rushed over to do what she could to help.

'What a pity Stanley didn't come,' said Connie.

Maxine thought the same but didn't want to show it.

'He's a busy man'

'Pity he's tied up with that Yankee wife of his. The one with the awful name.'

'Precious. It's because her surname was Diamond. What else would they call her?'

'Oh disgraceful, Americans are strange.'

'Never mind, Mum, her family call her Pussy.'

'My God, even worse.'

Despite her indignation Connie did not miss the presence of a tall bearded young man and she rushed across the room to him.

Jessica nudged Maxine.

'Ricky,' she said.

'How do you know?' asked Maxine.

Connie brought him over.

'My daughter Maxine,' she said in a peremptory manner – then, 'And THIS is Jessica Sherwood.'

Connie said Jessica's name as if she was a Music Hall chairman inviting audience applause.

Ricky nodded briefly at Jessica, but kept his eye contact for Maxine.

'I've always wanted to meet you,' he said.

Connie cast her eyes to heaven and Jessica quickly engaged her in conversation, slipping her arm under Connie's elbow. They moved away without attempting to compete for Ricky's favour.

'So you are my mother's friend,' said Maxine.

'Euphemism,' he said, 'I'm her lover, this month's edition anyway.'

'Flavour of the month,' she laughed. 'Reminds me of Marine ices. Are you Strawberry or Vanilla?'

'Don't bring me down,' he said. 'Try something more exotic.'

'Mango?'

And he said 'I'll settle for that' and he sang, 'She never was a man to let a mango.'

'You write songs?' enquired Maxine.

'Occasionally – but I think someone thought of this one first.'

He had a nice laugh.

'Are you shocked by the licentious behaviour of we folk in the sticks?'

'London does seem rather puritanical by contrast.'

'So will you be staying in this den of vice when Connie moves out?'

'Connie's moving out – where is she going?'

'To live with her husband of course. I hope you move here. It would be nice to see you now and again.'

From across the room, the authoritative voice of her mother cut short their conversation.

'Ricky darling. I want you to meet Mrs Johnson.'

He gave her a grin and left.

Jessica came over with a dish of crab and avocado toasts.

'Seems like a nice boy,' she said. 'He only had eyes for you.'

'Sorry, Jess, but don't worry, you'll soon win him over.'

Jessica picked up a crab toast and chewed it thoughtfully.

*

The party was over, Connie and Leslie had gone off for their honeymoon. Jessica and Maxine were left on their own while Ada dealt with the washing up. They poured out a couple of gin and tonics and settled themselves on the comfortable living room armchairs.

'You think I'm a whore don't you?' remarked Jessica.

'Yes,' said Maxine.

'OK.'

'I was once a scarlet woman,' said Maxine. 'It was fun. Stan and I had it off in a train.'

'Not the Yorkshire Pullman. What did all the camp waiters in Burgundy say?'

'They didn't see us. We did it in the Loo.'

Jessica giggled.

'That's funny – but it doesn't count. You and Stan were married.'

'Not then we weren't. It was where we met'

'In the toilet of the Yorkshire Pullman? How romantic.'

'Not exactly. We never stopped laughing long enough to do it properly'.
Maxine's laughter faded a little as she remembered.
'We never stopped laughing – except when we were yelling at each other.'
Jessica took a sip of her drink, looking at her quizzically.
'Why did he get involved with Pussy Precious?'
'I got tired of being ordered about and we both needed a bit of peace. So we got a divorce.'
'And he married Precious?'
'Thought it would be restful. They liked each other for about a month.'
Jessica laughed and looked closely at Maxine's face.
'It's nice to know things about you.'
'My life has always been an open book', she replied, 'not like yours. Mystery woman. But one day I'm going to make you confess and tell me everything.'
'Well, if we are going to run the school together, we'll have time for chats.'
'Are we?' Asked Maxine.
'Aren't we? It's your decision. Your house.'
How strange. This was something that had been running through her mind. It was good that Jessica had felt the same way.
'Oh yes, well then. Yes, I think so. Good to get away from theatre. Must be less stressful.'
'I feel the same way. I have begun to hate show business.'
'Will we get on well together, do you think?' asked Maxine.'
'Without all the stress of the profession – why not?'
They solemnly shook hands on the deal.

It didn't take long to work out the schedule, send out advertisements and the pupils came flocking in. All the local mothers had happy memories of their own experiences with Irene's dancing school and sent their little girls there in large numbers.

Irene and Jessica took care of the musical comedy side of things and Maxine taught elocution and drama. Ada was happy looking after the children just as she had in the old days.

Epilogue

Jessica suggested they should have their breakfast in the garden. Ada cheerfully laid out coffee and croissants, marmalade and butter on the Susie Cooper breakfast service that Connie must have acquired some time during the sixties.

Maxine wriggled herself into the old hammock that they had pitched between two trees in the garden and fell to remembering what it had been like when Connie was living there lying on the hammock with a box of milk tray gently melting in the sun. Her memories of Connie were most tranquil ones as if the war and everything that had happened to the family had been rubbed out of her consciousness. She only remembered the deep snow in the winter and the blissfully warm sun in the summer and how she had adapted her personality to match the weather. In the winter she would be an arctic explorer with a long stick, digging it in to the soft snow. In the summer she imagined she was in Lincoln green trousers and jacket, her bow strung across her shoulder and her arrows in a holder strung on her belt, which also held her wooden sword.

This of course was when she wasn't in public dressed up like Shirley Temple with blonde ringlets, pretty dresses, champagne socks and her white fur coat.

The white fur coat – the garment she had destroyed by fire, hoping to rid herself of whatever germs the dirty little girl had put on it. The smell of burning fire reached her nostrils just as Jessica came out of the house looking soignee and every inch a star as usual with a silken kaftan over her practice dress and a floral chiffon scarf tossed with apparent carelessness over her shoulder. Her red curly hair was dressed in a chignon with a few escaping tendrils on her slender neck. Despite herself Maxine was bewitched by her charisma. Was she wasted here, teaching dancing at Madame Renee's old stage school.

Come to that thought Maxine. Am I wasted lying here in a hammock after years of dressing rooms or getting up at the crack of dawn to go to studio and makeup. But then I no longer have that standing around waiting to be lit. Or live in that absolute terror of losing the lines. I'm content here.

'You are looking beautiful this morning,' said Jessica as she stroked Maxine's blonde head – a little darker these days but the few silver hairs that grew there gave it an ethereal quality.

'And you are ravishing,' Maxine laughed. This was a tradition paying each other compliments each morning. Kept them on their toes, kept them polite with each other. Stopped them falling into a slump of resentment.

Jessica loved the kids, empathised with them and loved teaching them the things she had learned. She also had a worshipful admiration for Irene who reciprocated the admiration. It was a highly satisfactory combination. The only fly in the ointment was the fact that she was enjoying the hospitality of Maxine Nevertheless, she smiled a lot, paid her compliments and life was continuing in a pleasant way.

Ada poured the coffee.

'Get off that hammock, you old lazy bones,' she admonished Maxine who was quick to obey.

Ada arrived to help out at Connie's wedding and had never gone away.

Jessica looked at Maxine and in her heart she knew she would never really enjoy her company. It was Irene that kept her here. She knew that Maxine was jealous of the relationship and felt a little left out when the two women were together. So Jessica knew she had to keep it sweet. Despite her misgivings she kept smiling. Better forgive and try to forget whenever possible

Jessica took a piece of toast from the wicker table where Ada had left it and spread butter and marmalade on it. She took a bite. She was going to have a class in just five minutes and she was feeling a little resentful that Maxine had cancelled her elocution lessons for a couple of weeks. She said she needed a holiday. Jessica never needed a holiday and couldn't understand anybody who would want one. Maxine was lying there on the Hammock, eating raspberries out of a big dish that Ada had prepared. She was obsessive about her figure. She was rather die than eat a piece of toast. Bread and potatoes had been banned from her diet for many years now and she had almost forgotten what chocolate tasted like. Jessica thought this was extreme. She thought everything about Maxine was extreme. Taking her son and seducing him, that would something she would never understand or forgive. Nevertheless, they were content together, weren't they.? The past wrangles had only been because of the stresses of show business. Now in this peaceful spot they could manage to keep bad memories of each other under wraps.

'It's going to be a beautiful day,' said Jessica, 'I'm so happy here, aren't you?'

'It's my home. I was born here and this is where I grew up,' said Maxine 'How could I not be happy?'

And then the phone rang.

'Hello light of my life,' said the familiar voice.
'Why Stanley,' said Max, 'what has happened now? Precious come back again?'
'Happily no. She's back in the good old USA. With that revolting child. Wonder if it still screams all day long.'
'So what do you want?'
'Why should I want anything – except to chat?'
'I know you Stanley, there is always a motive.'
'Ok then. Just to let you know I've got you another theatre job.'
'No, I'm retired from theatre. I am now a drama teacher.'
'Good God. What a waste.'
'I find it soothing.'
'You are not a soothsome person. This little job is something very interesting.'
'All right then go on.'
'I've been talking to Lazlo remember him? The director.'
'How could I forget?'
'We want to do the play again.'
'The play?'
'The one about the Queens. Philip bequeathed the play to me along with a generous production budget but with the proviso that you and Jess play your original roles. As Lazlo said, *those two broads are just about the right age now to play them.*'

Maxine was silent. She was thinking.
'Good idea? said Stanley.
There was no reply. Stanley urged her to answer.
'What do you think?'

Lightning Source UK Ltd.
Milton Keynes UK
UKOW05f2123160217
294596UK00023B/554/P

9 781782 224952